Accessory
After

Accessory
After

E. Charles Vivian

RAMBLE HOUSE
2018

First American trade paperback edition

Ramble House
10329 Sheephead Drive
Vancleave MS 39565 USA

www.ramblehouse.com

First published by
Ward Lock, London, 1934

ISBN 13: 978-1-60543-943-3

Preparation: Gavin L. O'Keefe.

To

MY FRIEND

JOHN FARQUHARSON

CHAPTER I

OLD BOOTS

"IT SHOULD BE easy enough," Inspector Head said to himself, as he set out to follow the trail of the old boots from the doorway of Westingborough Grange.

"But it isn't," he observed some twenty minutes later.

At the start, the trail was obscured to some extent by the marks of car-wheels and other footprints, both of men and women, for the late Mr. Edward Ensor Carter, as owner and occupant of the Grange, had given a party the preceding evening, and his guests had made a confusion of tracks round the doorway when they left, somewhere between one and two in the morning. But, since the trail of the old boots was superimposed on these others, both in approaching the house and leaving it, the muddle round the door gave Inspector Head very little trouble. He sorted out the track he wanted from all the rest, and followed it, slot-hound-wise, across a lawn, through an opening in the laurel hedge, and thence across the three hundred yards or more of meadow-land which divided the Grange garden from the road. As boundary between meadow and road, there was a seven-foot brick wall, topped with broken glass set in cement, but this precaution against trespassers was negatived by a break in the wall where what is usually known as a kissing-gate gave access to the road: Carter had had the break made and the gate put up when he bought the place from its previous owner, who had been a misanthropic hermit lamenting the passing of spring guns and man-traps.

Between the gate and the house was no regularly made path, but a sort of depression in the grass showed that the way was often used. Even at this present time, with an inch and more of snow veiling the earth, the trodden track showed, and along it went the prints of the old boots in two sets, one toward the house, and one returning away from it. And there was, Head noted, a slightly inebriated vacillation about those tracks: sometimes the toes of the boots pointed straight along the path; sometimes they inclined inward to an extent that might have indicated a broncho-buster as the wearer, and then again they would turn away from each other nearly to an angle of forty-five degrees each. There was no consistency about them.

Since the wearer of the boots had got away for the time—only for the time, Head felt convinced—a slow and thorough investigation was preferable to haste. Before he passed beyond the laurel hedge at the far side of the lawn from the house, he signalled to the man who had acted as chauffeur for himself and his party, a uniformed constable in a peaked cap who still sat at the wheel of the big police car. When the man got down to cross the lawn, Head gestured him to go round outside the laurel hedge, and then gestured a halt when he had his man within hearing distance. There was thus no muddle of tracks across the lawn, nothing beyond the two sets of prints made by the old boots, and Head's own marks, well away to the right of the others.

"See that nobody walks across this lawn, Jeffries," Head ordered, "and tell Williams—no, though—tell Sergeant Wells to go along the drive, out by the main entrance, and along to the kissing-gate, but not to obscure any footprints between the gate and the road."

"Very good, sir," said Jeffries.

"And tell him to stop anybody from coming through that kissing-gate, or even coming near it from the road," Head added.

"Right, sir."

"That's all, thanks."

He stood to watch while his man called the sergeant and transmitted the order, waited till he saw Wells set out from the doorway of the house. He appeared, then, as a kindly looking man, probably in the late forties, with greying hair showing from under his soft felt hat, and no indication of his calling either in his bearing or in his well-cut lounge-suit and overcoat. Long, dark lashes gave his brown eyes a rather sleepy expression, and his easy, deliberate habit of movement gave no hint of the almost abnormal physical strength and alertness he could bring into use at need. A certain cat-burglar, with whom he had coped single-handed successfully, had described him as a blinkin' thunderstorm disguised as a sofa cushion: the simile had been intended to define his physical prowess, but it fitted his mentality equally well.

Now, before turning again toward the gap in the laurel hedge, he counted both sets of footprints made by the old boots, and found that in crossing the lawn toward the edge of the drive—that is, toward the house—there were forty-three prints: returning, the wearer had covered the distance in forty steps, a natural discrepancy in view of the fact that he went to his task carefully and trepidantly, and hastened, taking longer strides, on the return journey. Then Head, who had kept well away to the right of the tracks, counted his own footsteps from the edge of the drive to this point, and found the total thirty-seven.

But, he knew, he had not been walking normally; he had been looking at those footprints all the time, and might have taken either longer or shorter strides than usual. He passed through the gap, taking care to leave the two footprints there quite clear, and, stepping off to the right again, walked steadily toward the kissing-gate, counting the footprints leading away from the lawn as he went, and ascertaining that there were two hundred and thirty-three separate prints. Then, as Wells had not yet arrived at his post at the gate, Head went back, treading in the prints he had made, and found that he had taken two hundred and fifteen steps for the distance.

Thus the difference between his length of pace and that of the wearer of the boots was fairly consistent: since he was six feet in height, and took thirty-seven steps to that other's forty, what was the height of the wearer of those boots? He trod in his own footprints yet again on his way back to the gate, where Wells was awaiting him now, and realised that he had no practical data for the solution of this problem. Some men of five feet nine took as long paces as his: length of leg in relation to that of the body counted for much, habit and exercise—or the lack of it—for more. But he was safe in assuming that the wearer of the boots was shorter than himself.

So he came to the gate, and there gave vent to his second conclusion regarding the two sets of footprints.

"What isn't, sir?" Wells inquired gravely.

"Stop where you are," the inspector bade. "Just so, out there on the road, you'll see that somebody wearing boots a tramp might have discarded stepped from where you are up to this gate, passed through, and went to the Grange, all since the snow fell last night. Also you can see the tracks of those same boots returning as far as the gate—my side of it, that is—and there they stop. Did he hook up on a passing aeroplane? I refuse to believe that the man who murdered Mr. Carter like that was an angel."

"Well, I'm damned!" Wells remarked wonderingly.

"Sorry to hear it," Head retorted, looking over the railings beside the gate. "Don't come any nearer—don't tread on that snow, whatever you do! Wells, hustle back to the car while I stay here and keep people off, and bring back the camera. I want photographs of this, at once."

The sergeant set off on his errand, and Head, leaning on the railings, took stock of his surroundings. There was a big ash tree growing just inside the wall, and from it a horizontal or nearly horizontal branch stretched out over the kissing-gate, but the most agile of men could not have caught hold of the branch by leaping up at it, since it was a good fourteen feet above the ground. And, even if one had caught at it and lifted himself up, he would have had to come to ground again and display footsteps within sight of where Head stood. A slack-wire walker would have found it almost impossible to keep foothold on the cement-bedded broken glass that topped the wall, which was angled, roof-wise, and not flat. Leaning over the railings, Head could see that the footprints were not continued anywhere within the circumference of the tree, and there was no other near it to afford a continuance of aerial progress. No, the footprints away from the house came just to the gate, and there ended. On their way toward the house, they came in from the road—from where Wells had been standing—and by the turn there showed that the walker had come from Westingborough. And, Head knew, within half a mile of this spot he would lose them: milkmen and other early workers would have trodden them out of existence.

He knelt beside the last of the prints, heedless of wet knees or damage to his clothes. There were a right and left close together, as if the wearer of the boots had come to a halt there, putting both feet together, and then had taken a leap into space. For there was absolutely no continuation of the track, and the maker of it could not have leaped over the gate and cleared the twelve or fourteen feet (later, Head ascertained that the distance was fourteen feet six inches) of untrodden snow to the nearest tyre-mark in the road. And, had he done this, the print of a boot would have showed in the tyre-track, but Head had already seen when he looked over the railings that there was no such print, nor any sign of the boots having trodden there except in coming toward the gate on the way to the house.

These two final prints, side by side, revealed the boots as of the heavy kind worn by agricultural labourers and the like, but worn to a point that would cause any self-respecting labourer to discard them. The heels had been iron-shod, but half the metal of the right heel had either worn or broken away altogether: the print of the nail that had held it to the leather showed clearly in the snow, while two-thirds of the hob-nails that had protected the sole were missing, and the leather forming the sole had completely worn through in the middle and toward the outer edge. It was a boot that would let in water, a boot that a tramp would hardly wear in such weather as this.

The left boot was in little better case. Its heel-iron had survived whole, but was evidently worn thin on its outer edge, and there were not more than half a dozen hob-nails left in the sole. Studying this print as he knelt, Head deduced that the sole itself had come partly unstitched, and probably flapped as the wearer walked. This might account for the irregular way in which the wearer had placed his feet—and again might not.

Finishing his inspection, Head rose to his feet again and dusted the snow off his knees. He looked at his watch, and saw that it was just half-past seven; the sky was leaden, and there was a threat of more snow or perhaps rain in the clammy air, and, since the snow already fallen was softening, it was urgently necessary to complete his knowledge of these tracks as quickly as possible. He looked up at the ash tree, and at a sudden thought stripped off his coat, removed his hat, and, hanging both on the railings before him, bent and then leaped with all the strength he had in an effort to grasp the lateral branch extending over his head. He missed it by a good two feet.

"Not that way," he told himself, and donned hat and coat again.

Wells came along the road with the camera, and halted, waiting for directions as to how to use it.

"A general photograph from there, first," Head bade, "Take two shots for certainty, and mind your exposure is long enough. Then come along and take a close-up of each print between the road and the gate and get another close-up of this pair inside. I wonder—could we get a cast, by any means?"

Wells shook his head. "Not in snow, sir," he said. "It'd ball on to the plaster, or clay, or whatever we might use."

"Well, then, make your photographs tell the tale. Meanwhile, I'm going up this tree. That chap hadn't got wings."

Leaving his man to take the photographs, he removed his hat again and swarmed up the trunk of the ash, to the grave detriment of his overcoat until he could get a grip on the lowest branch, when he lifted himself to a foothold and stood to observe what evidence the tree might provide. And, at what he saw, he save a little "Ah-h!" of satisfaction, and then, as he looked down at the road, cursed.

The snow, adhering to the upper sides of the leafless branches, had been rubbed off the bough running out almost horizontally and parallel with the railings on either side the gate. Similarly, it had been rubbed off another bough extending out over the road, showing that the wearer of the boots had by some means drawn himself up from where the final pair of footprints showed, and had lowered himself into the road from the other, rather higher bough.

But, Head concluded then, he must have had a car waiting, or something of the kind. For there was no footprint anywhere in the road corresponding to the tracks made by the old boots along the path—no sign of any kind that the wearer of the boots had descended to the road. And, assuming that he had been absent a mere half-hour or less on his errand of death, a standing car would have made impressions altogether different from those made by moving wheels. Had he by any chance an accomplice, who had driven slowly along the road to permit of his dropping into a car from the tree?

However that might be—Head put the problem aside for future consideration—he had not dropped on his feet from the tree, evidently. Nowhere within range of a jump or a descent by rope was there any trace of the old boots, and it was in the last degree unlikely that a murderer, unless he were altogether careless of his own safety, would leave an unattended car in the middle of a public road while he went to commit his crime. Four sets of wheel-tracks had been made here since the snow had fallen, and all were in the middle of the road: moreover, Head knew enough to account for all four sets, for those four cars had conveyed Carter's guests to the Grange the evening before, while there was no snow on the road, and had returned this way after the snow had fallen. Which went to prove that the wearer of the old boots had not continued his journey from this point by car—unless some one of Carter's guests had been an accomplice in the crime.

"That's the last of the second roll of film, sir," Wells said from the ground. "Twelve snaps, altogether. Will that do?"

"It'll have to do," Head answered rather irritably. "I've found out—he swung himself up into this tree with a rope. There's the mark of it out along this branch, where he slung it over."

"Pretty clever, slinging it over in pitch dark," Wells observed.

"We are not dealing with a fool, by a long way," Head said.

"But if he got up there, sir, he had to come down again."

"By the evidence of the boots, he didn't," the inspector retorted. "No, he spread his wings and flapped away, without touching ground. And who the devil's been along there, on that footpath? Two of 'em, by the look of it. No—don't go. I'm coming down to see."

He swung himself down from the tree on the inner side of the wall, and went through the gateway on to the road, still taking care to obliterate none of the footprints, though he knew that a record of them was in the camera that Wells had closed and put away in his overcoat pocket.

"I make 'em tens, sir," Wells observed. "My foot fits perfectly for length, and I take tens. He's a bit wider, though."

Head nodded acknowledgment of the statement, and surveyed the road thoughtfully. Then he looked up at the ash branch extending out over the road, and shook his head as he turned to his sergeant again.

"There must be an explanation," he remarked.

"I expect you'll hit on it, sir," the sergeant ventured.

"Problem." He stated it with a note of irritation in his voice. "X—we'll call him X, for convenience—X walks from Westingborough, presumably, or at least comes from the direction of Westingborough, goes into the Grange grounds by way of this gate, and walks up to the house, after this snow had finished falling. That is, after one o'clock this morning. At the house he commits his murder, presumably again, and then walks back as far as this gate. By means of a rope slung over a bough—I've seen the marks of the rope up there—he hoists himself up into the tree, and according to the visible evidence he doesn't come down again. Ergo, he must still be up that tree—and he isn't."

"Along the top of the wall, sir?" Wells suggested.

"The snow on it is undisturbed far beyond the reach of the tree in both directions—undisturbed as far as I can see," Head asserted.

The sergeant gazed anxiously up the road and down the road, in quest of more than the one set of tracks approaching the gate: had there been another corresponding set going away from the gate, he must have seen it, for apart from wheel-tracks the snow was undisturbed. He pointed at the stile giving access to a footpath, almost opposite the kissing-gate, and leading past Westingborough churchyard into the town.

"There's two lots of footmarks, and a bicycle," he remarked. "If they have anything to do with it—but that man's set is smaller boots, and I know who it is, too. Potter, the man that works at Parham's garage, lives up in his cottage just past the Grange, and he's due at work at half-past six every morning. That's his feet."

"We'll put Potter down for an inquisition," Head decided. "He may be able to tell us something. The other set—it's a woman's, probably with brogue shoes, by the wide, flat heels. She got off her bicycle just here"—he was standing, as he spoke, almost in the tyre-marks on the side of the road farthest from the kissing-gate—"and wheeled it up to the stile and lifted it over. Then, by the look of it, she wheeled it along the path without mounting again—which she would do, since there was snow on the asphalt and it was still dark. Potter's tracks are superimposed on hers. Here's where she stepped down off the bike and began to wheel it, and she dumped it down well to the right of the stile to give herself room to get over. Then she—yes, Potter's left us enough to see what she did. Just got over and wheeled the bike along the path. I don't see—" He broke off to cogitate.

"What she's got to do with a man wearing a pair of tens a tramp wouldn't look at," Wells suggested thoughtfully.

"M'yes. Look here, Wells, I'm going back to the house, now, and you stop here and keep everyone off those wheel-marks and footprints round the stile—don't let them be obliterated or damaged. Take measurements of that woman's feet—if it was a woman. It might have been a small-built man, for all we know. And keep it all as clear as you can. I'm going to send you another roll of film, and you can take me half a dozen good exposures of those feet- and tyre-tracks, and get one of where she or he dropped down off the bike and began to wheel it to the stile, and the rest on the path there. One good general one showing the feet beside the tyre-tracks as she wheeled the bike—if it happened to be a she, and the rest I leave to you. Get the average length of pace over thirty or forty yards, and then go through this gate and take another average of the length of pace in the old boots. Don't worry about Potter's tracks. We can check him up easily enough."

"Right you are, sir. You think the woman—?" Wells paused.

"Possibility of accessory before or after," Head pointed out. "It was a clever devil who threw the rope over that branch in the dark, without making a miss and leaving the mark of it in the snow anywhere, or making any extra footprints over it. It was a clever business altogether, and done by somebody more than usually resourceful, because X couldn't calculate beforehand on snow falling last night. That murder was calculated exactly to time, planned out to the last detail, and we're up against brains, good brains. I'm not what you'd call happy about this case, yet."

Wells shook his head gravely. "It may turn out quite simple, sir," he observed hopefully. " 'Ullo! Do I stop him?"

"You do not. But mind where you step out of his way."

A big, six-wheeler lorry, laden with milk-cans, bore down on them, going toward Westingborough. Head looked down at its tracks after it had passed, and then gazed toward the Grange gateway, the direction from which the lorry had reached this point.

"He did us all the damage he could do, before he reached here," Head remarked, "and if X went that way, those wheels won't have wiped out all his trucks. I'll walk back round by the drive and send you that roll of film as soon as I get to the car. Don't let anyone mess up those footprints and tyre-marks by the stile there."

CHAPTER II

AT WESTINGBOROUGH GRANGE

THE FRONT DOOR of the Grange stood open as Head approached it from the drive, and the pendent electric light switched on inside showed him Constable Williams standing on guard over the place where the body of the murdered man had been found, a matter of three or four paces inside the doorway. But, as Head entered, he saw that the body itself had been removed: Williams was mounting guard over the two clear impressions of the old boots that the inspector had tracked through the snow, a right and left as clear as photographs on the polished parquet. The mysterious X had left other prints as well, but these two, as X had stood beside the spot where the body had been found, were the best, and evidently Superintendent Wadden had thought it worth while to preserve them. Head, entering, gave the constable a questioning look.

"In there, sir," Williams said, pointing to the doorway on the left of the entrance hall. "All of 'em,"

Head directed him to send Jeffries with another roll of film to the sergeant by the kissing-gate, and entered the room indicated. It was a long, low-ceiled apartment, with no less than three windows giving on to the front of the house. On a long heavy highly polished mahogany dining-table in the middle of the room still remained nine empty champagne bottles, one empty decanter and another less than a quarter filled with whisky, several empty syphons, and a dozen or more glasses and tumblers. A still, sheeted figure lay on the floor between the table and the window nearest the door. The three living occupants of the room, two seated and one standing, looked round at Head as he entered.

The nearer of the two seated figures, that of Superintendent Wadden, was almost too fleshy for comfort; his neck lay in rolls over his tightly hooked uniform collar, and his fierce grey eyes under bushy brows gave him an aggressive appearance totally at variance with his real character, for a kinder man never put on a uniform. Beyond him Bennett, the doctor who had examined the body, looked rather disconsolate: the room was chilly, and the littered table gave it a depressing look; also Bennett, having finished his work, wanted to get away.

"I've been holding everything up till you got back, Head," Wadden said. "Jones"—he turned to the constable in attendance—"go and see if they've got a paraffin stove or something—this room's like the North Pole. Y'see, Head, I'm due to retire the beginning of May, and just in case this business isn't finished by then, I want you to be conversant with all of it. So we've just fetched the body in here—what have you got since you went out?"

"A man climbed a tree, and apparently flew away," Head answered composedly. "That is, I can't see that he came down again."

Wadden took a pair of handcuffs from his pocket and held them out. "Take these and put them on him," he suggested. "If he didn't come down, he must be still up there."

"That's my trouble," Head said. "He isn't."

"It's your case," Wadden said. "I'm too old to climb trees. D'you want to go through that part of it first?"

Head gestured a negative. "I'll go over it with you later. Wells is on the spot, finishing off taking the photographs I want. What have you at this end? I see you've brought the body in."

"Ye-es, the doctor's finished with it. We deduce he was shot from the doorway the first time, and that bullet went clean through him just under the shoulder and fixed the time of the murder. Then he fell on the floor, and the shooter came and stood beside him, put the pistol down on to his right eye, and pulled the trigger a second time. The eye is completely obliterated, you'll see."

Head went to the still figure on the floor and turned down the sheet from the face. It was that of a middle-aged man, almost white-haired; the sickening appearance of the eye-socket robbed it of all normal expression, and Head drew the sheet back and turned to the superintendent again as Jones entered, carrying a lighted paraffin stove.

"That's better," Wadden said. "Put it down here, between me and the doctor. Questions, Head?"

"What did you mean when you said the first shot fixed the time?" Head inquired, after a thoughtful pause.

"It went clean through, and ended up in a clock on the mantelshelf at the back of the hall, stopping the clock at two minutes past four," Wadden answered. "That is, if the clock was going. I've questioned nobody, waited for you to come back."

"Which means it was done with an automatic pistol," Head pointed out. "A revolver wouldn't have put enough force behind the bullet.

"We'll go through the arms register and check up on it," Wadden promised. "There can't be many of either, in Westingborough district."

"Somebody must have heard the shooting," Head suggested.

"There are four servants and a chauffeur," Waddell observed. "Jones, fetch in Arabella Cann—she's the one who found the body, Head."

They waited, and presently the constable escorted into the room a stout, middle-aged, frightened-looking woman. Wadden nodded at her, and gestured her to seat herself in the chair that Jones drew forward.

"Sit down, Miss Cann," he said, "and we promise not to eat you. We just want to know all you can tell us about this business."

"Only just—I found the master, sir," she said shakily. "And telephoned the police station at once. I don't know any more."

"Oh, yes, you do," Wadden said encouragingly, "but you don't know you do know it. Let's go back a bit, as far as the party last night. What was it—dinner, or just a social razzle?"

"We had six to dinner, sir," she answered. "Five and the master, that is, and the others came in about half-past ten—"

"Just a moment," Wadden interrupted. "Who were the five?"

"Well, sir, there was Mr. and Mrs. Quade, Mr. Pollen and his young lady, Miss Hurder, and that young Mr. Denham."

"Yes. They came to dinner. Now who came after dinner?"

"Miss Perry—the one that gives dancing-lessons, and her sister Miss Ethel Perry. Mr. Frank Mortimer fetched them in his car."

"And took them back?" Wadden suggested.

She shook her head. "I don't know, sir. The master rang for me about midnight and told me we could all go to bed after I'd brought in some more soda syphons. I asked if he'd want Adams—that's the chauffeur—and he said no, he could go to bed too. They'd look after theirselves, he said, and we wasn't to stay up."

"And did all five of you go to bed?"

"As far as I know, sir. I know we all went up-stairs."

"Will that be up to the floor above this?"

"No, sir, the next one—the top floor of all. We all sleep up there. Adams was glad to go because Minnie—that's his wife—she's poorly. She'd gone up about half-past nine."

"Minnie is the cook, I understand?"

"Yes, sir."

"Now, Miss Cann, you know there's a clock on the shelf at the back of the entrance hall. Does it keep good time?"

"Very good time, sir. It's always within a minute or two."

"Was it keeping its usual good time last night?"

"It was just right, sir, when I heard the wireless signal from the drawin'-room and looked at it."

"You wind it every night, I expect?"

"No, sir. It's an eight-dayer, and I wound it Saturday night as usual, and to-day's only Tuesday."

"Made for us, Head," Wadden observed, looking at his inspector. "Carter was shot the first time almost precisely at two minutes past four this morning. How does that fit your examination, doctor?"

"I placed death as between three-thirty and four-thirty," Bennett answered. "Do you want me any more before the inquest?"

"No. I'll ring you and give you the time for that. To-day."

"Then I'll leave you to it." He rose and went out.

"Well, Miss Cann," Wadden pursued thoughtfully, "didn't you do anything at all when you heard the shots? Mr. Carter was shot at four o'clock, and it was five-forty when your telephone call came through."

"I didn't think it was shots, sir," she explained. "You see, sir, Mr. Denham's got one of these sports cars, and it goes bang just like a gun. It did when he started away, and I got up and went to my window to look then. I heard a lot of laughing round the front door, and heard the master say Mr. Denham—Dennie, he called him—mustn't point that car at anyone. So when I heard two more bangs downstairs I thought it was Mr. Denham come back for something, and didn't take any more notice."

"And all the others thought the same, I suppose?"

"Minnie—that's Mrs. Adams—she said she did, and didn't take any more notice than I did. The others say they didn't hear anything."

"Two floors up—no. Well, Miss Cann, how did all you get on with Mr. Carter? Was he a good sort of master in the house?'"

"Well, sir, he never bothered us or took much notice of us as long as we got our work done. Never took much notice of me, I mean."

"I see," Head said, slowly and thoughtfully. "What is your position here, Miss Cann? What do you call yourself—housemaid?"

"Head housemaid, sir. Hetty is the second, and Phyllis is the parlourmaid. Then there's Minnie I've told you about, the cook."

"Any questions, Head?" Wadden shot out the query after a brief silence, looking up at the inspector.

"Not now. Possibly at the inquest," Head answered.

"Then we won't trouble you any more, Miss Cann," Wadden said, "unless by any chance you could produce a spot of hot coffee. And you might tell Phyllis—Miss Taylor, that is—that I'd like a word with her if she'd be so good as to step in here."

"I think there'll be some coffee ready now, sir."

"Excellent! Just ask Miss Taylor to come in for a word with us."

Jones ushered her out, and presently ushered in the parlourmaid, to whom both Wadden and Head devoted appraising glances. She was not in uniform, but wore a dark grey silk blouse and black skirt, both very well cut, while in the matter of shoes and stockings she was above criticism. There were marks of tears on her cheeks, and her pretty, piquant face showed deathly pale where the rouge failed to cover—she had made up hastily and none too well that morning. As she entered and caught sight of the sheeted figure under the window she reeled and appeared about to fall, and Head took her arm and led her to the chair that Arabella had vacated. Wadden gave her time to recover composure.

"Miss Taylor, I think?" he asked at last.

She nodded a silent assent, and crumpled a handkerchief even more tightly in her hand. Wadden nodded gravely, sympathetically.

"I suppose you were on duty here last night, Miss Taylor?" he inquired. "Waiting on Mr. Carter and his guests, I mean?"

"Ye-yes." She nodded again, and choked back a sob.

"How long have you been in service here?" he pursued.

"Four—four months. Since September."

"Do you belong in this district—have you lived here long?"

"I—I came from London," she answered shakily.

"Engaged there by Mr. Carter—is that so?"

Again she nodded, and gave no verbal reply this time.

"What salary was Mr. Carter paying you?"

"Si-sixty pounds a year." She looked slightly surprised at the question, though she answered it readily enough.

"Umm-m! Where were you in service before you came here?"

Again her expression registered surprise. "Nowhere," she replied.

"This was your first place, you mean?"

"First time in service," she assented.

"I see. And what were you doing before then?"

"I was—I was in the chorus at the Quadrarian—in revue."

"Miss Taylor, did you hear those shots fired when Mr. Carter was killed, at four o'clock this morning?" He leaned toward her and put the question with a sort of tense abruptness.

She shook her head. "I was asleep," she answered.

"Have you a room to yourself?"

"Yes."

"The first one at the top of the stairs, isn't it?"

She gave him a frightened look, and Head, standing a little behind her, nodded silent approval of his chief's astuteness.

"Yes, but on the top floor," she answered.

"What time did you go to bed?" Wadden pursued.

"About one o'clock, I think."

"In your own room, and alone?"

"Yes. Of course I was in my own room, and of course I was alone!"

"There isn't any 'of course' about it, Miss Taylor," Wadden said gravely. "I want to tell you, anything you say here and now stays inside these four walls, but if I have to instruct for questioning you at the inquest to-day, it may be a very different matter. I'm not accusing you of any connection with Mr. Carter's death, but I want to know all I can, to help me in finding who killed him, and though the things I ask you may seem silly, they've all got a reason behind them. Parlourmaids with no experience don't get sixty pounds a year round here, as you know very well. Now we'll carry on. You saw as much of Mr. Carter as anyone in this house, didn't you, and more?"

"I suppose I did," she admitted.

"What was the time when you last saw him alive?"

"About half-past eleven last night," she answered.

"You neither saw not heard any more of him after that?"

"I—no." But she hesitated a little too long on the negative.

"Ah! Not good enough. What was the time when he came to your room at the top of the stairs, Miss Taylor? Don't lie about it, or I may floor you from another source. Be careful, now—what time was it?"

"He—he knocked at my door after everyone had gone," she admitted in a low voice, gazing down toward the floor.

"And you got up and let him in?"

"I didn't!" She looked up at him again. "I told him to go to hell."

"By the look of it, he's—never mind, though. How often did he come up to your room after everyone else had gone to bed?"

"Not often, lately." Again she looked down toward the floor.

"Was this the first time you'd refused to let him in?"

She tried to look at him, and failed. "Yes," she whispered. "And now— Oh, he's dead! He's dead!"

She forced herself back to composure as Arabella entered with three cups of coffee on a tray. Each of the men took a cup, and by the time Wadden had sipped his and put the cup down Phyllis was composed again.

"Why wouldn't you let him in last night?" Wadden demanded quietly.

"He—he'd been carrying on in the drawing-room with that Miss Perry, the fair one—Ethel, her name is. I caught 'em at it when I went in. I didn't want him coming to me, after that."

"A pretty business—oh, a pretty business!" Wadden mused aloud. "Now I want to know, Miss Taylor, do you know any reason why Mr. Carter should be down at the front door at four in the morning? Somebody might have rung the bell, of course, or thrown a stone at his window, but do you know of anything or anyone he'd go down for?"

"Yes, I do," she answered, more readily. "Him and me was in the drawing-room yesterday afternoon—I'd taken tea in to him, and the 'phone went. I stopped in when he answered it, and he said—'Four o'clock—yes. I'll come down myself, since you want to be so secret.' It was either 'secret' or 'secrecy' he said. I think it was 'secrecy,' though. I know he said he'd come down himself."

"At four o'clock in the morning?"

"No, just four o'clock. I thought he meant come down to Westingborough at four next day, or something—it didn't strike me till you asked just now that he meant come down to the front door. Of course, that was it! He meant come down to be killed, at four this morning."

"He didn't know he meant that," Wadden suggested. "Could you hear the voice in the telephone—hear what it was like?"

"Only the sort of mumble you always hear. Just a noise."

"Was it a squeaky noise, or a rumbling one?"

"Just a mumble. It wasn't squeaky, and it wasn't rumble. Just an ordinary little noise, so you couldn't tell in the least who was talking or what they said, not even if it was a man or a woman."

"What time was this?"

"Eddie—Mr. Carter always had his tea at half-past four if he was in, and this was just after I took it in."

"Immediately after? I mean, you hadn't been billing and cooing before the telephone bell went and he answered it?"

"There's been precious little billing and cooing for me the last two months," she answered bitterly. "I'd made up my mind to go if things didn't alter, and I hadn't any hope they would."

"D'you get on well with the other servants?" Wadden inquired, with an appearance of kindly solicitude over the point.

"No, I don't! I hate the lot of them."

"Well, Miss Taylor, you've given us some very valuable information, and that bit about the telephone call will have to come in at the inquest, but I see no need to disclose your intimacy with the deceased man, for the present. Thanks very much, I won't keep you any longer. Head, d'you think we can find out anything about that telephone call?"

"I'll see what can be done," Head assured him.

"Ah-h!" He yawned widely. "We all knew what he was, of course, but that doesn't alter the fact that it's a dirty murder. Now there's the other housemaid, Hetty Fraser, and Adams and his wife Minnie to be seen, though it's my opinion we won't get another thing out of any one of them. Then we can get down to your side of it, this chap who climbed a tree and flew away. Jones, push that chauffeur bloke in here to us, and tell the gentle Arabella that coffee of hers is so good I'd like some more, if she's got any handy."

He looked up at Head as the constable went out.

"I've got it in my bones—and that's a long way down—that you won't get to the end of this case either to-day or to-morrow, Head," he remarked. "You'll have to use your wits if you don't want to find yourself up a tree."

"I've been up one already this morning," Head answered ruefully. "Look at my overcoat!"

CHAPTER III

WASHED OUT

RAIN HAD BEGUN to fall steadily when Superintendent Wadden and Inspector Head seated themselves in the back of the big car after instructing Constable Williams to remain in charge at the Grange, until Sergeant Wells could be sent to relieve him. Wadden lowered himself into his corner with a grunt; Jones was already seated beside the man Jeffries, who was at the steering-wheel.

"Now what d'ye make of it?" Wadden inquired, as Jeffries turned the car about to go along the drive to the road.

"Nothing, yet," Head answered, "except that X, the man in the old boots, committed the murder. Puzzle, find X."

"Let's see what we've got," Wadden suggested. "State it, man."

"In sequence, eh? Not a bad idea," Head concurred. "Well, then, four months ago Carter took a fancy to this girl Taylor while he was in London, and fetched her down here ostensibly as parlourmaid. The other servants didn't like the arrangement, but they like their jobs too well to make a fuss, and at sixty pounds a year she wasn't a mere parlourmaid, while the clothes she was wearing this morning prove sixty wasn't all she was getting. Lately, Carter was getting a bit tired of her, and had rather a crush on this Ethel Perry—and we know already he was that sort of man, eh? How's that for groundwork, chief?"

"Go ahead—but the Taylor girl had nothing to do with the shooting. She didn't hate him enough for that, yet."

"That's obvious. Yesterday afternoon, she took in his tea to the drawing-room, and overheard his end of a telephone conversation, in which he arranged to come down to the door at four o'clock this morning to interview X—it was X put that call through, for a certainty. And we want a far more detailed account of that telephone conversation—Carter's end of it, at least, from the girl Taylor."

"I know. I left that for the inquest. She'll have got her wits more about her by this afternoon, and from what I make of her she's regretful enough over his death to help us find out who killed him.

We already know that he made the appointment to come to the door himself, for secrecy, and that she hasn't any idea who it was calling up. Go on—Wells can wait. We'll stop here while you finish."

"Next, then," Head pursued, "Carter had that dinner-party and the razzle after it. I've been over the guests in my mind already. The Quades—we can practically rule them out. Quade is a racehorse trainer, I know, and a harmless sort. Young Pollen wouldn't hurt a fly, and he's lived in Westingborough all his life, and Betty Hurder would travel miles to get a smell at a champagne cork, and sing for her supper too—any old song that was asked of her. Denham—I don't see him at all in that galley. He's a lot better than the type Carter generally had round him. The Perry girls are much more in Carter's line, and Frank Mortimer is the darkest horse of the eight people Carter had at the Grange last night. But it appears from what the cook said that the party didn't finish till just past three, so any one of the eight would have had to hustle to get into those boots and come back and do the shooting at two minutes past four."

"You can go round the lot of them to tell them they'll be wanted at the inquest—give the summonses yourself," Wadden suggested. "If I fix it for three this afternoon, can you do the lot?"

"Easily, I should think," Head assented.

Jeffries had drawn the car to a standstill in the road about twenty yards short of where Sergeant Wells waited by the kissing-gate. Wadden made no move toward getting out, yet. "Go on," he urged.

"Me, sir?" Jeffries asked from the driving-seat.

"No. You sit here, and listen to the rest of this story, if you like. We'll get out when I'm ready. Carry on, Head."

"Some time between three and four, just after the party had left, most probably, Carter went up to the girl Taylor's room. I think he wanted to persuade her that he was only fooling with Ethel Perry, and she was still the light of his eyes, but however that may have been she wouldn't let him in. You see, he had to keep awake till four o'clock, since he was due to go to the front door himself and open it, and it would be well past three when he knocked at Taylor's door. And at that time, or a little later, X in the boots must have begun moving. He came along this road from Westingborough, went through that gate, and up to the Grange. Carter opened the front door to him, and he fired two shots, as we know, the first of them at about two minutes past four. Then he came back and climbed that ash tree by means of a rope slung over the branch, and he didn't come down again, but he isn't still up there. That is, he didn't come down to make any impression on the snow with those boots, and there's no other footprint near that corresponds remotely to the boots. All that's visible is a woman who cycled as far as the stile and wheeled her bicycle along the path after she'd lifted it over the stile, and the marks left by Alfred Potter on his way to Parham's garage—and he came later than the woman cyclist."

"And which way did X go?" Wadden inquired ironically.

"No way at all," Head asserted. "He climbed the tree, and the snow shows that he didn't come down—shows it far beyond the radius of the tree. And he didn't go along the top of the wall—I've made sure of that, while I was up the tree. No marks of any kind."

"Which is absurd," Wadden commented. "Good old Euclid! Let's see."

He got out from the car, and Head followed him. With an order to Jeffries to stay where he was, the two went to where Wells stood beside the road. Wadden looked up at the sky and shook his head.

"In a couple of hours all these tracks will be washed out," he observed. "You took photographs, I understand, Wells?"

"Eighteen altogether, sir," the sergeant answered.

"It should be a pretty complete record then. Yes, I see. He came from the top end of Market Street, and when you get to that road junction round the bend there's not a hope in Hades of trailing him further. Nevile's works are running two shifts this month, and the first lot goes in at five-thirty, which means that snow will be churned to mud a quarter-mile farther on. Potter—yes, that'll be his feet. Now the bicycle—yes, she dropped off here, if it was a she. It's doubtful, with those heels—might have been a small-built man. Wheeled the bike to the stile and lifted it over—yes. And Potter came along and planted his clumsy foot right over hers where she stood to lift the machine over. Walked it along the path—what's that other set coming and going, off to the left there?"

"Mine, sir," Wells explained. "Mr. Head told me to—"

"All right, sergeant. I want to see all I can before the rain distorts the prints too much. Now through the gate—yes. Both going to the Grange and coming back, and the coming back ones stop just as you said, Head. Swung himself into the tree, eh?"

"I found the mark of the rope on that branch over the gate," Head answered. "From there, he shifted the rope to the branch sticking out over the road, as if he meant to lower himself down by it from there. But you can see for yourself the boots don't come down there."

"Dropped into a car, then."

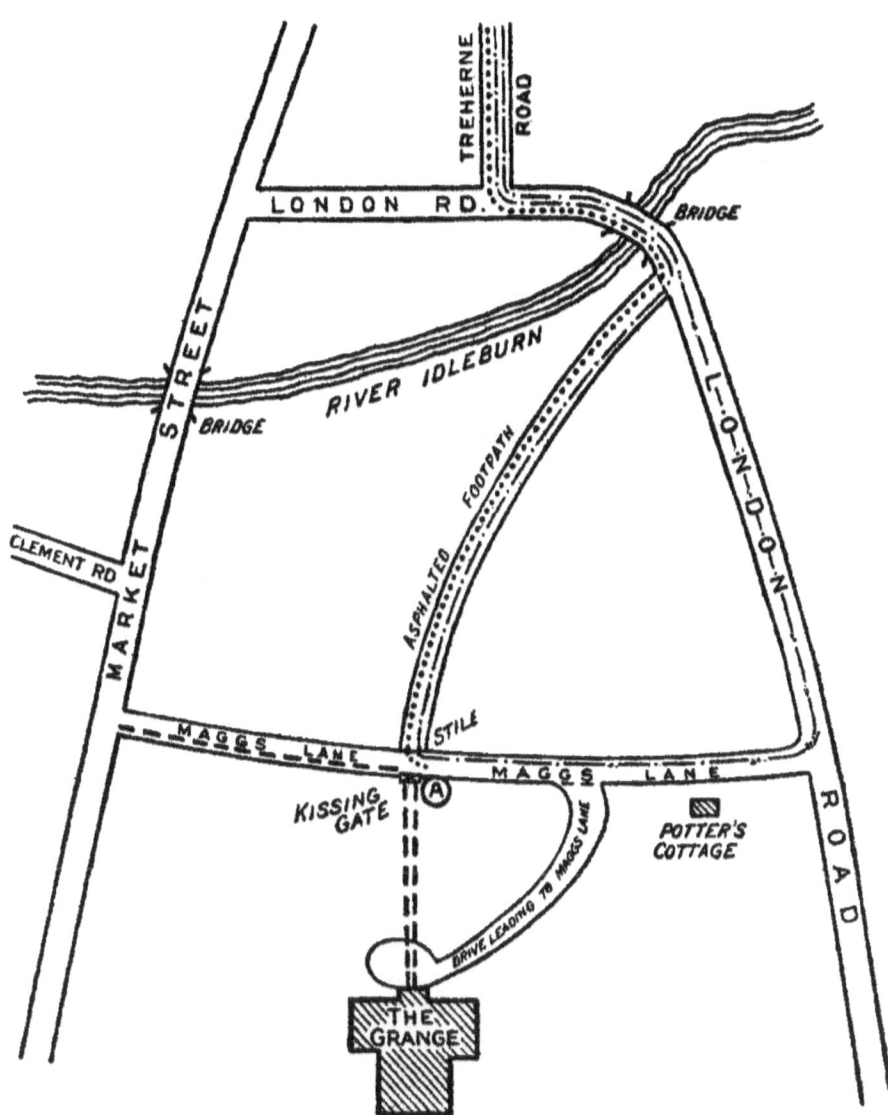

PLAN OF PART OF WESTINGBOROUGH GIVING RELEVANT DETAILS
TO THE UNFINISHED TRACKS OF THE OLD BOOTS.

- - - - - Tracks of Old Boots.
········· Footprints made by Cyclist.
—·—·—·— Tracks made by Bicycle Tyres.
(A) Ash Tree, one branch extending over Kissing Gate and
one out over Maggs Lane.

"If so, it was one of the four cars from Carter's place. Only those four had left tracks in the snow when I got here."

"Why didn't they leave tracks going to the house?"

"Because there wasn't any snow before midnight."

"Kick me, Head. Never mind, though. Have you made any cast round to pick up the prints of those boots?"

"Not yet. When I was up in that tree, I could see clean snow for a good two hundred yards in every direction, and apart from what we have here there wasn't a print on it. Nothing at all. You see, this Maggs Lane isn't overmuch used—there's only the Grange and Potter's cottage beyond it, and then you get Market Street and its continuation that way, and behind us, the other side of the Grange, the main Westingborough-London road."

"That cyclist. What's she or he doing here between midnight and four o'clock—or five o'clock, or whatever time it was?"

"We've got to find out," Head answered. "Evidently she came off the London Road—I traced her wheelmarks as far as the Grange gateway—and dismounted here to take the path and rejoin the road just before you get to the river bridge— Gosh! Chief, she's in it!"

"Why?" Wadden asked interestedly.

"Else why should she cycle down this lane from the main road, lift her bicycle over the stile, and walk along the path with it only to rejoin the road she'd left just before you get to the bridge? It's a good road for cycling, all the way, and by coming round this way and walking the path she puts a quarter of an hour on to her journey."

Wadden shook his head. "Maybe," he said, "and maybe not. Don't jump to conclusions, Head. Are you going to suggest that X dropped out of the tree on to her bike? If so, what happened to him and his feet when she lifted the bike over the stile? I'll grant she might have piggy-backed him along the path, and might have climbed over the stile with him on her back while he held the bike, but if that had been so she wouldn't have left this one even track. Look at it, man—as plain as print, though the footsteps are going a bit saggy in the rain. He'd have had to drop down on her shoulders, retrieve his rope, and sit tight while she wheeled the bike to the stile. Then one or other of them would have had to lift it over, and she'd have had to climb the stile with him on her shoulders and make that walk along the path. And that steady, regular set of footprints brings Euclid in again—it's absurd. Accessory in some way, perhaps, but not accessory after in that way. It would be far too damned conspicuous, for one thing."

Head went to the stile and gazed down at the footprints in the soggy snow. They retained enough character to tell their tale.

"You're right," he said disappointedly as he returned. "It wasn't done that way. But he went, somehow. Wells, did you get those measurements of the two sets of paces?"

"Yes, sir. The old boots average twenty-nine inches going to the Grange, and twenty-nine and a half coming back to the gate here. I took both averages over eighty paces. The feet beside the bicycle average just on twenty-eight inches over another eighty paces along that path. I'd just finished working the three sets out when you came along in the car. There's been nobody along here since the lorry."

"How far have you been along the path?"

"All the way, sir, up to where it goes out to the road between the white posts. It's a consistent track all the way."

"Right. Now hand me that camera and the films, and you go back to the Grange and take over there for the present. Tell Williams to report back at the station. Chief, we've got to find that cyclist."

"Also, a man who climbed up a tree and flew away," Wadden retorted dryly. "Well, I've seen all I want here. We'll get back, I think."

They went back to the car. At Wadden's instruction, Jeffries drove very slowly past the kissing-gate and along the lane to the point where it emerged to Market Street, and all the way they saw the prints of the old boots on their left, showing how the mysterious X had come along the lane, but no sign of his returning. Wadden gazed out, registering each footprint in his mind, but after a hundred yards or so Head appeared to lose interest, and sat deep in thought. Jeffries turned then into the churned slush and wakened activity of Market Street, and there put on speed until he slowed again to draw up outside the police station, where all three of his passengers descended.

"I'm coming in," Head announced. "It's too early to go round after Carter's guests, yet, and I've got an idea."

He retired to his own room, where he took a. large sheet of paper and set to work on it with his fountain-pen. A quarter of an hour or less passed, and then he entered the superintendent's office. Wadden had had breakfast sent in there to save time, and Head laid his sheet of paper down beside his chief's plate on the flat-topped desk.

"How's that?" he asked. "Do you agree?"

Wadden took a drink of coffee, and then read—

POLICE NOTICE

TO ALL CYCLISTS

Any cyclist who passed along Maggs Lane from London Road to the path leading from Westingborough Grange grounds to the Idleburn bridge, and went along the path toward the bridge, between midnight of January 19th and 6 AM. of January 20th, is requested to communicate at once with Superintendent Wadden at Westingborough head police station. Also any person who may have seen a cyclist in the vicinity of Maggs Lane or of the path between the above hours is requested to inform the police at once.

"Umm-m!" Wadden commented. "Might be worded better. D'you think it's going to fetch your cyclist here?"

"I don't," Head answered decidedly. "It's going to prove that cyclist accessory to the murder by showing that he or she is afraid to come forward. We can have it posted all over the town by noon, and it's pretty evident that the cyclist who came round by that path in the dark knows Westingborough well—is no stranger to the district. Whoever it is will see the notice, and if we get no response that person is either accessory or even the murderer himself."

"Accessory, yes," Wadden said thoughtfully, "but the footprints and the tree branches put the other out of our possibilities, I think. Here, you'd better have some breakfast, man. You'll think better on a full tummy, and this is no five-minute job. It's a pity about this rain, but you'd got pretty much all you could out of those footprints."

"We'll have the films developed," Head said. "Wells can be trusted for a complete record. It doesn't matter if the tracks are washed out, now. Yes, I do feel rather like eating, now you speak of it."

* * * * *

"Head! HEAD! Come back here, out of that car!"

Head, about to set out on a round of interviews with all who had been guests at the Grange the preceding evening, descended to the pavement again in response to the superintendent's agitated summons.

"What's happened now, chief?" he inquired.

"I haven't got apoplexy hurrying out to catch you, but that's not your fault," Wadden answered. "Come inside with me. I rather think we've got what used to be called a clue."

Head followed to the superintendent's office, and saw, standing by the desk, a young constable in uniform. Wadden blew out his lips and gave the man one of his fiercest looks, and then sat down.

"Story, Borrow," he commanded. "Tell Inspector Head what you saw, and make it a witness-box report. He's in a hurry."

"Very good, sir. At three A.M. to-day, sir"—he turned to address his report to the inspector—"I passed Parham's garage in Market Street as I patrolled my beat, and turned to go along London Road, toward the bridge. It would be five minutes later, or seven minutes at the most, when a woman on a bicycle passed me, coming from the direction of the bridge. She was in nurse's uniform. That is, sir, she had on one of those long capes nurses wear, and a little bonnet with strings. I saw that much clearly as she cycled under a street lamp, but she was on the far side of the street from me, and kept looking at the pavement on her side of the street, so I didn't see her face. She appeared tall, something between five feet eight and five feet ten, and as nearly as the cloak or cape would let me see, I should say she was slim too. I didn't take particular notice of her, knowing that nurses are out all hours, but I looked back after she'd passed me, and saw she'd turned into Treherne Road. The bicycle was fitted with an electric lamp—and that's all I can tell you about her, sir."

"You didn't see her till she was over the bridge—on your side of it, that is?" Head queried.

"No, sir. I'd stopped a lorry soon after turning into London Road to make the driver relight his off-side lamp—he was fitted with oil-lamps, and it had gone out. I looked back when I heard him start his engine again, and when I looked in front of me again, here comes this nurse on her bicycle. It would be between five and ten minutes past three, then—certainly not more than ten minutes past."

"Carry on, man," Wadden bade. "This isn't all, Head."

"I went on over the bridge, sir," the constable proceeded, "and saw the track of a bicycle coming out from the path that leads across a field to Westingborough Grange—"

"And footprints beside the bicycle track on the path?" Head interrupted questioningly, "Did you see them?"

The man looked puzzled. "I couldn't say, sir. I didn't look along the path. It was pitch-dark then, and what little light there was from the nearest street lamp only showed me the wheel tracks close to the side of the road—there's no pavement beyond the bridge, you know, sir. I just thought to myself that's the way that nurse has come, and turned about to come back over the bridge."

"You didn't notice any footprints, then?" Head persisted.

"No, sir, but they may have been there all the same. I'm not sure."

"I am, though," Head said, with a note almost of exultation.

"Sure of what?" Wadden asked sharply.

"Never mind, chief, for the minute. It's a theory, no more, and it needs testing, but down in my mind I feel sure I've got this clear. Is that all you have to report, Borrow?"

"No, sir, not quite. I'd gone back along Market Street and up Clement Road, and turned back to come into Market Street again. I could see Parham's clock, and the time was three thirty-five. I could just see a young man on the far side of Market Street from me, coming from the direction of London Road—"

"That is, going toward Maggs Lane—the end of it," Wadden interjected. "The way the old boots went, in fact."

"How could you see it was a young man?" Head asked the constable.

"He passed under a street lamp before I lost sight of him, sir," Borrow answered. "He was dressed in riding-breeches and either gaiters or knee-boots, and carried something under his arm, something that made him draw his hand up and keep the arm close to his side. Under his left arm, and I was on his right as I saw him, so I don't know what it was he was carrying."

"It was a pair of boots, size ten, and possibly a coil of rope as well," Head said with conviction. "Go on, though. What was he like?"

"Not very tall—five feet eight or nine, I'd say. He was walking quickly and keeping to the shadows all he could, I thought. Looked a gentleman, as nearly as I could tell—didn't carry himself like a groom or stable hand. What made me think of that was that I'd seen Mr. Quade, the racehorse trainer, driving the opposite way before I turned into Clement Road. This man was rather like Mr. Quade in build, thin and active, and light-footed, and he was hurrying for some reason. He had no overcoat on, only what looked to me like a double-breasted jacket, and a cap, not a hat. When I got to the junction of Clement Road and Market Street again, he was out of sight."

Head thought it over. "Is that all?" he asked at last.

"That's all, sir. When Jeffries told me about the murder at the Grange I thought I ought to report this to Mr. Wadden at once."

"Quite right, Borrow. Are the nurse and the young man the only two people you saw on your beat between three and four o'clock?"

"They are, sir, except for the lorry driver and his mate."

"Chief"—Head turned to Wadden—"has that notice I drafted gone for printing yet, do you know?"

"I sent it off while you were wolfing sausages," Wadden answered.

"Well, they'll send a proof. If you wouldn't mind adding 'And Nurses' to the second line in heavy type, and after 'Any cyclist' in the text add 'or lady in nurse's uniform with bicycle,' it'll make our check still more complete, especially if she doesn't come forward."

"And put her still more on her guard," Wadden pointed out.

"Not more," Head dissented. "The people concerned in that murder are very fully on their guard already. No fingerprint on the Grange door-handle or anywhere else, though the murderer must have closed the door after the shooting, since there was nobody else to close it—we start this without a single clue of the conventional kind, apart from those footprints, and the rain's washed them out by now. If she's innocent, she'll come forward. If she doesn't, we know we've two people to find, and that may be easier than finding one."

"Probably will be," Wadden assented. "I'll alter the notice to fit a lady cyclist in a nurse's cloak and hat, anyhow. Or do they call it a bonnet? I must get that from the hospital before I alter the proof. Strings under the chin, Borrow?"

"Yes, sir, as nearly as I could see. She kept her face turned away from me, though, and the street lamps don't give much light."

"And you didn't look for footprints beside the tyre marks?" Head inquired, returning to the point again.

"No, sir. You see, I should have had to focus my belt lamp, and for what looked like a nurse coming back from some job it didn't appear worth while. I'd no idea there'd been a murder, sir."

"Neither had we, then," Wadden remarked. "Well, Head, I thought you ought to have this under your thatch before you start your round. Meanwhile I'll have every nurse in Westingborough investigated, and find if there's one of any sort living in or near Treherne Road. Leave all that to me. And get on to Carter's past life as soon as you can. There's some old grudge behind a planned job like this."

"I hope to come back with a history of him," Head said.

"Old boots, nurses on bicycles, young men in riding-breeks, and a chap who flies up out of trees and doesn't come down —Gee-whiz!" Wadden soliloquised, and blew gustily ceilingward. "Head, it's a packet, and no bloomin' error! Off you go, man. Borrow, I don't want you any longer. Keep on the way you're go-ing, and you'll be a credit to us yet, but be a bit more nosey, man. No matter whom you see out between one and five in the morning, conclude they're up to no good, and act accordingly—in a quiet way, of course. There'll be a whole series of promotions on my retirement, and your name might get in among the recommenda-tions somehow or other. I'm keeping an eye on you,"

"Thank you, sir."

"That's the first time I've ever been thanked for keeping an eye on anyone. Now you go off duty and remember what I've told you."

He took up a sheaf of reports that had been lying on his desk, in token of dismissal, and blew at them as if he hated them.

CHAPTER IV

THE LATE MR. EDWARD CARTER

IN PLACE OF the steady rain of early morning, a chill drizzle caused Head to set his windscreen-wiper to work when he set out on his round of visits, not in the big car in which he and Wadden had gone to Westingborough Grange, but in a fast little coupé which he drove himself, and used for visits to village stations in the district. He went out, first, to Quade's training establishment, which was situated on the far side of Westingborough from the Grange.

He saw four stable lads walking rugged and bonneted horses round a yard as he descended from the car, and Quade himself, gaitered and horsey-looking, turned from watching them in the gateway of the yard as Head approached him. Borrow's description of the young man he had seen as resembling this man recurred to the inspector's mind. He nodded a casual greeting: Quade was the hail-fellow-well-met sort with whom such a form of salutation would pass.

" 'Morning, inspector. Come to see whether my crocks exceed the speed limit? I forgot, though—there isn't one, now."

"Good morning, Mr. Quade. No, I've come to warn you to attend the inquest on Mr. Carter at Westingborough Grange at three o'clock this afternoon. He was shot dead there at four o'clock this morning."

"Good God! Inspector, you're joking!"

If he had had any doubt regarding Quade's innocence, this reception of the news would have dispelled it: but he had had no doubt.

"I'm not," he said. "Carter has been murdered."

"At four o'clock? Why, we only left the place at three—about three, that is. My wife and I, I mean."

"I know. That's why you may be wanted for evidence. I don't know that you will, but both you and Mrs. Quade must attend. Shall I see her and tell her, or may I rely on you?"

"I'll— Oh, rely on me by all means! I'll tell her. Three o'clock, at the Grange. But who—who did it? Have you got him yet?"

The inspector shook his head. "You may hear something at the inquest," he said evasively. "And you left at three or thereabouts. Were you the last of the party to leave?"

"No. We all went pretty much together—I drove off first with my wife, and the rest followed us. At least, I believe they all did. I know Hugh Denham was just behind me coming along Maggs Lane."

"Alone in his car?"

"Yes. He'd left his hood down, and had to shake and wipe the snow off the driving-seat before he started up—it hadn't started snowing when we got there for dinner."

"And after," Head suggested, "nobody thought to see if it were snowing—or anything else, for that matter."

"Well, to tell the truth, inspector, I shouldn't have taken my wife there if I'd known it was going to be that sort of a party. Not that she didn't enjoy herself, but—still you say he's dead, and I'd better not say any more about that. I can't believe—" He broke off.

"On the other hand," Head said gently, "the more you say, the more help you may give. We've got to get his murderer, you know."

"You mean—yes, I see. Well, I'd only met him in the hunting-field, till then—he followed the Westingborough, you know—and rode like a sack on a barrel, if I may say so much of a dead man. He invited my wife and me last week, and told me Hugh Denham would be there. It was that made us accept. I thought Denham —well, you know, it was a sort of warranty. Mrs. Quade thought so, at least. It was a good dinner, with the bubbly flowing free, but everything quite all right. I thought Fred Pollen had quite as much as was good for him, and that Miss Hurder made one or two remarks I wouldn't care to hear from my wife, but it was pleasant on the whole. Then, after dinner, that Mr. Mortimer—do you know him, though?"

"I've seen him," Head assented. "Never spoken to him, though."

"Well, he came in with the Perry girls. Carter ordered out another case of champagne—another case!—and said something about making a night of it. By that time I was—well, a bit elated, if you like to call it that, and Mrs. Quade was quite safe with Mr. Denham, I knew, so—well, there we were. I thought of leaving about midnight, but couldn't find Carter. He'd strayed off and got lost with the younger Miss Perry somewhere, and she looked rather rumpled when they came back. By that time I'd forgotten about wanting to go. Somebody had set a gramophone going, one of the sort that changes its own records, and we were dancing out in the big entrance-hall—it's parquet, you know, and they rolled the rugs out of the way. And none of us left till three. It all broke up suddenly, then—I thought Carter wanted to get rid of us."

"Did you hear him say anything about an appointment for the morning—for any time in the morning?" Head asked.

Quade shook his head. "No—I hardly spoke to him after dinner, till we said good-bye to come away. He was too busy with Ethel Perry for any of us to get many words with him."

"Quite a cheerful party, eh?" Head suggested.

"Very nearly what the Yanks call a petting party," Quade responded. "There was Carter carrying on with Ethel Perry, and going off with her away from the rest of his guests, and I saw Miss Hurder sitting on young Pollen's knee after a dance, and Mortimer and the other Miss Perry tried out some steps as they called it, but it wasn't the sort of dancing you expect to see oft the stage—or on it either, in this country. As a matter of fact, I got my hair pulled when we got home."

"Mrs. Quade didn't enjoy it, I gather?" Head inquired sympathetically. "That is, she didn't quite approve?"

"You've said it!" Quade assented, with earnest gravity.

"And you all left at about three?"

"Somewhere about then, as nearly as I can tell. As I said, Denham followed us in that open Bugatti of his—and it sounded like a machine gun out of order when he started up. Mortimer had his coat on, and the two Perry girls had got into their wraps, and I saw Pollen hand Miss Murder into his car as we were leaving. About three o'clock."

"Ah! Thanks for all you've told me, Mr. Quade. Don't forget, three this afternoon at the Grange. I must get along, now."

He drove back into Westingborough, and drew up at a block of business offices at the corner of Market Street and London Road. On the first floor he found a door which carried a brass plate stating that "Hugh Denham, F.R.I.B.A.," occupied that particular office. A lean, elderly clerk took his name, and ushered him into a comfortably furnished inner office in response to his request to see Mr. Denham.

A tall, well-set-up man in the early thirties turned from a drawing-board at Head's entry, inquiry in his clear grey eyes.

"What have I been doing, inspector?" he asked. "And what can I do for you? Do sit down, won't you?" He indicated a chair.

Head took no heed of the invitation. "I want you to tell me what's wrong with the exhaust of your sports Bugatti, Mr. Denham," he opened.

"Ah! Forty shillings and costs for having an improperly silenced exhaust, eh? Well, if it's got to be, it's got to be. But I assure you it will be all right after to-day. I dropped some water on the exhaust manifold while it was nearly red hot and cracked it, but Parham himself told me this morning that the new manifold he put on order has arrived, and he's putting it on for me to-day. So I throw myself on the mercy of the court. Do sit down and have a cigarette."

He offered his case. Head accepted a cigarette and a light, and seated himself. Denham leaned against the stand that held his drawing-board, and in turn lighted up.

"Meanwhile, you've been making a noise like pistol-shots," Head affirmed with thoughtful gravity.

"Guilty, and I know it's an offence. But I have to use the car." He smiled pleasantly. "Can't you let me off?"

"If it hadn't been for that noise, Mr. Denham," Head said, without smiling, "we might be nearer than we are to catching the man who murdered Mr. Carter at four o'clock this morning."

"WHAT?" Denham almost jumped, and dropped his cigarette.

"The shots that killed Carter were mistaken for the explosions from your exhaust by the servants who heard them," Head pursued unmovedly, "so they made no attempt at finding out who fired the shots."

"Do you mean to say Carter's dead?" Denham gasped.

"Quite dead," Head assured him. "Shot, at four this morning."

"But—but I was up at the Grange last night!" Denham pointed out. "I didn't leave there till the early hours of the morning. I—inspector, you haven't come here because you think—" He paused, almost fearfully, staring at the seated man before him.

"If it were that," Head said, "I shouldn't be here alone, and you'd have had handcuffs on before now. No. You left the Grange at about three o'clock, and Carter was murdered at four—never mind that, for the present, though. Mr. and Mrs. Quade drove off first, and you followed them. Were you alone in your car?"

"Yes—except for a packet of snow, that is. I'd left the hood down when I went there—to the Grange—and had to clean some of the snow out before I got in myself."

"Did you put the hood up before you left?"

"No—it wasn't snowing, then. The car was open. I drove it to Parham's this morning for the new manifold, and told them to clean it out and dry it as well. I had to sit on my folded overcoat."

"You know the kissing-gate in the wall, opposite the path leading to the Idleburn bridge—in Maggs Lane, I mean?"

"Yes. What about it, though?"

"When you passed that gate, did you see anything or anybody?"

"Nobody and nothing," Denham assured him. "Not a sign. Why?"

"Did you slow up there at all?"

Denham shook his head. "No. I was just behind the Quades' car, and another—Pollen's I think it was—was close behind me. We all left at about the same time. But about Carter being murdered—"

"You'll hear all about that at the inquest at the Grange at three o'clock this afternoon," Head interrupted. "I'm here to warn you to attend the inquest. What sort of party was it last night?"

Denham hesitated. Then he looked his questioner squarely in the eyes, and shook his head gravely.

"I didn't want to go," he said. "But I don't know if you know that Carter employed me as architect for the new wing he gave to the Westingborough hospital. He made a point of my accepting this invitation. He's been trying to get in with Westingborough people ever since he took the Grange. And it needed only that party to prove that he'd never get in, if he tried for a thousand years."

"Like that was it?" Head inquired interestedly.

"The man's an utter bounder—God forgive me! You've just told me he's dead. I ought not to have said that."

"Mr. Denham, I want you to say everything you can, to help me in laying hands on the man who murdered him."

"Have you any idea who it might be?" Denham asked.

Head did not answer at once. He was utterly certain of the innocence of the man before him. What he wanted to say, he reflected, would in all probability be said at the inquest, and Denham might be able to help in some way if he said it now.

"I think," he answered at last, "it was a young man of about five feet eight to ten—not as tall as you, you realise—who passed along Market Street not long after you left the Grange this morning. He was dressed in riding-kit, and carried a pair of boots and a rope under his arm, and he walked from outside this office, I think, to where Maggs Lane comes into Market Street just outside the town."

In turn Denham was silent, gazing down at the floor.

"Why from outside this office?" he asked at last.

"By, that, I mean that he walked along Market Street," Head answered. "I don't particularise this office any more than, say, Parham's garage, or the Duke of York Hotel. He walked along Market Street at about half-past three, or a little later, on his way to the Grange."

Denham turned away and went to the window of his room, where he stood looking out for some seconds. His manner, Head noted, had completely changed. Abruptly he turned back toward his seated visitor.

"What can I tell you, inspector?" he asked.

"Did you see that young man, or anyone else, as you drove back from the Grange this morning?" Head demanded quietly.

"Except for a policeman here in Market Street and the Quades in the car ahead of me, I didn't see a living soul as I drove," Denham answered, with utter, patent sincerity.

Head thought over the reply. It was truthful, obviously, but he scented a reservation in it somewhere. But further questions on the point, he felt, would only put Denham on his guard: they might be put at the inquest, where the man would be on oath—he was the type that would heed the sanctity of a promise to tell the whole truth.

"So you didn't think much of the party?" he suggested.

"I—well! Quade got squiffy"—Denham appeared to answer more easily now—"and poor little Mrs. Quade almost turned to me for protection—not from her husband, but from the general rowdiness. And—yes, amorousness. Pollen and Betty Hurder cuddling openly, and that man Mortimer with Lilian Perry—there was dancing on the parquet out in the entrance-hall, and—I felt it served me right for accepting the invitation. Think me a prig if you like, though I've no objection to a general frolic, but it all seemed to me like a bad night-club being unusually suggestive—immorally suggestive, if you understand."

"Oh, I understand," Head agreed, "and we've had you up for speeding in the Bugatti, and know it was you put the pyjama jacket on the statue in the square on New Year's night. A pretty lively prig, altogether. And you say Pollen was close behind you, driving home?"

"Up to the end of Maggs Lane. He turned left, there, and I turned right to follow the Quades along Market Street. He lives along to the left there, and the Hurders live next door to him, you know."

"Yes, I know." Head rose to his feet. "I'll go and warn him for the inquest. Three o'clock at the Grange this afternoon, Mr.

Denham. You can take this as the official notification that you are to attend."

"I'll be there," Denham promised. "It seems impossible to realise this, though. Only an hour after I left him—"

Driving out to the Pollens' house, on the outskirts of the town, Head reflected over this last interview. Denham had kept back something: he had, Head felt almost certain, recognised or thought he recognised somebody in that description of the young man in riding-kit, and meant to keep whatever knowledge he possessed to himself. It might be possible to make him reveal something at the inquest, though.

A clean-living, high-spirited youngster, a general favourite in the town, well-connected, and doing well in his profession, he was neither murderer nor accomplice, Head felt certain. And, going over all the men whom Denham might know, the inspector could think of nobody in the least like that young man in riding-kit, with something under his arm, out at half-past three of a wintry morning. There were not so many young men in Westingborough of the class and type with which Hugh Denham associated that they could not be placed. Yet Denham's change of manner, his momentary unease, pointed to some knowledge. . . .

Head braked the car to a standstill outside the Pollens' gate, got out, and went along the path to the double-fronted, rather pretentious-looking house with its stucco-pillared portico. It marked the type of people, he reflected, who would be willing to associate with such a man as Carter: probably young Pollen had been quite pleased with his invitation, and evidently he had enjoyed the party.

"Yes, Mr. Fred is in the study," the maid informed Head as she stood back for him to enter the house. "I'll tell him, if you'll wait."

He waited, amid a collection of pseudo-artistic trifles with which Fred's mother had seen fit to deck the tiny entrance-hall. Fred himself, son of a retired builder who had made much more money than he ought, out of erecting rabbit-hutches to house people of the working class, was supposed to be reading for the law. He was a terribly slow reader, having been at it now for more than four years.

Head followed the maid to the study after a period of waiting, and found Fred Pollen standing before a good fire in his dressing-gown. An empty cup stood in its saucer on the table, and though Fred might have gone so far as to wash, he had neither shaved nor brushed his hair. He looked thoroughly unappetising, Head decided.

" 'Mornin', inspector. Take a pew if you feel like it. What's up?"

"So you've not heard what happened this morning?" Head inquired.

"Just got up," Fred answered. "Have a heart, man. I've been having a bit of a thick night—spun it out a bit."

"And evidently reeled it home," the inspector retorted sourly. "I merely want to warn you to attend the inquest on Mr. Edward Carter, which will be held at the Grange at three o'clock this afternoon."

Fred reeled to the armchair beside the fireplace and slopped down in it. "Dead?" he gasped, "Carter dead?"

"Dead," Head confirmed, standing immobile by the table.

"But—but he was alive when I left there a few hours ago!"

"He's dead now," Head insisted. "I want to know, Mr. Pollen, when you drove away from the Grange, who was in the car in front of you?"

"The car in . . . why, let me see. That racehorse man—no, it wasn't, though. He went first, with that prim wife of his. No, he'd gone. It was an open car—I know! Denham in his Bugatti sports. But you say Carter is dead?"

"Were you close behind the Bugatti?" Head persisted.

"I'd say I was! Betty—Miss Hurder, you know—she begged me to leave off stepping on it, for fear of running into him. You can't pass very easily in that lane. I was right on his tail all the way to the corner. But about Carter, how did he—?"

"Was there any car behind you?" Head interrupted.

"Why, let me see! Yes, Frank Mortimer's, with the Perry girls—Miss Perry and her young sister, the one Carter—but look here, inspector, what's it all about? I can't take it in, you know."

"You'll take it in at the inquest at three o'clock this afternoon," Head told him, "and mind you attend. You are sure Mortimer was behind you as you drove along the lane?"

"I'd say I'm sure! The blind over my back window won't work, and I had his headlights dazzling on my windscreen all the way to the corner of the lane. We were a regular procession along there. But—"

"That's all, thank you, Mr. Pollen, except that you are officially required to attend the inquest this afternoon. Good morning."

He left the rather discomfited young man gazing open-mouthed from the armchair, and let himself out from the house in a mood of angry disgust. Fred Pollen was a useless waster who would batten on his father until the old man's death, and then, either with or without the aid of Betty Hurder or some equally second-rate discard from Westingborough's matrimonial pack, would proceed to spend old Pollen's accumulated hoard with scant benefit to anyone else and certainly none to himself.

For a moment, as he held the handle of the car door, Head reflected over his next move. Eventually he decided that he did not want Betty Hurder: she was as brainless as Fred Pollen, and if Wadden felt that he wanted her at the inquest, there was plenty of time for him to have her warned in the normal way. Similarly, Wadden might deal with the sisters Perry, or Head himself might look in on them after he had found and interviewed Mr. Frank Mortimer.

He had planned his series of visits carefully, and from Quade, from Denham, and in a slighter degree from Pollen, had ascertained the general layout of the party and of the drive away from the Grange. Denham had checked Quade's statement with regard to the order of leaving, Pollen in turn had said enough to indicate that Denham had had no chance to pull up at the point where the kissing-gate gave access to the grassland in front of the Grange. Mortimer, presumably with the Perry girls in his car, had been last to leave.

Further, Quade, Denham, and Pollen had been obvious, easy witnesses to examine. Head knew them all in varying degrees, Denham least of the three, since he belonged in a different, higher order, while the other two could be approached almost on a footing of equality by one of the position Head occupied in Westingborough. The inspector's conduct of the Forrest case,[1] still fresh in the minds of local people, had given him a status far above that of an ordinary police officer; he was respected, equally with the racehorse trainer and far more than the builder's fatuous son.

Now he drove back into Westingborough to interview Frank Mortimer, far from obvious, but the one from whom he expected to learn most. For this man, almost certainly, was in a position to reveal the circumstances of Carter's past life, while none of the other three had known more than Head himself already knew, he felt sure. To that past life, the inspector felt equally sure, he must turn to ascertain the identity of the one who had shot Carter down before dawn of that day.

1. See *Shadow on the House*, by E. Charles Vivian, Ward Lock & Co.

CHAPTER V

EDDIE ENSOR

A RIGHT-ANGLED right turn out from Market Street, the principal thoroughfare in Westingborough, marks the beginning of London Road, which crosses the River Idleburn after about a third of a mile, and there the town gives place to country. On the townward side of the bridge, and on the right going out from the town, stands a white stone house in about a half-acre of gardens which slope down to the river-bank. It is double-fronted and bay-windowed, this house; between it and the road stands a mighty, ancient cedar, and there are other trees in the garden, notably a weeping ash, of which the curving branches have drooped to take root in the ground and form a pleasant arbour in summer. The house and grounds are trim-looking, well-kept, as is fitting for the residence of a man of leisure, and apparently of taste as well.

The last of the night's fall of snow had melted, helped by the rain of early morning, when Inspector Head got out from his car, went to the front door of Kerkmanhurst, as the brass plate beside the gate declared the white house, and rang the bell. A dour-looking woman told him not only that Mr. Mortimer was in, but that he was expecting his visitor, and ushered Head into a room in which the wall-paper was two-thirds covered with photographs, all autographed, and depicting apparently every kind of theatrical and music-hall performer. Irving, Dan Leno, Margaret Cooper, and Cinquevalli were easily recognisable; Head went to the cheery fire and stood, there trying to estimate how many photographs went to this collection, when the door opened to admit a stout little man in a black morning-coat and striped trousers, with a monocle slanting on his paunch at the end of a broad, black, watered-silk ribbon. He had bright, beady little eyes in a pale, expressionless face, and he kept his gaze fixed on Head as he paused just inside the door to bow formally. Then he advanced into the room.

"Good morning—good morning," he said. "I expected you'd call to see me, and had the fire lighted in here. Won't you sit down?"

"Thanks." Head seated himself in an armchair by the fireplace. "I've come to tell you, Mr. Mortimer, that you will be required to attend the inquest on Mr. Edward Carter, who was murdered at four o'clock this morning, apparently an hour after you left him."

"Ah, so I heard a while ago. The milkman, I believe. Won't you have a cigar, or a cigarette, Mr. Head?"

"No, thanks. Do you mind answering a few questions?"

"Not in the least—not in the least! Only too happy to oblige, if I can be of any service. Murdered, I think you said. Isn't that—well, rather a premature assumption, if I may venture the remark?"

"Possibly," Head concurred, "since we have as yet no verdict to that effect. But the facts are fairly conclusive."

"Well, well! In the midst of life we are, unfortunately, in debt."

He uttered the parody quite gravely, drew forward a chair, and seated himself immediately in front of the fire, having Head on his right. "And how would you like to question me, Mr. Head?"

"As a beginning," Head answered, "it appears to me that you must have been one of the three last persons to see Mr. Carter alive—apart from the one who shot him, that is."

"But I might have been the one who shot him."

Mortimer fixed the gaze of his heady eyes on his caller as he made the astounding statement. He appeared gravely earnest over it.

"It is a possibility," Head concurred, "but I consider it remote."

"Well, yes, I suppose it is," Mortimer remarked, gazing into the fire again. "The two ladies I had the honour to escort would certainly have raised objections to anything of the sort. And since I went back to the doorstep to shake hands with Mr. Carter—the late Mr. Carter, that is—after ushering them into my car, I suppose I was the last person to see him alive, apart from the one who shot him."

"All the rest of the party had gone, then?"

"Were going, rather. We played follow-my-leader down the drive and along the lane, and then—Pollen, his name is—turned off to the right while all the rest of us came through the town. Am I answering you satisfactorily, Mr. Head? I am most anxious to be of service."

"Quite satisfactorily, thanks. Did you see Mr. Carter close his front door before you drove away?"

"No. He stood on his doorstep with the light behind him, watching us go. Quite alone. I heard him tell the servants they could go to bed about midnight, so he would be quite alone."

"You had Miss Perry and her sister with you in your car?"

"Yes, Lilian and Ethel. Charming girls—most charming girls."

"And all four cars went along the lane together—one behind the other, that is?"

"Head to tail—yes, exactly. Follow-my-leader, as I said."

"Did you all keep a steady pace?"

"Yes, about twenty miles an hour, I should think, once we got outside the gateway of the Grange. About that, to the corner. No tear of other traffic on the road, at that hour."

"What are your headlights like, Mr. Mortimer?"

"Very good indeed. I could see the back of Quade's head in the front car of the four—through the back window, that is. His is a small saloon, as you probably know."

"You saw the back of Quade's head, over two intervening cars?" Head asked incredulously.

"In the dip of the lane," Mortimer explained. "Pollen drives one of those low-built things, and the car in front of his was an open tourer. And my headlights are very good indeed."

"They must be. Did you see anyone else along the road? Or anywhere beside the road, on foot, cycling, or anyone at all?"

"Not a sign of anyone," Mortimer answered gravely. "Not a sign of anyone all the way home. I dropped Lilian and Ethel—the Misses Perry, you understand—at their door in Treherne Road, and came on here, garaged the car myself, and went to bed after a whisky and soda. Which reminds me. Can I offer you a whisky and soda?"

"No, thank you," Head answered. He had felt, in his three foregoing interviews, that he knew the thought behind the words his subjects uttered, but with this imperturbable little man it was different: was Mortimer speaking frankly, or was he merely fencing watchfully?

"Never drink on duty, eh?"

"Did you hear Mr. Carter say anything at all, during the evening, about an appointment for any time this morning?" Head inquired, disregarding the comment on his refusal of a drink.

"Laddie—I beg your pardon, I should have said Mr. Head. But to tell you frankly, it wasn't the sort of gathering where anyone would say anything about anything. We were all very merry. And Eddie Carter, I mean—was very much engaged with the ladies—with one lady in particular. I may confess I was very much engaged with another."

"Then you heard nothing of any appointment he had this morning?"

"Nothing whatever, I assure you. Nothing whatever."

"Mr. Mortimer, who and what was Edward Carter? You know, until we have cause, we don't interest ourselves in the antecedents of a man in his position. I understand that he had been connected with the theatrical profession in some way, but who was he, what was he?"

Mortimer gazed into the fire very gravely indeed.

"If he were still alive, I should refuse to answer that question," he said at last. "It would have been utterly contrary to his wishes. But I divine your thought that his past career may hold the secret of his murderer's identity, and so you're welcome to all I can tell you. Edward Ensor Carter, to give him his full name, was Eddie Ensor."

"I'm no wiser," Head confessed. "Who was Eddie Ensor?"

"Man!" Mortimer gave him a pitying look. "You don't know that?"

"I may have heard the name, but it conveys nothing to me."

The little man gave a long sigh, in disparagement of this monstrous ignorance, and gazed into the fire again.

"Some people say Charles B. Cochran is the greatest showman, the greatest producer, the world ever knew," he said after a pause. "They may be right, but Eddie Ensor ran him pretty close, till he decided to give it up and turn country gentleman—give it all up, turn his back on it, and dissociate himself from it altogether. Eddie Ensor—yes. He began as a mere theatrical agent, finding jobs for chorus girls and boys, and one day he got hold of the script of *Green Mice* and put every penny he had and could raise into it. Put it on, produced it himself. It ran two years, as you may know, and he made sixty thousand pounds out of the production—clear, apart from what he'd borrowed and had to pay back. That was how he really began."

"How long ago?" Head asked.

"Nine—eleven years. It's nine years since *Green Mice* ended its West End run, but it's still touring. Ah, Eddie had a flair, if anyone ever had!"

"And after that?" Head inquired.

"After that? Success after success. I've heard him say he only had two failures out of all he produced. And he found people. He found Harry Quartz, the big comedian, and made him. He dug that

marvellous trio, Nita and Quita and Peter, out of a third-rate travelling circus, and made 'em the rage of the halls. He found Zela
Patrisky in Vienna, the most beautiful woman who ever appeared
on an English stage, and had half London mad about her. His
finds—laddie, he was a marvel, was Eddie. And that farce, *The Pig
that Snored*—it was another gold-mine of his. He bought the
Quadrarian and turned it from a bankrupt music hall into the finest
and most popular home of revue there is, and couldn't he pick 'em!
When Eddie Ensor put a chorus together, it wasn't merely a picture,
it was a galaxy. The eye that man had!"

"He made enemies," Head suggested after a pause.

"You're telling me, laddie," Mortimer said gravely. "In that line,
you've got to be hard. There's no help for it. Soften up, and you're a
lost man. I'll say Eddie was good to a girl if he fancied her, in a
general way, though there may have been exceptions even there. He
was no saint, or he'd never have got where he did, and if he had a
weakness, it was pretty and young, every time. He had an eye, Eddie."

"Can you recall any special enemies of his?" Head inquired,
ignoring the eulogy on the deceased—for it was no less.

Mortimer, gazing into the fire, shook his head. "That same thing
had occurred to me," he confessed, "but I can't. That is, nobody
who would go to the length of killing him. And I knew him pretty
well."

"You say he bought the Quadrarian?"

"*And* floated it, *and* made a handsome bit out of it. Retained an
interest—it's the Quadrarian Limited, now. It was the only interest
he did retain, after he got out from producing."

"And what made him get out?" Head asked.

"Ah! I knew him well, you see. It'd be about three years ago, or a
bit more, when I looked in on him in his office at the Quadrarian,
and he said to me 'Frank, I've made enough, old lad. I've always
liked a good horse, as you know, and I'm going to cut this life altogether and turn country gentleman while I'm still young enough
to follow a pack of hounds and make a girl lose her head over me.'
Just that, out of the blue—as far as I know, I was the first person he
mentioned it to. I knew the Grange was in the market, and there's
good hunting country round here, though I don't ride myself, so I
told him he couldn't do better. And inside a month he'd bought the
Grange and got four good hunters in the stable. Nevile bought one
of them, the one that killed his first wife, and he pretty much ruined
Carter's chances of getting into Westingborough society by what he

said about the deal at the inquest on her. Carter didn't warn him that the horse was a killer. All that's by the way, though—Nevile isn't the man to go shooting anyone, and besides, he's married again and happier than ever, I understand. But Carter came down here to settle and separate himself from the reputation he'd made as Eddie Ensor. Not that he made a graveyard secret of it, but he didn't want Westingborough generally to know him in that light, and as far as I know they didn't. You didn't."

"Because I had no reason to inquire, till now," Head pointed out.

"And now—perhaps you've still no reason to inquire," Mortimer suggested. "I know no more than that Carter was shot since I left there at three this morning. There were eight of us at his place last night, and it might have been any one of us, or one of his servants, or anyone on earth. And still I can't realise him as dead. He was too vital, too alive. He was, as you might say, a rhapsody of energy."

"And you—in what capacity did you know him?" Head pursued.

"I? Surely you've heard of me? Frank Mortimer, the greatest scenic designer of the century. Eddie himself told me that my designs for the scenery of *The Pig that Snored* did as much as the music toward putting it over—he acknowledged it frankly. Dear laddie, don't tell me you never heard of Me!"

"I'm afraid the details of theatrical production are new to me," Head confessed. "I've had no occasion before."

"Such is fame!" Mortimer observed regretfully. "But they still remember me.— Oh, they still remember me, though it's nearly five years since I decided for a life of quiet here. Not that I'm altogether out of things, even now. Eddie—I told you he'd retained an interest in the Quadrarian—he was putting me forward as the only artist living capable of doing justice to the settings for the next revue—*The Fire of Spring*, it's to be called. Most people know their Omar well enough to see the aptness of the title—the Quadrarian public does, at least. And it's a wow, dear laddie, a perfect wow! I've heard most of the numbers, and I can tell you the winter garment of repentance will be mere ash five minutes after the curtain goes up on the first night."

He stood up abruptly, and looked down at Head. "What more can I tell you?" he asked. "You've only to put the questions."

"Nothing at present, I think," Head answered, rising too. "I may want to ask you more, later, possibly."

"Always at your service, laddie—Mr. Head, I mean. Y'know, I followed your handling of that Forrest case last year, and I said to myself as I read it, here's as great a genius in his line as I am in mine, and that's a good deal for Frank Mortimer to say. To a man like you, a straight, simple case like this should present no difficulties. You need only eliminate possibles, analyse the probables, and there you are! Case complete. What could be simpler?"

"Exactly." Head took his cigarette-case from his pocket, offered it, and, as Mortimer shook his head, took a cigarette himself and lighted it. Mortimer smiled, for the first time during the interview.

"Since you wouldn't accept a cigarette from me, I conclude I'm not eliminated yet," he remarked quietly.

"You're a clever man, Mr. Mortimer," Head told him.

"I am a genius—I may say a great genius. And always at your service—always at your service. Command me at any time."

"At three this afternoon, at the Grange, for instance."

"For the inquest—yes. I shall be there—I shall not fail to be there. You may rely on me, Mr. Head. Always at your service."

He accompanied the inspector to the front door, bowed him out, and watched him go along the path toward his car outside the gate. He was still watching, a tubby, pompous little figure of a man, when Head turned the car about and set off, back toward the middle of the town.

But, a little way along London Road, Head turned off to the right into Treherne Road, having decided to interview the Perry sisters before returning to ascertain what Wadden had gleaned in his absence. He had come to the conclusion that the author of the crime had fired the two shots at Eddie Ensor, rather than at Edward Carter, and that he must learn more of the dead man's past history in order to solve the riddle of the disappearing boots. Still, one or other of the Perry girls might provide useful information: he would try them.

They lived, together with an aged and almost imbecile father and one small domestic, in a semi-detached, two-storied house about a hundred yards along the road. Lilian, the elder sister, gave pianoforte and dancing-lessons, and had a girl friend in to play for her for the latter: Ethel, the younger, had recently finished a four-year course of training as a nurse at a London hospital, and had come home to establish a connection in private nursing in Westingborough. Lilian herself opened the door to the inspector when he rang. She was about thirty, of middle height, fair-haired, and possessed a rather hard sort of prettiness: her lips were too thin for real attractiveness.

"Good morning, Miss Perry," said Head. "I've come to see what you and your sister can tell me about your visit to the Grange last night."

"Oh, but we had nothing to do with Mr. Carter's death!" she exclaimed. "And you can't possibly see my sister. She's far too upset."

He looked at her steadily. "After that, I think you'd better let me come in for a word or two about it," he said.

She drew back, and he followed her into the corridor which ran back from this door to the staircase. He noted two ladies' bicycles leaned against the wall—and Ethel, whom he could not see, was a nurse! But the time at which Borrow had seen a nurse cycling appeared to remove any possibility of connecting her with that night-rider. Still . . .

"Would you mind coming in here?" Lilian Perry opened a door on the right of the corridor, and led the way into a fairly large room, unfurnished except for a shabby-looking piano, a music-seat, and four cane-seated chairs ranged against the wall. "It's very uncomfortable, I know, but it's the only one available."

It was cheerlessly uncomfortable. Head faced the woman. "I merely want to know if you had much conversation with Mr. Carter while you were at the Grange, Miss Perry," he said.

"Apart from ordinary civilities, hardly any," she answered, after a pause in which she appeared to consider the question.

"Did you hear him mention any appointment he had for to-day, or any plans he had made with regard to to-day?"

"I did not." The reply was unhesitating, this time.

"How did you get to know Mr. Carter?"

"He came to me for tango lessons," she answered, equally readily.

"Tango lessons, eh? How long is it since he first came to you?"

"About a month—yes, just a month ago."

"I see. And how long is it since your sister finished her training and got back here from London?"

"Nearly two months, now. Late in November."

"Yes. Thanks, Miss Perry; I think that's all I want you to tell me. Now will you tell your sister I wish to see her?"

She shook her head. "But it's quite impossible, as I told you," she protested. "You really can't see her to-day, Mr. Head."

"If she's in bed, I'll see her there," he said inflexibly. "You must realise, Miss Perry, that I intend to see her, and will."

She tried to outgaze him, and failed. Her face paled, and her lips looked thinner than ever, he thought.

"I'll ask her, if you'll wait here," she said at last.

He waited six minutes by his watch in the bare, chilly room, and then Ethel Perry opened the door and entered. She was taller than her elder sister, and, like her, was fair in colouring, but there the resemblance ended. For she had red, full, tempting lips, beautifully glossy golden hair, and deep blue eyes set in a face of classic beauty, of which the normal expression was one of almost childish innocence and purity. But, as she faced Head fearfully, her eyes were ringed through weeping, her red lips tremulous, and she was unnaturally pale.

"I'm sorry to be compelled to trouble you, Miss Perry," Head opened crisply. "You've heard what happened after you left the Grange in the early hours of this morning, I see."

She inclined her head in silent assent. Her fingers twined and unclasped from about each other before her, nervously, as she faced him.

"But I want to ask you about what happened before you left," he pursued, "in the event of your knowing anything that might help us in finding who shot Mr. Carter. In the course of the evening, you and he were alone together for a considerable time."

He made almost a question of the final statement. She flushed deep red and her gaze went to the floor at her feet, but she made no reply.

"And, during that time," Head pursued, after waiting vainly for her to speak, "I want to know what were your subjects of conversation."

Still she made no answer. The flush faded out from her cheeks almost as quickly as it had arisen.

"What did you talk about, Miss Perry?" he demanded.

"A—a good many things." It was little more than a whisper.

"Such as—?" he prompted her.

"Mr.—Mr. Carter promised me a part in a new revue," she answered tremulously, hesitatingly. "I— he— Oh, I can't!"

"But you must," he persisted inflexibly. "Promised you a part in a new revue—that will be *The Fire of Spring*, the one coming on shortly at the Quadrarian theatre. In return for which—?"

"No— Oh, no!" she cried piteously.

But he had no pity on her. "There is the evidence of a girl called Phyllis Taylor, who entered the drawing-room at the Grange while you were alone there with Mr. Carter," he told her. "Miss Perry, do you want this story told in public, at the inquest?"

"Oh, please!" she sobbed, abandoning all restraint. "I did so want to go on the stage—I loathe nursing! And he promised to get me a part—he said he could, showed me letters. I didn't mean any harm, and now the chance has gone, and—and you'll ruin me!"

"Not if you pull yourself together and answer coherently all I ask you now," he dissented coldly. "You talked of that—of getting a part in the revue. Anything else?"

"He—he made love to me," she confessed.

"On that point, as I told you, I have other evidence," he pointed out. "Subject to my being satisfied with what you tell me now, that evidence will not be produced, and your association with this dead man, whatever its nature may have been, can remain a secret. You talked of this part you were to have, and he made love to you. Anything else?"

"About—about how stuck-up people are here, and how he'd like to kill Mr. Nevile for showing him up over selling him the horse—that swine Nevile, he called him. And—and all he'd done for Westingborough since he came here, the new wing for the hospital, and how he'd subscribed to the church restoration fund and other things."

"Yes. Anything else? Think hard. Anything at all?"

"He got rather—rather sad, I thought. He said he wished sometimes he could get away from his past life, but he couldn't."

"That's what I want most," Head told her. "Try to remember every word he said on that subject. Never mind the rest, for the present."

"He said—what was it? Yes, he said he wished ghosts wouldn't rise up and haunt him, and wished he hadn't a conscience."

"What he had of one appears to have been pretty rubbery," Head commented ironically. "Tell me, now, did he make any allusion to the nature of the ghosts, whether they were male or female, or anything else about them?"

"No. It was just before we went back to join the others he said that. He seemed to—to want not to be remorseful any more."

"Most of us do, too late," Head commented. "Can you remember, Miss Perry, if he mentioned any name at all? In addition to Mr. Nevile, did he speak of anyone by name?"

"Yes, Peter—Peter somebody. As if he were thinking aloud, and not as if he said it to me. Peter . . . it was a Spanish-sounding name. 'That poor young Peter . . . Vesci.' Yes, Vesci, Peter Vesci."

"Which sounds more Italian than Spanish to me," Head commented. "What did he say about this Peter Vesci, can you remember?"

"Nothing. Only that one sentence, and after he'd said it he looked at me as if he wondered whether I'd heard it—as if it had slipped out without his meaning me to hear it. Oh, Mr. Head, I am telling you all I can! You won't—won't let people know—" Her voice failed her.

"No, I think I can promise you I won't. I've no wish to show up a dead man, whatever he may have been in life. Did he mention any other name? Think hard over it—this is important."

"No, no other, I'm quite sure. And nothing more about this one."

"Peter Vesci." He repeated it thoughtfully. "Miss Perry, did you hear Mr. Carter say anything about appointments or arrangements for to-day, meeting or seeing anyone, or anything of that sort?"

"Only that he had to be up so early that it wasn't worth while to go to bed. But he didn't say why, or about seeing anyone, I'm sure."

"He didn't say, for instance, that he had an appointment with this Peter Vesci, did he?"

"No, nor with anyone, I'm quite sure. Not in my hearing."

"And he appears to have been more in your hearing than out of it, I gather," Head commented rather caustically. "I think, Miss Perry, both you and your sister had better attend the inquest at the Grange at three o'clock this afternoon, but we shall not call either of you to give evidence if we can possibly avoid it."

"Oh, must we go—must I go?" she pleaded.

"Yes, you must," he answered. "Both of you. Tell me one other thing, now I think of it. Do you wear nurse's uniform when you go out, or just ordinary clothes—ordinary outdoor clothes?"

She gazed at him through a long interval, possibly trying to fathom his reason for asking such a question.

"Only—only when I'm on a case," she answered at last.

"Are you on a case now?"

She shook her head. "I've only had one since I came home," she said regretfully. "It finished last week."

"Have you worn outdoor uniform since?"

"No. I—I hoped last night I should never have to wear it again."

"Then you didn't wear it last night, or early this morning?"

"Why—why no! I was—at Mr. Carter's. What do you—?" She broke off, regarding him anxiously, fearfully.

"That's all, Miss Perry. I shall respect your confidence as far as my duty will let me, especially in regard to your relations with Mr. Carter. Now I'll be getting along. This is rather a busy day for me."

CHAPTER VI

PERSON OR PERSONS UNKNOWN

"No," HEAD SAID thoughtfully. "There wasn't time."

"Time for what?" Wadden leaned back in his chair, which he had pushed back from his desk, and regarded his inspector interestedly.

"For that soiled butterfly to get her nurse's outdoor kit and her bicycle, ride round to the stile, lift the bicycle over it, and come out again to London Road beyond the bridge for Borrow to see her there at about ten minutes past three," Head explained.

"Why should she?" Wadden inquired again.

"Why should a man fly out of a tree instead of coming to earth?" Head retorted, rather wearily. "Why anything? Chief, I've had one hell of a morning, and don't like myself. I've told you all my story, and now what have you at your end of the table?"

"To begin with, that telephone call making the appointment for four o'clock can't be traced," Wadden reported. "We're on the dial system, as you know, and there's no record of the connections made for local calls, only an automatic record of each call made, for purposes of accounting. The gentle Phyllis has got to tell all she can at the inquest, and that appears to be all we shall get about it—which is as much as we've got now, probably, and no more."

"Item one," Head commented. "Next, please?"

"From Wells, at the Grange. It was an automatic, thirty-eight bore. You know they eject the empty shells with a whiz to make room for the next round. Wells found one empty shell down just outside the door of the drawing-room, and the other down by the outside wall."

"Which proves that the first shot was fired from the doorstep, probably immediately Carter opened his door," Head commented. "You've checked the arms register, of course?"

"Only one thirty-eight automatic in it—though there's six of thirty-two bore. That one belongs to Mr. Raymond Nevile, and I know he was at home last night, because his wife presented him with a son. He came down to his works this morning grinning from ear to ear. I saw him pass here. Then I had a word with him on the telephone, and he told me his automatic is locked away in his gun-room at Long Ridge. Offered to let us have it for inspection, if we liked. I told him he needn't worry, as long as he made sure of that, but he sent the gun, all the same. I took a look at it, and sent it back."

"And there's no other?" Head asked.

"A gun intended for unlawful use is *never* registered with the police," Wadden declared. "That's the blasted futility of registering 'em, giving us extra work to no purpose. You didn't expect we'd find it there, did you? I know I didn't."

Head made no reply, but gazed dreamily up at the whitewashed ceiling, where a solitary fly clung in immobility.

"Yes, I know it wants doing again," Wadden said rather peevishly. "You can indent for redecorating all through when you take over this office next May, but I'm not going to turn out for white-washers."

"I was thinking, we are up against very clever premeditation," Head said reflectively, "and damn the ceiling—and that fly, too."

"That's where he goes in winter—don't damn him. Or her."

"Yes, or her," Head repeated, still more thoughtfully.

"Meaning—?" Wadden looked the rest of the interrogation.

"Or her," Head said again. "A woman's foot would fit inside clod-hopping tens—a woman's shod foot, I mean."

"If you're thinking of that woman with the bicycle—and I don't see how you can connect her—there's the difference in the length of pace," Wadden pointed out. "A consistent difference, too, as Wells calculated it. You can rely on his arithmetic, I know."

"Consistent, yes," Head agreed, "but I said it was clever pre-meditation. I mean in every detail. For instance, the killer made that appointment the day before without knowing there would be snow on the ground. Probably it couldn't be made again—Carter wouldn't come down a second time in the dark and cold to open his front door, if he were fooled once, and since his party was on when the snow began the killer dared not telephone a postponement then."

"Go on," Wadden requested impatiently.

"Difference in length of pace. If you're used to wearing a shoe that would fit inside those old boots, you'd swing your foot to a pace of an extra inch or more with the extra weight of them on your feet. Apart from that, with snow on the ground and every chance of measurement, the killer probably extended his ordinary pace to prevent identification by measurement of a normal pace, and in hurrying on the return journey extended it still more, to an average of half an inch over the inward-going paces. And that reminds me—the photographs Wells took. Are there any prints available, yet?"

"Yes, two sets. But you need a magnifying glass to see the detail. I've ordered a complete set of enlargements—they're due in at not later than three-thirty this afternoon."

"When we shall be busy at the inquest! But will they stand enlargement—without distortion of detail, I mean?"

"Stand it? With our Goertz-Anschutz and Wells handling it? You know what he is when it comes to photography. Man, you could make Empire Marketing posters of the lot, or Hampton Court cartoons, and be sure every hobnail was to scale! Don't worry about that. Go on with your analysis."

"All right. I want a set of those enlargements, though. And now I think of it, have you checked up on Alfred Potter?"

"Well, naturally. He went along that path—after passing down the lane to the stile, of course—about ten minutes before we drove along to the Grange. Offered his wife as evidence for the time he left his humble cot, if we wanted it, and clocked in at Parham's at the other end. He's absolutely out of it, and wouldn't want to shoot Carter, in any case. We know him for that rarity of rarities, an honest working man—and they're about as plentiful as white blackbirds."

"You're a pessimist, chief."

"Why the devil are you worrying about me? Of all the long-winded, irritating rozzers ever pupped, you're the peach. Get on, man!"

"Peaches aren't pupped. Never mind, though. Finished with the feet of the mysterious X. Said X is a perfect rope-thrower, remember. It's no novice at the game who throws a rope over a bough like that in the dark, and judges length and height to make it first throw. He inspected it in the daytime, probably, but still it's a throw that wants making. Also, a tolerably good shot with an automatic, though that first bullet wasn't instantly fatal, as it was meant to be, and it was fired at five or six yards range. But a fair shot, all the same. A good rope-thrower, and a fair shot, which is narrowing it down a trifle. Ergo, probably a man—you don't get that combination in a woman, especially the throwing part of it."

"And maybe not," Wadden commented. "You've given me this Mortimer's eulogy of the deceased, a man who found everything in the way of circus and theatrical top-holers. He might have got a woman to combine the two. I'm not saying he did, but he might."

"And done her wrong, you're thinking, so she up and shot him. I thought of that, chief, while Mortimer was rhapsodising, but it's too melodramatic. It doesn't happen in real life, that sort of thing. She might have held a pistol to his head to make him pay up, but she would never have pulled the trigger. No, we'll put the lady back on her bicycle, and let her ride away."

He was silent awhile, and Wadden did not interrupt his cogitations. Suddenly he got up from his chair at the end of the desk, and looked down at Wadden, who returned his gaze questioningly.

"But she didn't ride," he said. "She walked, and wheeled the bicycle, along the path. Half a minute, chief, I want to get this clear in my mind. She walked, and wheeled the bicycle."

"On the evidence of footprints in the snow," Wadden said gravely. "And wheel-marks. Why the hell did that snow want to go and melt?"

"She walked, and wheeled the bicycle," Head repeated.

"Well, what about it?" Wadden snapped.

"I think—no, it's not clear yet. Was it a she? Or a small he? They might have been the riding-boots, and yet—"

"I don't get you," Wadden said doubtfully.

"He or she went up the tree with the old boots on," Head explained. "He or she is not still up the tree, so must have come down. Ergo, he or she took the old boots off before coming down—they didn't reappear anywhere in the snow. And apart from Potter, already accounted for, there's only one other track anywhere near the spot—"

"Also accounted for," Wadden interrupted. "Riding a bicycle from I.ondon Road as far as the stile, lifting it over, and walking it along the path. In a nurse's outdoor uniform."

"Are you sure about walking the bicycle along the path?" Head inquired. "One other set of footprints beginning near where the old boots leave off, footprints showing a boot or shoe that could easily have fitted into that pair of tens—"

"But why the bicycle?" Wadden interrupted again.

The snow," Head explained. "There had to be a complete, separate track all the way, so he or she rode the bicycle from London Road to the stile, lifted it over, and *rode* it along the path, not walked it. Leaving those half-dozen impressions of feet from the dismounting point to the stile, but getting on again carefully from the stile itself and riding along the path—"

"By the living shade of Sherlock, man, you've got it!" Wadden exclaimed enthusiastically. "Carry on."

"There was thus a complete bicycle-track, and half a dozen or more footprints on the road by the stile, footprints made by the riding-boots or whatever they were. He had the old boots slung round his neck by the laces, in all probability, when he lowered himself by the rope very carefully into the footprint, stepped in those half-dozen tracks to the stile, and *walked beside the bicycle wheel-marks*, this time, so that it looked to us as if he had only gone once along the path, wheeling the bicycle—"

"Where was the bicycle on this second trip?" Wadden interjected.

"Why, haven't you got it yet? He made the round with the bicycle, as I said. From the bridge, he rode on home, parked the machine, got rid of his nurse's bonnet and cap, and turned out again in riding-kit. In that, with the old boots and his rope under his arm, he went down Market Street, as we know from Borrow. At the corner of Maggs Lane he put on the old boots over his riding-boots, and laid the trail that led up to the Grange and back as far as the kissing-gate. Climbed the tree, took off the old boots, dropped into the footprint beside the bicycle-track that indicated dismounting, hauled his rope down carefully, and very carefully indeed stepped in his previous footprints—the ones he made on his first round with the bicycle. Once over the stile, all he had to do was to walk beside the wheel-tracks of his ridden bicycle, to give us the impression that he'd led it along the path."

"Head, I believe you've got it. Which means we didn't pay half enough attention to those half-dozen prints between the stile and the middle of the road, and we ought to have noticed that the bicycle had been ridden, not led—the deeper tracks."

"On that asphalt path, and with that soft snow, you'd hardly notice the difference," Head pointed out. "And we hadn't connected up the bicycle with the murderer, then, though of course I ought. Gosh, but we're up against a brain, chief! The simple cleverness of that little scheme, thought out after the snow began to fall. The idea of a nurse's cloak and bonnet, because nurses are out at all hours and nobody would remark one, then the riding-breeches and boots—ideal for climbing about in a tree, and in a horsey district like this less conspicuous than any other outfit. Planned to the last detail, and even then luck must step in to help him, in the shape of Denham's Bugatti exhaust explosions."

"It's hopeless looking for the rope, and hopeless looking for the old boots," Wadden reflected. "He was clever, as you say, damned clever, and he'll take good care of them—and of his bicycle and nurse's kit, too. Head, what the hell are we to look for?"

"For the motive—for someone who hated Carter enough to kill him in such a way," Head answered. "Someone he feared, for if he hadn't, he wouldn't have made an appointment to open his own front door at four o'clock in the morning. Let's consider Carter a bit."

"I'm all for a spot of consideration," Wadden agreed.

"Came here three years ago," Head began, with deliberate thoughtfulness, "and thought he could buy his way into Westingborough society. I've told you what I got on my round of calls, and it's evident he'd not given up hope, even yet. A sensualist, proved by the story we got from Phyllis Taylor, and this business of Ethel Perry, poor fool! But there'd be dozens of stories like that in his life as theatrical producer, for he was buying men and girls every day, in that, as you know. For his shows, I mean. And he'd take his personal pick of the girls, and fling them aside as he'd begun to fling Phyllis Taylor. Supposing he—but you suggested that, and as I said, it's too melodramatic. The betrayed maiden doesn't up and shoot her betrayer, and moreover she hasn't the brains, as a general rule, to plan and carry out a shooting like this. There might be a disappointed honest lover, of course, but I don't think so. The Taylor and Perry girls are a pretty fair index of the types that appealed to Carter, and they don't attract honest lovers of the sort that would hate him enough to bump him off."

"Then where—who—what?" Wadden demanded.

"Where—in London," Head answered seriously. "Who, a badly stung business rival, employee, actor, or something of the sort. What—a good rope-thrower, a fair shot, and probably something of an acrobat. Dropping cleanly into that footprint, I mean—and with good muscles, to haul himself up into the tree without scraping the gate or anything, and balance himself on one branch to haul up his rope, and on the other to let it down again—in the dark, remember. He had an electric torch, almost certainly—and it's no use looking for that, either. Torch, rope, old boots, nurse's uniform, and in my opinion it's no use our looking for any of them till we locate him."

"And gun," Wadden pointed out.

"And gun, as you say—we know the calibre and that it was some sort of automatic. But we'd be fools if we wasted time looking for it apart from him, since it's not on our arms register."

"If it had been, he wouldn't have used it," Wadden said glumly.

"A bitter, vengeful killer," Head reflected aloud. "A man who can drop the muzzle of a pistol on to another man's eye, and pull the trigger, must have a devilish hate. And you won't find that in Westingborough. The people here didn't hate Carter—they merely ignored him."

"Don't be too sure of that," Wadden dissented.

"Where can you find him an enemy bitter enough and clever enough for a crime like this anywhere in our district?" Head demanded. "Think over everyone whom Carter might possibly have known—I've done it, and I can't find one. Mr. Nevile is the only remote possibility, since Carter was indirectly responsible for his first wife's death, but we needn't even interview him. He's as much in love with his second wife as a man can possibly be, and he was at home last night waiting to know if it were a boy or a girl. Check that up with Bennett's partner, who was the doctor in attendance, if you feel like it. I wouldn't even take the trouble, myself. And who else?"

"No-o," Wadden breathed slowly. "And yet it was somebody living here, somebody who knew the district—"

"Who studied the locality of the Grange, and planned accordingly," Head asserted. "Was connected with Carter in his past life—Chief, we've got a population of ten thousand in the town itself. Mortimer—but he's out, on the ground of time and his physique. Somebody connected at some time or other with London and the theatrical world, as Mortimer is—or was."

"What was that you said about Denham?" Wadden asked abruptly.

"Denham knows something," Head asserted. "He didn't do it, and he didn't know it was going to be done, but I feel sure he saw somebody or something, and wants to keep it dark. Shielding —whom? Somebody he knows and thinks might be implicated—I can't see Denham actually associating with anyone capable of a brutal murder like this, but he might think there was an indirect connection, and someone he knows might get suspected, drawn in. I don't know. We'll get the coroner to put him through the hoop at the inquest. And to-night, chief, I'm off to London, before the trail gets too cold."

"As you remarked, there are ten thousand people in this town," Wadden observed. "I believe there are over seven million in London."

"And one of them happens to be my cousin, Inspector Terence Byrne," Head responded with unruffled confidence. "By the time he's told me all he knows, and taken me on a round tour of the people who know the rest, I prophesy I'll be able to write a history of Edward Carter from childhood onward, with explanatory footnotes on every page."

"It'd be banned by the libraries," Wadden prophesied. "Here, it's time to get going, if we're to be in time at the Grange for a word with the coroner. Wind it up to-day, of course—person unknown. Then we shall have a free hand and be able to carry on."

"And get me a set of those enlargements to take to London with me," Head asked as he rose to his feet. "I want to study those footprints in the small boots from the middle of the road to the stile."

* * * * *

Tuesday being press day for the local weekly, the *Westingborough Sentinel and District Recorder*, the editor ordered a stoppage of the machines when less than a quarter of the issue had been run off, although he knew deliveries of the paper would be late in consequence. He lifted out a page of sports reports and market news, and found a block which depicted Edward Carter, Esq., as he appeared at the opening of the new hospital wing, his gift to the town, and centred it on the page in question. The report of the crime and of the inquest occupied the rest of the page.

Meanwhile, the editor lifted out two short leaders, which could appear just as aptly in the following issue, and replaced them by a long one which he felt inspired to dash off. Thus the *Sentinel* blazoned forth an indignant lament which, the editor hoped, represented the sentiments of his fellow-townsmen.

"For the second time in a comparatively brief period," said the *Sentinel*, "an unspeakably ghastly crime stains the annals of our town, and rouses feelings of horror and indignation in every breast—save one! For again, on the verdict of a coroner's jury, we have a murderer probably in our midst.

"The atrocious ingenuity which characterised the foul crime for which Hector Forrest eventually paid the just penalty is lacking from this second outrage. In place of it, we find a callous daring, for the murderer actually made an appointment with his victim for the commission of the crime, called him to his door in the dark hour before dawn, and shot him down brutally, ruthlessly, horribly. Seldom, in the whole history of crime, has such sickening fiendishness been displayed as in this example of reckless, dastardly hardihood, of which the very daring character proved a means of escape for the murderer. For who would think that, in this law-abiding country, a man could be lured to his own doorstep at an hour when slumber wraps the world, and there be relentlessly, deliberately destroyed?

"To-day, all Westingborough sincerely mourns the heavy loss of a resident who, during the three years of his residence among us, attained well-deserved popularity and respect. His generosity in connection with local charities and the relief of suffering had become, it is not too much to say, a byword among our townsmen, and not only his large circle of friends, but the whole community among which he had made himself so well-known and respected, must mourn his untimely passing. Of the monuments he has left among us, the new wing of our hospital stands most prominent as a testimony to his liberality, his sympathy with the suffering, and his intense desire to further the well-being of the inhabitants of this town and district. He is foully and cruelly taken from our midst, but his name is, as it were, written in letters of gold for all to see, since such generous charity as marked his sojourn among us is more than fine gold. We are bereaved, one and all, and we cry aloud for just vengeance on the author of this awful crime.

"We have no fear of his escape from such a vengeance. Already we are permitted to see the beginnings of the quest which, we think it not too much to say, will end as did the search that ended in the arrest and trial of Hector Forrest. On another page of this issue will be found a verbatim report of the inquest held at Westingborough Grange to-day, and the admirable assiduity with which the knowledge possessed by persons not even remotely connected with the crime itself was elucidated, proves that the respected chiefs of our police force, Superintendent Wadden and Inspector Head, are fully alive to their responsibilities, and are exercising that unerring perspicacity which, a little more than a year ago, extended their fame far beyond the area in which our subscribers reside. Let this murderer do what he will, or hide where he will, we feel confident that he will not escape, with such men already on his track.

"Meanwhile, sufficient has been revealed to render it doubly essential that the authorship of the crime should be discovered. For, while it remains a mystery, the whole body of those heroic ladies who devote their lives to ministering to the suffering lie under suspicion of complicity in the crime. A nurse, cycling, was at least in the vicinity of the scene of the crime, and possibly was implicated. It may have been no nurse, but someone in disguise, and surely it is an index to the character of this brutal murderer that, possibly, he did not hesitate to implicate this noble profession as a whole by displaying its insignia, either on himself or on an accomplice.

"Another painful circumstance is the necessary severity employed in the production of evidence at the inquest. We realise the necessity of such methods for the full elucidation of facts which may be vital to the inquiry, and still more, in consequence, do we deplore the foul crime which places some of our citizens in such a position. The persistence with which our respected fellow-townsman, Mr. Hugh Denham, was questioned regarding whom he might have seen on his way home from enjoyment of the deceased's hospitality, admirable though it is from the point of view of justice, and necessary as admirable, could have been no other than a painful experience for Mr. Denham, who emerged, we may say, with flying colours, unable to throw any light on the tragedy, since he had seen nobody on his way home and knew nothing of its occurrence. This, and things like it, are regrettably inevitable concomitants to the tragedy itself.

"We believe that the murderer will be apprehended and justice will be done. Meanwhile, we are keenly, lamentably conscious of the notoriety inflicted on Westingborough by this second terrible crime, and conscious, too, of the irreparable loss our town has suffered in the tragic death of its public-spirited, honoured resident, Mr. Edward Carter."

Head, on his way to London that night, read the leader carefully after he had perused even more carefully the report of the inquest. Perhaps they had been a bit hard on Denham, and the strenuous and repeated questions to which the coroner had subjected him had been utterly fruitless. Denham had seen nobody on his way to his garage, which adjoined his home in Treherne Road. He had insisted that he had seen nobody at all on the journey, and Head had believed him at the end of his gruelling. And still, the inspector felt convinced, Denham was keeping something back.

"Guff!" he said to himself, as he threw the paper aside and looked into the darkness beyond the window of his compartment. "Washy, undigested guff, you sycophantic tripe-merchant!"

CHAPTER VII

REACTIONS

ALTHOUGH, AS HEAD had pointed out, it would have been a waste of time to concentrate on the search for the old boots, every police officer in Westingborough and the surrounding district was furnished with an enlargement of the photograph Sergeant Wells had taken, showing the impress of both boots together in the snow inside the kissing-gate. Wadden hoped for nothing from this, but he missed no chance.

And, that Tuesday evening, after the report of the inquest had had time to circulate, the boy scouts held their monthly gathering in the corn hall. The district scoutmaster was an enthusiastic young man, and during the next two days nearly every dustbin, ditch, and coppice in the neighbourhood underwent inspection. As a result, there were delivered at the police station one hundred and eighty-nine pairs of old boots before the end of the week, each pair bearing a label in youthful script, stating where the find had been made. Such a harvest of discarded footwear had never been reaped before, and Wadden blew fiercely and cursed, for he knew full well the futility of such a search. The haul included even a pair of elastic-sided antiques, and one of ladies' high-heeled shoes in gold brocade. The scouts were thorough.

The matron of the Westingborough and district hospital, on her own initiative, furnished a detailed report to the superintendent, showing the precise whereabouts of all nurses under her charge, with the exception of two who were on leave at the time. She also sent a copy of the report to the *Sentinel* for publication. Wadden put his copy in the fire in his office, and cursed again, even more heartily than over the torrent of old boots flowing in on him.

After the inquest had been concluded, Hugh Denham got back into his Bugatti and drove back to Treherne Road, where he lived with his sister Adela in a comfortable little house, some distance farther along the road than the one occupied by the Misses Perry and their father. He put the car in the garage, went in, and dressed for dinner in no pleasant mood, for the nagging inquisition to which the coroner had subjected him had left its impress on his mind. He had seen Head watching and listening while the examination proceeded, had seen him scribble on a slip of paper and pass it to the coroner, and knew that every Westingborough resident who was present had seen the incident. In consequence of it, he knew, he would be as prominent a subject of discussion as the murder itself, and might even fall under suspicion of complicity in the crime.

"But Marguerite will know better," he told himself by way of consolation, as he flattened his dress-tie before the mirror.

He went down to the drawing-room, where presently his sister joined him. She was slim, tall for a woman—or girl—chestnut-haired and attractive in an inconspicuous way until she began to talk, when she revealed an unusual turn of wit that made her an acquisition to any gathering. Hugh nodded casually at her, and looked at the clock.

"I suppose they'll turn up," he said.

"Why shouldn't they?" she asked, surprised.

"Oh, I'm pariah, after this afternoon," he told her.

She was silent for an interval. "I wish you hadn't gone there last night," she said at last. "You know I was against it all the time."

"Oh, any fool can say—'I told you so!' " he retorted savagely.

Any comment she might have made was arrested by the opening of the door and the entry of Robert Leigh, a prosperous young farmer of the district to whom Adela had become engaged at the New Year, three weeks before. He shook hands with Hugh after giving his fiancée a modified lover's greeting, out of consideration for Hugh as witness.

"Well, Denham," he said heartily, "this is a nasty business I've been hearing about, and it appears you were one of the party last night, from the gossip that's come my way."

"I don't feel like discussing it," Denham answered, with cold distaste. "I was one of the party, since you asked."

At the end of a minute's strained silence Adela turned and looked at the clock. "I do hope Marguerite won't be late," she said. "It's a very little dinner, Bob, and I made it seven-fifteen to give us time to get to the town hall. I've planned to arrive five minutes late, so that everyone can admire my frock as we go to our seats."

"But we're going for music, darling, not for a mannequin parade," Leigh objected, smiling at her.

"Silly old Bob! Every woman worth calling one likes to see the others envy her—and you haven't told me you like the frock, yet."

"Miss West, madam," the maid at the door announced.

Denham almost spun about to face the doorway. Adela advanced and kissed the new-comer. "Dear, I do hate you," she said. "I was hoping to create an impression when we get to the concert, and now I know what the other ducklings felt like when the swan flew away."

Marguerite West laughed as she gave her hand to Denham. "Isn't she the world's worst flatterer?" she asked him.

He shook his head slightly as he gazed into her dark, expressive eyes. The moody gloom that had characterised him had given place at her entry to eager interest, and it was easy to see how he regarded her.

"Swan is an apt simile," he said.

Silently, Leigh endorsed the comment. The perfection of modelling of her neck and throat was set off by the black dinner-gown she wore; she was slenderly graceful, and although no taller than Adela appeared to stand over her, almost. Her nearly black hair revealed copper-red tinges in the lamplight; vividly red lips that needed no art to enhance their richness, and her large, soft dark eyes, made contrast in her almost colourless face, and in spite of this natural pallor she radiated vitality as of perfect health. It was easy, in spite of her English name, to discern other than English blood in her parentage.

"Denham's right," Leigh said, as she shook hands with him in turn. "He and I are going to be envied, to-night, I think."

Denham, then busy with the cocktail glasses and shaker, frowned at the rather obvious flattery. He handed the glasses round in silence.

"Will it be a very impressive concert?" Marguerite West asked, as she took her glass from him.

"We've no data for guidance," he answered. "But it's our duty to go, as Adela impressed on me when she made me get the tickets."

"Oh, Hugh, how can you?" Adela remonstrated. "I didn't say—"

"Dinner is served, madam," the maid at the door interrupted her.

"How are we going?" Leigh inquired, as he seated himself at the dinner-table a little later. "My chariot is outside, and it can take the four of us easily—or are you turning your terror out, Denham?"

"Neither," Adela interposed. "It's a fine night, and five minutes' walking will take us there, you lazy sybarite."

"What made you say it was our duty to go, Mr. Denham?" Marguerite asked. "Do you anticipate a dull evening?"

"If I had, the fact of your being a member of our party would have consoled me," he answered. "But it isn't that. Irma and Haydée Carson are local talent, they're doing it for charity, and Westingborough has to second their noble efforts by taking tickets —paying up, in fact."

"Hugh, you're usurping a woman's prerogative, being catty," Adela reproved him. "He's omitted to tell you, Marguerite, that Irma Carson has a perfectly lovely contralto voice and knows how to use it, and Haydée is a gold medallist for violin playing."

"And are Haydée and Irma their real names?" she asked.

"They are, poor things," Leigh put in. "Irma was my first love, till she punched me on the nose and made it bleed. Now she's got a singer's chest development, and Haydée's all bony."

"Bob, you're perfectly horrid," Adela told him. "That's not the sort of thing you ought to say of any girl."

"Comparison with you, darling," he retorted unrepentantly. "With your picture imprinted on my 'art, as Mr. Guppy would say, all else is vanity. And artists like those two don't bother about appearances—at least, they needn't unless they like."

"The compliment to my intellect is too obvious," she said caustically. "Marguerite, you won't mind walking, will you?"

"Not in the least. It's such a little distance."

She glanced at Denham as she spoke, and the quality of the glance indicated that she would not have objected if the walk had been far longer, since the other two would expect her to pair with him. And, returning the glance, he smiled at her, as if he had divined her thought and shared her anticipation.

"Don't you wish yourself back in Italy, Miss West?" Leigh asked abruptly, after the inevitable silence that falls on every dinner-table sooner or later. "Snow one night, and almost a spring evening next—and quite possibly a blizzard before morning."

"I am quite content to be here," she answered. "Remember, I am as much English as Italian, and my two years here have taught me that the climate is not all bad. There are compensating days."

"It's rather surprising that you speak idiomatic English so perfectly," Leigh observed. "Living most of your life in Italy, I mean."

"Not till I was ten," she pointed out. "Till then, I was in England, and in every Italian city there is an English colony. In every city I have known, that is. Go to Florence, or Taormina, or even Ventimiglia, and you cannot get away from English speech for long."

"And you don't want to go back?" Leigh persisted.

She shook her lovely head. "Why should I, when people are so kind to me here?" she asked in reply. "Since Adela and I got to know each other, I have made friend after friend, and now I am quite happy here."

Later, as she walked behind the engaged pair toward the town hall with Denham, she laid her hand on his arm and shook it gently.

"Why the silence and gloom?" she asked him. "You are not like yourself to-night. What is it—what has happened to you?"

"Haven't you heard what happened to-day at the inquest on Carter?" he asked in reply, looking down at her.

"I have not," she answered decidedly. "I live in my little house with my one maid, and town gossip interests me very little."

"You know Carter was murdered last night?" he queried.

"I think there is nobody in Westingborough who does not know it," she said. "But what has that to do with your gloom? He was no friend of yours surely—such a man?"

"No, no friend, though I dined at his place last night. An invitation I wish I'd never accepted. Now there seems to be an impression that I ought to have seen the man who murdered him, and since I insisted that I saw nobody of the kind between leaving his place and putting my car away, I'm likely to be highly unpopular."

"What kind of man did murder him, then?" she asked.

"A young man in riding-breeches and boots, they say, who walked along Market Street toward Maggs Lane not long after I drove away from Carter's with the rest of his guests. A young man with a parcel under his arm—and I saw no such person on my drive home, as I told them. Still, I feel myself suspect —and here we are. *You* won't suspect me, will you? It would be the last evil, if you did."

"Have no fear," she answered very softly.

They went into the hall, five minutes late as Adela had foretold, and Denham had confirmation of his surmise regarding the reception that would be accorded him as they went to their seats in the front row. Old Mrs. Haddon, who in a normal way would have greeted him enthusiastically for the sake of her three unmarried daughters, became unaccountably interested in her programme as soon as she sighted him. Major Fenwick, usually very friendly, sat bolt upright and gazed straight before him from his seat in the second row—and these two were typical of the attitude of the majority. The coroner's severe inquisition had given them the impression that Denham knew something, and they acted accordingly. There were, of course, exceptions, people who nodded and smiled at him—the platform was unoccupied at the time—but in their greetings he saw or imagined a touch of commiseration or curiosity, and possibly they stung him more than did the frank cuts.

"Mr. Denham," Marguerite whispered, "don't sit down, just for a second. It may mean nothing, but I wish to do it."

Turning toward her in response to the request, he showed his profile to the audience in the seats behind him. As he stood so, she leaned toward him and laid her hand on his arm again.

"Now you may sit down," she said, smiling up at him.

"By Jove!" said Major Fenwick to himself, "that was a gallant gesture, and I feel ashamed of myself."

Mrs. Haddon, on the other hand, might have gnashed her teeth at the sight, if they had not been artificial. Few people in the hall could fail to realise the significance of Marguerite's act, a statement of her belief in Denham and of her contempt for their implicit suspicions. And, since Marguerite West ranked as the most beautiful girl in Westingborough, and hitherto had shown no more open preference for Hugh Denham than for any other of her many admirers, this challenge in the sight of all caused many a man to wish he could change places with Denham, and to question if he had not judged the man prematurely and unfairly.

Denham himself was glowing with happiness. "I don't care what anyone else thinks, now," he whispered to her.

They sat the concert out and contributed their share of applause, though Denham hardly knew whether Schumann, Chopin, Souza or Al Jolson were being rendered by the Carson sisters. He was lost in a great happiness that made the trial he had undergone that day a thing far-off and small: Marguerite would not thus have stated her belief in him publicly unless she cared for him, and of all things he wanted her love most, though as yet he had not told her his need of her.

He came out with her at the end to the hazed mildness of the night. Two or three people arrested their progress to shake hands with him—in all probability Marguerite's acknowledgment of her belief in him influenced them, for they were men of about his own age. By reason of these pauses the pair found themselves well behind Adela and Leigh when they got clear of the parties waiting for cars about the entrance to the hall. Denham took Marguerite's arm.

"There's no need to catch up with them," he remarked.

"Unless you wish," she answered.

But, at the junction of Market Street and London Road, they found the other two waiting for them, and Denham grunted inarticulate resentment at Adela's tactlessness. She had her own man—why could she not realise that he wanted nobody but Marguerite, then?

"I waited to ask you—will you come in for a minute or two, Marguerite?" Adela inquired.

"I think not, dear, thanks," Marguerite answered. "May I come in and see you to-morrow, some time in the afternoon?"

"Why, of course! Come in for tea, and then we can rend to-night's performers in peace. Good night, dear."

She went on with Leigh. When, nearing the end of Treherne Road, she glanced back, the other pair were out of hearing behind.

"If I were a man, Bob, I think I should be rather afraid of her," she remarked. "She's so—so terribly lovely, sometimes."

"I don't get you, darling," Leigh said.

"I mean— Oh, well! Perhaps it's the best thing for him—if she means to have him, that is. After we're married, he won't have me to mind the house and stand between him and the horde of would-be wives, and if Marguerite really cares for him she'll probably make him happy."

"Who is she, really?" he asked. "I mean, who was she?"

"Marguerite West, with an English father and an Italian mother—that's all I know, and all anyone here knows," she answered. "Perfectly charming—though I needn't tell you that, and in the two years since she came here she's gradually been accepted everywhere. She manages to win women as well as men, in spite of being so lovely."

"From Italy, isn't she?" he asked reflectively.

"Taormina—that's Sicily. She had a villa there when the Harrison family went to stay, and Mrs. Harrison invited her to look them up when she came to England. Marguerite's little house in Panlyon Avenue was for sale, then. She bought it, and moved in after a fortnight's stay with the Harrisons, and of course they launched her among their friends and gave her a start. And she stole my cook—that's how I first came to know her. I was so wholeheartedly grateful to her."

"For thieving your cook away from you?" he asked incredulously.

"I was afraid I should have to pension her, or something. Old Mrs. Pennefeather, you know. She'd been with us ever since I was a child, and was getting past doing all I want done, getting faulty in her memory, and deaf, and generally troublesome. Then she saw the chance of going to Marguerite, and took it, a single-handed post. A tiny house, only one person to please—and I believe she gets on very well there, from what Marguerite tells me. When there's no man in a house, it reduces the work by about two-thirds."

"Thoroughly domestic, aren't you, darling?"

"Women don't come into a drawing-room with muddy shoes, or leave oil-cans and spanners to make marks on furniture. Poor old Mrs. Pennefeather used almost to weep over some of Hugh's careless ways. We only keep two, you see, and she had a good deal to do besides cooking."

"And you've told me all you know about Miss West?"

"All I know? How do you mean, Bob?"

"Why, if there's nothing more known than that she had a villa in Taormina once upon a time, Westingborough seems to have been more trusting than usual, in her case," he pointed out.

"A girl obviously of independent means," she explained, "a thoroughly nice girl in every way, and she had the Harrisons behind her. Since they had accepted her, and in a way sponsored her, Westingborough as a whole couldn't question—didn't question, in any case."

"It's odd," he reflected. "I might say it's damned odd."

"What is?" she inquired.

"That a frowsy old buffer like Harrison and his musty freak of a wife should be social arbiters of a place like this, just because he happens to own the hall and a big estate."

"Mrs. Harrison is quite nice, when you get to know her," she said severely, pausing at the gateway of her home and looking back along the road. "Bob," she added, with a total change of tone, "they're not even in sight round the corner, yet."

"Shall I come in?" he asked.

She took his arm and urged him forward in the direction of the door. "Didn't you hear the joy in my voice?" she demanded.

CHAPTER VIII

TO NO PURPOSE

A SCORE YARDS or less from the junction of Market Street and London Road, a copy of Head's "Police Notice" showed clearly in the light of a street lamp as Denham and Marguerite West, walking slowly to give the other pair time to make an interval from them, approached it. Marguerite hesitated, glancing at the heavy black type which stated that the notice was addressed "To All Cyclists and Nurses."

"Is that connected with—with what happened last night?" she asked.

"It is." He took her arm and drew her forward, away from the notice, as he answered: it appeared that he wished to avoid such a reminder of the tragedy in which he was remotely implicated.

"Cyclists and Nurses," she repeated, as they walked slowly on.

"A policeman saw a nurse cycling from the bridge into London Road, and saw her turn into Treherne Road, about the time I left the Grange this morning," he explained, after a brief silence. "Later on, he saw a young man in riding-breeches and boots walking along Market Street toward that end of Maggs Lane, and they won't believe I didn't see that young man somewhere between the Grange and Treherne Road, on my way home. So I'm under suspicion of complicity, you see."

He spoke with hard bitterness. For the moment, his remembrance of the initial reception that had been accorded him in the town hall outweighed that of her championship of him, or perhaps he resented the need for such championship, from her of all people.

They walked on slowly and in silence for awhile. Ahead of them, Leigh and Adela Denham steadily increased the interval between the two pairs. Denham kept his hold on the girl's arm, and felt her lean toward him as she walked, and in the consciousness of her nearness his bitterness lessened, and passed. They turned the corner of Treherne Road in time to see Adela and Leigh go into the house.

"It was wonderful of you, to-night," Denham said abruptly.

"But I believe in you," she answered, very softly.

Momentarily, he paused and faced her. Then, still holding her arm, he led her on again along the road, and crossed to the opposite side, toward the point where Panlyon Avenue branched off at right angles.

"I may see you all the way home?" he asked. "Adela and Leigh will be glad of the interval, if you'll let me."

"I shall not resent the interval myself," she said, looking up at him and smiling. "And we can count it our good deed to them."

She lived in one of four tiny residences set next each other in fairly large gardens. The builder who designed and erected them had reluctantly abandoned the idea of giving the general title of "Honeymoon Terrace" to the four, since a childless couple and one servant was the limit of occupancy any one of them could accommodate. Denham opened her gate for her, the third of the four from the Treherne Road end of the avenue, and stood back for her to enter.

"Won't you come in for a minute?" she asked, pausing and facing him.

"If I may," he answered hesitantly.

"We shall be extending our good deed," she pointed out. "Look back at your drawing-room window—you can see they're in there. And they won't welcome you if you go back there now."

"No, but—your maid. Has she a long tongue?"

"Mrs. Pennefeather? She's deaf, and sleeps in the back bedroom. No, you needn't fear for my reputation through her. Besides, it's not yet eleven o'clock, and, as a final reason, I simply don't care. So why not come in for a little while?"

"I hoped I might," he said, and followed her into the house.

She switched on a light, and led the way into the small, front sitting-room, where she took a box of matches from the mantel and lighted a gas-fire. Denham had left his hat and overcoat in the tiny hall, and he faced her as she stood looking down at the fire, still wearing her furred evening cloak over the black frock.

"And now tell me all about what happened this afternoon," she bade without looking up at him. "Why you are suspected, I mean."

"I think it is because of a momentary loss of self-control this morning, when Inspector Head came to see me at my office," he answered. "When he told me about the young man in riding-kit with a parcel under his arm. Somehow he gleaned an impression that I'd seen that young man on my way back from the Grange, and they badgered and bullied me to make me say I had seen him."

"And you had not?" she queried, without looking up.

Denham regarded her intently, steadily. "I told them, from the time I left the Grange until I locked my car in the garage and went into the house, I saw nobody but the Quades in their car," he answered.

She looked up then. "I believe you," she said.

"You mean—?" he asked, and paused.

"I believe you are incapable of lying," she answered steadily.

"Possibly," he said, with a note of doubt. "And yet—Miss West, I want to make a confession to you—a confidence. May I?"

"You may tell me anything you wish," she answered. "Anything."

"It's this. I answered every question put to me at the inquest truthfully, and yet—because of you—" He broke off abruptly.

"Because of me?" she asked, surprised.

"I've got to tell you the whole of it," he said, rather shamedly. "I left the Grange at about three o'clock this morning in my car, and drove to my home at the end of this road and put the car away in the garage. From the time I turned into London Road from Market Street, while the Quades drove straight on, I didn't see a soul. I heard Mortimer and the Perry girls laughing and talking farther down the road as I went into the house, but didn't see even them. That was after I'd put the car away and locked the garage."

"And so the suspicion of you is utterly unjust," she commented.

"To that point, yes," he assented, "but although I answered every question put to me truthfully, I was jesuitical about it, because of you, as I said before. I put the car away and went into the house."

She was looking down at the gas-fire again, standing with one foot on the brass fender. "And then?" she asked quietly.

"I felt like a whisky and soda, and had it," he went on. "In the dining-room. I wasn't in the least sleepy, and lighted the gas-fire in there just as you did with this one when we came in here. I sat over the fire wondering if it were worth while to go to bed at all, and heard the church clock strike four and chime a quarter past. Then I remembered that when I backed the car into the garage I'd stopped the engine by letting the clutch in too suddenly with the reverse gear engaged, and so had forgotten to switch off the ignition."

"What does that mean?" she asked, glancing up at him.

"It's battery ignition, and the battery was already partly run down," he explained. "It meant that, unless I went out and switched off, the battery would be discharging all the time, and quite probably. I shouldn't be able to start the car in the morning. So I went out to the garage, switched on the light, and switched off the car ignition. It would be then about twenty minutes past four, I think."

"Still I don't see why you say it was because of me," she said, gazing steadily at him, with the suggestion of a smile about her lips.

"I switched off the garage light," he went on, disregarding the comment for the moment, "locked up, and turned to go into the house again. The garage doors, as you may know, are exactly opposite the end of this road—Panlyon Avenue. It was very dark, and just a little misty. I saw a man, and as far as I could tell he was a young man in riding-kit—I saw him just for a moment or two under the street lamp nearly outside this house, and it appeared to me that he opened your gate and went to your front door. I know there are four houses exactly alike, and the street lamp didn't give me a chance to see clearly, but—can you understand? I'm confessing to you, no matter what you may think of me over it. It appeared to me that he came to this house."

He waited for some comment from her. She looked down at the gas-fire again. "I see," she said coldly. "Yes, I see."

"Then Head came to me this morning," he went on rather desperately. "I didn't know, you see, and my one thought was to keep you out of it. Whether my eyes deceived me or no, I had to keep you out of it. If I'd said I thought I saw a man come to this house at that hour, it would have damned your reputation for ever in Westingborough even if you disproved it —you can never overtake and kill a scandal like that altogether. I had to keep you out of it, at any cost, short of actual perjury. They can suspect me of lying if they like, though actually I didn't lie—they can suspect me of anything, as long as I save you from any question of that kind. I had to save you, and did."

She put her left hand on the mantel beside the right, and drooped her head between her wrists, so that he could not see her face. And, so posed, she stood silent and quite still.

"So now you know what I am," he said bitterly. "Incapable of lying, you said, while all the while I'm a jesuitical hound who went as near lying as I could without actually committing perjury. But I had to tell you, felt I must make the confession, though it's an insult to you."

After awhile she let her hands fall to her sides, and turned to face him. He could see her lips quivering slightly.

"Will you believe me when I tell you that no man, young or old, came to this house at any hour last night or this morning?" she asked.

"Of course I believe you," he answered. "I never thought it, but being on oath, I should have had to say what I felt convinced I saw, if I'd said anything about it. I knew, really, it must have been one of the other houses, or he went between two of them and over the fence at the back, but it looked to me as if he came to your front door. I should have had to own it looked like that, and people are only too ready to believe evil on the slightest grounds. It would have put you under suspicion, no matter what you said."

After a long silence, he backed a step toward the door.

"Now I'd better go," he observed. "I can guess pretty accurately what you're thinking of me after that."

She smiled. "If you can," she said, "you will not go yet."

"You mean, I suppose, you want me to wait while you tell me in full what I am," he flung back bitterly. "It isn't necessary—I know."

"And I tell you, when you know what I feel, you will not wish to go," she said again. "If I could tell you—"

"To no purpose!" he broke in, with harsh self-condemnation. "After what you've told me now, all to no purpose—since there was no man here. I might have known—I did know—and yet it would have brought you in, brought your name in. And now, if you despise me half as much as I despise myself—but I'll go. You needn't tell me."

"Wait!" She turned to him momentarily, and then again laid her hands on the mantel and so held her head that her face was hidden. He stood irresolute, and after a long pause she spoke again.

"I am thinking of a man to whom honour and truth are first things, treasured things," she said slowly and only just audibly. "I am thinking how he set those great possessions of his against my good name, as if he put it at one end of a balance against them at the other, and let the balance swing until it showed that his care for me was the greater. And I ask myself, what can I give to prove—what can I say to prove how much this gift of his means to me? And there is no answer—I can find no answer. For nothing I could say or give could ever repay such a man, yet if I could I would compensate." Again she let her hands fall, and faced him. "Prove it!" she almost whispered tensely. "Ask of me—tell me to kneel to you! Set me some hard thing to prove how I honour the sacrifice you made for me?"

"Marguerite!"

She saw the wonderful glow of happiness in his eyes only for a moment, for then she was in his arms, strained close to him, her face hidden, and her sobbing breath a warmth against his neck. So through a tranced interval they stood, and at last she looked up at him.

"But I bade you ask," she whispered.

"Darling, can I ask more? How could I ever gain more than you?"

"Ah! This is not asking, but giving! Every moment of to-night I have been longing to feel your arms round me. Yes, so, as if you would not have me breathe any more—as if you would be life and breath for us both! As if you knew me all yours, my dear."

"Did I hurt you, darling?"

"You?" She smiled up at him. "You could never hurt me, you strong, gentle lover. My lover! How can I tell you all you mean to me? My dear, how I love you!"

* * * * *

"Darling—Marguerite! Do you see it's midnight? I must go."

"I know, Hugh, but I don't want you to go. I love you so."

"One thing, sweet. I must get in touch with Inspector Head and tell him what I thought I saw, now—but no, I can't, though."

"You . . . why not, my dear?"

"Drag your name through the mud of a murder trial, even though you were not called as witness? No, not that, darling. And I couldn't say I didn't know which house I thought he entered—it's a matter of telling all or nothing. To say my muddled sight made me think I saw a man come to this house at that hour—no!"

"What will you do, then?" Seated, with his arms round her, on the settee he had drawn forward for her before the fire, she lifted her face toward his to ask the question.

He kissed her, held her closer, in renewed forgetfulness of all but her presence. In the end she laid her cheek against his.

"What will you do, dear?" she asked again.

"Nothing," he answered decidedly. "Head will get the man—I feel sure he will run his quarry down in the end, and then there will be no need for me to do anything. What that man was doing in this road must have very little connection with the crime itself, and the one I saw may not even have been the murderer. No, I shall say nothing."

"But then suspicion will still rest on you," she pointed out.

"It will rest on me still more if I speak now, after keeping silence to-day," he said. "Also it will look as if I'd conferred with you, agreed with you as to what to say—if I did speak at all, I couldn't keep this house out of it, and I might be putting the people in all four of these houses under an unjust suspicion, not only you."

"He might have come to one of them," she suggested, and Denham felt her shiver suddenly as she sat in his clasp.

"Afraid, darling?" he asked tenderly. "You need have no fear. A man like Carter would easily make enemies who might want to destroy him, but no harm can come to you. Have no fear."

She released herself from his hold and stood up. He too, standing, faced her, and she reached out and laid her hands on his shoulders.

"My dear," she said gravely, "I did not think—no, do not hold me again just now—I did not think there could be such happiness in the world as you have given me to-night. I did not think a man's love could be so great, so wonderful, as yours. And sometimes, my dear, I am foresighted, but I will not tell you what I have seen in this time of happiness you have given me. Only—yes, hold me quite close while I tell you this—I will be very selfish, now. I will ask, give me every hour, every minute you can spare, and ask every minute of my time you will. I want you with me, my darling, want you close to me. I am not all English, as you know, but in part of the warm south, and that part of me loves you so intensely—so far more intensely than you can realise, I know. There is another reason, but I will not tell it you. I ask, give me every hour that you have to give, and take every hour I may give to you. Be selfish too, and ask of me."

He looked down into her eyes, intently, tenderly.

"Is anything troubling you, darling?" he asked.

She smiled rather wistfully. "Only that I must let you go, strong lover, and ache alone for your strength and gentleness. And to-morrow I shall go to Adela in the afternoon. Will you be there?"

"I shall certainly be there, now I know you will," he assured her.

"Tell her that I belong to you before I see her. If I stay a little while, you can come back here with me and we can be together again. Adela will understand, and nobody else counts—except you."

"Marguerite, darling—I'm sure there's something worrying you, something you haven't told me—not that I've given you time to tell me anything. What is it, sweet? Tell me."

She drew his head down to kiss his forehead, and then clung close to him. For awhile he felt the beating of her heart.

"I am afraid," she said at last. "Afraid of so great a love as this I have found to-night, in myself as in you, my lover. Lest it should be only for a little time, lest through any cause we should lose it—as I shall be afraid when I have to see God. So few hours ago, I did not know if you loved me, and I was apart from you and cool. And now I am on fire, my soul a part of you as my body would be, and in my mind fear lest it should be too great a thing for such a one as me, and lest it should be taken away. So I ask—every hour, while the gift is mine, and apart from you I can only be afraid."

"Will it make any difference if I tell you that you have made me very happy—happier than I have ever been in my life?" he asked.

"This difference—that I too am happy because of such a telling. Now, heart of me, I let you go, not easily, and to-morrow—"

"All the to-morrows—every hour I can give and take from you," he promised. "And I'm not in the least afraid, darling, now I know you love me, though I too find it almost too wonderful to be true."

But, as he went slowly back to his home after a final leave-taking, a quarter of an hour later, he realised vaguely that the phrase, "too wonderful to be true," was a mere banality which did not nearly cover the meaning of the words in which she had told him she was afraid. She knew well that it was true, knew all that she meant to him and that she need have no fear of his love failing, and yet . . .

He planned a future, with Marguerite as mistress of his home instead of Adela, and, in the farther future, a small Marguerite in her arms. There was a species of intoxication in that glimpse of the crown set on their destined happiness, and silently, as he walked, he worshipped his living Marguerite, and prayed to be worthy of her.

Adela gave him a long look as he entered the drawing-room. "So you've settled it," she observed in a satisfied way.

"I don't see how you deduce that," he answered, smiling broadly.

"No? Then take that dark hair off your shirtfront, and brush the powder off the shoulder of your coat. A man of your age ought to have had experience enough to look for things like that himself. Did you find it difficult to propose to her, or did she make it easy?"

"Did I . . . ? Adela, she's wonderful!"

"Yes? Bob told me I was. I suppose we all are in the mating season. Plumaged in the man's eyes for the great occasion."

"Don't be so beastly cynical, girl!"

"I'm not. It's the practical streak I inherit from mother—she didn't bequeath you any. Hugh, Bob and I agreed to get married in April, and if you ask Marguerite, we might make it a foursome."

"Make it a— Oh, good Lord, Addie!"

"If you're looking for my bump of reverence, I poulticed it out of existence. I've always understood that two and two make four, so why not call it a foursome? It isn't blasphemy, is it?"

"I'm going to bed," he said, with grim determination.

"On your way," she retorted, "you'll step into the dining-room and mix yourself the usual nightcap. Mix me one too, and bring them both in here. I knew something was happening to keep you out with her so long, and sat up in hope instead of going to bed myself after Bob had gone. Now I want to drink your health and Marguerite's, and tell you how very much I hope you'll be happy."

He went to her and kissed her. "You're a dear, Addie," he told her.

"Over the drink," she pursued, "I'm solemnly going to forgive her for turning up in a frock like that and making me look a worm and no man, though it's 'ard, bitter 'ard! Make mine as strong as yours, and I think you need a good strong one to brace you after all you've been through."

CHAPTER IX

AT THE LONDON END

A CASUAL OBSERVER, to whom Inspector Terence Byrne was once pointed out, remarked— "He looks more like a poet out of a job than a police inspector," and there was aptness in the description. It fitted him when, having heard Head's story of the discovery of Carter's body and of the tracks of the old boots, he fixed his soulful, melancholy gaze on the rough plan of Westingborough Grange and its surroundings which Head had drawn to illustrate the tale of the boot-tracks.

Holding the plan in one hand to study it, he groped with the other hand over the table at which the two men sat—the fact that the concert at Westingborough town hall was then in progress fixes the time of their conference—and in the end Head reached for the glass for which that hand was seeking and held it for Byrne to grasp.

"You can't do two things at once," he said reprovingly.

"Don't be obvious, Jerry," Byrne objected. "You're the world's worst draughtsman, by the way. Feet—more feet—what's that? Oh, I see. Bicycle-track. Coming from London Road. Didn't you follow it along London Road to where it started out?"

"Some hope!" Head retorted. "Carter was shot at four o'clock. We got it by telephone at five-forty, turned the car out, and picked up the doctor on the way. By that time, London Road was churned mush—we came round by it. Lorries and farm carts, bicycles, people on foot, milk-floats—we start work early down there."

"More fools you," Byrne remarked unsympathetically. "And for the same reason, I deduce, you couldn't track the old boots past the other end of the lane—the Market Street end?"

"Nothing short of an elephant-track would have survived along Market Street till six o'clock that morning," Head confirmed the surmise. "A lot of the Nevile dye works employees go that way, in addition to other traffic. No, we only had Maggs Lane and the footpath—and the trail of the old boots to and from the Grange, of course."

"I get it. How was the body found?"

"Arabella Cann, head housemaid at the Grange, came down to light the kitchen fire and get things going at about five-thirty, because the cook was seedy. She found it, and telephoned us."

"You've acquitted the servants?"

"Easily. That is, as far as I'll acquit anyone till I've got my man. Acquitted all the party he had at the house till three that morning, too. They check each other's movements rather nicely."

"What was that you said about this man Denham, though?"

"I had an idea he saw something or somebody, but he swore he didn't at the inquest this afternoon. We toused him to the limit."

"Anybody can swear," Byrne commented, rather derisively.

"Yes, but Denham's a man of honour," Head pointed out. "I can't see him lying over that or anything."

"Ah-hum! Is the paragon married?"

"No, nor likely to be, as far as I know. Lives with his sister."

"Find the woman, Jerry—find the woman. Even a man of honour will sometimes glory in making a rogue of himself for a woman's sake. Now let me have a look at those photographs you say you had taken, and get me another drink. The rozzer is worthy of his booze, when his country cousin makes him work overtime. Same as before, and don't drown it."

Head took the photographic enlargements from his attaché-case and put them on the table. Then he took up the two glasses and went to the bar of the Captain's Cabin, in which he had run Byrne to earth after failing to get him at his office. When he returned with the refilled glasses, Byrne was intently studying one of the prints.

"Your solution fits," Byrne remarked. "I'd say it was a small he, rather than a she. And look at this. You'll see—here—the three footprints nearest the stile have been trodden twice. Look at that edge and that toe. Jerry, my lad, he didn't dismount from the bicycle in the middle of the road. He rode it to within three paces of the stile, and then got off and lifted it over. On the second trip, when he dropped down out of the tree, he did it so cleverly that it looked as if those footprints from the middle of the road were made in dismounting from the bike, and he only had to duplicate three footprints."

"Obviously. Yes, I see. Two heads are better than one."

"As the woman said when she took the dog to market. Here's luck, Jerry. And you need it, with a man like this."

"Yes, I'm giving him credit for brains," Head assented.

"As I see it, the old boots and the rope were part of his original plan, but not the bicycle," Byrne declared thoughtfully. "He'd have laid that trail to and from the Grange with the boots, swung up into the tree, and chosen hard ground to get away in his own small boots or shoes, whatever they were. But the snow upset that, and he had to improvise this scheme between midnight and four o'clock, make himself an apparently invisible getaway. A hell of a bold crime, Jerry, and very clever planning leading up to it. But it looks to me as if the solution to your problem is simply this. Who had enough influence over Carter to get him to come and open his own front door at four in the morning? Answer that, and then don't wait to get a warrant for arrest."

"And I've come to you to help me to find the answer," Head said.

"Blinkin' optimist, as usual," Byrne grunted. "Haven't I got work enough of my own, without tackling yours as well?"

"You gave me the help I wanted over the Forrest case," Head reminded him, "and gratitude is a lively remembrance of favours to come, as you know. All I want this time is to dig up Carter's past, and incidentally to find out what he had to do with someone called Peter Vesci."

"Peter Vesci," Byrne repeated thoughtfully. "I seem to know that name from somewhere, but I can't place it. Where does Peter come in?"

"Just that Carter had a girl on a string at his party—"

"That's inevitable," Byrne interrupted. "He always had, from what I've heard of him. Rows of 'em, all his life."

"And this girl," Head pursued, "told me when I questioned her that Carter mentioned the name. 'That poor young Peter Vesci,' were the words he used, according to her. He appears to have been meditating on his past sins at the time, and sort of thought the phrase aloud without intending her to hear it. There may be nothing in it, but it seems to me worth while investigating, in case Peter can give us any light on the problem, or let me into some of the secrets of Carter's career."

"I dunno," Byrne said doubtfully. "What's the time?"

"Just on half-past nine," Head answered, glancing at his wrist-watch. "Have you fixed up anywhere to stay, yet?"

"Strand Palace. It's central, and I know what it's like."

"Country cousins always head for the Grand Palace." Byrne finished the contents of his glass. "Pack that picture gallery of yours in your cabin trunk—why can't you carry a decent attaché-case, man, so I don't have to be ashamed of you?—and we'll hoof it up to the Quadrarian and see if we can catch Jimmy Weeds. He's your man."

"Never heard of him," Head said, putting his photographs away.

"No? You've a lot to learn. Jimmy is the stage manager there, and if he wrote half his reminiscences there'd be enough libel actions to keep every barrister in the country busy for a couple of years. He'll talk, for me. Have you eaten?"

"In the restaurant-car on the train. Why?"

"Never go and see Jimmy Weeds on an empty tummy—that's why. He keeps a mellow twenty u.p. whisky, and it's most insidious. Let's go."

They went. A short walk took them to the brilliantly lighted frontage of the Quadrarian theatre, where Byrne, ignoring the entrances to the garishly prominent vestibule, pushed open an inconspicuous swing-door at the side and entered a short, bare corridor along which Head followed him. They ascended an angled staircase and came to a half-glazed door at which Byrne knocked: a throaty voice bade them enter, and Byrne led the way into a comfortably furnished office, decked quite as fully as Mortimer's room at Westingborough with signed photographs of theatrical personalities.

From a comfortable armchair, placed beside a glowing coal fire, a big, middle-aged, fleshy-faced man rose up and held out his hand.

"Byrne, by all that's holy!" he exclaimed, and his rich, deep tones reminded Head of a celebrant intoning a ritual. "But I had an idea some one of you might look me up soon, when I heard of Eddie's sad end."

"And here we are," Byrne confirmed him. "I want to introduce my cousin, Inspector Head, from Westingborough. I told him you might be able to give him some information that might help. Jerry, this is Mr. Jimmy Weeds, and if you can pump him dry you're cleverer than I am."

"Well, this is an honour!" Weeds remarked, as he shook hands with Head. "I never thought I should meet the man who solved the Forrest case. Sit down, Mr. Head, and just wait while I get the bottle out. I hope you're not teetotal, though?"

"Strictly, Mr. Weeds, between drinks," Head assured him.

"Ah! Aha! A noble principle. And I take it you want some particulars of the life of our late chief, eh? Once more, I may remark, the words of our immortal dramatist may be evoked, as it were over the prostrate corpse of this foully murdered man. For, as Macbeth was made to say, this is indeed a bloody business!"

He busied himself with a bottle and glasses in a cabinet as he spoke. Then, advancing with a tray that held three glasses and a soda-syphon, he offered it to his guests.

"I refer, as doubtless you divine, to Eddie's death, not to his life," he added. "I've left you to help yourselves to soda."

"And, as usual, left none too much room for it," Byrne commented.

"Ignore the persiflage, Mr. Head," Weeds advised as he seated himself again, "and tell me how I can help you. If any information that I may give can assist you in bringing the cursed miscreant to justice, it will double my pleasure in becoming acquainted with such a man as yourself. I am, I may tell you, a keen follower of great criminal cases."

"You know a Mr. Frank Mortimer, a scenic artist?" Head opened.

"Frankie? *Do* I know him!" He rolled out the confirmation with melodious emphasis. "But surely you don't suspect Frankie. He and Eddie had some fierce quarrels at times, but our Frankie is no cold-blooded murderer! Oh, no, Mr. Head! I can't admit that!"

Head smiled. "I had a fairly long interview with him this morning," he said, "and he gave me a pretty good idea of the personality of Carter. If you'll forgive the epithet as applied to a dead man, there appears little doubt that Carter was a libertine."

"I will admit that a pretty face was his weakness," Weeds assented cautiously. "But, if you will allow me the comment, Mr. Head, you must not judge the members of our great profession by the standards of conventionality. Conventionalise us, and we die—we are as if we had never been. From our very frailties we mould the mimic passions that stir the hearts of men, and—if I may be forgiven the paraphrase—our little lives are rounded by our loves. Rounded, and sweetened."

He enunciated his dictum with sonorous delight in his own phrasing, took a sip at his glass, and gazed at Head as if he expected signs of overwhelming conviction from the inspector. Head nodded gravely.

"I gather that Mr. Carter did quite a lot of rounding," he suggested.

"He sipped," Weeds assented. "Oh, yes, he sipped the honey from many a flower. And who shall condemn him now?"

"I'm not condemning him, but looking for the man who killed him," Head pointed out. "Some one of his sips may have made him an enemy capable of killing him, for all I know, and if you could tell me—"

"Mr. Head," Weeds interrupted solemnly, "if I am to recite that side of our Eddie's life to you, we must make another appointment. To-night I could no more than touch the fringe, with the aid of summoned memories. He was here, intimately here, for more than ten years."

"Overhauling the beehive all the time?" Head queried.

"Overhauling the—?" Weeds looked his lack of comprehension.

"Sipping honey, as you put it," Head explained, and saw that rarity, a smile, on Byrne's face.

"Ah, I see! Yes, certainly. Yes. Genius has its prerogatives, and who shall deny our Eddie genius? We shall not look upon his like again. I regard his frailties as buried with him."

"Yes, but his funeral isn't till the day after tomorrow," Head pointed out, "so we've got till then, at the least. Now, Mr. Weeds, do you know if he ever had anything to do with somebody named Peter Vesci?"

"Why, yes—the Vesci trio! He discovered them. And—but surely . . . And yet— Is it possible? Peter Vesci!"

"Will you tell me all you can about the connection between the two, as full a history of it as you can give?" Head asked.

"The full history!" Weeds cogitated, with his hand to his brow in true theatrical fashion, for awhile; then he rose, took a large portfolio from a side-table, and turned its millboard pages. Eventually he returned with it to where Head sat, and laid it open on his knees. "There they are," he said. "Peter is the middle one."

It was a large platinotype print depicting three figures, all dressed exactly alike in trunk hose and doublets—they might have been pages of the Tudor era, with their wasp waists and puffed sleeves. All three had luxuriant mops of hair, apparently black or very dark, and big, soft dark eyes, and they bore so great a resemblance to each other in feature and form that, as far as this photograph was concerned, there would appear to have been a difficulty in distinguishing which was which, if any one of the three were regarded apart from the other two. Stage make-up, probably, had increased the resemblance, but apart from such a factor it was strikingly noticeable.

"Brothers, apparently," Head remarked.

"A brother and two sisters," Weeds corrected him. "The Vesci trio. On the left as you look at them, Nita—Anita, that is. In the middle, Peter. And on the right, Quita. Eddie found them, made them, and in the end broke them. And it may be that you have lighted on the author of his extinction in that central figure, Peter Vesci. I do not know, but it may be. Nita, Quita, and Peter, a dazzling combination in their day, a breath-taking turn. Alas, a turn no more!"

"What was it?" Head inquired prosaically.

"Ah, what was it not!" Weeds lamented wistfully. "I have heard the applause go on and on, on and on, till we had to send them back."

"On and on like time," Head said gravely, looking at his watch. "What did they do to get applause like that?"

"You would have to see and hear them to appreciate what they did," Weeds told him. "I can tell you one item of the turn. Quita would come out from the wings, wearing a little metal cap. On the cap was a small cylinder, like a circular ruler, about six inches long. On the top of the ruler was a pad, and on that pad Nita lay—it was a tiny thing on which she balanced herself, lying on her back and keeping herself rigidly extended in a horizontal line, and singing one of her wicked little songs that always set the house rocking. At the far side of the stage Peter would be standing with a coil of rope, and as his two sisters came on he would swing the rope and fling it as a cowboy does. And with the end of that rope he would flick the little cylinder away, so that Nita on her pad dropped down on to Quita's head—and went on singing! That was just one little feature of the turn."

"I'm looking for a good rope-thrower," Head remarked thoughtfully. "What else could they do? Was there any shooting in it?"

"A modification of the William Tell business," Weeds said assentingly. "Quita, swinging head downward from a trapeze —swinging, not merely hanging by the backs of her knees—broke glass balls on Nita's hair, and shot the end off a cigar that Peter held between his teeth, while they were standing on the stage. It was a trick cigar, of course, but shooting and smashing the crystal balls was real."

"I don't need quite as good a shot as that," Head commented. "What other peculiarities had they? They look harmless enough, here."

"They were brilliant—you would have had to see the turn. And hear them sing, too. Unaccompanied harmonising, and they sang as well upside down as on their feet, all three of them. They were as inventive as Grock—I've heard the whole house sobbing with laughter, and then seen it one vast horde of open mouths and goggling eyes. Variety? Those three were an unending variety show in themselves!"

"And you say Carter found them?"

"Not long after he found Paul Bellerby. And that reminds me—I was questioning in my mind whether Eddie's action over Paul had anything to do with his death. It came into my mind as I read my evening paper. I really ought to tell you about it."

"What was it, then?" Head asked with an air of resignation.

"Paul had a marvellous voice, ranging from a yodel down to the lowest possible note, and Eddie booked him at twenty pounds a week. He was a bargain at that. Then he got some throat trouble that killed his voice entirely, spent every penny he had trying to get it back, and the throat trouble developed till it was certain he wouldn't recover. He was dying in a workhouse infirmary, and his wife came to Eddie to see if she could get any help—Eddie had his office just across the passage from this room—and I was in here when she came up to see him. He didn't wait for her to speak when she went in. 'Mrs. Bellerby,' he said, 'I can buy all the sob-stuff I want for my shows. If ever I want any free, I'll let you know—Get out before you're thrown out!' I heard that myself—he could be hard, could Eddie. And I wondered to-day whether that woman had some man behind her after Paul died, some man that might boil up enough inside to go and kill Eddie."

"You make me feel like regarding it as justifiable homicide, whoever did it," Head observed. "I'll mark Mrs. Bellerby down in my mind as a side-line, but for the present I want to know more about these Vescis. If there's time—have you time, though? I appear to be asking a good deal of you, Mr. Weeds."

"Say no more, Mr. Head—the honour is mine. And let me refill that glass for you—yours too, Byrne. Anything I can tell you, you know."

"Well, then, you say Carter found this trio. Let's begin at the beginning—how and where did he find them, as you phrase it?"

"He was up north—I believe it was Sunderland—and he was always on the look-out for talent of every kind," Weeds said from the cabinet, where he was busy with the bottle again. "There was a circus—Aldeni's Mammoth Circus it was called—and the Vesci trio were one of the turns of the show. It was a second-rate sort of show, and Aldeni was really Alden, English, and uncle to these three. They'd only just left off being kids, and apparently they'd been with him all their lives. He'd had them well-educated, though—you could tell that as soon as any one of them spoke. Their father and mother had died while they were still infants, and Alden had taken them over and cared for them. One other thing—they were all children of one birth, triplets."

"Any physical defect in any of them?" Head inquired.

"Why, no," Weeds answered, with a note of surprise. "Perfect physiques, and any one of them could lift and carry the other two. Why?"

"Merely that triplets are often lacking in some way physically," Head explained. "Never mind, though—tell me the rest."

"Eddie saw their possibilities," Weeds went on. "They weren't nearly what they became after he took them over, of course—he developed their possibilities and made them a star turn. Aldeni knew his circus was a dying industry, and when Eddie said he was willing to sign them up for a year at twenty pounds a week for the three, Aldeni let them go willingly enough. Later on, he died and left them a little money, and they put it into insurance premiums, a ten thousand pound policy on each of the three lives, because if any one of them died it would ruin the turn, and they knew it. Eddie worked them up and up, and their contract was renewed at a hundred a week. They were worth far more than that, and he knew it, and got them at that figure." He paused to take a drink. "I hope I haven't overdone the soda for either of you," he suggested. "I risked mixing it myself."

"A most noble mixture," Head assured him, and Byrne nodded satisfied concurrence. "A hundred a week between the three, you mean?"

"Inevitably," Weeds assured him. "They were happy on it, too. They didn't mix in with any theatrical set, but took a little house at Twickenham—I went down there to see them for Eddie, once, one Sunday afternoon. The Mallows, it was called, a pretty little house with a garden running down to the river, and that garden plays a part in the tale. They lived there quite simply together, and quite happily—had a little saloon car, and Peter used to keep it clean, I believe. Pastoral simplicity, in their off time—Arcadia up to date."

"No liking for grandeur," Head suggested.

"For a gay life," Weeds corrected him. "But refined, quite refined. They were partly of foreign extraction, and when you looked at Peter's delicate little hands and feet, and his dark eyes and black hair, you could well believe his father had been a Spanish grandee, or his mother some passionate Andalusian. Not that they gave any hint of it in their talk, for there wasn't a trace of foreign accent. And both girls were something more than pretty—you don't get a hint of their real looks in that photo, with their hair all buzzed up as they used to appear and grease-paint and make-up to make them as much like Peter as possible. I always thought Quita the better-looking of the two, but Eddie's fancy strayed to Nita, and so the serpent entered their Eden."

"And this," Head suggested, "is where the story begins."

"The end of the comedy," Weeds said assentingly, "and the beginning of the tragedy. I didn't see the details of the tragedy, but this much I can tell you—what Eddie wanted, he got, and I don't know a single exception to prove that rule. There was delay in signing up the third contract for the Vesci trio, and eventually it went through at a hundred and fifty a week for fifty-two weeks. Less than three months after it had been signed, Anita walked down their garden and into the river in a fog, and the post-mortem before the inquest proved that she didn't stray from the way she meant to walk. Did I say they were all three passionate, impulsive?—fierce, they could be. I've seen them with each other, and still more in defence of each other. Tigerish."

"Was there a verdict of suicide?" Head asked.

"Obviously—unsound mind, though, out of compassion for the two left alive. And they got the insurance—the policy ruled out suicide within the first twelve months, but made no limitation after that, and it had been in force over a year. I think they'd saved a good deal as well, living simply as they did. Of course, the act was at an end till Quita and Peter could cook up a show between them, and Eddie claimed that Nita's death broke the contract, and refused to pay any more—"

"He being actually the cause of her death?" Head half-questioned.

"Undoubtedly, but Eddie was a hard man when it came to personal relationships. He always said he had to be to survive and flourish. I believe, too, that legally he was right, though Quita and Peter never contested it. He'd booked three people for an act, and with only two left alive the contract became void. So he said, at least, and I know there was no saving clause in the contract to cover the contingency."

"How long ago did this happen?" Head queried.

"Not more than two months before Eddie chucked it and went to live in the country," Weeds answered. "Indirectly, it was the cause of his retirement, I think. I always put it down to that, myself."

"But if Peter Vesci had meant to have vengeance for his sister's death, he wouldn't have waited over three years," Head pointed out.

"Wait—I haven't come to the end of the story yet," Weeds urged. "Yes, Tommy,"—to a man who looked in at the door—"put everything on to Samuelson to-night. I'm busy, as you can see. Where was I, Mr. Head? Oh, yes, I remember! Nita had been dead about a month, and we hadn't seen anything of the other two up here, when there was hell's own ringing of Eddie's bell late one afternoon. Three of us rushed up these stairs—it was a matinée afternoon—and into his room, and there he was standing over Peter Vesci. Peter was lying on the floor beside Eddie's desk, and there was a stiletto not much thicker than a hatpin down beside him and red and black ink splashed all over the front of his vest. Ordinary clothes he had on, of course. He'd been going for Eddie with that stiletto, and Eddie, being a quick and powerful man, just heaved up a malachite inkstand he had on his desk—a presentation thing—and took Peter on the breast-bone with it. Stove his ribs in—it was a heavy thing, and there were three ribs broken—and I heard after that one of the ends of broken bone had gone into the lung, or something. We three were trying to do something about it when I was pushed aside as if I'd been a mere rabbit—and I'm just on fifteen stone!—and Quita stooped and picked up her brother in her arms and went to the door with him as if he had been a small baby. He was quite unconscious. She turned in the doorway and looked at Eddie. 'This is reprieve, not escape for you,' she said to him, and went out."

"Carrying her brother," Head supplemented.

"Carrying him all the way down the staircase and out to the car, and she put him inside and drove away. And none of us ever saw either of them again. Eddie hushed it up, took no action, and they took none. They left The Mallows, and I heard she'd taken him abroad, Algiers or somewhere, as soon as she felt it was safe to travel him. About that, where they went, I'm not sure, but it's more than possible that she nursed him till he got well again, and it took a very long time. Being well again, he came back to England and put paid to Eddie's account for his dead sister's sake—that's only conjecture, of course. But if you have to choose between a snake and a Spaniard with a grudge against you, kill the Spaniard, or else he'll get you in the end. The snake's animosity isn't personal."

"Carter made other enemies," Head suggested after a thoughtful pause. "You've told me this story, and it's a possibility, I admit. But were there no others with equal cause to hate him?"

"Oh, plenty! It's getting late, Mr. Head, but you come round again to-morrow night, and I'll tell you some more histories, if you like. But he made no enemies as vital as Peter Vesci—no others with that deep capacity for hate, and the passion for vengeance that's inbred in a Spaniard—in any southerner, for that matter. Naturally, being so intimately connected with the Quadrarian and with Eddie while he made this his headquarters, I'm deeply interested—and shocked too —and since I read of the murder, before we got the account of the inquest, I've been casting about in my mind for the ones who might have done it, I put Peter Vesci top of the list, with Mrs. Bellerby second, and the rest of the field nowhere. You may not think it worth while, but in your place I think I'd look up Peter and at least get an alibi out of him. That is, unless you've stronger reason to suspect anyone Eddie met after he retired, down in your part of the world."

"I shall think over it." Head rose to his feet as he spoke. "And I'm very grateful to you, Mr. Weeds, for all you've told me—and still more for your offer to tell me more. I'm afraid we've trespassed on your time almost beyond pardon."

"Not at all—not at all. I feel myself honoured in meeting such a famous member of your profession as yourself. Ask for me at any time, and regard me as happy to place myself at your disposal. Good night, sir—good night. Good night, Byrne. Don't forget that little matter I rang you about this afternoon."

"It's already in hand," Byrne said. "I hope to let you have some definite news about it to-morrow."

"Thanks so much. *Good* night, Mr. Head!"

CHAPTER X

THE QUEST FOR PETER

"TRIPLETS," BYRNE REMARKED thoughtfully, as he accompanied Head from the Quadrarian entrance in the direction of the Grand Palace hotel. "There's a definite significance in it."

"Gosh, how that man enjoys his own voice!" Head mused. "What definite significance do you see? I'd hate it to happen in my family."

"I dunno. You'd have to get a three-seater bassinette specially built—couldn't get one from stock. Then there'd be three christening robes, and three names to find, and I believe you're entitled to apply for Queen Anne's bounty or the Chiltern Hundreds or something. But on balance, you'd lose. Don't you begin to feel hungry?"

"A bit, but it's past midnight. I suppose at the hotel—"

"Not so, my bucolic buck!" Byrne interrupted solemnly. "You're not in the wilds of barbarism now—this is London, not Westingborough. I know a little place round the corner where you can get oysters and vintage stout by just whispering. Come along."

"Oysters? After that whisky we've had?" Head protested.

"It's evaporated," Byrne assured him. "There was a high alcoholic content in it. Besides, I always think better when I've got indigestion. Two dozen each, and a spot of mellow cheese, and we shan't know ourselves. The night is young, and so are we."

He led the way to his place round the corner, where, evidently, he was well known. Head brooded in silence till the oysters appeared, following two pint tankards of stout. Byrne took a draught from his tankard, and rubbed his hands with grave satisfaction.

"I should, if I were you," he observed, taking up his fork.

"You'd what?" Head demanded, gazing at him suspiciously.

"Follow up and find Peter Vesci," Byrne explained. "From what I know of your man Wadden, he'll take care of the more obvious lines."

"Obvious?" Head derided. "A marvellous rope-thrower, exactly the height and build we're looking for, used to pistol-shooting, delicately small hands and feet, and no mean acrobat—isn't all that so damned obvious that it can't possibly be true?"

"And a triplet," Byrne pointed out. "The man who invented the oyster was a benefactor to humanity, Jerry."

Head stacked four empty shells, and reached for more brown bread and butter. "What's the special significance of that?" he asked.

"The ante-natal association," Byrne explained. "Those three were together from the first hour of their existence, and they're bound to each other by far closer ties than two separate children —or three—of the one mother—children of different births, I mean. They are one in spirit far beyond ordinary relationship, and when that girl committed suicide, the other two lost a part of themselves. And any injury to one would wound all three, unforgettably. Then add the Spanish hunger for revenge—you see it in Peter's first attempt at killing Carter, the blazing recklessness of going for the man as he did—and you've got the picture. For this second attempt, he substituted careful planning for recklessness, and made a success of it."

"And in spite of the way he did it, I could almost wish he got away with it," Head observed. "Carter's treatment of Mrs. Bellerby, and what I know about him already—whoever bumped him off did humanity a service, since his blasted cruelties and selfishness are not punishable by law. No, don't worry. I know it's heresy, and I shall do my job."

"Then put a call out for Peter Vesci," Byrne advised.

"What? Send him to earth by telling him we're looking for him?"

"No, no, man! A confidential, not a placard. It's murder, so you can have the whole country covered by to-morrow night."

"If he's the one, I see it as a world-chase," Head reflected. "He wouldn't stay in this country to be caught."

"I wonder whether Jimmy Weeds has gone home yet?" Byrne queried. "You want that photograph and any others he may have, and particulars of height and build and colouring—you're going for him, I take it?"

"It's too promising a line to leave alone," Head assented.

"Then don't eat any of my oysters while I go and ring up for you. I'll see if we can still get at the pontifical Jimmy."

But he returned within about three minutes, shaking his head. "All closed down," he reported. "Night watchman reports nobody in the building, now. Never mind—you'll find Mr. James Weeds' private address in the telephone book. Make an appointment with him for as early in the morning as you can get him to his office, and get all you want out of him. You won't have any trouble—he owes me quite a lot of good turns. Then go ahead, and the famous Westingborough police inspector goes up one more notch, thanks to his faithful cousin Terry. What about another dozen each, Jerry? I've still got a crevice or two left."

"It couldn't be done," Head dissented, gazing at his two plates of empty shells, and reaching for his tankard.

"Right. Then a slab of soft and soapy cheddar, and another half-tankard of the same to drown it. I am being a dog!"

"Yes, and if you're not careful you'll bark in your sleep," Head retorted. "That is, if you get to sleep at all."

"It was worth it," Byrne said solemnly.

* * * * *

Fresh and alert as usual, and apparently suffering no ill effects from his oyster supper following on Jimmy Weeds' hospitality, Head put through a telephone call to Wadden's private address at seven o'clock the next morning, and got the superintendent himself.

"You, is it?" Wadden apostrophised him. "Well, let me tell you I've put the geyser running for my bath and my wife hasn't left off raising hell about last quarter's gas bill, yet. Whaddye want?"

"Any fresh developments down there?" Head inquired.

"Not a smell. Bowman found out about Mrs. Platts' three ducks—it was Penley, the Westingborough Parva poacher, lifted 'em out of the pen. Footmarks, same as in this case of yours, and indubitable feathers to clinch it. What have you at your end of the table?"

"How about the notice to cyclists and nurses?" Head inquired.

"No reply. You didn't expect one, did you?"

"I don't, now—now I know the cyclist and the old boots are one and the same. That is, I feel sure of it. Chief, I've got a line at this end just as I thought I should, one I feel ought to be followed up. Will you take care of things down there till to-night or to-morrow morning—or longer, if this doesn't prove a blind lead?"

"Carry on, man. I'm keeping a hard eye on Denham, and everything else too. Anything else? That geyser's still running."

"You'll get a confidential through as soon as I can get the details and put it in shape, and then you'll see what I'm on. It won't go over the wire now, and wouldn't make any difference if it did. When you get it, don't take it as conclusive, only as a very strong line."

"Right. Carry on, man, and I'll see that nothing gets missed here. Now can I get away and turn that geyser off ahead of my wife?"

"You can, chief. You know where to get me if you want me—"

The click of the receiver at the other end terminated this piece of information. Head also hung up, and, consulting the directory, ascertained and then rang Mr. James Weeds' private address. A woman's voice, with a definitely tart intonation, informed him that Mr. Weeds was not up yet, nor likely to be for some time.

"I want you to waken him and tell him Mr. Head wants to speak to him," Head said, as authoritatively as he could. "It may he unusual, but he will realise at once that the urgency of the matter justifies me in asking such a thing. Mr. Head, who saw him at his office last night."

"But—but it's impossible!" the voice protested incredulously.

"Oh, no, it's not," he assured her. "I am a police inspector. I'll hold the line while you go and tell him, please."

"Well . . ." The solitary syllable implied that the speaker regarded it as a desperate venture. "If it's police—I'll see, if you hold on. But I don't think he . . . Hold on, please!"

He held on for a long time. Eventually, with some preliminary clicking, and a few distant, booming curses spoken away from the receiver, Weeds' voice came through, very coldly indeed.

"Mr. Head, I understand. What is it, Mr. Head?"

"In consequence of the story you told me last night, Mr. Weeds," Head said crisply, "I want to ask your further assistance. Could you let me have that photograph you showed me—lend it me long enough to get a reproduction made, I mean—and any other photographs you have of Peter and Quita Vesci? I want them to accompany an inquiry memorandum. And I must apologise for troubling you at such an hour, but it's urgently necessary to lose no time."

"Strike while the iron is hot, eh?" Weeds boomed back, far more cordially. "Well, Mr. Head, the fact that you are acting on my advice compensates for any inconvenience I might feel over being called from my soporific bliss. At what hour would you require the photographs?"

"Would nine o'clock be too early?" Head felt that he dared not suggest an earlier hour for an appointment.

"Expect me to alight outside the Quadrarian at nine, Mr. Head," Weeds assented. "I fear you will have to await my arrival on the pavement, for the door will not be unlocked at so fell and uncanny an hour, but I will keep tryst with you. Await me at the portal, Mr. Head."

But when, fifteen minutes later than the appointed time, he appeared and led Head up to his office, he could produce only the photograph of the trio and prints showing them singly in costume—he had no portraits of any of them in ordinary attire, nor could he tell Head where such might be available. He made no demur about lending all that he had of Peter and Quita, and Head took them all, for, obviously, any "confidential" that he might send out must contain descriptions of both Peter and his surviving sister, since in all probability they were still together. And Weeds was able to give the particulars of height and colouring that Head required: the photographs gave the rest.

But, facially, Head knew, they told little. The pair were rendered as alike as possible by stage make-up, though according to Weeds the resemblance was little more than that ordinarily existing between brother and sister, when they were seen as normal people. Peter was far more manly than these photographs made him, while Quita was a very charming and attractive girl, as feminine as she could be, and with no trace of the boyishness she assumed for her stage turn. And though, at Weeds' invitation, the inspector rang up nearly a dozen theatrical and other photographers before leaving the office, he could learn of no existing photographs that would show either brother or sister as they appeared in real life—nor could he find any of the dead girl, Anita.

"There will doubtless be snapshots, taken by their friends," Weeds suggested. "But they, usually, are not very lifelike."

"Who were their friends?" Head inquired.

"There, my dear sir, I am at a loss. One would think that such vivid and attractive personalities as these three would undoubtedly have made friends, but their social circle, if it existed, is beyond the bounds of my horizon. We are, in our profession, a world apart from the throng beyond the footlights, and into this world of ours the Vesci trio entered only in the hours in which they won the plaudits of our patrons. To me their private life is a sealed book."

Head went away with the photographs and particulars he had ascertained concerning the two survivors of the trio. Byrne collaborated with him in the composition of his "confidential," snatching half an hour from his own work, and making more than one useful suggestion.

"And now what?" Byrne inquired, when they had done all they could.

"Twickenham," Head answered. "Obviously. Tradespeople, possible acquaintances, possibly even a local photographer with natural portraits of them. And possibly information as to where they went, whether it were Algiers, Monte Carlo, or Wigan. Weeds told us they'd saved a bit and had the insurance money on the dead girl as well, so they could afford any one of the three. Gosh, I forgot to ask him where they were insured! Through that, I might get their bankers."

He rang Weeds again. In reply to the query, the golden-toned stage manager intoned the information that the Globular and Universal Insurance Company had paid ten thousand pounds in respect of Anita's death, and at the same time had terminated the other two policies at the request of their holders, and made a cash payment in respect of premiums received. Next, Head rang the Globular and Universal, who told him they were quite unable to say where the Vescis had had banking accounts. They offered specimen signatures, if he wanted them, but he already had these from Jimmy Weeds, and so declined the offer.

He felt, as a suburban electric train took him toward Twickenham, that the Grange tragedy was settling down to a very ordinary, unexciting piece of work, a steady, plodding quest for Peter Vesci, and possibly for others after him, since he might not be the author of the crime when found. There was a probability that he had committed it, but Head did not intend to devote himself exclusively to the determination of that probability. He was putting a day into the quest for Peter, but he had other possibilities in mind as well. It was comforting to reflect that just as keen a mind as his own was at work in Westingborough: Wadden would let nothing escape him there, and Head knew that on his own return he would find no difficulties caused through neglect or lack of perception and of consequent action.

He found The Mallows easily enough, a rather small, two-storied house set with its back toward the river, and before it a board announcing that it was for sale or to let on lease. The sodden garden was overgrown and neglected, and what had been a pleasant lawn was now a tract of rank, yellowish grass; the house itself looked dingy and unkempt, with blistering paint on window-frames and doors, and more than one broken pane of glass. It was depressing as long unoccupied habitations usually are. Head took the agents' address from the board, and went to them.

There, a suave young man with a beautiful permanent wave and a wart on his chin had little information to give about the Vescis. They had taken The Mallows on a yearly tenancy, and had paid their rent in advance and promptly; when the surviving sister and brother left the neighbourhood, they had given no information as to where they were going, and had left no address. The young man himself had gone to take over the keys, the day they left, and had received them from Quita Vesci, who had subsequently carried her brother out to a big Daimler, probably a hired car, in her arms. The brother had had some injury to his spine, or something of the sort, the young man believed. As far as he knew, they had made no friends in the neighbourhood. The house had not been let again since they left; possibly the fact of a suicide having occurred there put some inquirers off, and then, of course, those riverside houses were only attractive in summer. He concurred in both these final suggestions as Head made them, though rather unwillingly. In fact, he remarked that it was not his business to crab property that they had on their books, and he hoped the suggestions would go no farther. Head comforted him on the point, and took his leave.

The post office had had no address for forwarding correspondence. Head looked in on a druggist, two grocers, an off-licence, a butcher, baker, and dairy, and found and called on four photographers, all to little or no purpose. Nita and Quita, apparently, had shared the business of housekeeping between them, for one was as well-known as the other—which was very little—at the establishments they patronised. They had always paid cash, either at the time of ordering goods or on delivery, and Head could not find that either of them had ever given a cheque to anyone. In no place could he find that they had had any local friends: they appeared to have been a self-contained trio. About three months before Miss Nita drowned herself a man had begun coming to the house in a big car on Sundays and taking her out—but Head knew already the identity of that man, and did not pursue the subject.

Then he found Miss Craylaw, angular, simpering, and voluble, who kept a greengrocer's shop, and, it being a slack time of day for her business, hailed him as an Event and unburdened herself of her tale.

"Where they've gone, sir? Well, I don't know no more than Adam, as the sayin' goes—tee-hee! I went to the funeral of the one they called Nita, because I'd supplied so many of the wreaths—had 'em made to order by the firm I deal with, of course, and the flowers was simply lovely. Sim—ply lovely! Over a man, it was, poor girl, and they said she wasn't in her right mind when she done it, of course. But we girls never are in our right minds when it's a man, are we?—tee-hee! Then the poor lad Peter had that accident—it seemed as if there was a fate against the three of 'em. I always say astrology's got a lot to do with it. They were under the wrong planets just then, and if they'd paid attention to astrology they might of escaped. Perhaps, that is. There's some things you can't escape. Like love, for instance—tee-hee! Or chilblains. I get chillblains every winter."

"But you mean they ought to have consulted the sacred flat and round sticks," Head suggested gravely, with a view to encouraging the spate of monologue, and also with a memory of Ernest Bramah's *Kai Lung*.

"I don't know about sticks, but there's a woman I know'll give you a wonderful reading for eighteen-pence, and a chart from birth for half a crown. She's wonderfully correct, too. My niece went to her when she was—well, you know—tee-hee! and she told her the stars were favourable to her in two aspects. And my sister had twins! Would you believe it, now? Twins, and such a bonny pair they are!"

"The Vescis were triplets, I believe," he suggested, to bring her back to the subject of his inquiry. "Would you say they were well liked by people round here?"

"Well, I really don't know if they knew anyone—I never heard of anyone being invited there or their going out among Twickenham society. And I hear most things, I assure you, sir! I never heard that they were *not* liked—I can say that much. But then, not only were they foreigners, as you could tell by the name, but theatricals as well. Not that you'd guess it when they spoke to you, because they talked just like properly educated people, and spoke as good English as I do. And I went to the high school till I was sixteen, and I've still got a whole writing-desk full of certificates, and beautiful prizes, too."

"Theatrical, and foreign." He brought her back to the Vescis again. "And how did you get on with them in a business way? I gather they dealt with you. Did you find them nice people?"

"Very nice people. Mr. Peter used to come in for fruit sometimes, and you'd take him for a gentleman if you didn't know he was a mere theatrical. Always polite and affable—' 'Morning, Miss Craylaw,' and 'I couldn't think of troubling you to send them, Miss

Craylaw,' as if he really knew how to talk to a lady. Juggled with ropes on the stage, I heard, though I never went to see them act. And the girls were quite sweet, and perfect ladies as far as manners went—you'd never think it of theatricals, but they were. Not a bit loud and rowdy, but beautifully dressed, and quiet-speaking. I used to like Quita best. She was so—so sincere, if you know what I mean. And she always paid for what they had—if Nita came to order anything, she used to say Quita would pay when she came in next. And she did, on the nail."

"Have you any idea what became of the other two after the sister died?" Head inquired. "After they left The Mallows, I mean?"

"Quita came in—I think it was sprouts, but I'm not sure. It may have been cauliflower. But it was about two days before they went, and she said she wouldn't see me again and thanked me for the good quality and service she'd always had here. She told me then she was taking her brother to bally-something or other in the Mediterranean, to get him out of this climate, in the hope he'd get well there. I looked all over the map, and wondered if she meant the Beleeric Islands, but she didn't pronounce it a bit like that. I couldn't see any other bally on the map that was in the least like what she said. But then foreigners are funny about some words, aren't they? —tee-hee!"

"Did she say the Balearics?" Head inquired, giving the word its more usual and more nearly correct pronunciation.

"That was it! Yes! Tee-hee! And to think it must have been staring me in the face all the time when I was looking at the map, and me not to see it! All I could see was the Beleeric Islands."

"Well, thank you for telling me so much, Miss Craylaw. I suppose you don't know if any photographer round here has a portrait of the Vescis—or of any one of the family?"

"No, I don't, sir. What might you be wanting one for?"

"Oh, it's not that I want it. A young friend of mine—sentimental memories, and all that sort of thing. I told him I'd make a few inquiries, to find out if he could either trace them or get a portrait, since I happened to be coming into this locality."

"Ah! 'In the spring a young man's fancy'—even though it is only January—tee-hee! I'm afraid I can't tell you, sir. You might try the one on the corner, going toward the station."

"Yes, they might have one there, of course. Very many thanks, Miss Craylaw. I'll go along that way now."

He went that way, but because it was the way to the station. He had already drawn blank at that photographer's. The Balearics—it was a specific destination, unlike Weeds' "Algiers or somewhere," and it was sufficiently distinctive for him to feel sure that Quita had said it, though possibly with intent to mislead. The Balearics were Spanish possessions, with Barcelona and Valencia as their normal points of communication with the mainland. A cable to the consulate at Barcelona, evidently, would reveal whether the Vescis had gone there, and whether they had remained there or gone farther.

He felt that he had to work to the end of this Vesci line, now. Quita's threat to Carter before she carried her unconscious brother down the staircase recurred to his mind. "This is reprieve, not escape for you."

"Whether they did it or no, they meant it," Head told himself.

CHAPTER XI

RESULTS OF A STRUCTURAL DEFECT

SOME FIVE MINUTES after eleven o'clock of the morning following the inquest at Westingborough Grange—and while Inspector Head was on his meditative way to Twickenham—Hugh Denham's clerk entered to his room from the little outer office and informed his employer that Miss Ethel Perry had called and wished for an interview. Denham frowned at the information: up to the night of Carter's party, he had had a distant, nodding acquaintance with the two sisters; Ethel had made eyes at him before Carter annexed her and took her away from the rest of his guests. If she hoped to improve the acquaintance with that ill-fated party as a groundwork, he reflected, she was badly mistaken.

"What does she want, Joslin?" he demanded.

"Just said she wanted to see you, sir, if you could spare the time. I didn't ask her what it was about."

"You should. Never mind, show her in."

Ethel entered, and Joslin closed the door on her. In her way—her pale, almost ethereal way—she was attractive, Denham decided morosely, but nobody would give her a second glance if Marguerite were in sight! And in five hours he would see Marguerite again.

"Won't you sit down, Miss Perry? What can I do for you?"

"I—my sister asked me to call, Mr. Denham," she answered nervously, and took the chair he indicated. "About the house—our house, it is. Lilian has lessons to give all the morning, you see, and she thought—we thought—well, I suggested consulting you."

"That's very kind of you," he commented, rather ironically. "About your house—yes? Alterations, enlarging it—what?"

"Oh, no! Nothing of that sort. But—father bought it not long after the war, you know, and it's been a constant trouble and expense to us, ever since we moved in. He bought it from Pollen, you know."

"Yes, I do happen to know it was one of Pollen's houses," Denham assented. "He put up six or seven there, I believe."

103

The worthy builder, he knew, had bought the tract of then un-developed building land at the London Road end of Treherne Road, which at that time had been almost open country, and had jerried his erections to completion almost at the beginning of the building craze that set in at the end of the war. His son Fred was now helping to dissipate the profits of this and similar enterprises.

"Yes, just after the war," she agreed. "We're always having to get repairs done—it was the roof, last time, a lot of new woodwork wanted to replace unsafe beams. But this seems so much more serious that Lilian and I agreed we ought to get really expert advice, so I suggested coming to you. I thought—we know we can rely on you—"

She paused, and gave him a slight smile which indicated that she would like to rely on him for more than architectural advice. He inclined his head in acknowledgment, but did not return the smile.

"Suppose you tell me what the trouble is?" he suggested.

"It's a crack," she explained. "You know, we keep the one big room—on the right as you go in—we keep it for my sister's pupils, and I'm afraid I have to confess that it's rather more cold and damp than it would be if we lived in it. And in the last few days we've noticed a crack in the wall—the outside wall, quite near the actual corner of the house. Lilian and I went and looked at it outside this morning, and near the ground it shows in the brickwork, nearly half an inch wide. I believe, too—I'm not sure, but it looks to me as if the whole wall had sunk. If you look up at the ceiling inside the room, it seems that that corner is a little lower than the rest, and the plaster shows cracks, too. It frightened us, when we examined it this morning. I think something ought to be done at once, and it seemed too serious for us to go to an ordinary builder and trust to him."

In other words, Denham thought, it formed a good excuse for her to come and see him. He was far from conceited, but Ethel's manner was not that of one engaged solely in conducting a business interview.

"What do you want me to do?" he asked bluntly.

"Simply to advise us," she answered. "If you could come and see it for yourself—as soon as possible, of course—and then tell us what we ought to do and how much it is likely to cost."

He rose from the chair in which he had seated himself, went to a large chest of drawers, and took from it a series of sheets which recorded a geological survey of the area in which Westingborough was situated. Choosing out one of the sheets, he studied it for awhile.

"Yes," he said eventually, "you come just on the edge of the clay belt lying up from London Road—my house is quite off it. In addition to that, Pollen didn't build my house. To put it frankly, Miss Perry, he didn't build the six or seven that include yours. He scratched the ground instead of putting down sound foundations, and then threw those houses together, scandalously and immorally threw them together, instead of building them. I'm open to tell him or anyone that, and let him take what action he likes. He set those houses on the clay, instead of bedding his foundations soundly under it, and the corner of your house has begun to sink. It was inevitable that it should, sooner or later. I'd like to expose Pollen and a few of his kind."

"But—but something can be done, surely?" she asked in a frightened way. "We—you don't mean the house will fall down on us?"

"It can be underpinned," he told her. "Put it in the hands of a decent builder—Allen, or Marwood, for instance—"

"Mr. Denham," she interrupted, "since I've come to consult you about it, will you come and see what ought to be done, and arrange it all?"

"I can," he assented rather dubiously, "but it will probably cost you more than if you went straight to a good builder. You'll have my fee on top of his, and I should insist on the best workmanship?"

"But that's what we want," she interrupted again. "It may cost a little more, but—but I know we can rely on you. Even the best of them might think they'd leave something to make more work. We've had builders about the place almost continually since we've been there, and a serious defect like this ought to be put quite right, even if it does cost more—we ought to be quite certain it is right. So if you could come and examine it, and then put the work in hand for us—" She paused, gazing at him pleadingly.

"I could come and make an examination, and draw up a report on which a builder would submit an estimate to you," he said.

"Whatever way you like, so long as we feel you are in charge of the work, and will make sure it is properly done," she agreed.

"Very well, then." He put his plan back on the top of the others, and returned to face her. "When shall I make my examination?"

"How soon could you do it?" she asked in reply.

He paused a moment to reflect. If he looked in to examine the subsidence at three o'clock that afternoon, he could then go on home, and arrive there before four o'clock—soon enough to be on hand when Marguerite arrived to visit Adela. Well in time to greet her, in fact.

"Shall we say three o'clock this afternoon?" he suggested.

"That will do nicely," she agreed. "Lilian will probably be out, but I shall be there to show you, and I can tell her all you tell me."

"Then we'll make it three, or possibly a few minutes after," he promised. "Expect me then, and we can get the work put in hand in a few days. From what you tell me, delay would not be wise."

"Thank you ever so much, Mr. Denham." She rose and offered her hand. "And—quite another thing"—her nervousness returned—"we are so sorry about yesterday afternoon, if you don't mind my saying it. The—the unfairness to you at the inquest, I mean. We both saw you go into your house, and I could have told them that you couldn't possibly have seen anyone, any more than we could. Both Lilian and I felt quite distressed about it—the way you were questioned, I mean."

"That's very kind of you, Miss Perry," he answered stiffly. "Expect me at three o'clock this afternoon, and I'll do my best for you."

It was very nearly, but not quite, a snub. He saw her through Joslin's room to the outer door of the office, and returned to his own room, where he took up a blotting-pad, flung it savagely on the floor, and jumped on it, so that the tenant of the floor below looked up at his ceiling apprehensively, and saw his lamp-shade quiver.

"Oh, damn and blast all Westingborough!" Denham ejaculated.

* * * * *

"Yess. Oh, yess-s!" Wadden said that evening, after Head had walked in on him, sat down, and delivered a full report of his adventures since leaving for London the night before. "And you cabled the Barcelona consulate before you left, eh? Got a copy of the cable?"

"Here." Head produced it and handed it over.

"Just so! Confirming letter and photographs follow, you say. Got the photographs with you, or have they gone yet?"

"I didn't take a secretary with me," Head responded rather caustically, "and you'll own I haven't been lazy. Here are the photographs. I'll get the letter off to-night, with a copy of the confidential for particulars of the pair. They're only stage photos, unfortunately. I couldn't find any trace of a natural one."

"And yet his face seems to remind me—I can't place it, though," Wadden mused as he studied the portrait of Peter. "P'raps it's because I took the missus to see their turn at the Quadrarian, while we were on a bust in town. A hair-raiser that turn was, too. He could lipstick a gnat's mouth with that rope of his; and the girls—the one that sang, especially! But you've got enough of that. Head, my lad, a copy of this cable to the consulate at Valencia, and duplicate letter and photographs to follow there, too. I went a cruise round that coast once—didn't take the missus with me, and believe me Valencia can give Paris points, over some things. But what I wanted to say was that there's a regular service from Valencia to the Balearics, as well as from Barcelona. Let us miss no chances. Get Wells to go round to the post office at once and get the cable away, and then come back here. Developments at this end, quite apart from this Vesci line of yours."

Head complied with the order, and presently returned. "He'll just do it," he reported. "Post office closes at eight."

"Oven door opens at seven-thirty, or a bit earlier," Wadden replied plaintively, "but I knew you'd come off that train, and Mrs. Wadden's going to comb my hair when I do get home. It's mutton, I happen to know, and mutton's the very devil half cold. Never mind, this is more important. The time factor, Head—we've been damned careless."

"We've been damned busy," Head retorted. "Do you realise, chief, that Carter hasn't been dead forty-eight hours yet—only forty hours, as a matter of fact—and we've done quite a good deal in that time?"

"Oh, yeah? Go on patting yourself on the back. We ain't done it thoroughly, as far as time is concerned, let me tell you. At least, we hadn't till I butted in to-day and checked up on the given times."

"I don't get that. What given times are these? The clock with the bullet through its works gave us time clearly enough, and—"

"Not that at all, man! The given time or times for the end of the party—when those eight left the Grange. I say times, because they're variously inexact—and all wrong, too."

"All right, chief. If the mutton can wait, I'll listen."

"Not all right. All wrong, I said. Instead of going to sleep when I got to bed last night, I began thinking. Now take what we got at the inquest with regard to the time they left—we know they all left together. Quade first. He thought it was about three o'clock, but didn't note the time definitely. Naturally, he was too full up with either whisky or champagne, or both. Mrs. Quade wasn't called.

Denham said it was a little before three, and he couldn't say how much, but he estimated it as between ten minutes to three and three. Pollen had no idea, but reckoned it somewhere about three from what the others said—and he couldn't say which others said it. More fuddled than Quade, obviously. Betty Hurder wasn't called. Lilian Perry wasn't called. Mortimer agreed with Denham that it was just on three o'clock, as nearly as he could say, but he had two ladies on his hands—we put a circumflex accent over 'ladies', I think—and he didn't observe the time. Ethel Perry had no idea, but heard Mrs. Quade say it was just on three o'clock, and Quade had to be up at seven, so they really ought to be going. Out of all that we assume they all set off at three, don't we?"

"We did. And since they all checked each other about going home—"

"Wait, man—wait! This nurse's uniform, and Denham stuffing something up his sleeve and then putting an elastic band round the cuff to prevent us from getting that something down, make the time of leaving enormously important, especially after what happened to-day. But it struck me we ought to get it more accurately, before that happening began to affect my view—I'll tell you about it later. I know the Vesci line is promising, but so is this, let me tell you."

"I wish you would tell me," Head observed, looking at his watch.

"You don't tell a story in one paragraph yourself," Wadden reminded him. "Never mind. I cast about in my inner consciousness, and hit on Mrs. Quade. We know she was keeping her wits about her and keeping an eye on Quade, who had to get up early in the morning, and was tolerably tight. I took the car and went to see Mrs. Quade, about eleven this morning—and as I told you over the 'phone, I was keeping a hard eye on Denham. He went to his office at ten, as usual."

"This morning," Head remarked encouragingly.

"It wouldn't be usual if he went at ten at night, would it?" Wadden inquired acidly. "But to get to Mrs. Quade—I got her on her own, because Quade was out with a string of his last hopes for the bookies. She was scared, as they all are, but I told her what I wanted—and got it! And we've been led up the garden, Head—led up the garden!"

"It's proving a hell of a long way back to the conservatory," Head pointed out unsympathetically. "You'll have frozen mutton for dinner."

"Blast the mutton! Mrs. Quade stuck to Denham most of the evening. He wasn't tight, he's perfectly respectable, and also he's a cut above the Quades, as you know. Runs in a different pack. So she felt more peaceful with him than anyone else. Now you remember that grandfather clock standing in the corner of the Grange dining-room?"

"Yes, quite well. It was fast—but they had their watches."

"Oh, yeah? I've told you what state most of 'em were in when it came to gazing at watch-hands—the ones who hadn't an interest in altering the time, that is. Well, Mrs. Quade says to Denham that it's time they were going, since Quade would stop for ever if he was let and the whisky held out, or words to that effect, but she had to get him up by seven in the morning. Says Denham, I'll soon fix that for you, and he gets hold of Quade and points at the grandfather clock, tells him it'll be three before they get away if they start saying good-bye at once, and Mrs. Quade wants to go home. Quade sees reason—being in the state he was, he saw double reason—and tells Mortimer it's three o'clock, and his wife wants to go. Mortimer collects Pollen, Denham gets his coat and goes out to start annoying the night with his cracked exhaust—to warm the engine. He'd already said good night to Carter, having nobody to take with him. By the time he's dug the snow out of the inside of his old iron, the rest are ready to go. Now get this. When Mrs. Quade said good night to Carter in the dining-room, that clock hadn't struck three. And it was Denham who hustled the lot of them—she remembers it, because she was grateful to him for getting Quade out and away with such a rush, and told him so when she bade him good night. She told me all this, this morning."

"I'm still listening," Head said interestedly.

"Y'see, we were so proud of ourselves getting the time of the murder exactly checked for us by the shot clock in the hall, that we didn't check up on the grandfather clock—didn't realise the importance of being quite sure of the time these people left. Now when I came back from seeing Mrs. Quade, I got a report that Ethel Perry had gone to see Denham at his office, and stayed there a good half-hour—that was while I was away at the Quades. Oho! says I to myself. And we let her down very gently at the inquest, too, although she's got a nurse's uniform. We thought it was impossible for her to get into that uniform, and the brogue shoes or riding-boots—but was it? Let's see. It was you who said she couldn't do it, I believe."

"She was in evening dress at the party," Head pointed out, but rather doubtfully, as if impressed by his chief's reasoning.

"And still in it for some while after, if there's anything in what I'm trying to tell you," Wadden retorted with some asperity. "I had Mrs. Quade's version of the time they left, and when I got that report on the fair Ethel as well, I rang through to the Grange and commanded Arabella to my presence. Head housemaid, local woman, and reliable, as far as anyone is in this business. Questioned her about the grandfather clock. Head, it was sixteen minutes fast by the one that got shot, and Arabella had checked that by the wireless signal and found it correct. Now do you see why I'm trying to give you cold shivers?"

"The whole party left, practically, by two-forty-five," Head said.

"Thereabouts. And they didn't gather daisies by the wayside, either. You ascertained that they were doing about twenty miles an hour along the lane, and that's going some with snow on the ground. Quade wanted to get home and to bed, and the others kept close to him. Denham hung on his tail till it was time to turn off into London Road, and it's not more than two minutes from that corner to Denham's own door, the pace he was making. Mortimer wouldn't lag, either—he landed the Perry girls at their home almost as soon as Denham got to his. Give them seven minutes altogether, say they did twenty miles an hour average over the whole course, and you get a distance of over two miles—which it isn't, from the front door of the Grange to Denham's, coming by Market Street. Denham and the Perry girls were home by seven minutes to three. You agree with me on that, now?"

"Yes, it might have been as early as that," Head conceded.

"Damn it, man, it *was* as early as that! Now Mortimer, as we know, was persuading himself he wasn't as old as he thought he was, and getting Lilian Perry to help him. While he was telling her she was the only girl he'd ever loved, outside the Perrys' house, what was to prevent Ethel from slipping into the house, taking off her evening shoes—not making any other change in her dress, mind—but just taking oft the shoes and slipping on a pair of riding-boots? Then she could hang her nurse's cloak on the handlebars of her bike, with the bonnet concealed in the folds of the cloak. Lilian would finish saying good night to Mortimer, he'd drive away, and she'd come into the house. Probably she'd go straight upstairs, and Ethel would say she'd be up in a minute or two, but wanted a breath of fresh air or something first. As soon as Lilian was out of sight, she'd run the bicycle out, put on the bonnet and cloak, and do the round we know some bicycle did—and we know it came back into Treherne Road, too, from Borrow's report."

"He said, about five minutes past three," Head pointed out. "I don't think it could be done in the time, chief."

"I've had him up again, and he owns it might have been as late as ten minutes past," Wadden replied. "He calculated by the time that had elapsed since Parham's garage clock told him it was three o'clock—and we thought the party were just leaving the Grange then, instead of a quarter of an hour earlier. And Parham tells me his clock is two minutes slow, too, but he's putting it right, now. Head, it could be done. Ethel Perry could have been the nurse that Borrow saw coming back into Treherne Road. Mind, she rode all the way, didn't walk along the path, that first trip. That walk was after four o'clock, after the murder."

"It looks possible, the way you put it," Head said in a way that indicated his doubts of the theory. "And on this assumption, Ethel Perry killed Carter, if my view that the cyclist wore the old boots over her own is correct. When she walked up to the Grange, I mean."

"Why not? She got back home and put the bicycle away by a quarter past three at the latest. Then she had twenty minutes to get into riding-kit and reach the point where Borrow saw that apparent young man in Market Street—he gives the time of that as three thirty-five. She could do that easily. Lilian, champagne-fed and tired, would be asleep while all this was going on. We know Ethel's got nurse's uniform, and I've seen her out riding astride, though not lately. But she's got riding-breeches and boots, undoubtedly. And at school she was a star hockey player, and probably a good gymnast, too."

"And you think she'd shoot Carter like that?" Head asked dubiously.

"Who is as callous as a nurse?" Wadden asked in reply. "They have to be, to keep on at their jobs. They have to live with pain every day, see men and women carved and chopped in operating-theatres, and keep their nerve through it. They see things ten times worse than putting a pistol-muzzle on a man's eye and pulling the trigger."

"Still it doesn't seem feasible, to me," Head objected.

"Well, now take Denham's side. He caught sight of her, possibly as she came back on the bike, after he'd put his car away and come out of the garage. Our egg-brained coroner consented to shake out of him anything he saw up to when he put the car away, but didn't carry it beyond that point, though you passed him a note on it. I'll own he'd almost accused Denham of complicity in the murder, by then, and possibly felt he couldn't do any good by stretching the rack another notch. But this morning, thinking Denham might have seen her, Ethel went to his office to make certain. Quite possibly she didn't say anything directly, but put up a pretext of some sort for going there, and then either commiserated him on what he'd had to go through or mentioned the murder in some way, just to find out whether he'd tell her she's laid herself open to suspicion by being out with the bike, and saying nothing about it in answer to our notice to cyclists and nurses. I don't know what they said to each other, of course. But I do know this, Head. He called at the Perrys' place on his way home this afternoon, and had the best part of half an hour's talk with Ethel—Lilian was out at the time. Then he went on to his own home, and didn't come out from Treherne Road again before seven o'clock, when I got my last report on him. Y'see. Her half-hour at the office this morning wasn't enough, but *he* had to have another half-hour with her this afternoon. Why? Have you got a better theory than mine to account for all this?"

"Why did she kill Carter, then?" Head demanded thoughtfully.

"Search me. But when Phyllis Taylor caught them together in the drawing-room at the Grange, Ethel might have told him her good name was a thing of the past once that girl began talking, unless he married her, being a single man who might try marriage as a new form of amusement. Then he might have answered her something after the fashion he tried on that Mrs. Bellerby you told me about, being that sort of man. Then, of course, she'd hate him like hell, which hath no fury—the rest is in Shakespeare, I believe. And in that sort of fury, a woman will kill, sometimes. Especially if she hasn't had too long a time for cooling down."

"And the preceding telephone call that Phyllis overheard?" Head asked. "How do you fit that in?"

"Carter had been angling for Ethel for weeks, as you know," Wadden answered. "I haven't tried to fit it in yet, but I don't doubt I could with a few minutes to think over it."

"And she planned all that business of the rope and tree and old boots, and got the gun and everything else, all in the one evening?" Head queried again. "Chief, it doesn't appeal to me."

"One thing that ought to appeal to you is the possibility of separating the identities of the cyclist and the murderer," Wadden retorted. "You've got them definitely and finally in your head as one and the same, but we've no proof that they are one person, man or woman. Even your interpretation of the footprints and bicycle-track doesn't justify you in making that a final and unalterable conclusion."

"The only conclusion I've got of that sort is that somebody murdered Edward Carter, and I've got to find that somebody," Head said. "It's an interesting theory you've put up, and certainly Denham knows something. And your mutton's grown whiskers, by now."

"Therefore," Wadden answered, rising from his chair, "let us hie to the Duke of York and speak peaceably to Little Nell. I want a bracer of some sort before I go home and face my wife."

CHAPTER XII

AN ITALIAN ANTIQUE

"YES." ADELA DENHAM made it as much a sigh of resignation as an indication of assent. Marguerite had said that it was time for her to go. "I suppose it's as well that you should go, really."

Hugh, standing over the tea-table, and so facing Marguerite as she leaned back in the corner of the settee in Adela's drawing-room, stared hard at his sister. She returned his gaze steadily.

"You're a pretty sort of hostess," he observed scathingly.

"What would you?" Adela retorted calmly. "Marguerite, I'd planned it all so nicely, and here I was, ready to settle down with you, just our two selves, and discuss everything from the Carson girls' performance last night to undies, and before you even appear in walks this long brother of mine! And you two—well, I suppose he felt that he'd had to put up with Bob and me for the last three weeks, so he'd give me a taste of what he's been through. I forgive you, children. After all, you only began your ante-nuptial ecstasies yesterday evening. Hugh, is that intended for a soulful gaze at her, or have you got indigestion? I thought you were inclined to bolt your lunch to-day."

"For two pins, Adela, I'd put you across my knee and spank you," Denham said, with a trace of real annoyance.

"Please don't," she requested calmly. "Your knees are so horribly bony—not a bit like Bob's. His are nice and cushiony, and he's got smaller feet, too. There won't be such acres of hole when I have his socks to darn, instead of yours. You'll despair, Marguerite—"

"Do you think I'd let her darn my socks?" Denham interrupted.

"Of course you will! It's in the marriage service—part of the cherishing," Adela pointed out, while Marguerite laughed amusedly. "No, I've got it wrong, though—it's the man who has to do the cherishing. I wonder, how does one cherish, exactly? I must consult Bob. I suppose I shall have to be cherished, whether I like it or no."

"You're a perfect idiot, to-day," Denham told her.

114

"Bob always tells me I'm perfect, but he doesn't finish it as you do. Well, Marguerite,"—she stood up, for the other girl had risen to go—"I shall get you to myself some day, when we're both followers of sober and godly matrons, as the marriage service says. Judging by to-day, there won't be much chance before."

"I'm so sorry, dear," Marguerite said. "It was my fault. I told him last night I should come to see you this afternoon."

"Aiding and abetting—yes. Being an angel, I forgive you both," Adela promised. "Marguerite, darling, I know you're both going to be perfectly soppy and unspeakable as soon as you get alone together, but I do believe it's the very best thing that could have happened to him. Now just one word of sisterly advice before you go. Don't let him adopt a he-man attitude toward you. Do as I did with Bob, and begin it now. Get him down and hold him down—keep him meek."

"I won't promise," Marguerite said, with a glance at Denham that showed how little the adjuration meant to her. "One other thing, Adela. Have you told anyone yet—about Hugh and me, I mean?"

Adela shook her head. "Not a soul," she answered. "I've had no chance, and of course I shouldn't tell anyone until you wished it. Besides, you're not officially engaged, yet, to my knowledge."

"I wish—please don't tell anyone, yet," Marguerite asked.

"No? Not even Bob? Surely I can tell him? He's quite discreet."

"If you're sure he won't tell anyone else," Marguerite conceded.

"But—Marguerite—" Denham began, and paused.

"It makes it more thrilling and mysterious," Adela remarked with a touch of satiric amusement, "as the curate told his wife when—"

"Adela!" There was peremptory reproof in Denham's interruption.

She looked at him with frowning surprise. "And he used to like that story!" she told Marguerite. "Never mind, I'll tell you the rest of it when we're by our two selves. And you're both dying to get away, I can see. Perfectly natural—dinner at the usual time, Hugh?"

"I don't know," he said, with marked displeasure in his tone. "I may go back to the office after I've seen Marguerite home."

He moved toward the door. Marguerite kissed Adela good-bye and followed him. The pair crossed the road and went along Panlyon Avenue, silent for awhile. Denham opened Marguerite's gate and followed her toward the door, waited while she opened it.

"Adela goes a little too far, sometimes," he remarked then.

"Need we think of her, now?" She went along the tiny hall as she voiced the suggestion, and opened the door of the front sitting-room. Glancing into the room, Denham saw that the gas-fire was alight and the settee drawn up beside it. "I told Mrs. Pennefeather I expected a visitor when I came back," Marguerite explained. "I'm sorry—I really must clear some of those pegs of my things. You can put your hat and coat down on the chest, for this time, if you don't mind."

He looked down at the heavy, iron-bound, antique chest to which she referred. Its lid was secured by two heavy, intricately orna-mented locks, and a large steel plate inlaid in the lid itself was en-graved with a shield on which were many quarterings. The decora-tive ironwork on the chest itself covered fully half the wood of which it was made.

"That's a noble trophy," Denham observed, as he removed his overcoat and put it down. "Very old, isn't it?"

"Sixteenth century," she answered. "I believe it's the most val-uable thing I have, though I bought it quite cheaply in an antique shop in Taormina. A treasure-chest that once belonged to an Italian noble family, but I forget the name. The family is extinct now."

He followed her into the sitting-room and closed the door. When, by the settee, she turned to face him, he took her in his arms.

"Marguerite—my dear?" he asked.

"I have been living for this, since you left me last night," she answered. "Waiting—longing for you to hold me. . . ."

"Do you know I've been here with you nearly an hour?"

She laughed, happily. "But I told you—I want every hour you can give. Surely—there's no need for you to go yet?"

"No—I don't want to go. But I mean I've been here without telling you anything of what I meant to tell you."

"My dear, I don't care. You've told me what I wanted most to know."

"And knew already. . . . But, Marguerite, I had a great idea."

"Yes? About me? Say it was about me!"

"It was, shining eyes. I thought if I turned the Bugatti out and put the hood up, we might go along the London Road, over Condor Hill, and down to the Carden Arms in the village beyond. We should get the hotel dining-room practically to ourselves at this time of year."

"But I thought you wanted to go back to your office?" she asked.

"That," he confessed, "was merely camouflage for Adela."

She laughed, and tightened the clasp of her arm round his neck. "Now I shall know what to believe when you tell me you've been kept late at your office," she told him. "But aren't you happy here?"

"I'd be happy anywhere, with you. But we've both got to dine somewhere, and it would mean keeping you with me longer."

She released her hold on him. "No, let me go, please," she bade. "I want to go and tell Mrs. Pennefeather you're dining here with me. We can go to the Carden Arms some other time—to-morrow, perhaps."

"Marguerite—you darling! That means—"

"I said, let me go!" she admonished him severely. "We must dine somewhere, and there isn't a minute to spare if you're to dine here. You don't know what Mrs. Pennefeather is, but I do."

Some minutes later, after she had released herself from his hold and got away, he heard her giving instructions regarding the dinner—at least, he concluded that the dinner was the subject of her talk, though her words were indistinct, since the sitting-room door was closed. She returned, and drew a long breath of relief as she smiled at him.

"That's over," she said. "I must change her—she gets deafer every day. Did you hear me screaming into her ear to make her understand? And even now I'm not sure that she does."

"Make her use a trumpet, or something of the sort," he suggested.

"She won't. Dinner will be ready in a little more than an hour, and I'm going to put on the frock I wore last night, because—because it will always remind me of your first kiss."

Holding her, he laughed, looking down into her eyes. "It'll get horribly crumpled," he prophesied. "Have you thought of that?"

"I don't care. Except . . . I always want to look my very best, for you. And yesterday, darling, I wasn't sure whether you loved me."

"Marguerite, why don't you wish anyone to know?"

He saw or imagined a momentary change in her expression: it passed so quickly that he could not tell if it were surprise at the query, or any other emotion. She laid her cheek against his shoulder.

"Does it make any difference—any great difference—to you?" she asked in reply. "Will you mind not telling for awhile?"

"Not in the least," he assured her. "I wouldn't care if an earthquake swallowed up Westingborough, as long as it left us together—and Adela, of course. The rest of the town can go to the devil, as far as I'm concerned. I merely wondered—" He did not end it.

"A nice, discriminating earthquake," she reflected. "We should have to get it specially made. But I thought—after yesterday—if we made it public at once, people would say you had been trying to shield me, and so we should bring about the thing you made such a sacrifice to avoid. Do you see, dear? And a week or two later they would not be so likely to connect the two things. Some other sensation or piece of scandal will occupy their thoughts, then."

"The arrest of Carter's murderer, possibly," he suggested. "Yes, I see, darling. And when they get him, I shall be forgotten."

"We shall have nothing more to fear," she amended. "Hugh, dear, I'm going now to put on *the* frock, and you'll find the bathroom half-way up the stairs. And if you know exactly how much the burgundy should be warmed, I don't. The bottle is on the sideboard in the dining-room, just through the folding doors there."

"I'll see to it," he promised. "But you needn't go quite yet."

"Well, perhaps not quite yet," she conceded. "If you—but do you really want me to stay as long as I can?"

Denham convinced her that he did.

* * * * *

"A repetition of the dose, chief?" Head inquired.

"No," Wadden answered firmly. "One's enough—I haven't been to London, getting into bad habits. I'll go and see about that mutton—feel fit to face anything, now. Come along—it's time you were getting home, too. We've done all we can, for to-night."

"Except that I've got to get those letters off to Barcelona and Valencia before I hit the hay," Head pointed out.

"When a chap bumps another chap off," Wadden remarked as they emerged from the main entrance of the Duke of York, "he never seems to think of all the extra work he's putting on chaps like us. I might have finished my mutton by now if it hadn't been for this."

"Yes, they're all so damned inconsiderate," Head agreed, as the two walked back toward the police station—Wadden's home was situated some distance beyond the station. "Chief, an idea occurred to me when I looked round the smoking-room and recognized so many of our old friends of the press—the ones that came hunting for copy while the Forrest case lasted. But I didn't think it wise to mention my idea while we were within hearing of anyone."

"Quite wise," Wadden agreed. "It's not safe to talk about anything but the odds on the National, with those chaps within sight of you. They'd lip-read what they couldn't hear, and imagine the rest. But what's this lonely little idea of yours?"

"That it's quite possible, assuming that Peter Vesci is the man we want—quite possible he's been in Westingborough for weeks or months, getting the lay of the land and choosing his time."

"Not probable," Wadden dissented at once. "If he had been, Carter would have told somebody one of the Vesci trio was here."

"That's just what he wouldn't do," Head dissented. "He wanted to dissociate himself entirely from his life as a theatrical producer. He wouldn't give away his knowledge of that world by saying he recognised Peter Vesci—or his sister, if the pair came here together. No, Carter would have kept quiet about them, and hoped they'd leave him alone."

"Then that other bird, Mortimer—he'd have talked about them," Wadden said. "From what you told me, he's making no secret of his association with the stage. Great scenic artist and all the rest of it—he's proud of himself. He'd have been calling Peter Vesci 'dear laddie' before now. No, it was a sudden raid, if Peter made it."

"I doubt it," Head dissented again. "That ground was studied very thoroughly, and the plan wasn't made in a day. Besides, Mortimer might not have recognised the Vescis, or either of them, in their ordinary kit. Weeds told me you'd hardly know them from the stage photos—the eyes are about all there is left, and the make-up round them doesn't leave a lot of the original for recognition. Mortimer was a scenic artist, which doesn't mean he'd fraternise with the Vescis in their dressing-rooms and see any of them in a state of nature."

"Well"—they halted on the pavement, having reached the entrance to the police station—"you go and get those letters off, and I'll go and tell the missus I'm sorry and won't do it again. And to-morrow you can look round among Ethel Perry's list of friends for dark-eyed strangers to us, one male and one female, and when you get your Vesci we can put Ethel alongside in the dock as accessory before, and produce her bicycle as an exhibit at the trial. She hasn't got the nerve to commit the crime, I know, but she's capable of doing the ride round—and we know now she had time for it."

"If she had, the rest had," Head pointed out.

"Don't you chuck any more ideas at me to-night, my lad. I'm off after cold mutton and a hell of a lecture for being late. If you want me as evidence to your wife that you came off the nine-twenty to-night instead of the seven thirty-five, I'll stand for it. One more lie makes very little difference, and we married men have got to hang together. See you in the morning, Head—good night."

* * * * *

"Was it a good dinner?" Marguerite asked hopefully.

Denham shook his head.

"What's the use of asking me a thing like that, darling?" he answered. "You were there, so naturally I didn't think of what I was eating. I just ate."

" 'Just' hardly describes it," she commented, with a reminiscent smile. "I wonder—shall I always mean as much to you? I don't mean to an extent that prevents you from seeing anything but me, for that's absurd, but—would this love of yours endure against everything?"

"My dear, since we seem to be talking seriously, that love of mine has been a slow growth. Not that it didn't exist very soon after I first met you—came in and found you at tea with Adela, do you remember? And from that point onward it's been growing till a day without seeing you was no day at all. That's been going on for over a year. And at the inquest, you stood before everything for me, as I told you. You always will stand before everything, for me."

"In spite of—Hugh, dear, supposing I tell you I didn't mean you to know I cared for you, last night? Tell you that the way you'd put me before even what you felt you ought to say—at the inquest, I mean—literally forced me to let you see all that I meant to hide. I meant—"

"But why, darling?" he interrupted incredulously.

She shook her head. "It was self-betrayal, a sudden impulse," she said. "Don't think I'm sorry, or that I'd retract—one hour of the hours we have had already is enough to make me glad I let you see how much I love you, and how much your love means to me. And now there is no reason why I shouldn't let you see?" Suddenly she clung to him. "I hate letting you go, Hugh! I shall not so much live as wait for to-morrow, after you've gone and left me to-night."

There was sudden, almost fierce passion in the final sentences. He placed his hand on her dark hair and made her look at him. Tears stood in her eyes, he saw with amazement.

"Marguerite—what have I done, or said?" he asked.

She shook her head, and two tears fell. "No," she said, "not you. I myself—my dear, you're so simply straight, so far above me—"

"Hush, Marguerite! Since yesterday I am what you make me. And nothing in earth or heaven or hell will ever alter my love for you, or make you mean less to me. Since you let me take you and hold you, I make you a part of every thought, a part of my whole life."

"Is it so big a thing?" She looked up at him wonderingly, almost in an awed way. "Am I—so much to you, my dear?"

He smiled. "It will take all the rest of my life and yours to tell you," he said. "Just so much you are to me—all."

"And now you must go? Really?"

"It's nearly midnight," he pointed out. "And tomorrow, dear?"

"To-morrow—yes. Hugh, you spoke of going to the Carden Arms for dinner. Shall we go there to-morrow? Will you have time to spare?"

He nodded. "Supposing I come along with the car at about half-past three," he suggested. "Then, if you like, we could have tea and go out there in time to get the view from the hill before dark, and go on down to the hotel. It won't matter what time we get back."

"Yes, tea here with me. But we'll take my little coupé—it will be warmer than your car, and—and we shall not be so conspicuous on the road. I mean, if we stay to look at the view, or—or anything."

He laughed. "It's quite likely I shall want to look at the view I can see now," he remarked. "Such lovely, soft eyes, Marguerite, each a mirror to reflect love. Yes, we can go in your car if you wish. The Bugatti is a bit faster, but yours will be warmer."

"Faster?" she queried dissentingly. "Mine will do seventy."

"Will it, by gum? Well, I have had mine up to seventy-five, but it isn't exactly comfortable at that pace. Anyhow, we'll take yours, and I'll be here at half-past three. Now I must go, darling."

She followed him out to the entrance hall, took up his coat from the antique Italian chest and held it for him. He stooped, with the coat on, to look at the delicately wrought ironwork of the chest.

"Some artist in metal made that," he remarked, turning to her again. "Do you think, darling, when we have our own home—?"

She nestled close in his hold. "All I am and all I have will be yours, Hugh, all there is of me and about me, since last night gave you to me. As you said of yourself, a part of my whole life—yet more! For since yesterday you *are* my life, not merely a part."

He looked back from the gate and saw her standing in the doorway of the house, slender and tall in the red-trimmed black frock, her hand raised in a gesture of parting, her face in shadow, and the light shining on her dark, glossy hair. So, until he slept, he saw her in his thoughts, and wished he had gone back to hold her close and kiss her just once more. For it had seemed to him that the gesture of her upraised hand beckoned him, though she would not call him back to her.

CHAPTER XIII

MORE INTERVIEWS

"OOMPH!" HEAD GRUNTED, putting down the telegram "flimsy" Wadden had silently held out to him for inspection—the message was in code, and Wadden had pencilled the translation over the code words. " 'Communicating with Balearic consulate(s) at once, will let you know result by cable'—that's a hell of a lot to get into three words. What's the code, in case I want to decode the next in a hurry myself?"

"Bentley's," Wadden told him. "The book is on the safe."

"Right. Now what's the big thing for to-day, chief? I don't see that we can proceed to any extent on this Carter case until we either eliminate Peter Vesci or fix it on him."

"You can't proceed on anything else, because there isn't," Wadden pointed out. "Petty sessions next Tuesday, and all we seem to have is two drunks, that N.S.P.C.C. case, and Penley with the feathers oft Mrs. Platt's ducks. I'm thinking of putting you up as an independent expert to swear they are duck feathers, and didn't come off an ostrich."

" 'Sno good, chief—I've never plucked an ostrich. I think, if you don't want me this morning, I'll do another round of visits on the Carter case. I don't like leaving it alone, and might get a line on it."

"More aeronautical pigs," Wadden remarked sceptically. "All right, you go and amuse yourself. But never own that you're not an expert, Head, on duck feathers or anything else. You've only got to say you are, and the vulgar herd—which is everybody except us—will believe you. Now buzz off where you like, and let me know the result."

Head went out. Pausing in the doorway of the police station, he looked up and then down Market Street, and saw, in the entrance to the Duke of York, a London agency pressman who had been sent down to "cover" the Grange murder case, and was remaining on the spot in the hope of developments. The inspector turned the other way, and sauntered in leisurely fashion away from the centre of the town, toward the point where, as the street became a country road with occasional villa residences on either side, Maggs Lane branched to the left at right angles.

He came to the end of the lane, and paused. Somewhere near here, he decided, Carter's murderer had stopped to put on the old boots before going on toward the kissing-gate. Boots of every description were still piling up at the police station, but Head knew there was scant hope of the pair he wanted being among them: the author of such a crime would not commit the error of leaving that pair within reach of enthusiastic boy scouts—or of anyone else, for that matter. After a brief meditation, Head walked on along the lane slowly, and visualising the murderer going that way through the darkness until he reached the kissing-gate, passing through and on to the Grange, where Carter had opened the door to him—opened the door to death!

And then back. Back to the gate—Head paused again there and looked up at the ash tree, with one branch running out over the gate itself, and another, equally convenient, extended over the road. Yes, it must have been a very good rope-thrower indeed who had flung his rope over the branch in the darkness, getting it over the first time—for, had he not got it over, the end would have fallen and marked the snow. And Head knew there had been no marks of a rope, nothing but the footprints ceasing just inside the gate.

The position and form of the tree, probably, had given the murderer his plan when he had made his initial survey for the crime. Had there been no snow, he would have left the prints of the boots on the soft soil of the track to the Grange, and here they would have ceased, with no indication of emergence across the slightly muddy border of the road to hard macadam. The rope would have been used just the same: it was part of the original plan. The bicycle, to permit of the tracks ceasing, must have been a sudden inspiration at sight of the snow falling. And the fall had been just so slight as to permit of riding the machine without forming a noticeably deeper tyre-track, in order to make it appear that the one who had made the footprints later beside the tyre-marks had walked beside the bicycle and wheeled it. A little more depth of snow would have made the deception obvious.

Neat, simple and neat—and the footprints beside the tyre-tracks might be those of a small man or of a woman. Head had studied the photographs exhaustively, but still he was not able to decide the sex of the murderer. Peter Vesci had delicately small hands and feet; Peter Vesci was a good rope-thrower—a miraculously good rope-thrower. Yet Head hesitated over fixing the crime on Peter; he fitted all requirements—he fitted too well for Head's liking, was too obvious altogether. He had already tried to kill Carter, he wanted revenge on the man, and had the temperament for executing a plan like this, as well as the physical agility. Had he murdered Carter? If not, who had?

Thinking over the eight guests at the party that had preceded the crime, Head mentally ruled out the Quades as possible suspects. The distance at which they lived on the other side of Westingborough put them out of his list, apart from the possibility of motive: neither Quade nor his wife could have got back to do the bicycle ride and commit the murder before four o'clock—or to do either of these things, in fact. Then he ruled out Fred Pollen and Betty Hurder; they were mere ineptnesses, out for a good time—as they counted good times—at the expense of anyone who offered it. Now he had Denham, Mortimer, and the Perry sisters left for consideration. Denham knew something—of that Head felt convinced; he was almost equally convinced that Mortimer knew something: the man had been plausible, fully self-contained, but he had been a little too self-possessed and watchful when Head had interviewed him, a little too ready to give selected bits of information, to be altogether trustworthy. One glance at him was enough to show that he was neither a rope-thrower nor a good tree-climber; he was a corpulent, sedentary sort of man. But he knew something.

Then the Perry sisters. Ethel was a nurse, and Head felt certain that the person in nurse's uniform whom Borrow had seen had some connection with the crime. That person might be either woman or small man, and if the latter, where did Ethel come in? Had she lent her uniform cloak and head-dress, and if so, to whom?

Lilian—he considered her next. She might have inadvertently passed on to Mortimer the bit of information that had put him on his guard when Head went to interview him. About her sister having lent the cloak and bonnet to somebody. About anything! She might be worth closer and more detailed questioning than he had accorded her.

Nothing had been said at the inquest about a possible connection between the bicycle-tracks and the crime, nor had any explanation been given with regard to the apparently futile "police notice" to cyclists and nurses, though Westingborough had immediately connected it with the murder, and the editor of the *Sentinel* had made it an excuse for rhetoric. The fact that the murderer's footprints had led to and from the kissing-gate had, of course, been made public; and now, looking over the gate, Head could see that the earth all round it had been trodden to mere mush by pressmen and sightseers.

While he stood cogitating, the man whom he had seen in the entrance to the Duke of York came briskly along the lane and joined him by the gate with a hearty "Good morning, Mr. Head."

"No," Head answered, "nothing for you to-day. That is, so far."

"Do you mind if I go along to the Grange and have a word with Arabella Cann?" the pressman asked. "I must send something off."

"I do mind, most desperately," Head answered. "Until I get this investigation a bit more developed, I've an objection to anyone connected with the case being questioned by you or anyone else. It forms their opinions, you know, and makes them more difficult for me."

"All right, I'll leave her alone," the man promised, rather regretfully. "But can't you give me a line about something? As it is, I'm merely kicking my heels down here, and that means a wigging."

"You can say that we have a promising line of investigation, and hope for developments in the course of the next few days," Head told him. "I know your editors will consider that mere guff, but it's the best I can give you, until I know a bit more myself."

"Guff?" the journalist echoed gratefully. "When you open your paper to-morrow morning and see what I've made of it, you'll find you've spilled a bibful. It's a column and a half, easy!"

"Well, good morning, Mr. Simpson," Head said. "I'm going on, now."

He passed through the gateway and made his way up to the Grange. Incidentally, he read in one of the papers the following morning that "Inspector Head, whose name will be familiar to all our readers, interviewed by our special representative at the scene of the crime, communicated to him the fact that a special line of investigation with regard to the identity of the murderer is at present in progress, but in the interests of justice we are compelled to withhold further particulars of the direction in which the activities of the Westingborough police, and especially of its directing brains, are trending. Important developments may be expected within the next few days, and it is confidently anticipated that the Westingborough Grange murder—"

Etc, etc., for the column and a half—and a bit more —that the journalist had seen as possible in Head's simple statement. But then, the space had been reserved for the case, and it had to be filled somehow. Cross-heads and heavy type helped the padding, which included a description of the winter landscape, the unusually mild weather following wintry conditions, and a forecast that startling revelations might be expected to appear in to-morrow's issue.

But all this was hidden in the future when Head walked along the path and, crossing the laurel-hedged lawn, approached the Grange. The windows of the long front, each masked by a down-drawn blind, had an unfamiliar, depressing appearance—Carter's funeral was to take place that afternoon, and the residuary legatee under the deceased man's will, a tall, hungry-looking Nonconformist minister rejoicing—or not—in the name of Septimus Snood, evidently intended to observe the proprieties. He was a distant relative of some sort, Head knew, and the only one who had appeared, so far, though two others were mentioned in the will, and he had installed himself at the Grange and taken charge. Among other things, he had given all the servants and the two grooms who looked after the horses a choice between a month's notice and wages in lieu. He intended to sell everything by auction as soon as he could get probate of the estate, being sole executor of the will.

Outside the entrance to the house, Head saw as he approached, stood a local taxicab, and, as he crossed the stretch of gravel beyond the edge of the lawn, the driver and a girl emerged, carrying a big fibre trunk between them. The man heaved the trunk up beside his seat and went back into the house, possibly to fetch more luggage, and as the girl stood waiting on the doorstep Head recognised her as Phyllis Taylor. She was wearing faultless make-up and beautiful silver-fox furs.

" 'Morning, Miss Taylor," Head said. "It struck me it would be just as well to look along and get your future address, in case we want to get in touch with you over Mr. Carter's death."

She gave him a startled look. "But—but who told you I was leaving to-day?" she asked, staring at him.

"Oh, we have our own ways of finding things out," he answered. He had not known that she was leaving, but had no intention of confessing his ignorance of the fact to her.

"It's one of that herd of spying cats in there, I suppose," she suggested, gesturing toward the interior of the house. "Well, if it is, I don't care what they say about me, the self-righteous sneaks."

"I should have thought you'd have stayed for the funeral," Head suggested, abandoning the other subject as unprofitable.

"I would, too, if it hadn't been for the devil-dodging sniveller here after Eddie's money," she declared. "Why, he wanted us all to come down to prayers before breakfast this morning! I'm not standing for anything of that sort from him or anyone else."

The cabman came out with a large suit-case. "Is this all, miss?" he asked. "I've put the little one inside."

"Then put that one in with it," she answered. "Yes, it's the lot. I'll wish you good morning, Mr. Head, and hope you catch your man."

"Also, you'll give me an address where I can find you at need," he told, rather peremptorily. "Here's a pencil and paper."

She took them, placed the paper on her handbag, and wrote the address. Head, taking it from her, scrutinized the words.

"Bow Road, eh?" he commented. "Is this Mrs. Merriman a relative?"

"Married sister, since you must know everything," she retorted.

"Well, I can check up on it while you're on your way," he said.

"I—I made a mistake," she faltered. "It should be fourteen, Connaught Rents, Bow Road. Not fourteen Bow Road itself."

Head gave her a grave look. "The sort of mistake, that," he said, "over which people sometimes get detained on suspicion. I'll have you watched young lady, every stage of your journey, and I'll have Mrs. Merriman looked up for inquiries while you're on that journey. You're quite sure you haven't made a mistake about Connaught Rents?"

"I'll take my oath on it," she protested earnestly. "Fourteen."

"If it's not correct," he warned her, "you'll step out of your train just in time to be arrested at the ticket-barrier—or sooner. All right, you can go—but don't think you're going out of my reach."

He turned his back on her to face the entrance, and saw the Reverend Septimus standing in the doorway, gravely shaking his head. The inspector advanced toward him, and nodded a greeting.

"I want to use your telephone, Mr. Snood, please," he asked.

"Why, certainly, inspector. I fear"—he shook his head at the cab, then on the point of starting—"a daughter of Babylon."

"Ye-es," Head agreed slowly, "and she might come to a hanging garden, yet, if she keeps on the way she's going."

"It was such a one who let down the spies from the wall of Jericho by a cord," Septimus pursued mournfully. "My late cousin, it grieves me to say, was a man of many frailties."

"Gosh!" Head looked round at the retreating cab. "Let down by a cord! That's hitting near the bull's-eye, if you only knew it. Not that she— I'll go and telephone, if you don't mind."

And entering the drawing-room, he got through to Wadden and informed him of Phyllis's "mistake" over her address. Wadden, by the resulting sound, blew gustily into his receiver before he spoke.

"All right, Head, all right! I'll get through and have this Mrs. Merriman looked up at once, in case the girl's still trying half-larks. If so, there'll be time to take care of her when the train gets in. You carry on—keep on amusing yourself. It's quite probable Phyllis only wanted to get shut of us so we couldn't call her as a witness."

Head hung up and went to the dining-room, where the coffin stood on trestles beside the table, and in the corner behind the door the grandfather clock ticked solemnly. The Reverend Septimus followed the inspector into the room, and stood gazing at the coffin.

"It is a sad thought that he should have been hurried into eternity from the midst of his sins," he announced. "Struck down unrepentant, as it were, and heedless of the wrath to come. Hurried forth—"

"I'm concerned with the one who did the hurrying," Head interrupted impatiently, "and I'd hate to waste time passing my little human judgment on any man instead of getting on with my job. Have you been through his papers, as Superintendent Wadden asked?"

"I have inspected such documents as are available," Septimus answered stiffly. "They appear to consist of accounts with local tradespeople, correspondence in connection with the wing he gave to the local hospital, and similar matters, and some—er—some unduly affectionate communications from sundry females with whom he appeared to have been on—er—terms of close acquaintance. But nothing of importance, I am sure. Levity, evidence of intemperate gaiety—nothing more."

"You'd better sort everything of that sort out from the purely business correspondence, and let us have it," Head suggested. "I'll see that our Sergeant Wells comes back here after the funeral, and you can hand over to him all correspondence apart from ordinary business letters. About four-thirty, say. Will that suit you?"

"Are you not taking a good deal on yourself, inspector, in making such a request?" Septimus inquired with solemn displeasure.

"I'm not making a request, but giving you an order," Head retorted sharply—the note of sanctimonious reproof irritated him. "What's more, I expect it to be carried out, since you're executor here."

"Oh, very good, inspector—very good. All documents shall be handed over as you request. I trust they will be returned to me."

"Any that we don't want in the event of having to produce them as evidence will be returned," Head assured him. "That's all, thanks. Oh, one thing, though. Is that girl the only one who has left?"

"The other servants will stay the month out," Septimus said. "The two grooms, further, will remain until the horses have been sold."

"Right—I don't want to see any of them at present. Good morning, Mr. Snood. I must be getting along, now."

He went out, and slowly made his way down the drive. The Grange had nothing more to tell him, he felt; apart from the correspondence Septimus had promised to hand over, it could offer no clue as to the identity of the one who had shot Carter down. Possibly a report would come through from one of the two consulates in Spain, something that would put him on the track of Peter Vesci —and his sister! Head kept in mind her parting words to Carter before she carried her brother away: she might have acted as accessory to Peter, might be equally guilty with him. And, as he had told Wadden, the pair might be here in Westingborough now. Denham might be capable of giving information about them, Ethel Perry might have lent one of them her outdoor uniform. But this latter was in the last degree unlikely: whoever had planned the crime had had far too much wit to give a girl like Ethel Perry so much knowledge of the plan as that. Yet Head suspected her, could not yet acquit her of possible complicity, mainly because he felt sure there was a woman in it somewhere. A woman's brain was behind that use of a nurse's uniform, and Ethel Perry possessed one.

The riddle of the murderer's identity seemed to him no nearer solution as he made his way back to the town, going this time by London Road, across the Idleburn bridge and past Mortimer's white house, and so back to Market Street. There he turned into the business block on the corner, entered Denham's office, and asked Joslin to tell Mr. Denham that he had called and wanted a few minutes' interview.

Joslin, emerging again from the inner office, reported that Mr. Denham was sorry, but he was very busy. On that, Head pulled forward a chair for himself, and sat down on it.

"Tell Mr. Denham I'll wait till he can see me," he said.

Joslin went in with the message, and Head overheard Denham's voice in loud and apparently excited remonstrance. Presently Joslin emerged.

"Will you go in, Mr. Head?" he invited very coldly.

Head went in, and saw Denham standing by the side of the room, with his back to the fire in the grate and his hands in his pockets. He gave the inspector a steady, resentful stare.

"Well, what do you want?" he asked. "Have you come to arrest me?"

"If I had, I should not be here alone," Head answered evenly. "I'm here for two reasons. The first of them is that an accessory is equally guilty with the principal in the eyes of the law, no matter how small his or her share in the offence may be. It's worth remembering sometimes, Mr. Denham, and your attitude made me remind you."

"First catch your principal," Denham retorted contemptuously. "If you feel like trying some more third degree on me before you get on with that main business, carry on. But make it as short as you can. Sometimes, though you might not think it, I work in this office."

"I will make it short," Head answered coolly. "My second reason for coming to see you again—when did you last see Peter Vesci?"

Watching his man as he thus drew his bow at a venture, he knew the name conveyed nothing to Denham. He saw a frown of curiosity, and then a gleam of interest, but of an impersonal kind.

"I don't know the name," Denham said at last, slowly, as if his interest had conquered his hostility. "Peter Vesci— Ah, I remember, now! Yes, the Vesci trio, Nita, Quita, and Peter—if that is the man you mean. Well, inspector, I last saw Peter Vesci on the stage of the Quadrarian, three—no, it must have been nearly four years ago. I saw the trio in their act one night, and have seen none of them since. Does that answer your question, or do you want to go on badgering me over it as the coroner did over another matter at the inquest on Carter?"

"The answer is good enough for me," Head said quietly.

"And having got it—you said you had only two reasons for coming, and this appears to be the second—having got it, do you think you could turn your attention to the business of finding out who murdered Carter, and leave me alone?" Denham asked caustically. "That is, I conclude you can hardly arrest an accessory to a crime until you have managed to find the principal. You've got to arrest the principal first—isn't that so?"

"Not if there has been active complicity," Head dissented.

"Well, I don't know who killed Carter, and my activities are confined to my work and my amusements—and murder isn't one of them," Denham said. "You needn't bang the outer door as you go—there's a spring on it, and it closes if you just release the handle. I'm sorry to have wasted so much of your time, inspector."

He lifted his hand and regarded his finger-nails closely, as if interested in them. Head turned without replying, and went out, leaving both the door of this room and the outer door to close themselves.

CHAPTER XIV

ON CONDOR HILL

"WHAT MAKES YOU so morose to-day, Hugh?" Adela inquired, as, having finished lunch with her brother, she pushed back her chair and sat regarding him. The frown with which he had watched Inspector Head go out from his office still creased his brow slightly.

"Things, and people." He rose as he answered and, going over to the fireplace, lighted a cigarette and stood there, still frowning.

"I don't see why," she said reflectively. "They'll get whoever it was killed Carter, and then this slight unpleasantness will wear off when it's proved you had nothing to do with it—it's only the fools who think there's anything in the way you were questioned, in any case."

"Fools are plentiful," he pointed out, rather grimly.

"Well, why worry?" she retorted. You've got Marguerite, and she's a dear—and it isn't often a girl says that and means it about another girl better-looking than herself. And she's really in love with you."

"Are you in love with Bob Leigh?" Denham asked abruptly.

"Why on earth do you think I'm marrying him, if I'm not? Daddy left me enough money to live on if I wanted to remain single, and I'm not man-hungry. Of course I'm in love with him!"

"In your own practical way," he suggested.

"That's all you know." She smiled reminiscently. "We're going to have two children, a boy and a girl, I hope. Neither Bob nor I believe in having more—it splits up the inheritance too much. Will you be in for dinner to-night, Hugh?"

"I shall not," he answered decidedly. "I'm taking Marguerite out, and we've settled to dine at the Carden Arms, beyond Condor Hill."

"Oh, I know where the Carden Arms is," she told him, with another reminiscent smile. "And that reminds me. I met Vere Langton when I was shopping in the town this morning, and she told me her father was taking her over to Carden this afternoon."

"Well, they won't interfere with us," Denham remarked.

"They're going to look at a hunter he might buy for her, if she likes it," Adela pursued, following her own line of reflection. "I wished—wished—and I still wish—that Marguerite hadn't insisted on postponing an official engagement between you two."

"What on earth difference does it make to you?" Denham demanded irritably. "She had good reason for it, as she explained to me."

"My dear infant, any reason Marguerite chose to give you at the present time would be a good one," Adela pointed out. "And it does make a difference to me, more especially over meeting Vere. Do you remember the week we had in London, nearly four years ago?"

"You're the second person to remind me of it today," he answered, with Head's reference to the Vesci trio in his mind.

"Am I? Life's full of coincidences, isn't it? But I was thinking. Vere and her sister were there, too, you remember—but I expect you'd rather forget how you and Vere paired off all the time and left me to amuse myself with Mary as best I could. And up to six months ago I still hoped you and Vere would make a match of it."

"What's that got to do with Marguerite's wishing to keep our engagement quiet for awhile?" he asked sceptically.

"Just this, you very unobservant infant. Vere is as fond of you as ever she was; she's a sweet girl who would have made you an ideal wife if Marguerite hadn't happened, and she'll go on hoping for that fate till she knows it's out of the question. And you're not altogether free of blame over it, Hugh. You and she were very much together, up to a year ago or thereabouts. We used to go over to the Langtons, you remember—Vere asked me this morning how it is that we never come over now, and I had to put her off when she suggested an evening."

Denham stood silent for awhile. There had been a time when he and Vere Langton had been very close friends indeed, and he knew they would have become more than friends if Marguerite had not appeared in Westingborough. He felt the justice of Adela's half-accusation.

"It's a good three months since I even saw Vere," he said at last.

"She's not the type that forgets easily." Adela rose to her feet as she spoke. "But perhaps I ought not to have said all this just now. Vere is a might-have-been, and Marguerite is a reality—you've every reason to be proud of her, too. Tell her you want to be proud of her—to let everyone know you are, and get her to lift the ban. An appropriated man is in a different position from a free-lance, and as soon as Vere knows you're engaged she'll stop thinking about you—or stop hoping over you, which will come to the same thing in the end."

Denham pressed the end of his cigarette down into an ash-tray. "In a week or two, Marguerite said, we'll let people know," he answered. "Quite possibly I'll tell her some of what you've said this afternoon."

"I doubt it," Adela retorted. "Once you get together, you'll think of nothing but your two selves. Speaking from experience, I don't blame you. Give her my love if you do happen to come back to earth for a moment or two—though I haven't much hope of that."

She went out from the room, and a little later Denham went back to his office to see if any of the builders' estimates he had requested for underpinning the corner of the Perry's house were in yet, and also to tell Joslin to take charge from three o'clock to closing time, since he himself would not be there. As he walked toward the office, he reflected rather self-accusingly over Adela's statements. He had been very nearly in love with Vere Langton once, he had to confess—perhaps he had been in love with her, though this absorbing passion with which Marguerite had inspired him made any other love seem an impossibility now. But there had been a time when Vere had appeared very desirable, and he had let her see that he was content to be with her, had paired with her on occasions that brought them together, and had not resented it when Adela, a match-maker at heart as is every woman, had made opportunities for them.

Even after Marguerite had appeared he had continued his friendship with Vere for a time, and had given her no hint of any kind that the relationship between them was doomed to change. He ought to have—what ought he to have done? What could he have done? There had been no open declaration, only a drifting together that she had very evidently welcomed, and then a drifting apart. Yet, he knew, Vere might with justice feel resentment when she heard of his engagement, for the attraction existing between man and woman is not expressed in words alone, and she had let him see that he had only to put his feeling for her in words to win the answer fitting to such words. And had there been no Marguerite, he knew he would have spoken them, had been very near speaking them, little more than a year ago.

His regrets over Vere, however, were short-lived. Two of the three estimates for which he had asked were awaiting him, and by the time he had finished with them and given Joslin his instructions, he had to hurry to avoid being late for his appointment with Marguerite. He saw her car, a small, low-slung coupé, standing outside her gate in readiness, and as he reached the door she opened it, cloaked in readiness for the drive. But she drew back into the hallway, and Denham entered and took her in his arms to kiss her.

"Darling, you look lovelier than ever," he told her. "Ah, but you're looking at the little weasels and the hat, not at me at all," she said reprovingly. "I'm just the same."

"Don't be silly, Marguerite. What little weasels?"

"My sables. Didn't you know it's sable? And sables are weasels, or at least they belong to that family. Hugh, dear, I thought we'd go straight out, instead of having tea here. Otherwise, there will be no light to show us the view when we get to Condor Hill. We can go on down to the Craven Arms and have tea there, and then go for a drive through the Craven woods and come back to the hotel for dinner. It won't be cold in the car on a day like this."

"Just as you like, dear. As long as I'm with you."

They went out to the coupé, and Marguerite took the wheel. It was a hazily sunlit afternoon, giving that promise of spring over which nature recants so many times in the first three months of most years. Denham gave a little whistle when, after starting, they swung round the corner into Treherne Road: his Bugatti cornered fairly easily at speed, but this car with its shorter wheel-base seemed to spin at right angles like a doubling greyhound, an uncanny movement.

"It felt as if you turned on two wheels," he explained, as Marguerite gave him a questioning glance. "Keep it up—I'm not worried."

She laughed, and swung them on to the London Road with similar suddenness. Then, depressing the accelerator, she hurtled over the Idleburn bridge, the end of Maggs Lane fled away behind them, and a three-mile straight stretch showed almost level ahead. Denham glanced at the speedometer and saw that it was already past the sixty and still rising.

"High ratio of power to weight," he commented. "Some time, if you don't mind, I'd like to take that wheel and find out how it feels."

"You'll find the steering and everything else so light that you hardly know you're driving," she said. "And, of course, you can drive it whenever you like. Would you care to change places now?" She slackened speed as she asked it, and glanced toward him.

"No—carry on," he answered. "I'm perfectly happy as I am—which is more than I'd tell most women drivers if I sat beside them."

She accelerated again. For nearly eight miles they kept almost an average parallel with the course of the Idleburn, along the floor of the valley drained by the river. Then came a slight rise of three miles or more, bearing to the right away from the river, and on that followed the long, steady climb which would take them over the crest of the western range of hills bounding the catchment area of the Idleburn. It was a new road, cut since the end of the War to avoid the twists and sudden, sharp ascents by which coaches had made their way Londonward, out from the Idleburn valley, in the old days.

The little coupé went at the hill with only a slight abatement of its speed. Denham watched the speedometer-hand, expecting it to quiver down to the forties and thirties at least, and perhaps so low as to involve a change of gear: Marguerite, glancing at him as she drove, noted his intent expression, and laughed amusedly.

"No, you don't believe it, do you?" she said. "But it's true."

"It's a marvellous little engine. Ten horse-power, you said."

"Racehorses, all the ten," she remarked. "You see—still forty-three, because we had a clear run at it. If I'd had to slow at the foot of the hill for anything, it would probably have meant changing down. As it is, we shall still be doing nearly forty at the top."

"We'll stop this side of it and look back," he suggested.

She drew the ear into the side of the road and stopped it, before they came to the quarter-mile or more of cutting in which the road crossed the crest of the low range of hills. When they looked back Westingborough roofs showed clearly, together with the filter-beds of Nevile's works, Westingborough Parva, a sleepy little village, in the distance beyond, and the line of the river running like a pale thread and receding into dim haze, with the branches of leafless trees forming a mesh over its whiteness. From the blue indistinctness clothing the slopes of the farther range of hills, beyond the river, rose mysterious shapes, church towers distorted and exaggerated to faery battlements, trees and house-roofs blending to form giant castles, and over all there lay a great stillness, a perfection of peace.

"I'm so glad it's not summer," Marguerite said abruptly.

Denham nodded agreement. "I should want to smash the ice-cream barrows," he remarked. "As it is—just us two. The view down into Carden is more abrupt and striking, but I think this is lovelier."

"I'm glad to see it with you," she said softly.

"And you here beside me—lovelier still." He laid his hand on hers on the steering-wheel. "What should I have done if I hadn't found you, or if you hadn't cared for me, Marguerite?"

She shook her head. "I didn't mean you to know I loved you," she answered. "And now for the first time in my life I know real happiness. But it's nearly sunset—shall we go on and see the Carden side?"

He nodded assent, and she drove the car on over the crest of the rise. On the downward slope, where the cutting fell away, there stood beside the way a "Danger" signal, studded with red reflectors to render it visible in the light of car-lamps at night, and just beyond it the road curved sharply and steeply to the left, to go down the hillside in a long diagonal. White railings, also studded with red reflectors, guarded the right-hand, outer edge of the curve, and beyond the railings the hillside sloped downward at an almost un-climbable angle for two hundred feet or more. At the lower edge of the descent a belt of pixies uprose, and in summer hordes of motor-cyclists leaned their machines against the railings and sat at the edge of the steep, looking down at the tree-tops beneath them. But to-day Denham and Marguerite had the height and its famed view to themselves.

Almost opposite the danger post, the road had been built out, for a distance of fifty feet or more, to four or five times its normal width, and the concrete extension of its outer edge formed a wide platform on which, throughout the summer, fifty or more cars would park on Sunday and holiday afternoons. To this point Marguerite drove now, and halted the car half-way along the widened space, close by the railings. There was no other vehicle or human being in sight, then.

"It's early to go down for tea, yet," she remarked. "Shall we get out for a little while and pay our homage to the scenery?"

Without replying, Denham reached over and opened the door on her side. Then he got out from the near side of the car and joined her by the railings, leaning over beside her to gaze.

"If this rail gave way, we should probably be unconscious by the time we stopped down there among the pines," he observed.

"Dead," she amended. "But why think of it? The rail is quite safe. And these funny little circles of red glass-like big rubies."

"They look more like it at night," he remarked. "Put there to re-flect back the light of headlamps, and warn drivers of the curve."

"Yes, I know. Are you really trying to educate me, Hugh, or just saying that because you can't think of anything else?"

"Neither. Saying it just to keep you talking, because I love the sound of your voice. It makes the miracle of your caring for me so much more real—when you're not with me it hardly seems real."

"You'll get tired of the sound of my voice, dear, if—" She paused abruptly, and turned her head away to gaze downward at the pines.

"Never, darling," he dissented confidently. "But if—if what?"

"Nothing. Look—there's someone coming up the hill. A saloon, and a woman driving. And we've not got it to ourselves."

Denham glanced down toward Carden village. "It's Langton and his daughter Vere," he said. "Adela told me they were going over to Carden to-day. I think—we'd better stay where we are, Marguerite. It would look as if we we're trying to dodge them if we got back into the car."

Marguerite made no reply. They stood side by side against the railings, and Denham prayed inwardly that the Langtons would go straight on up the hill. But the saloon came along by the railings and stopped within a few feet of the coupé, and Langton, rubicund and cheerful, looked out.

"How do, Miss West?" he said genially, and opened his door. "Hullo, Denham! Admiring the view, I see." He got out from the car, and revealed himself as a tall, middle-aged man, still active and vigorous. "Vere told me she met Adela in the town this morn-ing—and that's the first any of us has seen of either of you for the last age or two. And you seem to hide yourself away pretty well, too, Miss West, since the hunt ball. It's Westingborough's loss, you know."

Marguerite shook hands with him, with no reply other than a smile. Denham made some indistinct remark about being con-foundedly busy lately. Then Vere Langton came and joined them from the driving-seat of the saloon: she would have been more than woman if she had remained in the car, having seen Denham and an evident rival together.

The contrast between the two girls as Vere faced her was akin to that between an English rose and, say, a perfect magnolia blossom. Vere, chestnut-haired, blue-eyed, daintily patrician in figure as in feature, was definitely of her country: Marguerite appeared darker and more foreign by contrast with her. They greeted each other with cool friendliness, and even Langton felt the tension of their meeting.

"A wonderful view," he said, to cover the constraint of the pause since his last words. "I never tire of it, always want to get out and see it again, when I'm driving this way. And to-day I've been buying a new hunter for Vere—we're just on our way home."

"We are on our way out," Denham replied, with a glance at Vere which might have denoted a challenge, or a question as to her opinion of his choice. But she missed it, gazing out over the hillside.

"This always reminds me of Malvern, to a certain extent." Langton addressed Marguerite with the remark. "Don't you think so?"

"I'm afraid I don't know Malvern very well," she answered.

They talked, or tried to talk, a little longer, but found no subject that could remove the almost hostile coolness between the two girls. Langton alone maintained a cheerful friendliness, to which Denham tried vainly to respond: Marguerite's presence prevented him from showing how much he appreciated Langton's unchanged demeanour, in spite of the vague suspicion the inquest on Carter had set wandering among Westingborough gossips. In the end Langton turned to go.

"We must get home, Vere," he remarked. "I'm glad to see you again, Denham, after this long interval. You know where we live."

Denham smiled for the first time. "I ought," he answered, "but I appreciate the reminder all the same."

"Well, fetch Miss West along some day—if you'll forgive such an informal invitation, Miss West. And drag Adela out of her shell—tell her we're still alive, all of us, and not quite a hundred miles away."

Something that he was missing or had missed troubled Denham's remoter consciousness momentarily. He could not have explained or accounted for the impression, and it lasted only till he glanced at Marguerite again and realised the contrast between her and Vere. Then, as Langton turned to shake hands with her, Vere faced him fully for a brief interval, and he saw her quite cool and self-possessed, mistress of all the weapons a woman can hold against a man she has desired and lost.

"Give Adela my love, won't you, Hugh? It's quite a coincidence, meeting both of you in the same day after not seeing you for so long."

Marguerite could hear her, he knew. The words were no different from her usual way of speaking to him, except that perhaps she stressed his name a little, as if to emphasise the friendly intimacy that existed—or had existed—between them. And she offered her hand—a totally unnecessary gesture, it appeared to him, with Marguerite there.

"And as daddy says, we're not quite a hundred miles away," she said, in reply to his rather confused rejoinder. "Tell Adela that, too."

She went to the car and took the driving-seat. As Langton seated himself beside her, she pressed the self-starter, and then slammed in first gear with totally unnecessary vigour. A glance past her father showed her Denham and Marguerite faced toward them: perhaps she imagined relief in his expression. The car moved off with a jerk.

"Gear-box—clutch," Langton said reprovingly. "What's happened to your driving, Vere? Replacements are expensive, you know."

"Yes, sometimes," she agreed, and changed up to second sweetly and noiselessly. "I'm sorry, daddy—wasn't thinking what I was doing."

"I'd no idea of this—Denham, I mean," he remarked.

"Hugh or any other man—one look at her is enough to tell you she has only to lift a finger," she said, with caustic irritation.

"I saw her at the hunt ball," he observed, "and she seemed pretty popular, I thought. Foreign, it's easy to see, though there's no accent when she speaks. But that's not an English face."

Vere glanced up into the driving-mirror, and saw the tiny reflections of Denham and Marguerite as they stood by the white railing.

"And as you're so fond of saying when you get talking on economics, there are some departments in which home products can never hope to compete with the imported article," she remarked acidly.

Langton made no reply. He had known that Denham and Vere were very good friends indeed, and would have welcomed a closer relationship between them—had hoped for it, in fact. The discovery of this meeting had been just as much a surprise to him as to Vere, and he wished he had not asked her to stop, now, but had driven straight on. His daughter's tone, even more than her words, told that she was hard hit, but she would get over it in time.

"Please light me a cigarette, daddy," she asked abruptly. "I am looking forward to trying out my new horse to-morrow."

CHAPTER XV

RE-ENTER THE BOOTS

MARGUERITE WATCHED THE Langtons' saloon until it disappeared over the crest of the hill. Some of the constraint the encounter had caused appeared to remain between her and Denham, even after they had lost all sight of Langton and his daughter.

"Do many girls call you by your first name, Hugh?" Marguerite asked at last, turning toward him again.

He shook his head. "She, and Adela," he answered. "Nobody else, as nearly as I can remember. But we've known the Langtons a very long while. Mary was a great pal of Adela's before her marriage, and Adela felt her death rather badly. They're old friends."

"And Vere is the only remaining child," Marguerite suggested.

"All Langton's got left," he assented. "He thinks the world of her, too. He's a very decent sort, is Langton."

"I like what I've seen of him," she agreed. "Who—what are they?"

"Why, you know, surely? They live at the big house on the town side of Quade's place—and make it open house for their friends, in a general way. We might go along some day if you like."

But Marguerite knew they would not go along, any day, in the absence of a formal invitation, and even then she would evade it if she could. "I meant, what are they?" she amended. "I know where they live."

"Langton was a parliamentary barrister till his elder brother died," Denham explained, "and then he gave up practice and came to live here for the sake of the hunting—and he's fond of a rod and line, too. Very much an outdoor man, and has plenty of money in addition to being very well-connected. And a thorough good sort."

"For the second time," she observed with a smile.

"The way he made a point of stopping to speak to me makes it worth emphasising," Denham said with some warmth. "After the inquest, I mean. You remember the attitude most people showed at the concert the night before last, when you were so perfectly wonderful over it."

"I wasn't," she dissented, smiling in a different way. "I could see how you felt about it, and that was all."

"But it was wonderful, my dear, all the same," he insisted.

"And you're 'Hugh' to her, and she's 'Vere' to you," Marguerite reflected aloud. "I'm a very jealous person, Hugh, as you see."

"Darling, it was all before I realised there was any chance of your ever caring for me," he protested. "Almost before I knew you."

"What was?" she asked. "Was there anything, then—anything more than the casual use of each other's first names?"

"Nothing—nothing definite," he answered, rather awkwardly. "She and I were together a good deal—just good friends. I—I liked her more than most girls, and we got on well together. That's all."

"It was not all for her," Marguerite said gravely. "It is not all now, on her side. And if it had not been for me—"

"My dear, no other girl exists for me, now I know you care," he interrupted. "It was Langton himself to-day—the way he showed me he cared nothing for scandalmongers and what they might say, but believed in me as you do. For that, I was glad they stopped as they did."

"I'm so sorry anyone should think ill of you, my dear."

"Oh, it's nothing." He tried to speak as if it were indeed nothing to him. "Besides, they'll all kick themselves once the man who killed Carter is caught, and it's proved I knew nothing about him."

"Except for what you saw, and held back from saying you saw for my sake," she reminded him. "But do you think they will get the man?"

"I don't need to think," he answered with conviction. "Perhaps you remember the Forrest case. Not a sign or sound for months after the murder, apparently no clue of any kind, and then suddenly Head—much as I dislike him now, I've got to own he's almost unbelievably clever at his work—suddenly he arrests Forrest and produces an unshakable case against the man. Oh, they'll get this one, too!"

"But the two cases are utterly different," she urged. "There was definite motive for Forrest to wish to kill Nevile."

"You'll find Head will go on ferreting, and eventually discover who had a definite motive to kill Carter," Denham asserted. "He's got his nose down to it, and he'll miss nothing. Patient work, apparently to no purpose and even foolish, as his trying to get something out of me is foolish, but in the end he'll get on the scent, track his man down, and produce just such a complete case as he did against Forrest."

She thought over it in silence for awhile, her face averted from him as she gazed down at the tops of the pines before and beneath them. Then she faced about abruptly and took his aim with a smile.

"Don't you begin to feel like tea?" she asked. "I do, I know."

He followed her to the car and seated himself beside her. The constraint induced by their encounter with the Langtons had quite worn off, but still Marguerite appeared withdrawn into herself, thoughtful and a little apart from him. He remembered and resented Vere's attitude, and especially the almost possessive quality in her parting words to him. Adela was right—Marguerite should consent to a formal announcement of her engagement to him. But he did not like to approach the subject until she was in a different mood from this.

She started the engine and engaged the gear. Beyond the widened portion of the road the steep slope took them down toward Carden with swiftly increasing momentum, but Marguerite touched neither brake-lever. They shot down the curve, swayed to the right-hand, outer edge of the road, and for seconds Denham held his breath, since it appeared that they must crash on the railings and perhaps go down to death among the pines below. Marguerite held the wheel with apparent placidity, swung them back to their own side of the road, and turned her head to glance at him with a smile as they faced straight descent to Carden village.

"Will you still say you're content for me to drive you?" she asked.

"I almost thought we were gone, then," he answered. "But you know your car, of course, and what it will do. I wouldn't have risked that curve at anything near the speed in mine."

"And if we had gone?" she asked. "At least we should have gone together. And Westingborough would have had something else to talk about. I won't do it again, Hugh, I promise. It was a silly freak."

A freak, he knew, that had taken him as near death as he had ever been. There was some perversity about her to-day, some strangeness of mood not altogether due to Vere Langton's appearance, for he had sensed it when she started and drove out from Panlyon Avenue, spinning the car round the corner and then pushing it nearly to the limit of its speed. Now he saw her hands steady on the wheel, and her face turned to the road before them in purposeful, immobile gravity—this was a new Marguerite to him, one he could not yet understand. So, without speaking again, they came to the

Carden Arms, and presently faced each other with a tea-table between them. Marguerite poured and gave him his tea, and then poured her own and set the cup beside her plate.

"Hugh, dear, I want you to promise to do something for me," she asked. "To promise, I mean, before I tell you what it is."

"Anything in my power, darling," he answered.

She shook her head. "It is in your power," she said. "I want you to make it an unreserved promise before I tell you."

"Very well, then, I promise. It sounds terribly mysterious."

"A definite promise—that's what I wanted. Now you remember when we were coming down the hill, and you thought for a moment we might crash through the railings and be killed?"

"I didn't actually think it," he protested. "There was just the apparent possibility for the moment, but I've got more confidence in you and your driving to think you'd wreck us like that."

"But there was the possibility?" she insisted.

"A very small one," he hedged. "But what has that to do with this promise you've wrung out of me? Not to grab the steering-wheel if I get really scared, no matter what you seem to be doing?"

"Not that." She did not smile as she answered. "Just that—the ordinary chances of life. If I were driving alone, say, and some accident made an end of me, as it might any day—"

"Marguerite, for heaven's sake don't talk like that!" he exclaimed.

"But I want to talk like that, just for a minute or so, Hugh. And it might happen to me as well as to anyone—do be sensible about it, dear! I'm not being morbid, only practical for just this once."

"Well?" he asked doubtfully, reluctant to pursue the subject.

"In that case, and if there were no me, I want you to go back to Vere Langton. Not at once, of course, but after you'd—"

"Marguerite, darling, what are you talking about?" he interrupted again. "Even if Vere would want me back, which I very much doubt, I should never look at her or anyone else if I lost you now."

She smiled then. "I have no doubt that she would want you back," she said. "And when you say never, you overlook the fact that you have forty or fifty more years of life before you, and it would be a very evil thing if the loss of me doomed you to spend all those years alone. It would be unnatural, for such a man as you. No, don't tell me I'm silly, Hugh—I'm providing against a very remote possibility, no more. In reality, I want a very happy life with you—it will be happier than any I've known, so far, and I asked that promise only in the event of fate robbing me of it. Such fate as might come to anyone, I mean."

"I wish you wouldn't talk like that, dear," he urged.

"I won't, any more. I merely wanted that promise," she explained.

"Which, to me, seems the limit of absurdity," he said complainingly.

She smiled again. "Quite possibly," she said, "but you gave it—"

"Marguerite!" A sudden thought caused the interruption. "That first evening—you told me then you were foresighted sometimes. Is this—your asking this promise—because of that?"

"It may be, just a little," she admitted. "And perhaps not foresight at all, but merely seeing how she realised she had lost you, and all it meant to her. I know, Hugh, I know you're all mine while I live, and all that it means to me, and I'm not too jealous to feel what her loss must be. She knew you first, cared for you before I knew you."

"And will forget me while you still love me, I hope," he completed. "Well, I've made the futile promise in the event of an impossible contingency—there's a limit, even, to the cruelty of fate. Now let's be our natural selves, darling, and let me see you as happy as you make me by merely being here. Three days ago I should have said that sitting here alone with you was an impossibility—and yet here we are!"

* * * * *

The sergeant on duty in the charge-room at Westingborough police station grunted with disgust as Sergeant Wells and Constable Borrow entered, escorting a burly, filthy, ragged specimen of humanity whom they jerked to a standstill before the desk at which the other sergeant sat. Since the daylight was beginning to fall, he reached out and switched on the light beside his desk, and then drew forward a form, took up a pen, and lifted the lid of an ink-well before him.

"Usual charge, eh?" he suggested wearily.

"And using obscene language this time," Wells confirmed him.

He wrote, without querying the object of his entries on the form, and read aloud the particulars as he wrote—

"Erastus Donnithorne—aged forty-one—no fixed place of abode—no occupation—soliciting alms—using obscene language—where was it this time, Herbert? Market Street as usual?"

"No, Thorpe Place. Time, four-forty P.M. Constable Borrow, me, and a Miss Jane Tempest of nine, Thorpe Place, as witnesses. Miss Tempest is a permanent cripple, it appears, and Rastus begged of her as she was being wheeled along in her bath-chair. Borrow and I both heard what he said to her after pestering her to give him something."

"Oho!" The charge-room sergeant looked up from his writing. "And she'll come forward to give evidence?"

"Willingly," Wells answered, "but she'll have to be wheeled into court. She's totally unable to walk."

"Gosh, that's good! Our friend goes up for a good stretch this time. He might be very nearly clean when he comes out."

"Ye're a lot o' plurry liars," Erastus growled.

The charge-room sergeant, taking no more heed of the remark than did the other two auditors, finished filling in his form. Then he read out the charge to the accused man, and ended with the usual caution.

"Ye're a lot o' plurry liars," Erastus declared again.

The charge-room sergeant yawned. "Now, I suppose, we take the usual inventory before locking him away for the night. I know all the items pretty much by heart—clasp-knife, clay pipe with broken stem, quantity of tobacco in paper, and all the rest of the shoot. Why the hell can't you work like other people, man?"

"Don' wanna work," Erastus stated defiantly. "You sen' me up, they gotta keep me, ain't they? Only silly bastards what work."

"Here, you mind how you talk, or I'll put another charge against you on this sheet!" the sergeant warned him.

He made no resistance when they began emptying his pockets, having got used to the routine of police stations and magistrates' courts long since—this would constitute his eighteenth appearance on a charge of begging in Westingborough, and other towns knew and suffered from his presence as did this. Wells called out each item discovered as he took it from his man, and the charge-room sergeant whistled softly when "Two pounds one shilling in silver, and nine pennies" was announced.

"No," he said, "of course he won't work. Making a general nuisance of himself pays better. Gosh, there are some fools in the world!"

"And that's the lot," Wells said, when the last pocket had been explored. "Now, Rastus, go over there and sit down on that form against the wall, and hold up your feet one at a time so I can see the soles."

" 'Ere, this ain't reg'lar!" Erastus protested.

"Never you mind whether it's regular or no. Go and sit down on that form—do as you're told, and don't make trouble over it!"

"But it ain't reg'lar!" Erastus insisted. "I ain't never been made to do that before. I sh'll make a complaint, thass' what I'll do. You gotta treat me reg'lar— 'Ee-ee-ere!" Wells had taken him none too gently by his ear, and was impelling him toward the form. "Wotcher reckon you are? Orright, sargint, I'll go quiet. I'll set down there."

Wells let him complete the journey alone, and he seated himself, facing the uniformed trio. "Now wotcher want?" he asked sullenly.

"Lift your feet so I can see the soles, one at a time," Wells ordered. "Right foot first. Come on—up with it!"

Placing his hands under his right leg just above the knee, Erastus elevated his foot until the sole of his boot was almost vertical. Wells took a brief initial glance, and then knelt for a fuller scrutiny.

"Kee-hee!" Erastus chuckled. "Kee-hee-hee! Fust time a copper ever went down on his knees to me. Ye'll wanna kiss me next."

Wells took no heed—it was possible, even, that he did not hear the words, so absorbed was he in his examination of the boot-sole. Eventually he signed to Erastus to lower his foot. "Put that down and let me have a look at the other one," he bade. "Lift the left foot."

Erastus complied, with a pretence of frightened haste and a grin that displayed fangs as grimed and ugly as his face. Wells gave this sole a far briefer examination than its fellow, and stood up.

"Found 'em," he announced. "We'll take him straight in to the supe, Borrow, before we lock him away. And I'm prepared to bet it'll be the first time in his life he's ever been any use to anyone."

But Erastus, overhearing the proposal, instantly objected that it was not reg'lar. He had a definite antipathy toward Superintendent Wadden, who had a virulent tongue and—in Erastus's opinion—gimlet eyes that bored into you and let light in on your soul, Wadden was, possibly, the one man who could make this useless derelict ashamed of himself, and so the plea of irregularity was advanced again.

But all in vain. Wells and Borrow administered the police grip, and marched their cringing, whining victim to Wadden's room, where Wells knocked and was bidden enter. They propelled Erastus into the room, and brought him to a standstill in front of Wadden's desk.

"He's wearing the boots we're looking for, superintendent," Wells stated in explanation of their presence. "We took him up on the usual charge, with obscene language added, at four-forty P.M. to-day."

"With boots, eh?" Wadden observed, and pushed back his chair a little. He gave Erastus a fierce stare. "Take those boots off, Donnithorne, at once," he ordered in a totally different voice.

"Bu-but—it ain't reg'lar, Mr. Wadden," Erastus whined.

"TAKE—THOSE—BOOTS—OFF!" Wadden repeated, and the windows rattled. "COME ALONG NOW! AT ONCE!"

Erastus went down on one knee, and then changed to the other, and stood up again, displaying his feet as wrapped round with bits of dirty rag in lieu of socks. Sergeant Wells took a boot between each finger and thumb, gingerly, and laid them on their sides at the end of the superintendent's desk, so that the soles were plainly visible.

"Yes," Wadden said, "we don't even need to look at the photos. It's the pair, past question. Now, Donnithorne, where did you get those boots? Come on, now, and tell the truth about it."

"I come by 'em honest enough," the hobo whined.

"I'm not asking you how you came by them, but where you got them," Wadden said sharply. "Where did you get them?"

"I 'ad 'em so long, I fergit," Erastus lied.

Wadden stood up and put his hands in his pockets. Then he came round to the front of the desk and stood gazing at Erastus, and his eyes were far more than mere gimlets. They were more like pneumatic drills.

"You have not had those boots three days, you lying swine," he said with quiet, deadly incisiveness. "Do you know we can twist your arms till you howl like a dog, and not leave a mark on you, if you keep on at this lying? Now, you stinking piece of useless carrion, where did you get those boots? Who gave them to you?"

"I foun' 'em, Mr. Wadden."

"You . . . Here, Wells, give him a taste of what we can—"

"Oh, Mr. Wadden, I take me dyin' oath I foun' 'em! Day afore yistiddy—day arter the murder, it was. Take me dyin' oath!"

"All right, Wells." The sergeant had no more than taken Erastus gently by the wrist, but possibly it was the gentleness that frightened the man. "Where did you find the boots, Donnithorne?"

"Take me dyin' oath, Mr. Wadden, I foun' 'em up that road goin' off London Road, day afore yistiddy. It's the Gord's truth, Mr. Wadden, I did. That road—the las' one afore you come to the bridge——"

"Treherne Road? Is that the one you mean?"

"Thass' the one, Mr. Wadden. My las' pair—one o' the soles fell right off. The's a piece o' buildin' land nigh the end o' Treherne Road as you go in from London Road, wi' lots o' old tin cans an' things on it, an' I see these boots there. So I got through the railin's an' got 'em, an' they was a fit, so I jes' took 'em an' lef' the others there. Take me dyin' oath it's the truth, Mr. Wadden, I will."

Wadden blew at him, so fiercely that he recoiled, startled.

"Put him away, Wells, and get him another pair of boots—take it out of petty cash, and buy him a pair. He'll get a long stretch with the obscene language thrown in, so he'll be handy as a witness. There's no doubt this is the pair we want, and Treherne Road comes into it again. Tell Mr. Head I want to see him as soon as he comes in."

They marched Erastus to his cell. As he went, he protested that new boots were useless to him. They spoilt his trade, and were not reg'lar. Might as well give him wings and a harp, right off.

"You're not likely to get near anything of that sort," Wells said with conviction. "A fire-shovel's more in your line."

* * * * *

When, after passing the crest of Condor Hill on the return journey that night, Marguerite drew the coupé in to the side of the road and switched off the headlights alter stopping the engine, she sat with Denham in the black, still darkness of starless winter night. Far beneath them the lights of Westingborough showed, and a yellow snake crawled along under the opposite line of hills—a late train going Londonward, so distant from where they sat at gaze that no sound of its passing came up to them. Denham put his arm round the girl and drew her close to him. Her mood of separateness had vanished before they went back to dinner at the Carden Arms after a drive through the woods, and now they were very quietly happy together.

"Most of the little people down there are asleep, now," Marguerite said. "Isn't life full of compulsions? Why must we go back?"

"Very soon," Denham answered, "I hope we shall be glad to go back."

"And then to go again—together," she reflected. "Hugh, we'll go south, don't you think? Capri, perhaps—south to the warmth, and the singing peasants, and olive trees on the hills. You and I."

"Anywhere, with you," he assented. "It must be quite half an hour since I kissed you, and as you say, we've got to go back."

There was an interval in which he remedied the omission.

"I feel, now—you remember that promise I got you to make," she said later. "I feel now—to-night—that no harm can come near us. I'm already so much a part of you that my own identity seems small to me, and I don't want to keep it, Hugh. I want my life to be yours, my will and desires yours, so that the Marguerite who was before you found me ceases to exist. Can you understand that, dear?"

"Not quite," he said slowly, "but—it's your identity I know and love. And if you lose it entirely—don't you see—?" He paused.

"Ah, not this identity you know! The one it rose from at your touch—the one that was before you held out your arms to me and made me own I love you. It's vanishing fast, Hugh, leaving just your Marguerite, glad of you and glad she is yours. . . ."

* * * * *

"Oh, Hugh! Look at the clock! We're lost and abandoned people for evermore! What will Westingborough say of us?"

"What it damned well likes," he answered grimly. "You here with me are worth more than all Westingborough, darling."

"But we must go back." She released the handbrake and, as the car began to travel downhill, engaged top gear and released the clutch. The engine picked up, and she switched on the headlights again. "Adela will wonder what has happened to you."

"Adela will be comfortably asleep by the time I get in," he dissented. "Besides, I shall be very little later than I was last night."

"And to-morrow?" she asked. "When shall I see you?"

"Supposing I come to tea? Between half-past three and four."

"Yes, I shall be waiting for you."

"And stay to dinner, as I did last night?"

"Yes, or we could go out again, if the weather is still good."

"No, I know!" he said. "I'll come along to tea, and then take you back to dinner with us. Leigh will be coming along to take Adela out after dinner, I happen to know, and then you and I can have the evening to ourselves till he fetches her back. And that won't be too early, by my past experiences of them. No earlier than this, in fact."

"Then we'll do that. Oh, Hugh, I am so happy, to-night!"

"You shouldn't tell me things like that while you're driving," he warned her. "If you do, it may land the car in a hedge, yet."

She laughed. "Wait till we get home," she suggested.

When they reached her home, she drove the car straight into the garage beside the house, and after Denham had closed the doors for her he followed her into the darkness of the entrance-hall to bid her good night. Since they were so late, the good night took no more than twenty minutes, and then he turned to go.

"Half-past three to-morrow, darling. Mrs. Pennefeather hasn't heard me here with you, has she?"

"I don't care if she has. But there's no likelihood of it—she's far too deaf to hear anything downstairs, once she's gone up to bed. Good night, my own man—good night."

When he had gone, she switched on the light in her front sitting-room and entered. She lighted the gas-stove, drew her writing-desk over toward its warmth, and, instead of going to bed, sat down to write.

CHAPTER XVI

NOT SO CLEVER

SOME TWO HOURS before Erastus placed himself within reach of the law for the eighteenth time in Westingborough Magna—to give the town its full and original title—Inspector Head set out for Westingborough Parva, where Tom Mullins, husband of Martha Mullins, had inflicted such grave injuries on his wife that she was now in the Westingborough hospital. Martha was licensee of the Dewdrop Inn at Westingborough Parva, and Tom ran the village wheelwright's shop attached to the inn premises: his mentality may be estimated from the fact that the hoary pun embodied in the name of the inn never failed to afford him amusement—as long as he remained sober, that is.

His treatment of Maria was one of the scandals of the district, but she persistently refused to prosecute him for his cruelty, fearing that such a course might imperil her licence, and also, possibly, having still a kindness for the man, who was a quiet oaf as long as he left the stock behind the bar alone. On this occasion he had not only inflicted on her injuries which involved hospital treatment and might prove permanently disabling, but had also "gone for" a neighbour who had tried to interfere, and had broken the man's arm in his berserk fury.

Such persistent scandal as Tom's conduct provoked was a discredit to the district, and both Head and Wadden decided that, since the man with the broken arm would stand as prosecutor with no persuasion at all, it was their business to obtain for Tom a good, stiff sentence, in the hope that it might bring peace to Martha thenceforth. So Head himself went out to interview the injured man, rather than trust the sergeant in charge on the spot, and returned with a *dossier* of the incident that eventually procured Tom a sentence of six months' hard labour at the quarter sessions, and incidentally made him a total abstainer after he had served his sentence and returned to work. Which goes to prove that the penal system is not always injurious in its effects on offenders.

The incident is relevant to the Carter case only in so far as it took Head out from Westingborough when the old boots were discovered, and went to show that in a normal way his work was many-sided, as was inevitable in a district inhabited by some thirty thousand souls. Erastus Donnithorne had been locked away for the night and left to brood on irregularities when Head returned, made report to Wadden of his afternoon's excursion, and in return received the news of the eighteenth arrest of Erastus and the discovery of the boots. Wadden produced them in evidence, and Head, examining each in turn, eventually put them down and nodded with grave satisfaction.

"Oh, yeah!" Wadden said sourly. "You go on looking happy, by all means! But how much farther does this take us?"

"A long way—a very long way," Head asserted confidently.

"Because Treherne Road comes in again, eh? Is that it?"

"Up to a point, but I don't attach much importance to that. Heaven only knows where our man went after dumping the boots in that vacant plot at the end of Treherne Road. You can go all the way along it and come back on to the London Road the other side of the river, or turn left and get to the Nevile works—and nearly a dozen new roads branch out of it. No, it's an indication that the cyclist and the murderer who wore the boots were connected with each other, and quite probably were one and the same person. But there's more in it than that."

"Well, put it down, man! Weigh it out and let's look at it."

"The inevitable flaw in the plan," Head explained. "Till now, I've been crediting our man with enough cleverness to commit the perfect murder. The only clue we had, the footprints, was left designedly to puzzle us, and even now we're not finally sure that we've got the correct solution to that puzzle. Till Rastus walked in here with these boots, there was absolutely no flaw in the planning and execution of the murder. We had nothing at all to go on."

"And what the hell have we got now?" Wadden growled.

"The fact that the planning was not perfect," Head answered. "Whoever was fool enough to dump those boots in that building-plot is not the genius in crime I've been thinking him. It's a bad, bad slip, from his point of view—it narrows the location from which he set out, fixes it as somewhere beyond that building-plot, going away from London Road. If he'd maintained the care with which he began, he'd have kept those boots, taken them home and hidden them safely, instead of linking himself up with the bicycle that Borrow saw going into Treherne Road less than an hour before Carter was shot. He's made one bad break, and now we can hope to find others. I hadn't that hope, before."

"Actually, though, you're no nearer finding him," Wadden objected.

"I feel myself a very long way nearer finding him," Head dissented. "I don't know if you realise, chief, that Mortimer's house is very nearly opposite that building-plot. That is to say, he's only got to cross the road and pass the house on the corner of Treherne Road."

"But you've acquitted Mortimer, I thought," Wadden said.

"Of the crime itself—yes. Of climbing trees—yes. But not of knowledge of the criminal's identity. Possibly, even, of sheltering the criminal till he could get clear. I've had one talk with Mortimer, chief, and he's a very dark horse indeed—considerably darker than friend Denham. Whatever Denham knows, he's entirely innocent of active or willing complicity—I feel sure of that. But Mortimer's different. I'd put nothing past a man like him."

"Even the murder itself?" Wadden inquired doubtfully.

"No, I wouldn't put that past him, but I do say he's physically incapable of the exertion it involved. We're as certain as we can be that the man who swung himself up into the ash tree was the one who committed the murder, and Mortimer couldn't swing himself up into a tree and change to another branch as the man we want did. More conclusive still, the paces in the snow averaged twenty-nine and a half inches coming away from the Grange, back toward the kissing-gate. Mortimer couldn't take paces of that length, a fat little man with short legs like his—he's long-bodied and short-legged, and simply could not take paces of that length over the distance. My normal pace is about thirty-two, and I doubt if his is more than twenty-seven. His little legs twinkle as he walks—twenty-six to twenty-seven is his average."

"And still you suspect him?"

"Of complicity—yes. I don't know what sort of complicity—I don't know where he comes in, or why. His liking for Lilian Perry, and Carter's little amour with her sister—Lilian getting all het up about it and— Oh, search me! That side of it is all dark, so far. But I don't acquit Mortimer of knowledge that I want for the case."

"Well, what are you going to do about it?" Wadden demanded.

"I'm going to tackle him once more, and I think I'll make it to-morrow morning. But before that, I've got another detail to settle."

The detail in question caused Hugh Denham some surprise next morning. For, as he looked out of his bedroom window after shaving, Denham saw two uniformed policemen and Inspector Head standing on the sidewalk outside the railings that guarded a vacant building-plot near the end of the road. In the plot itself, Denham saw, a very shady-looking individual stood and pointed to the ground at his feet. Presently he returned to the railings, crawled through, and yielded himself up to the escort of the two uniformed men, who marched him away. But Head remained, and presently went through the railings to the spot on which the disreputable one had stood, and appeared to cogitate. Then Denham went on with his dressing, and reflected disgustedly that the inspector's brain must be softening. He would be climbing telegraph-poles, next, or setting men to climb them while he took notes.

But Head was not wasting time, either for himself or for the men he brought with him to the building-plot. Very early that morning he had visited Rastus in his cell, had a talk with him, and convinced him that there was no third-degree motive in the visit by commanding for him an excellent breakfast of eggs and bacon and coffee. Thus fortified, Rastus was quite willing to set out under escort, and to point out the exact spot at which he had found the boots.

"You're quite sure that's where they were lying before you picked them up?" Head inquired. "I want you to be absolutely certain of it."

"Sure I am, Mr. Head. Dead sure. Thass' where they was, an' there's the same old bully-beef tin—they was jus' on touchin' it, before I took 'em in me 'and. Laces was tied together—good laces, they was."

They had still been good laces when Head had examined the boots in Wadden's office—abnormally good laces for such disreputable boots.

"And you left your old boots here, you say?" Head asked.

"Lef' 'em just down there, Mr. Head." Erastus pointed downward again. "I dunno where they're gorn—I don' see anybody wantin' them."

Head knew where they had gone, and silently cursed the enthusiasm of the Wolves and Red Rovers, Westingborough's two troops of boy scouts. It was not worth while, he decided, to go over the heap of old boots in the yard of the police station, to check up on Rastus's story. The story itself was both circumstantial and credible.

"Right you are," he said. "Now take that bully-beef tin, and put it down on the exact spot where the boots were lying when you found them. Make it as exact as you can, and then come back here."

Rastus moved the tin a few inches with judicial deliberation. "Jes' 'longside that there thistle," he announced. "I r'member that there thistle, 'cos I got a spike off'n it in me wrist. Thass' where."

He returned to the sidewalk, and his escort marched him back to his cell at Head's order. Then Head climbed through the railings, and paced carefully to the spot where the empty bully-beef tin lay. He paced back to the railings, and then back again to the tin, and stood there cogitating, gazing toward the road.

Eventually he went back to the railings and gained the road again. He looked back at the tin, thoughtfully, as if calculating. He shook his head in a doubtful way and, reaching through the railings, picked up a derelict brick which lay just inside. He broke it in half on the top of a post, took a piece of string from his pocket, and tied the two halves of the brick to each other with about a foot of loose string between them. Then, disregarding the absorbed interest of an errand boy who watched him from the other side of the road, he threw the two pieces of brick into the building-plot, swinging them by the string. They landed just two feet beyond the bully-beef tin.

Head went into the plot, retrieved the bricks, and returned to the sidewalk. He backed a dozen paces away from the spot at which both he and Rastus had got through the railings, and then went forward at a steady pace. As he walked, swinging the halves of brick by the string, he swung them over the railings again, aiming for the bully-beef tin. They landed a good four feet beyond it this time.

He climbed through the railings again, untied the pieces of brick, and put the string back in his pocket: a piece of string was always useful. For awhile he stood there, gazing at the railings.

"Impetus of the walk lengthens the throw. With a normal pace of twenty-eight inches, he was a smaller and shorter man than I am, so he'd make that much shorter throw. Yes. Not a woman, almost certainly, or else an abnormal one. The ordinary woman wouldn't throw that distance. No, a smallish man, with unusually small feet. And so we come back to Peter Vesci again, whether we like it or no."

He regained the sidewalk and went thoughtfully back to Market Street by way of London Road: it was too early, as yet, to call on Mortimer, as the down-drawn blinds of the white house's upper story showed. He went home to breakfast, and his wife told him she hoped Superintendent Wadden would hurry up and retire, for then she might know when to expect him to meals. He would be able to do as he liked, then, but this being sent here and there at all hours, and his coming in late nearly every day, or not coming in at all after she'd kept meals waiting till they were spoilt, was a perfect nuisance.

"It must be," he agreed calmly, and moved his egg-cup to the far side of the table. "Emily, my dear, that egg wants air—lots of air. I think you'd better turn it on its face and move its arms up and down a few times. It might run right out into the dustbin, then."

"Oh, Jerry, I am so sorry! I'll skin that dairyman!"

"Make him smell the egg—that'll reform him. Now if I whistled hard, do you think that bit of cold gammon would walk out of the larder and sit quiet under the carving-knife? Because I've been heaving bricks about, and knocked down a healthy appetite and brought it home."

She hastened to produce the gammon, and dropped a kiss on the top of his head before he carved himself a substantial slice.

"Jerry, you're a trial, but I wouldn't be without you for worlds," she told him. "And I do like to see you make a good breakfast—it's a lining for the day, and I know you have to work hard."

* * * * *

Simpson, the pressman who had followed Inspector Head as far as the kissing-gate in Maggs Lane the day before, was standing in the doorway of the Duke of York as Head returned along Market Street after his late breakfast, and he came out to the street to waylay this possible source of information, having been told by telephone that morning that he must Buck Up and Get Something, or else come back to headquarters.

" 'Morning, Mr. Head. How's the case going?" he inquired eagerly.

"Quietly," Head answered with profound distaste. "I've had a look at what you made of the little bit I told you yesterday, and I assure you it's going very quietly. In fact, not another word."

"I didn't say anything more than you told me," Simpson protested.

"Oh, no! But anyone reading that would think I put my arm round your neck and whispered in your ear till you rattled with concealed facts. I'm a simple country josh, Mr. Simpson, not a smart alec, and I don't know a thing. Neither will you, as far as I'm concerned."

"I'm very sorry, Mr. Head. I've got to send something every day."

"Send yourself, then, carriage paid and delivered free to consignee. And for heaven's sake make sure he doesn't refuse the consignment! I love solitude, Mr. Simpson—I'm never happier than when I'm by myself in these rural wilds. Nice weather, isn't it? Good morning."

He turned away just in time to encounter John Langton, who had handed over his horse and was about to enter the Duke of York—there was a meet of the Westingborough hounds that day, and Langton, being early, anticipated a preliminary meet in the hotel smoking-room.

"Ah, Head! Grand day for the hounds, isn't it? Have you got a moment to spare? I thought I might see something of you, some time."

"Why, certainly, Mr. Langton," Head assented, rather puzzled at the request. He could not think of anything over which Langton might wish to see him, and almost stood to attention for a moment or more.

"Come inside," Langton invited. "It's not too early to see the inside of the smoking-room. That is, unless you're busy."

"Not too busy, sir," Head assured him, and followed him into the hotel smoking-room. There Langton ascertained the nature of the refreshment Head favoured at such an early hour—a very innocuous beverage—and gave his order to Little Nell, the six-foot Hebe of the establishment, who presently executed the order and retired.

"I'm surprised at you, Head," Langton informed him, after Little Nell had left them alone, and Simpson, entering in an aimless way, had observed them together and wandered out again.

"A lot of people are, often," Head assured him, with a smile. "Not that I make a habit of surprises, but it just happens."

"But this is an unpleasant surprise," Langton pointed out.

Head smiled almost indulgently. "Now, Mr. Langton, you're a lawyer," he said. "At least, you've been a barrister. Surely you know the unwisdom of trying to make the other side give away a case before all the facts have come to light! It's an impossibility."

"Once upon a time, Head, I was a parliamentary barrister," Langton told him. "I know nothing about criminal procedure, and don't wish to know anything. But having got hold of you, I do want to know why you instigated this hounding of a very good fellow I happen to be acquainted with—a man I feel certain is no more connected with Carter's death than I am. I'm speaking quite plainly to you over it, and you know what I'm talking about, so don't smile and look mysterious, for it doesn't go down with me. What is the idea?"

"Hounding, Mr. Langton?" Head caught at the word and echoed it with an appearance of surprised innocence. "I'm perfectly certain we have not exceeded our duty in any way, in any connection."

"Oh, don't be a damned fool, Head!" Langton retorted impatiently. "You know quite well I'm not talking to you now as a police inspector, but as one man to another—we know you're considerably more than a mere officer, and I'm crediting you with the intelligence I know you possess. And you've made young Denham a suspect, acting through the coroner at the inquest. It's no use denying it."

"I'm afraid I cannot discuss this with you, Mr. Langton," Head said stiffly. "I may not be in uniform, but I am no less on duty."

"Well, forget you're on duty for the moment," Langton invited. "Forget the difference in our positions—I'm really interested, though there's no reason why I should be since yesterday afternoon. But I feel I ought to tell you—since the inquest there's been a feeling steadily growing against young Denham, and you're responsible for it! You can't talk to one of the blasted gossip-mongers in the town without realising that Denham's regarded as having something to do with Carter's death. Between ourselves, Head, do you think he had?"

Head paused long before replying. The man before him, he decided, had laced his breakfast pretty liberally—Langton did himself well, if Westingborough rumour were correct in regard to him—and, with a run behind the hounds in prospect, would call for a stirrup cup before he left home. Hence his open defence of a man who had not been definitely accused.

"I do not," he said at last. "Consciously, that is. I think he is incapable of anything of the sort, and would be the last man to shield anyone involved in Carter's death or what led up to it. But—"

"Then why put him under a cloud like this?" Langton interrupted. "I'm talking for Westingborough—I live here, and regard myself as a part of the town. I see a decent man who is also a part of it exposed to what I might call scurrilous gossip—and you instigated it! Don't tell me the coroner's badgering was not instigated by you, because I know it was. If you regard Denham as innocent, why do you do it?"

"We have our own ways of getting at facts, Mr. Langton," Head said. "I want certain facts—I'm still speaking to you as one man to another—and I'm going to get them. I don't suspect Mr. Denham of active complicity any more than you do, and when the case is completed I expect to see him stand clear of it. But I go my own way."

"A damned unpleasant way as far as a friend of mine is concerned," Langton commented with some heat. "Head, I've invited you to talk plainly, on the understanding that what you say is strictly between ourselves, and it appears that I've wasted my breath."

"I'm sorry, Mr. Langton," Head answered. "As a barrister—even as a parliamentary barrister—you ought to know it's quite futile trying to get me to discuss an incomplete case. *Sub judice*, you know."

"I was trying to talk *inter nos*," Langton retorted. "You, apparently, prefer to approach the subject *cum dignitate*. I think we'd better postpone the discussion *sine die*, and regard it as *non est* till you say *resurgam* and regard me as *frater sapiens*. Agreed?"

"*In veritate et in amicitiæ*, if that's not presuming," Head fired back. "I don't mean it to be. I appreciate your interest, Mr. Langton, but I must do my work in my own way."

"Well, good luck to you, Head, and the sooner you remove this suspicion from Denham, the better I shall like you. We're somewhat proud of having a man like you in Westingborough, but Denham's well liked up to now, and I know you can have no real reason to suspect him. Which makes a very good reason for removing suspicion from him. I must go—my daughter is probably waiting outside by this time."

He went out. As he had anticipated, Vere sat her new hunter outside the hotel, and he mounted and went off with her to the meet. Head followed them out from the hotel, and watched them ride away.

"Yes," he said to himself, regarding Vere's trim figure in the saddle, "that's easy. Almost too easy, in fact."

CHAPTER XVII

GONE AWAY!

HUGH DENHAM LOOKED out on the morning and decided that mere office work was altogether out of the question, since hounds would be out to-day. There was a moist, warm wind, veering between south-west and west, and spots of blue showed ever and again behind masses of cloud: it was such a morning as would have heartened Whyte-Melville or John Peel, and made John Jorrocks forget grocery. Denham got into riding-clothes, went downstairs, and telephoned Marguerite. He had first seen her at a meet, and decided that such a day must appeal to her.

"I'll ring up and get a horse," she answered him. "Half-past eleven at the Dewdrop Inn—I should love it, Hugh. Expect to see me there—I'll ring Parbury's stables at once."

"And we can come back for tea together," he suggested.

"Of course! Think of it—a whole day with each other!"

Parbury's, Denham knew, jobbed reliable mounts, and she would be creditably turned out on anything with which they provided her. But he himself always got a horse from Quade, who stabled half a dozen hunters in addition to his string of racing thoroughbreds, and jobbed them to riders whom he knew he could trust with good stock. Denham rang him, and stated that he wanted a horse for the meet.

"Oh, that's easy," Quade answered heartily. "I've got the chestnut you had last time and that bay mare of mine, both doing nothing. Either of them is up to your weight, though you're no feather."

Denham kept back a sharp retort. A week before, he knew, Quade's reply would have been—"Certainly, Mr. Denham," or an equally business-like equivalent. This familiar cordiality was a result of Carter's dinner-party—and it was not the only disagreeable result.

"Either will do, thanks," he said. "Outside my office at eleven or thereabouts, and I'll see it sent back to you."

"Right you are," Quade responded. "I'll see it's there."

Denham hung up and went in to breakfast, fuming at the altered manner of the trainer. Adela gave him an appraising glance.

"So Marguerite has decided to go to the meet," she observed.

"I'm going," Denham retorted, with irritation in his voice. "I'm going to show them I don't care a damn what they think, and give them all the chance they want to cold-shoulder me. And since you're so keen on deduction, Marguerite is going, too. I rang and asked her just now."

"Try a piece of bacon rind," Adela suggested.

"Bacon rind? What on earth has that got to do with hunting?"

"Something to bite on," she explained composedly, "to save you from biting me. I don't know whether you talk to Marguerite as you do to me—in that snappy, growling way, I mean—but love's young dream must be rather like a nightmare if you do. I'm terribly fond of you, Hugh, and I hate to see you in this state of permanent ill-temper."

"I'm sorry," he said contritely. "It's the general cussedness of things just now. Head and his suspicions, the way people either look the other way or sympathise—it all puts my hackles up."

"And your long-suffering sister gets the benefit. Well, have a good day out with the hounds—and finish it with Marguerite, of course—and come down to breakfast to-morrow looking more cheerful."

"To breakfast?" he echoed questioningly.

"I don't expect to see any more of you before breakfast to-morrow," she answered with decision. "You and Marguerite will come back—"

"But I'd arranged for her to come in to dinner to-night," he interrupted. "I know you're going off with Bob after dinner."

"I'm glad you told me," she observed. "If you hadn't, you'd have come in with her and found rissoles for one, since Bob isn't calling for me till after dinner. Now I can go out and buy things for a real meal. Housekeeping is the very devil, and I always think there ought to have been a scene in Dante's Inferno showing a crowd of women planning meals. Sitting on rocks, and trying to think of something new."

"Then don't marry Bob," Denham advised.

"Ah, but there's a deep sympathy between Bob and me. We both like steak and onions. And mushrooms on toast, all buttery."

"Greasy pigs!" Denham ejaculated, with amused aversion for such a diet. "Still, if you're both of one mind about it."

"Oh, I know! You and Marguerite are up in the clouds, now, but you'll both come down to earth with such a heavy thud, one of these days. Bob and I began in just the same state of dreamy bliss—"

"Don't I know it?" Denham interrupted. "Adela, I'm off—must see to things at the office. I'll fetch Marguerite in at about a quarter-past seven, which will give me just time to dress if you make dinner a quarter to eight. Will that suit you?"

"Make it seven, and dinner at seven-thirty," she amended. "Good luck, Hugh—forty minutes without a check, and in at the kill."

He kissed her and went off to his office. Coming out again to the street at eleven o'clock, he mounted the high-withered, long-necked bay Quade had sent for him, and rode along Market Street so absorbed in reflection that he did not see Langton's horse being held for him outside the Duke of York, or Vere Langton coming into the town behind him on the neat little chestnut her father had bought for her the day before. He kept to a walk along Clement Road, past Nevile's Works, and along the valley road leading past Long Ridge to Westingborough Parva. A couple of hundred yards ahead of him, Major Fenwick and another man also rode to the meet at a walk, and Denham, remembering the major's attitude at the concert, had no mind to overtake the pair. He would be in reasonably good time for the meet if he walked the bay the whole three miles to the Dewdrop Inn, and Marguerite was probably behind and might overtake him. If she were on ahead, he could join her before hounds moved off, and in any case they would ride back together.

Hoof-falls at a trot behind him—Marguerite? No, for Langton reined in to a walk on his off side, and Vere, on the grassy strip beside the road, pulled up from a canter, so that he was between the two. A good horsewoman, perfectly at ease on the chestnut, she looked very capably attractive as she gave him a smiling greeting.

"Your first time out this season, isn't it, Denham?" Langton inquired. "I don't remember having seen you before."

"I'm afraid it is," he answered soberly. "I don't get much time."

"Oh, Hugh!" Vere reproved him laughingly. "Why, yesterday—"

But then she broke off suddenly, realising the *faux pas* she had made. Denham tightened his reins and looked straight ahead.

"Yesterday was an exception," he said.

"Well, I'm glad for your sake to-day is an exception, too," Langton remarked. "The going should be very nearly perfect if we get a good run, and it's an ideal day for scent and everything else."

"Adela is not turning out?" Vere half-questioned after a silence.

"Obsessed with housekeeping worries," Denham answered. "She's gone into strict training for her marriage with Leigh."

"He's a very lucky man to get her," Vere asserted. "It's difficult to realise that she's sister to a scatterbrain like you, Hugh."

"The compliment shall be filed for reference," he told her.

Langton reined in close to Denham at the sound of a motor klaxon behind them, and Marguerite's coupé passed them swiftly and almost silently. Vere gave Denham a glance which he did not return.

"Wise girl," Langton observed after a pause; "she's had her mount sent on, and means to pick it up at the meet."

"If she's following hounds to-day," Vere suggested.

"She wouldn't be driving in riding-kit if she were not," Langton pointed out. "Driving in this direction, that is."

"She is following," Denham asserted after a pause.

He felt Vere's gaze, and reluctantly returned it. She was smiling, he saw, but the cost of that smile was beyond his divining.

"It's rather obvious, Hugh," she said, "and now you've made it more so. And Adela's getting married in April. I hope you'll both be very happy, and you can tell her so from me."

"There's—we haven't said anything to anyone," he pointed out.

"No?" She laughed at him. "Out for the afternoon together yesterday, when you get so little time, and both you and she turning out to hounds to-day for the first time this season—and the colour of your face now! I promise not to tell anyone, and I know daddy won't."

He had a glimmering consciousness, then, that she was showing him a gallant acceptance of the inevitable. She appeared almost—but not quite—glad that he had won Marguerite: her expression and tone were very nearly perfect, but there was an unmistakable wistfulness in her appeal to her father for support that did not escape Denham's notice.

"I've nothing to tell, Vere," Langton remarked. "I know nothing."

Since Denham gave him no enlightenment, they rode on in silence to the general assembly outside the inn, and within a minute of their arrival—as Marguerite edged her mount toward where Denham waited near the Langtons—hounds moved off to covert at the edge of the woods behind Long Ridge, and the hunt, forty or more members in all, followed. Major Fenwick ranged himself alongside Marguerite, and since his restive grey took up nearly three-quarters of the narrow lane, Denham had to keep behind the pair. So they came to the covert, and before Denham could manœuvre himself round the outskirts for a word with Marguerite, an old dog fox stole away and the huntsman laid his pack on, while Spot and Fanny and all the rest gave tongue.

"Gone away! Gone away!"

Over rich, close-cropped meadow land and far ahead the red speck showed, hounds straining after it and pouring through and over a quick-set hedge—promise of a run in a thousand. Denham saw Marguerite, a score yards ahead of him and away to his left, go smoothly over, and laid his hands down for the jump. Langton, a little to his right, held straight, and Vere followed him, though the point he aimed to clear was beyond a hollow that made it a risky leap. And, though not three minutes had passed since Reynard stole out, Denham felt all the thrill of the run, prayed there might be no check. He, with Marguerite and the Langtons, formed a little group almost by themselves; fully half the field, knowing the country, had gone crowding through an old gateway some distance off to the right, but if hounds kept straight these four would come in ahead of the rest beyond the next fence, having kept a straight line from the covert.

Over! Denham's bay gathered himself after the leap, but then an iron pressure on his mouth restrained him, for his rider had heard Vere's long, shrill scream, and as he turned his head he saw Langton lying at the foot of the poplar just beyond the hedge, his horse scrambling to its feet, and Vere dragging the chestnut back on to its haunches to dismount. He swung the bay about, and saw Marguerite turn to come back. When he dismounted by the poplar, Vere was kneeling beside her father, bent over him with his head on her arm. She looked up at Denham.

"He—thrown against the tree, Hugh," she said. "He—look—do you think—? Against the tree—the horse came down on his knees—"

One look was enough. Denham knelt beside her, and very gently drew her arm away and let Langton's head fall back, and as he eased it down he felt or fancied he felt the grating of the broken vertebra. He lifted her to her feet and drew her away, and Marguerite dismounted, let her horse go, and came to them.

"My dear," Denham said, "let her—go to her. I'll see to him."

Marguerite took the other girl by the arm, and Vere looked at her.

"Gone away!" she whispered. "Did you hear—gone away!"

Then Marguerite put an arm round her shoulders and led her from sight of Denham and the still figure by which he knelt. Major Fenwick rode up, leading Langton's horse that he had caught.

"My God!" he exclaimed at sight of Langton's queerly twisted neck. "He's dead! How did it happen?"

"Shut up, you fool!" Denham growled fiercely. "Can't you see his daughter there?"

He looked up. Five or six more men were cantering toward the spot, sensing more than an ordinary fall in the field. Fenwick dismounted, and stood holding the two horses beneath the tree.

"I'm sorry, Denham," he said. "It was—I ought not—"

"All right," Denham said. "The inn's nearest, I think. We must get him back there, somehow. That gate, and four of us. Carry him."

"All right—I'll see to the horses—there's plenty of help coming. Denham, leave it all to me. You know her well—get her away. You and Miss West between you—get her away, somehow. Persuade her."

Denham paused to take out his handkerchief and cover Langton's face. Then he rose to his feet and saw the two girls standing at a little distance; Marguerite's arm still encircled Vere's shoulders, and it appeared that she was restraining Vere from looking toward the tree and that which lay beneath it. Two more men dismounted.

"For God's sake get her away before she can come back here, Denham," Fenwick said. "We'll see to all the rest. If she breaks down here—tell Miss West we'll see to everything—"

He broke off. Denham went toward the two girls, and as Vere looked round at him he saw that her face was stonily calm, while Marguerite's was already marked with the tears she could not keep back.

"Vere, we'll take you home." He could think of nothing else to say.

"I think—mother is there," she said, and looked at Marguerite and then again at him. "I knew—quite dead. Before you came, before I could get near him. Daddy—and mother there. She doesn't know."

He took her arm. "Come away, Vere," he urged. "We'll go with you. It's . . . nothing can be done, here. Come away."

Unresisting, Vere went with them across the meadow, and no one of the three spoke till they came to the forecourt of the inn. Then Marguerite turned slightly so that they went toward where her car stood. She opened the door and looked at Denham.

"You can drive it," she said. "It's quite easy. Take her home."

"But—" he said, and paused, gazing at her incredulously. "You—"

"No," she said. "I have no place in it. He was your friend. Hugh, please! Take her home." She turned to Vere. "Will you let him drive you? It is my car, but he can drive it if you let him."

"You—you are very kind to me," Vere said tremulously.

Marguerite took her arm again and urged her to enter the car and seat herself. Denham went round to the off side and took the driving-seat. He started the engine and looked at Marguerite.

"I shall be waiting," she told him. "Somebody will bring my horse back here, and I can ride home. You will find me there."

She stood back from the car, and Denham engaged a gear and turned about. Vere gazed straight before her as they went out into the road.

"Gone away," she said whisperingly. "My daddy—gone away!"

Along the valley road, with the river in sight beyond the hedge that bounded the park land of Long Ridge—less than an hour ago Langton, good man and good friend, had ridden here, hale and cheerful. Denham's thoughts went to Marguerite: to-day, for the second time, she had shown him a rare fineness of character. As, unhesitatingly and without thought of the effect on herself, she had challenged the audience on his behalf in the concert hall, so now she handed Vere over to his care, put them in her own car, and herself stood back, knowing that she had no real part in this tragedy, and that Vere would find some comfort in his presence and help until she reached her home. Not one girl in a hundred, he felt, would have done such a thing, were she placed in Marguerite's position and knew as did Marguerite his relationship with Vere. She was very wonderful, his Marguerite!

He drove on through Westingborough, and idlers marked the fact that it was Miss West's car that Mr. Denham was driving, and that he had Miss Langton with him—an incredible mix-up of personalities and belongings! When they came to the gateway leading from the road to Vere's home, she asked him to stop, instead of driving in.

"I—I'm afraid, Hugh," she said. "It's so terrible—to tell her. To go in such a little while after he kissed her good-bye—"

"Let me break it to her for you," he offered. He would have hated the task, but knew what it would mean to her to undertake it.

"No," she said. "If you did—I didn't tell her we saw you yesterday, and if you did that, she might think—what I let her think once. You bringing me home like this, I mean. I—I didn't think,

Hugh— perhaps I ought not to have said that. But— No, I'll tell her, soon."

He sat silent. That "what I let her think once" had a stabbing quality. He had not dealt fairly by this girl, he knew now.

"Hugh, will they bring him home—back here?"

"Yes, of course they will, Vere! Don't think of it too much."

"But—but she and I will want to bid him goodbye. It's so—and she knows nothing of it! I'll go, but—please tell Miss West she was very sweet to me, and I don't wonder you love her. I'll go, now."

He got out and opened the door to hold it for her, gave her a hand out from the car, and saw how she tried to smile her thanks.

"Good-bye, Hugh. I'll try to tell you how grateful I am to you, some time. Not now. Don't forget to tell Miss West."

He saw her go along the drive toward the house, and, before he turned back to the car, remembered how Langton used to stand on the doorstep as he himself came toward it with Adela on summer afternoons. Again the sense of something missed, some vague, elusive quality of life that had been his and no longer belonged to him, went like driven cloud across his mind. He looked at his watch and saw that it was only just noon: hounds would be called off, of course, and the day's hunt abandoned: red Reynard would steal back to his earth in the covert and lick his chops over his reprieve. Fenwick and the others would take Langton's body to the inn and then go their ways, somebody would realise that he, Denham, had been riding one of Quade's horses, and would take it back to the trainer; he himself would go back to Marguerite as they had planned, and life would go on just as before, except that one good man, having gone away, would ride no more.

Denham got back into Marguerite's car and turned about.

* * * * *

The editor of the *Westingborough Sentinel and District Recorder* scratched the back of his ear with his pencil, and looked at the blank writing-pad on the desk before him. Then he looked at his chief sub-editor, district representative, interviewer, and sports reporter, but that person was busy correcting a proof, and did not look up.

"Our luck's in," said the editor. "A good front-page splash for the special sports edition to-morrow night. Inquest and biography of the deceased—the whole blessed shoot. Hot stuff, us."

"M'yep," grunted the c.s.-e., d.r., i., and s.r. "That is, if Head doesn't rake the Carter murderer in to-morrow and knock the whole bally paper sideways. That's quite a possibility."

The editor, frowning at his pad again, did not reply. Presently he began to write: a leader was distinctly indicated.

"Once more," he wrote, "the hand of calamity has fallen in our midst and with desolating suddenness removed a well-known and respected figure from our ken. Twice within the limits of a week is it our painful duty to record a tragedy, and we may well echo the words of the wisest of kings—" He ceased writing, scratched behind his ear again, and looked up at his quadruple-titled assistant.

"Jones, what's that bit in Ecclesiastes about the mourners going home, or something of the sort?" he inquired.

"Mourners going home?" Jones echoed incredulously.

"You know the bit I mean, surely. Mourners going home, or mourners in the streets. Something like that, I know, but I'm not sure of it."

" 'Man goeth to his long home, and the mourners go about the streets,' " Jones quoted. "Is that the bit you want?"

"That's it—that's the one! I must work it in somehow. Say it over again slowly, so I'm sure I get it right."

Jones, obviously concordance in addition to his other uses to the *Sentinel*, repeated the quotation, and the editor wrote it on his blotting-pad, so that it would be handy for working into the leading article. He might also knock out a poem to go on the leader page, if he could find time: the odd spot of verse, he reflected, always went down well with the wurzel-worriers of the outlying villages; they liked to cut it out and paste it in scrap-books. . . .

CHAPTER XVIII

EXIT PETER VESCI

IN ALL PROBABILITY Horace Marwood, the principal builder in Westingborough, would have been highly indignant had he heard himself described as a side-wind. Such, however, was the term Inspector Head applied to the worthy man, for Head, in reporting to Wadden his discovery that Denham's interest in Ethel Perry was purely professional, and was due to the fact that the Perrys' house would fall on them if it were not underpinned, confessed that he had obtained this information by a side-wind. And Marwood, highly derisive of Pollen's rabbit-hutches and everything else he had thrown together and sold to his clients, was the side-wind in question.

On that, Head nearly—but not quite—ruled out the possibility of complicity between Denham and Ethel Perry, so far as the Carter murder—which he was beginning to call the Carter mystery in his own mind—was concerned. Then he, among others, saw Denham driving Vere Langton through the town in Marguerite West's coupé, and, knowing nothing of Langton's fatal accident at the time, felt that Mormon elders had their prototypes, even in a peaceful district like this. He went in to see Wadden before going home to lunch, and from the superintendent's expression decided that he had brought his problems to a bad market.

"I hoped you'd drop in, Head," Wadden said, regarding him with a severe eye. "The chief constable's been on the 'phone to me, and I'm feeling woeful. I want comfort of the real solid sort."

"It's on order, chief, but I'm out of stock at present," Head responded. "Almost certainly, but not quite, it was a man who chucked those boots into the building-plot in Treherne Road. A woman wouldn't be muscular enough. An average woman, that is, of that size."

"Is that all you've got?" Wadden inquired sourly.

"All I've got so far," Head assented. "I want to hear what Barcelona and Valencia have to say about Peter Vesci, and then I think

I'll go and have another word with this man Mortimer, to see if I can trap him into giving anything away. He's got something to give, I feel sure."

"So have I," Wadden told him grimly. "The cable's in from Spain—but first of all I'll tell you what the chief constable said. He suggests calling in Scotland Yard, says we've got nothing ourselves."

"Let him call in Scotland Yard, by all means," Head retorted acidly. "I'm not in love with the damned case, if he's so impatient with us."

"Well, take it easy, man, and don't blame me. He wanted to know what we've got, and I told him. He said your solution of the boot-tracks was interesting, but not conclusive, as Casey remarked when the half-brick missed him—he didn't mention Casey, but I'm putting him in as an illustration. Then I told him of your Vesci line, and he was dubious, because I couldn't point to a half-baked Dago in the town who might correspond to our vague description of Peter—the cable was still to come in, then, and I've only just finished decoding it, by the way. I told him you had a couple of promising lines you weren't talking about, having the Perry girl and Denham in my mind, and he said he wasn't a newspaper man, and that sort of guff didn't go down with him. Then he told me it was a perfectly plain case. We had the bore of the gun that killed Carter, and knew it was an automatic. We had the footprints, and we were on the spot not much more than two hours after the execution had been carried out—and we hadn't a thing to show for it, after three days to think it over."

"Did you tell him to go to hell?" Head inquired very acidly.

"I thought of my pension, and restrained myself," Wadden confessed. "Head, that man had devilled kidneys for breakfast this morning, and overdid the Worcester sauce on them. He said, if we hadn't anything definite to show for our work by to-morrow, he'd have to think about getting Scotland Yard to send a man down, to see if they had more brains in stock there than we keep here. He was thoroughly nasty."

"And Carter was only buried yesterday," Head observed.

"Quite so—corpses keep well in winter. I can see that man's trouble, though. Those footprints were put there to make it look simple, and you've got to own it does, on the face of it. To go up to a man's door, shoot him down, and walk away—it looks as if we ought to have caught up before now. We haven't. What about it?"

"What about this Spanish cable?" Head asked in reply.

"Yes, that's my second bomb under your feet. I've decoded it, as I told you. From Valencia. Head, Peter Vesci died in Iviza, two years ago last June, so you can put paid to that account. He and his sister Quita were British subjects, and after his death and burial she left and went to Valencia. From there, they lost track of her."

"British subjects—hell and damnation!" Head exclaimed disgustedly. "Yes, call in a Scotland Yard man by all means—my brain's gone to sleep. Chief, we could have got the real life photographs of the pair long ago, from the passport office! And it never occurred to me."

"Kick me, too," Wadden adjured. "Of course we could."

"So she's been gone from sight—Quita, I mean—nearly two years and a half," Head reflected. "Let me see the cable, chief."

Wadden handed it over, and waited while Head scrutinised it and shook his head over it. At last he laid it on the desk.

"So he never recovered," he said thoughtfully.

"He died, if that's what you mean," Wadden assented. "Why?"

"Weeds told me Carter threw a stone inkstand at him, and drove his chest in with it—smashed his ribs in on his lungs, and laid him out so that his sister had to carry him downstairs to the car," Head explained. "The house agent at Twickenham told me she carried him out from the house when they left, and here, a little more than four months later, he dies in Iviza. Lung disease, and hæmorrhage of the lung, given as cause of death. Carter's inkstand drove a broken rib in on his lung and punctured it, and there may have been a weakness there as well. In any case, he didn't get better, but died."

"Sound reasoning, but the premises are obvious," Wadden commented.

"And they mean something," Head assured him gravely. "Peter blamed Carter for Nita's death, and went to kill him in consequence, with a stiletto. Instead of killing Carter, Peter gets knocked out, and in the end dies of the blow—and you've got Quita left, Quita who'd told Carter that the end of the stiletto incident was only reprieve, not final escape. Triplets, chief, don't forget, and she's the only one of the three left alive, an acrobat, one who would have learned quite a lot about rope-throwing from her brother, and is used to handling a pistol, shooting from a trapeze on the stage. And a triplet."

"What you might call a certain amount of consanguinity," Wadden suggested. "Related, in fact. Fairly closely related."

"One of three who have been together from the first hour of their existence," Head asserted very gravely. "The only one left, knowing that Carter is responsible for that, and feeling her loss far more than an ordinary sister would feel it—and add to that the southern mixture in her blood and the consequent instinct to put revenge before every other motive in life. I'm not saying she killed Carter, chief, but I'm feeling far nearer the end of the case now we've finally got rid of Peter Vesci. I haven't been happy about him, till now."

"And still I don't see anything tangible to make you happy," Wadden objected. "You've eliminated Peter, but you've nothing to put in his place—unless you count Quita something. And I don't."

"No, nothing tangible," Head agreed, "but call it an instinct. If I were American, I should probably say I have a hunch. If Scotland Yard must come in it, that's that—after only three days, and I'm pretty certain they can do no more than I'm doing. Which reminds me I'd better go back to London and see if I can get a passport photo of Quita, since she's the only one of the three left alive."

"And a fat lot of use it'll be, judging by the average passport photo," Wadden retorted. "It's nearly four years old for a certainty, and probably it's a flashlight thing that makes her look like a nanny-goat. Why not ring through and get it sent to us?"

"Because I'm going to have another shot at getting a real pho-tograph of her as well," Head explained. "I was in a hurry last time, for one thing, and for another, I was concentrating on Peter rather than on her. I'll find her in some studio or other, you'll see."

"You mean you'll go to-day? If so, you'll be late getting there."

"No, I'll go to-morrow. I want to know, first, what Denham has to do with this Miss West, driving her car—she's rather a dark horse, too, when you come to think of it. Not that she ever had anything to do with a man like Carter—she doesn't run in that class, any more than Miss Langton does. But when I suddenly see him driving Miss Langton in Miss West's car, I want to know something about it?"

"Hold on a bit." Wadden reached for the telephone instrument as he spoke, for the bell had rung. He put the receiver to his ear. "Yes, Wadden speaking," he answered his caller. "Who are you?"

Head, waiting, saw incredulous amazement on the superinten-dent's face. "Yes, where have you taken him?" Wadden asked after listening to a long statement from the other end of the wire.

"The Dewdrop—right, I'll come out myself. I—this is awful! I'm more than sorry, Major Fenwick. Just happened, you say?"

He heard the rest, hung up, and looked at Head with a very grave face. "No, you'd better not go to-day," he said. "Mr. Langton was killed in the hunting-field this morning, a very little while ago. They've taken the body to the Dewdrop Inn, Martha Mullins' place, and, of course, we've got to see about an inquest. Head, Westingborough's getting it hot and heavy—Carter and Langton in one week. And this was a good man—we don't want to lose his sort."

"It accounts for the car, too," Head observed. "He'd take any car to take Miss Langton home. Gosh, chief, this is bad news! But you won't want me on it, I hope, since I heard you say you'd go out yourself. I mustn't lose sight of the case, if I'm to keep Scotland Yard out of it. And only this morning Langton was talking to me—"

He broke off, realising the terrible suddenness of this new tragedy. Langton had been liked and respected by everyone who knew him, and these two men who could regard the death of a man like Carter as no more than a mere case felt this event as a personal affair, a definite loss to the town and to themselves. Wadden stood up.

"I'll have the car out and get along," he said. "You carry on with your job—get on with it in your own way. I'll be back here in an hour. Good Lord! Langton, of all men! And look at the number of second-rate wasters we've got who insist on going on living!"

He put on his uniform cap, hooked up the collar of his tunic, and struggled into the overcoat Head held for him. "Don't you worry about it, man—I'll see to everything," he adjured. "You just take *carte blanche*—Carter *blanche*, I should say—and follow your instinct as far as it leads you toward the Grange murderer. I've got faith in you, and I'd hate to see Scotland Yard called. You carry on."

He unhooked his tunic collar again. "I'm no living skeleton," he observed, "but I believe that collar's shrunk. It can stay undone till I get there, anyhow. I'll be back lunch-time."

He went out. Head followed more slowly, and reached the corner of London Road in time to see Denham returning from the Langtons' home in Marguerite's car. He held up a hand as Denham caught sight of him, and the car drew in to the kerb and stopped. Head went alongside.

"I've just got the news, Mr. Denham," he said. "Of Mr. Langton's death, I mean. There's nothing to be done, I suppose? I heard only the vaguest account—do you know how it happened?"

"Thrown, and killed instantly," Denham answered. "Is that all?"

There was impatient, bitter hostility in the query. Head stood back from the car, and gave him a steady look.

"Practically all, Mr. Denham," he said incisively. "Except that he talked to me before he went out to the meet, and I know you have lost a generous friend. And there isn't a man in Westingborough who won't feel his death as a personal loss. I'm sorry I stopped you."

He turned away before Denham could reply, and went on his way along London Road. Presently Denham passed him in the car, gazing straight ahead as he drove, and knowing that Head had made a friendly gesture in stopping him to inquire with regard to Langton, while he had responded in a way that made him feel himself an ill-conditioned boor. It all arose, of course, out of his own suppression of vital evidence at the inquest on Carter. If he had told all the truth then, confessed to having seen the young man in riding-kit in Panlyon Avenue—the young man who had *not* gone to Marguerite's house!—there would have been none of this suspicion against him, and he would not have had this irritable dislike for the inspector. It was the first time he had ever let himself be tempted from strict truthfulness in a matter of vital import, and he was beginning to find the consequences far from pleasant: he knew perfectly well that Head's suspicion of him was well-founded, and hated himself for it far more than he hated Head.

He drove on, and left the car in the road outside Marguerite's front gate while he went to the door to inquire. Mrs. Pennefeather, conscious after he had rung three times that there was somebody at the door, hurried to open it, and shook her head.

"Miss West is out, sir," she said, before he could question her.

"Not come back yet?" he inquired.

"Beg pardon, sir?" She cupped her hand behind her ear.

"She has not come back yet?" he repeated irritably.

"I didn't quite catch that, sir. She's not in."

He bent toward her and made a speaking-trumpet of his two hands. "I said, she has not come back yet," he shouted at her.

"No, sir. Oh, no, sir! She went to the hunt, sir. I'm sorry, sir, my hearing is not what it was. Is there any message?"

He shook his head. Marguerite would see the car outside, and would know he was at home—in any case, she would know that he would be with her in the afternoon as they had arranged. And getting any message to penetrate to this woman's consciousness meant telling all the surrounding residents: certainly Mrs. Pennefeather's hearing was not what it had been. He shook his head, and formed "No" with his lips.

"I'll tell her you called, sir," Mrs. Pennefeather promised.

He went back to his own home, and Adela met him in the hall-way.

"I saw you in Marguerite's car, Hugh," she said. "There's nothing wrong, is there? Is she all right? Your coming back like this—"

"She's quite all right," he answered. "Probably she rode back to Parbury's with the horse she jobbed from there. Adela, Langton was thrown and his neck broken in the first five minutes of the run."

"Mr. Langton?" She almost whispered it. "Hugh, was Vere there?"

He nodded. "She saw it," he answered. "I took her home in Marguerite's car. That's why I came back here in it."

"Vere? Oh, Hugh, what will she do? They were everything to each other! I—but we can't do anything. And you took her home?"

He nodded. "Marguerite insisted on my taking her, in her car," he answered. "She was—she's just wonderful, Adela. No thought of herself, or even of me. Forgetting everything to help Vere."

"Hugh, I can't—I can't think of Marguerite, over this. Poor Vere, and her mother—and nobody can do anything for them! Only yesterday she asked me to go and see them, said Mr. Langton hadn't seen us for so long, and wondered if we'd forgotten them?"

Denham turned away and went into the dining-room. He had in mind, then, Vere's hopeless tone as she said—"What I let her think, once." In forgetfulness of all but her great loss Vere had made that self-betrayal, and he knew that he himself had given her cause to believe she might have turned to him for comfort in such an hour as this. No, he had not dealt fairly by her: unconsciously, Adela was emphasising the fact, and he felt he did not want to talk about Vere any more.

If Marguerite had let him announce their engagement—or rather, if she had not requested Adela to keep it secret for awhile—none of this situation with regard to Vere need have arisen. For he knew his Westingborough well enough to realise that Adela had only to whisper the tidings to one friend in the course of a morning's shopping, and it would be all over the town by lunch-time. He must persuade Marguerite to let him state openly that he intended to marry her, before any fresh complications arose. It was not that he saw any further difficulties as likely to arise, but between Head, Adela, and Vere, he was in a state of mind in which it appeared that irritations arose in his way persistently and unescapably. If he had told the whole truth at Carter's inquest, he knew, none of this need have been.

There remained yet nearly an hour before lunchtime. It was not worth while to go back to his office, he reflected: if he went, somebody was certain to buttonhole him and inquire as to the circumstances under which Langton had been killed, whether Vere had been there, how much he knew regarding it—the whole petty round of questions that few people refrain from asking in such a case. And he would feel more like swearing than answering civilly; they might make it an excuse to offer sympathy with regard to the treatment that had been accorded him at the inquest on Carter. He had no sooner reached that conclusion than the telephone rang, and he went out into the hall and took off the receiver.

"Mr. Denham? . . . Yes, Mr. Denham. It's Superintendent Wadden speaking, from Westingborough Parva. I want to tell you, from what I can gather, you were present when Mr. Langton was killed this morning, and we shall require you to attend the inquest as a witness. It won't be till to-morrow morning—I find we can't get the coroner over this afternoon. I tried to get you at your office, but you were not there. We shall let you know the time—it will be held at the Dewdrop Inn here, probably at about eleven o'clock to-morrow. This is to save you from making any other appointment for to-morrow morning."

"That's very kind of you, superintendent," Denham answered, in a tone that implied scant appreciation of the kindness.

"Merely that I want to get this through as quickly as I can, and with as little fuss as possible, for the sake of Mrs. and Miss Langton," the superintendent answered. "Medical evidence, identification, and a straight story from you should finish it, and even so it'll be a pretty bad ordeal for Mrs. Langton and her daughter. That's all, Mr. Denham, thank you, as long as we're sure of you to-morrow morning. Good-bye."

Denham hung up. More publicity, more questioning by that supercilious, infernal coroner! And Vere, probably, giving evidence, too, with Westingborough tattlers watching him and her, and hearing that he had been first to join her as she knelt by Langton's body and had taken her home. Marguerite *must* consent to the engagement being announced! This secrecy must not go on.

CHAPTER XIX

SOMETHING UP MORTIMER'S SLEEVE

A DARK-EYED, weatherbeaten gipsy girl gave Head a challenging glance as he pursued his way along London Road after Denham had passed him in Marguerite West's car. She was wearing a pair of men's boots, and, with an apparently heavy sack slung over her shoulder, was striding along as if the burden were nothing at all. Her lifted arm that held the sack, with the sleeve fallen away almost to her shoulder, revealed muscles that would not have disgraced a man. But Head did not even look back after she had passed him.

"The Scotland Yard man can run her in and put her through the hoop," he told himself grimly, "and the rest of the gang with her."

There were quite a number of gipsies in the neighbourhood, he knew. They had a camp on a piece of waste ground beside the old coach road to Carden, and sold baskets, clothes pegs, and other oddments in and about Westingborough, and saved stray chickens the trouble of walking home, and got servant girls to cross their palms with silver, all after the fashion of their kind. Any one of them might have had a grudge against Carter, for all Head knew: a dozen girls like this one might be Quita Vesci. The Scotland Yard man, if he materialised, might set to work on them: he, Head, would go his own way.

Wadden, he knew, was badly upset over the chief constable's suggestion, though he had affected to treat it lightly. They had worked together, superintendent and inspector, for a long time, now, and Wadden, in addition to feeling the suggestion as a reflection on his own acumen, was angry on Head's behalf, felt that in passing on the suggestion he might appear to have lost faith in his own man. And that, as he had been careful to point out, was far from his actual state of mind, though in the three days that had elapsed since the discovery of Carter's body at the Grange Head had produced nothing tangible, in spite of all his inquiries. He had, moreover, no definite line on which to work, apart from this of Quita Vesci, who might never have been near Westingborough in her life.

179

She might be a triplet, and thus more keenly alive than a mere ordinary relative to injuries inflicted on her brother and sister: she might be Spanish in origin, and therefore more passionately revengeful than one of non-Latin parentage—but she was, as Miss Craylaw of Twickenham had pointed out to him, an intelligent, educated person, and thus would have sense enough to know that the commission of such a crime must inevitably lead to her arrest, in view of her brother's attack on Carter and her own words to him at the time. That she would endanger her own life by seeking revenge, even on her sister's seducer and the man she could regard as responsible for her brother's death, was in the last degree unlikely. Yet, apart from her, Head had no man or woman in his mind as suspect: if she had not killed Carter, now that Peter was dead, who had?

The chief constable had reason on his side, Head had to admit. A plain trail had been left to and from the scene of the crime, and the calibre and type of weapon with which it had been committed was virtually beyond dispute—but Head knew he would never recover that weapon, for the one who had committed such a murder would certainly dispose of it, and the Idleburn alone was a safe hiding-place for such a thing. The murderer had been seen certainly once, possibly twice, or else the cyclist in nurse's uniform was an accomplice, if Head's interpretation of the footprints and cycle-track were correct. Almost certainly the wearer of the old boots and the cyclist were one and the same person. And within two hours of Carter's death, the police had been on the spot. Even the old boots worn by the murderer had been traced, and the place where they had been thrown discovered.

Yet, Head had to own, he was unable to say whether the crime had been committed by a man or a woman. He had in mind two men who might be, and in his opinion were, in possession of knowledge bearing on the crime, but he had nothing to justify him in accusing either of them of being in possession of such knowledge. He had warned Denham of the danger of concealing vital information, but without result: strictly speaking, he knew, he had no right to give such a warning; it was tantamount, almost, to an accusation, and procedure forbade him to use any such means to attain his end: he was hedged round by the ultra-humanitarian decrees which protect the criminal at the expense of the general public, and hamper the police at every turn in their work of protecting the law-abiding against the lawless. Already, in his second interview with Denham, he had exceeded his prerogatives, and now he was on his way to repeat the transgression of crime-abetting rules.

He was, as is every successful exponent of business methods, of industrial enterprise, or any other department of activity in which brain is matched against brain, a psychologist, dependent to a certain extent on intuition and measurement of his opponent's limits of resistance, and he went, now, to see if anything more could be learned from Mr. Frank Mortimer, the occupant of the white house near the river. Mortimer was accommodatingly near the spot at which the old boots had been discarded: he was also in easy reach of the Idleburn, into which the automatic pistol might have been thrown after the murder. His manner had already indicated that he knew something: he had been altogether too effusive, too willing to convey information which told nothing, and Head felt that another talk with him, and such a warning as Denham had apparently disregarded, might be productive of results.

So he rang the bell at Kerkmanhurst and for the second time was admitted to the room in which he had interviewed Mortimer two days before. He had time to descry among the photographs with which the walls were decorated a framed print showing the Vesci trio, and to decipher the inscription and signature. They told him—"It's a wow, Frankie! Lord love you. Jimmy." He realised that Weeds had been responsible for the donation of this item, which was merely a reproduction of the one he had seen in Weeds' office, and then he turned to face Mortimer, podgy, watchful, and effusively friendly as he waved his visitor to a chair.

" 'Morning, Mr. Head, 'morning!" Mortimer greeted him. "Do sit down, won't you? What can I do for you this time? I've not been up long—just had breakfast, in fact. It's a pleasure to see you —you'll find that chair quite comfortable. Now count me at your service."

He sat down himself, fiddling with the monocle at the end of his watered-silk ribbon, and fixed the gaze of his beady little eyes on Head as if he would drag from him the reason for this interview. Head, settling himself in the armchair on the other side of the glowing fire, felt that he had a hard proposition in this man. Mortimer would tell what he intended to reveal, and no more. He was watchful already, careful both in manner and phrase. And he knew something.

"Just a general talk about this murder of Carter, Mr. Mortimer," Head said easily. "By the way, I don't know if you know that Mr. Langton was killed in the hunting-field this morning?"

"Another murder?" Mortimer ejaculated, horrified. "Surely not, Mr. Head! In the hunting-field, too—and such a popular man—"

"No, not a murder," Head interjected. "An accident—thrown and his neck broken. Quite an accident. I just mentioned it as news."

"Terrible! Terrible!" Mortimer commented gravely. "I didn't know him personally, but I do know Westingborough is the poorer for the loss of such a. man. Well, in the midst of life—"

He did not complete the quotation, this time, but gazed at his visitor in a way that indicated he expected more than this, as reason for the inspector's second call on him. He exhaled cautious watchfulness.

"But that, of course, has nothing to do with my being here," Head pursued thoughtfully. "Since I last saw you, Mr. Mortimer, I went to London, and among other things had a long talk with a Mr. Weeds, at the Quadrarian theatre. The stage manager there, I understand."

"Ah! Good old Jimmy! One of the very best, Mr. Head. And you learned some facts which might be of assistance to you?"

"Quite a few which might be, and might not," Head replied. "One thing—do you know anything about a Mrs. Bellerby? She was among the people he mentioned to me. I wondered if you knew her."

"Norah Bellerby— Oh, yes! Yes, certainly. Poor old Paul's widow. Married again—let me see! Ah, yes, she married Ted Halloran, the film producer, and I believe they're living down at Harlow now. In any case, Ted's one of our coming men, and she's made a good bargain."

"Did Weeds ever tell you about Carter's final interview with her?" Head inquired, watching his man closely.

Mortimer shook his head. "Not he!" he answered. "What goes on inside those offices is not for any outsider—and as far as they're concerned I'm an outsider. Jimmy's the most loyal soul ever pupped, and he never gave away any of Eddie's private affairs."

Possibly Byrne's presence, or the fact that Weeds might be contributing to the arrest of Carter's slayer, had induced the stage manager to break that rule, Head reflected. In any case, Jimmy had showed no reluctance to giving away all he knew regarding Carter and his private affairs, in spite of this encomium on his loyalty.

"I see. One other small point, Mr. Mortimer." Head made it as small as he could. "I suppose you heard of the Vesci trio, while they were starring under Carter's management—or whatever you call it?

They would be under his management, I conclude, since he engaged them for practically all their appearances on the London stage."

"Heard of 'em, dear boy—I mean Mr. Head?" Mortimer responded with enthusiasm. "I loved 'em, and Eddie simply raved. The most wonderful ever! Thrilling, side-splitting, inimitable—I assure you, there was not a solitary adjective you couldn't splash in the biggest caps on a poster, and know the crowd would endorse it when they saw that act. It was not merely a joy, it was an experience. I'm telling you!"

"All that, were they?" Head asked, with stolid reflectiveness.

"And then some!" Mortimer assured him. "I groan with pain to this day when I remember how that act was broken up. I don't know if you know, though probably you do, that Nita committed suicide down at Twickenham, and left the other two in the air? An awful crime against art, it was—they were *artists*, those three! Real artists! And her death broke the act to pieces—the other two were lost without her."

"Most inconsiderate of her," Head commented, watching Mortimer carefully. There was something behind this enthusiasm, he felt sure.

"Inconsiderate? It was criminally indefensible! To ruin a production like that—I never heard of anything like it!"

"Do you, by any chance, know why she committed suicide?" Head asked.

"Not an idea. There was a rumour that she was in love with Eddie, but he was running May Blumenberg at the time—you remember May—married Lord Grimbury about two years ago, an old devil with no teeth and a glass eye. Eddie was after her when Nita drowned herself, so that's out, and heaven only knows why she did it. But she did—ruined the act, and the other two never came back. They simply vanished."

"Have you any idea where they vanished?" Head inquired gravely.

"Not a smell, dear laddie—not a solitary odour. Eddie cancelled the contract, I happen to know, and there was some talk of possible trouble about it, but Peter and Quita hadn't a leg. Hadn't as much as a big toe, let alone a leg. And I heard that Peter had some lung trouble, so that he had to get out of the country, in any case. They'd made a bit, lived quietly, and didn't burn their money as most artists do, so possibly they could afford to go off while he recuperated, and think up a fresh act. Not that I expect to see them again in anything prominent. Nita's risky little songs, and that marvellously intriguing voice of hers, were half the act. By heck, they got over, that trio! I've never seen anything like it."

"And Nita was the star of the three?"

"Undoubtedly. Un—doubtedly! She was *the* big noise, the voice and the ultra-attractive cat's whisker. Without her, the other two were not merely lost, they were desolated. Annihilated, in fact!"

"I see. Now, off the stage, Mr. Mortimer, did you ever meet them?"

"Meet the Vesci trio?" Mortimer inquired in reply, as if this were an equivalent to asking whether he had ever met a king, or a heavyweight boxer. "Well, I once met Nita, up in Eddie's office, but I never saw either Peter or Quita off the stage. She happened to be there, one day when I walked in on Eddie, and I saw her for a few minutes."

"What was she like?" Head pursued calmly.

"Like? Oh, dark and Spanish-looking. Not in the least what you would expect, after seeing her in her act. I don't know how to describe her. Large eyes, soft eyes— Oh, you know! Typical Spaniard, the appealing type. Charming voice, dark and beautiful, and a trifle obvious. Castanets—no, guitar. That sort, and I don't think I can tell you any more about her. Passion in every line."

"And you never saw either Peter or Quita off the stage?" Head persisted. "It may be important—did you see them?"

"Ah, you've reminded me! I came out from Jimmy's office one night, it would be near on midnight. They'd had a reception from the audience—man, you couldn't hear yourself think while the applause was going on! And they were just going off, Quita driving the car, and Peter sitting alongside her, and Nita all alone in the back. And I went to the car and congratulated the trio, and Nita shook hands with me through the back window, or whatever you call it. That's the only time I ever saw all three of them apart from greasepaint. She was a wonderful child, was Nita. She made the trio."

"And Peter?" Head inquired casually.

"Oh, just an ordinary southerner. Un-English, apart from his speech. You'd think, from the way they all three talked, that there was no foreign blood in any one of them—you couldn't help realising that they were a brother and two sisters, but as far as speech was concerned they were quite English. Peter seemed a nice chap."

"And the other sister, Quita?" Head persisted. He had a sense that Mortimer was growing uneasy under this inquisition regarding the Vesci trio, and felt encouraged in consequence.

"Very much like Nita," Mortimer told him frankly. "As her normal self, that is. You might almost think they were twins, and they may have been, for all I know. Charming girl, by the look of her. Didn't say a word, but just smiled. I hadn't met her before, you see."

"No," Head said gravely, "but have you met her since?"

"I have not seen Quita Vesci from that day to this," Mortimer responded unhesitatingly, as if he had expected the question. "On that night, I saw the three of them together. Since then, I have not seen any one of the three, as I knew them then."

"What do you mean by 'as you knew them then'?" Head demanded quietly.

"I mean, I have not seen any one of the Vesci trio," Mortimer answered. "Why—what could I possibly mean?"

The final query, Head felt, anticipated his next question, and in effect neutralised it. He was dealing with a very clever man, one who had something to conceal, and meant to go on concealing it.

"You have seen nothing of any one of the Vesci trio since that night?" he persisted, watching his man carefully.

"No," Mortimer answered, after a perceptible pause.

The pause lasted too long, far too long for Head to be satisfied with the reply. Yet, short of accusing the man of lying, he had to accept the negative. Obviously, Mortimer was not happy under this inquisition, and was growing unhappier as it proceeded.

"Did you know that Peter Vesci threatened to kill Carter after his sister's suicide?" he asked after a pause.

"Threatened him? Why, no! Why should he?"

The surprise that accompanied the query was apparently genuine. Yet Mortimer fiddled with his monocle ribbon again, uncomfortably.

"Because of his sister's death," Head explained.

"No, it's news to me," Mortimer said slowly. "I remember Jimmy's telling me there was a possibility of their trying to raise trouble when Eddie cancelled the contract after Nita's death, but nothing more."

"You don't know that Peter attacked Carter in his office with a stiletto, and that Carter laid him out with his ribs broken?"

"Good heavens, no! Did he really, though?"

"So Weeds told me, when I went to see him. Now another thing altogether, Mr. Mortimer. Do you remember the Gutteridge murder?"

"I'm afraid I don't. Why—has it anything to do with this?"

"Only indirectly. Two men, Brown and Kennedy, were executed for the murder of Constable Gutteridge, and he was shot very much as Carter has been shot. Only one of those two men could have shot him."

"I'm afraid I don't see the relevancy," Mortimer said.

"Well, take another case, one you probably do remember. The Thompson-Bywaters affair. It was plainly evident that Bywaters committed the murder, and as far as the actual killing was concerned, Edith Thompson was innocent. As far as the act of killing was concerned, that is. Yet she was hanged, as surely as was Bywaters."

"Quite so—yes, quite so. Where is the connection, though?"

"Simply that Edith Thompson was found to be accessory both before and after the fact, and was regarded as equally guilty with Bywaters. She attempted to conceal information bearing on the crime."

Mortimer frowned thoughtfully at the fire. "Still I don't see—are you suggesting that Peter Vesci was accessory to this murder?" he asked after a long pause in which Head watched him intently. "Because if not, I don't see the relevancy of the case to this."

"Aren't you being rather wilfully dense, Mr. Mortimer?" Head demanded sharply, losing patience over this obvious fencing.

Mortimer looked up at him, gave him a cold, prolonged stare. "I think you rather forget yourself, Mr. Head," he said stiffly. "I have placed myself entirely at your service in connection with this affair, and now you appear to entertain some obscure doubt, I might even say you give me the impression that you suspect me. Me! I fear any continuance of this discussion would be futile, under the circumstances."

"I agree with you entirely, Mr. Mortimer." He rose to his feet as he uttered the concurrence, and felt that he wanted to take the little man by his shoulders and shake him until the knowledge he was concealing, whatever it was, rattled out from between his lips. "And, that being so, I'll bid you good morning."

With that he went, and let himself out from the house. A momentary glance back from the road as he turned toward the town showed him Mortimer standing at his window and looking out, and it appeared to Head that the man's chubby, normally expressionless face wore a look of anxiety, as if the warning with regard to the danger of acting as an accessory had sunk well in. Possibly, although the interview had been productive of no immediate result, the time spent over it had not been wasted: Mortimer might yet reveal what he knew, for the sake of his own safety, and Head was convinced, now, that he was concealing something which had a bearing on Carter's death.

He looked in at the police station, and learned that Wadden had not yet returned from Westingborough Parva. Then he put through a trunk call to London, and learned that Inspector Byrne was out, and was not expected back till late in the afternoon. On that, he sat down and wrote a fairly long telegram, stating that the Vescis had been British subjects, and passport photographs would be available. Could Byrne help him by getting in touch with the passport office and obtaining those photographs? He signed the telegram "Jerry," feeling certain that cousin Terry would make the effort on his behalf. And, if he himself went to London by a late afternoon train, he could return with the photographs either by the last train down or by the first one in the morning. He might possibly get a line on the case in that way, something sufficiently enlightening to avert calling in Scotland Yard.

But why, he asked himself, should two men so utterly dissimilar as Denham and Mortimer, so diverse in their ways of life and in their social proclivities, each conceal information that he wanted? The only link between the two consisted in their both being present at the party Carter had given, the night before his death. Were they both keeping back the same fact, or had Denham some different knowledge from that in Mortimer's possession? And why were they both withholding it?

Inspector Head went home to lunch, puzzled and irritated. It appeared as if Scotland Yard would be requisitioned to take a hand in unravelling the mystery, unless the passport photographs provided a clue.

CHAPTER XX

AN INTERRUPTION

GAZING THROUGH THE dining-room window as he sat at lunch with his sister, Denham could see that Marguerite's car remained outside her gate in Panlyon Avenue, as he had left it. Since the sky had cleared after the morning's threat of possible rain, there was no reason why Marguerite should garage the car, especially if she wanted it out again. But, as Denham was going to see her in mid-afternoon, and would be with her for the rest of the day and evening, it was unlikely that she would want to use the car again. Therefore, he reasoned, she had not yet arrived back home, or else she would have put the coupé away.

Adela, observing his gaze, turned her head to look out. "Marguerite has gone home, Hugh, if that was what you were looking for," she remarked. "I saw her turn into the avenue a good half-hour ago."

"Rode her horse back to the livery stable, and then walked home," he suggested. "It was good of her to insist on my taking the car for Vere as she did. Even Vere herself remarked on it."

"I don't see what else she could have done," Adela observed rather doubtfully. "One thing, Hugh—you must get her to announce your engagement. This taking Vere home as you did—all of it, in fact—creates a wrong impression. And it can make no difference to Marguerite."

"Vere knows, in any case," he pointed out.

"Whether she does or doesn't, you should make your engagement public," Adela insisted. "It alters your standing at once."

"I've already made up my mind about it," he retorted, with a frown of annoyance, "and I'm telling her this afternoon. So there's no need for you to worry about it. She'll do it if I ask her,"

"And Vere knows," Adela remarked thoughtfully. "I wonder—"

"Couldn't we discuss something else?" Denham pushed his chair back from the table as he made the interruption, and his frown deepened.

"I was going to say, I wonder if I ought to go and see Vere," Adela pursued calmly. "Quite possibly she won't want anyone, and on the other hand she might be glad to see me. I'm quite willing to discuss other things than your affairs, Hugh, and to tell you the truth they seem rather small to me now, compared with this tragedy for poor Vere and her mother. Your future appears happily settled. They're desolate."

"Now tell me I'm damned selfish, and finish it," he snapped.

"Since you realise it, I don't see why I should go to the trouble of telling you," she answered evenly. "But I will tell you your thin-skinned fretfulness is getting absolutely insufferable, and if you begin talking to Marguerite as you talk to me, your engagement won't last long. You seem altogether changed, and for the worse, too, since—well, since you went to that dinner at the Grange on Monday evening."

"I'm sorry, Adela," he apologised frostily, rising and turning away from the table. "For your part, I notice, you've been careful to lose no opportunity of rubbing in your disapproval of my having gone to that dinner, though you know perfectly well why I accepted the invitation. As for the length of my engagement to Marguerite, she and I will settle that without help from anyone. I suppose my invitation to her to dine here to-night can stand? It should have come from you, I know."

"I am expecting her to dine with us," Adela retorted with equal stiffness. "This is your home, and you have every right to issue any invitations you choose. I shall have my own home, soon."

Denham stalked out from the room without replying, and she heard him ascend the stairs to his own room. After a minute or so of reflection she rose from the table, and stood looking down at it.

"So that's how it takes him," she observed to herself. "But if ever I catch Bob behaving like that, I'll skin him!"

She busied herself over necessary household tasks for awhile, and, after lunch had been cleared away, arranged the flowers on the dining-table in readiness for dinner. Then, debating in her mind whether to go to the Langtons, she eventually rang through, and Vere asked her if she would go there on the following afternoon, in response to her suggestion. So she took a book and settled herself by the fire in the drawing-room: Hugh could come and apologise properly to her when he had had time to cool down; she was not going to look for him.

Punctually at half-past three she heard the outer door close, and, looking up from her book, saw him go along Panlyon Avenue and turn in at Marguerite's gate, looking very spruce and brisk. She smiled, and returned to perusal of the book. Probably, by the time he returned with Marguerite to dress for dinner, he would be quite ready to bury the hatchet; she made up her mind to give it an imposing funeral.

Marguerite herself opened the door to Denham before he could ring, and led the way to her sitting-room. She looked very grave, he saw, and made no move toward him after he had closed the door.

"What is it, Marguerite?" he asked anxiously. "Has anything happened? You look as if—not a bit like your usual self."

"I am not," she answered. "I have not got over this morning, Hugh. The awful suddenness of Mr. Langton's death, and his daughter's seeing it. She—I'm glad you were there to take her home as you did."

There was a slight emphasis on the "you" that did not escape him. After a second or two he went to her and placed his hands on her shoulders, looking into her eyes steadily.

"Marguerite, do you know how I love you?" he asked.

"Yes, I know," she answered. "I have known, now, for three days."

"Dear, what is it?" he questioned desperately. "What has happened to cause this difference in you—for you are different?"

"This morning—the shock of it," she answered slowly. "That in part, and then there was last night, after you had gone—"

"What then—what happened then?" he broke in, almost fearfully.

She shook her head. "Nothing—it was not a happening. I came in here, and—" she was silent through a long pause—"and—do you understand how one may be altogether reckless through stress, feel that only the one thing counts? That one must grasp and hold—?"

Again she broke off, and Denham regarded her in a bewildered way. "Grasp and hold—" he echoed, as if the words conveyed nothing.

She smiled. "Leave it," she bade. "Of course, you cannot understand. Hugh, dear,"—in turn she laid her hands on his shoulders—"I'm shaken and afraid, cold—not cold to you! When you hold me as you hold me now, all the fears and questionings disappear. And then again, alone, as when I sat here writing last night—"

She laid her head down on his shoulder. "If I could rest!" she whispered, with tense desire. "If only I could rest!" She drew away from him as the door opened. Mrs. Pennefeather entered with the tea-tray, and Marguerite, cool and outwardly quite herself again, stood still while the old woman put the tray down on a sutherland table, opened out the table, and brought it over toward the fire. Denham, puzzled and anxious, moved to the hearthrug, and so they two waited until Mrs. Pennefeather left the room.

"My dear, you've said so much, and yet so little, that I want to know the rest," he said when they were alone again. "There's something wrong, I know, something you ought to let me share with you."

She came slowly toward him, and paused by the end of the settee. "No," she answered. "In reality there is no difference, nothing, more or less, than has been since you came home with me the night of the concert—and that night seems an age away, now. To me it seems a very long time since you drove Vere Langton home."

"Is that—my driving her—?" he asked, and paused.

Again she shook her head. "No. I—you could do no less."

"She told me to tell you—she was very grateful to you," he said.

"She may yet be more grateful—or less," she observed enigmatically. "The loss—I can see her now, as I tried to prevent her from looking back, and as she went away with you."

"But—I thought we might put it aside, for this time together," he said. "We can do nothing—nothing more for her. And you—"

There was reproach in the final word. She was so remote, so separate from him: he had anticipated an utterly different reception from this, and felt that he did not know this Marguerite.

"I disappoint you." She moved forward as she spoke, and, drawing the small table closer to the settee, seated herself behind it. To Denham it appeared that she used the table to keep him away from herself. "Hugh, dear, sit down and we'll have an early tea—sit down there as if we'd been together so long that you were quite used to me. Just give me time, time for this mood to pass."

But he went behind the settee and leaned over her, his hand on her shoulder. Then, looking up, she reached out and drew his face down to her, returning his kiss eagerly, passionately.

"My dear, if you could know how terribly I love you!" she said.

"I think I know, now, Marguerite," he answered.

"Now go and sit down, and let me give you your tea, and then we shall have all the rest of the time." She smiled up at him as she issued the command, and after a moment of hesitation he complied, going back to the hearthrug and drawing forward an armchair. He seated himself facing her, and shook his head rather ruefully.

"This is the first time that settee hasn't held us both," he said.

"But it will hold us again, soon," she promised.

He took the filled cup she held out to him, and stirred the tea thoughtfully. "Marguerite, there's one thing," he said abruptly. "I want—I want you to let it be known that we are engaged."

"Soon," she answered. "Not quite yet."

"But what reason can there be for delaying it?" he protested.

"I do not wish it to be known quite yet," she insisted gravely.

"But—but Adela and Leigh know," he pointed out, "and this morning, when the Langtons overtook me on the road, Vere told me she had guessed. What object is there in delaying an announcement."

"Still I wish to delay it," she said inflexibly.

"My dear, what difference can it make to you?" he pleaded. "And I find it does make a difference to me, if we don't let people know. It puts me in a . . . I want to be proud of you openly, darling, to let everyone know you belong to me and I to you. And Adela suggested that we might be married with her and Leigh—I shall be all alone after she goes to him. So the sooner we make an announcement—don't you see it would make a difference? I don't want to wait one day longer than I must for you, darling, and the sooner we make it public—"

He broke off, for the slight movement of her head indicated dissent. Again he felt both puzzled and hurt.

"No," she said, "not quite yet. I have a reason."

"Then what is it?" he asked. "Is it—aren't you sure?"

She smiled, and at sight of it he felt himself childishly impatient. Vaguely he resented her expression.

"Haven't I given you proof that I'm sure?" she asked in reply. "Sure of this, Hugh, that the time since I let you know I love you has made you mean more to me than everything else, more than myself or my own future, and in that is my reason for delaying this."

"But I don't understand in the least," he objected. "Surely, dear, your future is mine, and you know that nothing can alter me—you mean as much to me as I to you. Marguerite, my dear, it's such a small thing, this. And I ask it of you—why refuse like this?"

While she sat, as if framing a reply, they heard the rattle of the door-knocker, followed by the bell's ringing. Marguerite stood up.

"I'll go," she said. "Mrs. Pennefeather won't hear till the third or fourth ring. It's the post, probably."

"Let me go for you," Denham suggested.

"No—stay here, dear. I'll see who it is."

She went out. Presently he heard her voice in the hall, and the sound of the outer door's closing again. Then, through the window, he saw a youth go out by the gate, mount a bicycle, and ride away toward Treherne Road. Marguerite came back into the room, an open letter in her hand, and Denham could see that the envelope was unstamped—it had been sent by messenger, not through the post.

She stood just inside the door, gazing at him almost absently. He took a step toward her, but she gestured him back.

"It is—I think . . ." she began, and did not end it. Then she went to the writing-desk under the window, put the letter down on the flap and stood there with her back to him, as if in indecision.

"I must go out for a little while, Hugh," she said, turning and facing him. "This is—it concerns what we were talking about, in a way. I must go out, leave you for a little while?"

"But I can't understand," he protested. "What is all this about?"

"Nothing—nothing you could— Oh, my dear!" She came to him and put her arms round his neck. "Trust me to put it right, to put everything right. And I must go, for a little while."

"Marguerite, I'm sure there is something desperately wrong! Your eyes tell it—you can't deceive me. What is it, darling?"

"Nothing new. Nothing in which you could possibly help. Hugh, I'm going out, going to take the car, and leaving you here—for a little while. Will you trust me—ask no more, but trust me?"

She looked up at him earnestly, pleadingly. He gent his head in assent, and then kissed her as he held her.

"Of course I'll trust you, dear, though I don't understand it."

"No, I know you don't. Such a little while, Hugh, that I won't even put on a hat and coat. It—it isn't worth it. You see? And you'll wait here? I must go alone."

"Yes," he answered doubtfully. "I'll wait for you, Marguerite."

"Bless you, darling!" She spoke more easily, with less of intense earnestness. "It's such a little thing to make a fuss about, such a very little thing, but I feel that I must go. One minute, though."

He saw that she went to the writing-desk again; took a bulkily filled envelope from a drawer, and put it down on the flap, over the letter she had just received and read. Then she came back to him.

"Only for a little while, Hugh," she said. "Come out to the gate with me. I know you're puzzled, and perhaps a little bit hurt at this secrecy of mine, but I shall soon be with you again."

"And explain it all, perhaps," he suggested, smiling at her.

"And explain it all," she assented. "Now I'll go. One kiss, darling, and then—only a little while."

For that one kiss she clung to him with a passionate strength of which he had not thought her possessed. Then, releasing herself from his hold, she went to the door, and he followed her to open it. They went out, and he opened the car door and held it for her.

"Sure I can't come with you, dear?" he asked.

She shook her head. "I must go alone," she answered.

For seconds she stood irresolute, gazing at him. Then she entered to the driving-seat of the closed coupé, and looked out at him.

"Hugh, dear, while I'm away—I put a letter down on the writing-desk—you saw it, perhaps. One I took out and put there."

"Yes. Do you want me to post it for you?"

She shook her head. "I think you'll have time, before I come back, to read it," she answered. "I wrote it after we came back last night, for you. Read it while I'm away, will you?"

"Marguerite, what is all this?" he demanded, almost angrily.

"The letter will tell you," she said, and smiled slightly. "And now, before I go, lean in to me for just one more kiss, and remember I shall be gone only a little while. Don't question, dear—just that!"

He stepped close to the side of the car, and kissed her as she had asked. Then, as he straightened himself again, she pressed the starter-button, and in a little while the engine picked up.

"I wish you'd let me come with you," Denham said.

"But that's quite impossible," she answered, smiling again. "You will know why, when I come back." He saw her hand move on the gear-lever. "Not long, Hugh, dear. Good-bye."

The car almost leaped away from beside him. Watching, he saw her turn it about to face toward Treherne Road, and she did not look at him again. He saw how, at the corner, she spun at right angles toward London Road, with the uncannily sudden twist that had startled him when he sat beside her. He stood by the kerb, listening, and the sound of the engine grew faint and died away. Then he went back into the house, puzzled, a little angry, and still more afraid.

If she meant to be gone only a little while, why had she bidden him good-bye?

CHAPTER XXI

TO THE CREST—AND BEYOND

MARGUERITE'S COUPÉ, HEADED toward London Road, was passing the unused building-plot into which the old boots that Erastus Donnithorne found had been thrown, when a big saloon with four men seated in it swung into the road, and pulled up with the whir-ring, grating sound of all four wheels skidded by the brakes, just as she took the corner into the main way and headed away from the town, over the Idleburn bridge. If she had looked into her driving-mirror as she accelerated over the bridge, she must have seen the saloon come back out from Treherne Road, swing to face in the direction in which she was going, and gather way again. And with only the briefest of glances she must have known who were the four men that larger car carried.

Over the bridge and away, with the meandering river on her left—the way she had gone with Denham just a day before. He, beside her, had seen the speedometer pointer creep up and up, but it moved up faster, now. She had a clear road with a good surface; the afternoon was hazily sunlit, an ideal day for driving. Did she think of Denham, back in her sitting-room in Panlyon Avenue? What were her thoughts, then?

Unwaveringly she held to the crown of the road while the coupé increased its speed. Fifty-five, sixty, sixty-five—and now the pointer moved more slowly toward the limit of the car's speed, but still it moved. Far ahead she saw the up-and-down movement of a horse's head in a side-lane, and the horse was advancing toward the road along which she drove. She blared a warning, and kept the accelerator pedal down: behind her, the big car was gathering way, threatening to overtake her. The horse came out to the road, a blinkered trace-horse with another between wagon-shafts behind it: an open-mouthed, stupid farm lad stood in the wagon, gee-ing and haw-ing at his cattle, and suddenly tugging at the rope rein he held as he saw the coupé bearing down to what appeared inevitable disaster. But a blinkered farm horse does not stop in the fraction of a second, and the trace-horse had made the middle of the road when, with a sudden almost unbelievably quick swerve, in view of the speed at which the coupe was travelling, Marguerite shot under its nose and went on, with only the slightest diminution of pace, and that only for seconds. Ignition a fourth retarded, throttle full open, and the dynamo charging shut off—she was making seventy miles an hour before the wagon was half a mile behind.

Its egress to the main road, just too late to stop or crash her, caused the driver of the saloon to snatch at his hand-brake lever and apply his four-wheel footbrake as well, so that the heavy car went gliddering on with locked wheels until its radiator was barely a yard from the trace-horse, and it came to a stop almost diagonally across the road with the impetus of the long skid. The lad was tugging at his reins to turn his leading horse: he heard such a volley of profane abuse as had never assaulted his ears before. The saloon went forward, straightened to the road, and gathered way again—but by the time its driver got back to top gear the coupé was a good mile ahead.

Stern chase, long chase. In spite of the far smaller weight-to-power ratio of the coupé, the bigger car crept up toward it again, but the miles were slipping behind them both, and now Condor Hill loomed before them with its three miles of steady, slow rise, and then the far steeper gradient of the hill itself. For that three miles the lighter, smaller car kept its distance, a little more than half a mile dividing the two, and both cars were down into the fifties again, then, for the ascent was not so slight as it looked. Two cars in succession, going toward Westingborough, flashed past the pair. Their occupants must have seen the hatless, silk-clad girl in the coupé, holding her steady way toward the hill, grave-eyed, immobile as fate as she grasped the steering-wheel. They must have seen the eager-eyed, almost breathlessly anxious men in the saloon behind her, and possibly they realised that they were witnessing an incident in a chase. But they went their ways, and pursuer and pursued too went on.

On to the end of the three-mile rise, neither increasing nor diminishing the interval between the two appreciably—the saloon might have gained or lost a mere matter of yards in the whole distance, but no more. Then, as the real ascent began, the coupé lost way, and for a time it appeared as if the saloon must overtake it. But this heavier car, feeling the pressure of the grade, slowed too—its driver changed down to third, and Marguerite must have heard the whining of the intermediate gear, a harsh, singing note that went up the scale as the engine responded to its fully opened throttle. If she heard, she took no heed: with the rush at the foot of the hill, and only her own weight in the car, she took the ascent on top gear, as she had taken it with Denham beside her the day before.

She was gaining again, ever so little. Just where the cutting began she looked back momentarily—perhaps she looked at the car in pursuit, perhaps over it, at the quiet valley of the Idleburn, at Westingborough roofs showing clear in the sunlight, and all that quiet stretch of country about the town. It lay like a picture opened and placed on a desk for one to view, its details minutely clear. For the moment in which she looked back, the coupé swerved: then she turned again to watch the road ahead, and held straight on the way she had planned.

From the Westingborough side, Condor Hill is steepest for its last hundred yards, and here Marguerite lost the greater part of her lead over the other car. It may have been that, driving with throttle full open and ignition retarded to get the most out of the engine on the ascent, she had risked and incurred overheating. Whatever the cause, the car appeared to flag and almost pause for a moment—and the saloon, singing up the hill in third, was coming on fast. But again she gathered way, and, though unable to increase her lead, kept the distance between them, a distance of less than a hundred yards, now. So they came to the very crest of the hill, where the sides of the cutting rose up fifty feet and more to right and left of them, and still went on. And, mindful of the danger of the curve with which the road went down the hillside toward Carden, the driver of the saloon left his gear-lever alone instead of changing to top speed again, for in the lower gear the idling engine would help his brakes until he could accelerate again with safety. He had proved that the smaller car could not outdistance him, but in the end he must pass and stop it.

* * * * *

"Pull up! JEFFRIES! For God's sake, man, PULL UP!"

Inspector Head, seated beside his driver, roared the command as the saloon turned into Treherne Road, for he had seen Marguerite driving the coupé out to London Road, and saw her turn toward the bridge. Sergeant Wells and Constable Borrow, occupying the rear seats in the saloon, just saved their noses from making contact with the backs of the two front seats as Jeffries skidded the saloon almost to a stop.

"Round you go—out on the London Road!" Head barked. "That car that passed us just now—chase it and catch it!"

The saloon came about, its near front wheel mounting the kerb and bumping down to the road again on the turn. Jeffries swung into London Road, changed up to third, and eyed the coupé going away over the bridge ahead of him. Then he changed up again to top, and eased the throttle open until he could get no more from his engine.

"Chase it, sir, yes," he said. "About catchin' it though—"

The doubt was evident in his voice. Head gazed at the coupé, growing smaller ahead—they had hardly got way on the saloon, yet.

"How much petrol have you got in the tank?" he asked.

"I'd say, two hundred and twenty miles, sir," Jeffries answered.

"Right. When that tank's empty, we'll stop, unless we pass and stop that car first. Nurse it up, man, and get all you can."

They had three times the power of the smaller car, he knew, but they had, too, more than three times the weight, with four six-foot men aboard, and fully twice the wind-resistance. But the weight of Wells and Borrow over the back axle was more aid than hindrance, for it held the chassis down to the road, gave the back wheels a grip, and made for steady riding. Head sighed relief as he saw the interval between the two cars diminishing, and knew he would pass the other car before the petrol in the tank had run out—and then the trace-horse came out from the lane to the road, and Marguerite shot under its nose.

Wells let down his window to help his chief in telling the farm lad the mixed quality of his immediate ancestry, the advisability of taking his team home and burning it and himself, and other thoughts engendered by the heat of the moment. The trace-horse moved aside, and Jeffries, murmuring quiet lewdnesses independently, released his brakes and moved on. Again he changed up and up as they gathered way.

"Lost us a mile," Head groaned. "A mile, if not more! And it'll be dark in two hours. And fools like that go about without keepers! Drive wagons about, too! We're a long-suffering people. Keep it up, Jeffries—keep it up! We're beginning to gain again, and there's the hill to come. You should make it there, if not before."

"She may turn off on to the old coach road, sir," Jeffries pointed out. "If she does, that car can slither round the hairpins while we're swearing at 'em, and gain a couple of mile on us."

"Then heaven send she doesn't think of it. Two miles lead, and the road divides beyond Carden—it's unthinkable!"

He breathed more freely when Marguerite shot past the end of the old road, holding straight toward Condor Hill. But he groaned aloud when, on the three miles of rise, she held her distance before them.

"Can't you get more out of it, Jeffries? Is that the best?"

"It's her limit, sir. She's not what she was when she was new, and I'm shoving her all I know. Third gear on the steep part should give us a bit of an advantage—I've had her up to fifty-seven in third."

"Ah! That's better. Now hoot like the devil and pass, and hold the middle of the road and make that car stop—or crash."

He gave the order when, as the coupé began the hill, the interval between it and this car diminished swiftly. But then the saloon began to mount the steeper part, and it became evident that Jeffries would not pass before they reached the crest, though he might be close behind. He roared a long warning from the klaxon, and Marguerite must have heard it, but she went on. Through the rear glass of the coupé they saw her look back, and it appeared to Head that her expression was one of steady confidence, that she was not perturbed by their nearness. She seemed not to look at him or the saloon, but over and behind him, he thought.

He saw, too, that the coupé swerved and checked, but then again it went on to the crest. He leaned back in his seat.

"Now you've got it, Jeffries," he said. "Steady to the bend and round it—steady, with as much speed as you can hold, allowing for the outward swing and the danger of getting too near the railings. Then go all out when you hit the straight, and our weight should take us past her before we're anywhere near the foot of the hill."

Like Marguerite, he turned and looked through his rear window before they passed over the crest of the hill. The confident expression he had seen in her face made him vaguely uneasy—was there something behind them to account for it? But the road showed clear and empty as far as his gaze could trace it, and he turned to look ahead again.

"Yes, steady. She's going away—she's got to slow for the bend. We've got— Oh, my God! Look there! Stop, man—for heaven's sake—!"

For, less than a hundred yards ahead of them, the coupé appeared to leap toward the big, red-studded "Danger" sign. They heard the purr of its exhaust deepen as Marguerite opened the throttle and rushed down and away from them.

They could see her head through the rear glass of the coupé, her little dark head held up, tilted a trifle backward, and the swift, straight rush of the car showed that her hands were steady on the wheel. They heard the crash, almost as of an explosion, as the radiator made impact on the railings guarding the road from the hillside, and Jeffries, braking as he had braked twice before that day, brought them to a standstill, faced almost squarely toward the near side of the road.

They almost fell out, all four, and Wells was muttering incoherently as he ran down toward the railings. Head outdistanced him, and came to a standstill to lean on the rail beside the gap through which the coupé had gone. He saw a break in the foliage of the pines, nearly three hundred feet below, and as he gazed down at it there rose up a swiftly thickening spiral of smoke. In the heart of the smoke he saw a little flicker of flame that grew and spread. He took off his hat.

"Ho—how do we get down, sir?" Wells asked.

"As best we can," Head answered, "but there is no hurry."

He stepped back, and for a second or two stood at attention.

"She was a brave lady," he said. "May God have mercy on her soul."

* * * * *

Lying against the almost perpendicular slope outside the railings, Head held himself from slipping by gripping at one of the posts, while Borrow climbed down beside him and, holding on to his feet, made another seven feet or so of human ladder. Down beside this Sergeant Wells clambered, and got foothold on a narrow sheep-track stepped in the hillside. When Jeffries had got down beside him, Borrow first, and then Head, let go and slid down, steadied to safety by the other two.

They made the rest of the descent without danger to themselves, for the sheep had worn tracks almost to the top of the slope. For some part of the way they were half-suffocated by the smoke of burning pine branches, but in the end they reached the almost level, needle-carpeted stretch in which the trees grew. Jeffries had fastened to his belt the fire-extinguisher from the saloon, and he sprayed its contents on the charred wreckage of the coupé, and on that which it held. They burned their hands in getting out the unrecognisable body that had been Marguerite West, and Head, looking up after they had laid it down, felt deep relief that the pines had not fully caught. Had the fire spread among them, it might have run on and destroyed half Carden village before means could be found to extinguish it.

"Your coat, Wells—and mine. Jeffries, go back and get the car, and fetch it round on to the forest road. Borrow, go and get that hurdle. We'll get to the edge of the road with her as soon as you can get there with the car, Jeffries. We must take her back with us."

Little more than an hour before, he reflected later as he sat beside Jeffries again, she had passed them—had she known then how the drive would end, or had that final rush that had its end for her in eternity been a sudden impulse, born of her realisation that she could not outdistance her pursuers? However that may have been, she had made a gallant, unswerving end—Head knew that her hand had not faltered on the wheel, but she had driven as surely and steadily toward death as ever she had driven her car. Yes, a brave lady!

He felt a vast contempt for Mortimer, the cunning, watchful devil who had ratted to save himself. Nothing could be done to the man: his written confession absolved him of complicity, and he had delayed it only for three hours or a little more—four hours, it would be, between Head's last interview with him and the time when he wrote the letter. That letter saved him: if he were charged with complicity, the charge would be dismissed, Head had to own to himself.

Denham—different stuff, Denham. Nothing would make him speak, and in the absence of anyone whom they could charge with the murder itself, they could not charge him with complicity. How much had he known—what had he known? Had he merely suspected something, and felt that the suspicion must be unjust? Anything was possible, and, Head felt sure, he would never know what Denham had kept hidden, now.

Apart from such revelations as might be made at an inquest, the case was closed—Mortimer's letter, together with what Head already knew, had closed it. There would be no trial, and very little credit, if any, would accrue to him over his investigations—he might even incur slight censure, but he felt no regret that it had ended this way. Thinking back over all that had come to light concerning Carter and his past, Head felt that the man had got no more than he deserved, and that there was a defect in the legal system, since it could let such a man inflict injury after injury on others, and had no means of punishing him. No wonder that one of his victims, either a direct or indirect one, had in the end seen fit to repair the omission in the penal code. It was wrong, of course, but . . .

"That'll be two inquests to-morrow," Sergeant Wells, in the back of the car, observed abruptly. "Looks as if Westingborough's getting it in the neck lately. Three in one week."

"She was a fine-looking girl," Borrow remarked. "You'd never think to look at her—big, dark eyes, she had. I used to see her drivin' her car about the town sometimes—"

"And now, dust to dust," Wells said gravely.

"Seems more like ashes to ashes to me," Borrow dissented. "Gosh, you'd never think it had been a car to look at it! And me with my arm scorched half-way up to the elbow—I noticed you nearly sung out, too."

They went on, all four men bareheaded, now. Head looked back at the cut in the crest of Condor Hill, and again in thought saw Marguerite rushing on to the white rail on the far side of the hill, saw the outward leap of the car, and how it began turning in the air as it fell. She could have known nothing after striking among the trees—death must have been mercifully swift, in spite of its apparent horror.

"What strikes me about it, she had Nerve," the sergeant observed after a silence. "A thing like that, it takes Nerve. I could no more bring myself to do it than I could fly. I saw the car suddenly begin to gain speed, and then, instead of taking the curve as it should, it kept straight on and crashed through the railings?"

He broke off, and Borrow realised that with the final statement he was practising, rehearsing the evidence he would be called on to give at the inquest.

"And disappeared," Borrow completed for him.

"Since the lady's body is lying at your feet"—Head turned in his seat to rasp out the admonition—"you might save those comments till you get to the end of this journey, both of you."

CHAPTER XXII

RETURN

UNDER THE LETTER Marguerite had asked Denham to read, he saw as he took it up from the desk, lay the one she had just received. He saw the stamped address at the top of the sheet— "Kerkmanhurst, London Road, Westingborough," and the opening words —"Dear Miss West," before he turned away and seated himself by the fire to read the closely written sheets he took out from the envelope. It was clear, steady handwriting, easy to read:

DEAR,

"Nothing in earth or heaven or hell will ever alter my love for you, or make you mean less to me."

These were your words to me last night, not long before you left me here. I knew then, as I knew when you first took me in your arms, that they are not true.

I did not intend you to know I cared for you. It was easy to conceal the fact that you meant more to me than any other man, until we came back here from the concert. Then, when you told me of what you had done for my sake, and what it meant to you—when I knew you had put me before honour, even—I knew I must make some return. Yet was it that, or was it the ache for your arms to hold me? I cannot tell, now—I know only that these days with you have been very wonderful, perhaps more wonderful because I have known all the time that they must end.

I do not know when you will read this letter, or if you will ever read it. Quite possibly I shall go away, as I meant to go without letting you know that I love you, but even then I think I must make confession to you in some way. In this way, perhaps. I am not sure.

You see that, in beginning, I call you dear, but not "my" dear. For when you have read this you will not be mine any longer. I know you well enough to realise that you will not acquit me as I acquit myself, since it is not in your nature to understand that what I have done is just. I saw my sister's body brought home, and knew that she had died because of Edward Carter. I sat beside my brother while he died, and knew that Edward Carter had killed him—and before his death I promised him that Edward Carter should die by my hand, since no law could punish him. I did not murder Carter, but killed him justly, one life for two.

Though I tell you this, I know you will not understand it as I do. Even as I write, I think I can see the horror in your eyes as you read, know that when you have read, there will be no love for me left. Why have I loved you so intensely? I ask myself this question, and can find no answer.

I came here two years ago—more than two years ago—to find and destroy the man who had destroyed all I loved in life. Before coming, I found out that the Harrisons were going to Taormina, and myself went there and became acquainted with them, knowing that if they accepted me I should find no difficulty in making myself the place I wanted here. One man, Mortimer by name, knew me under my real name of Maraquita Vesci—one man beside Carter, that is, and I knew that for the sake of his own position here Carter would not wish to reveal my identity as that of the sister of his victim. For he knew that my sister was dead because of him, but not that my brother was dead, too, and he still feared lest my brother should take vengeance on him. Mortimer promised to keep my secret, and has kept it, even though he must have guessed that I killed Carter, or that my brother killed him and I knew of it.

I was patient. Had I taken this vengeance too soon, a new-comer here, there might have been suspicion of me at once. I planned what I must do, planned that he should be killed in such a way that his death could not be traced to me. You said, this afternoon, that in the end Inspector Head would trace the murderer, but I do not believe it. For moments, sometimes, I think it may be possible, and then again I know it is not. For in these two years I have lived past the possibility of recognition as Maraquita Vesci—I, Marguerite West. And few people know, as I know, that my sister Anita's death was due to Carter's evil lust and heartlessness. Even if I were recognised, it would not connect me with his death.

It seems strange to me, as I write this, that you unconsciously helped me in the plan I made. For the defect in the engine of your car prevented anyone from thinking that shots had been fired, and then, when you saw *me* enter this house before dawn, you kept back your knowledge for my sake, though it was not for my sake in the way you thought. In the antique chest in the hall, at this present time, lie the clothes I was wearing when you saw me, together with the pistol, with the rope I used to get up into the tree, and the nurse's cloak and hat. Some time, when it is safe, I shall destroy them all.

I am telling you, so that you may have no doubt, but may know that I killed Carter—justly, not murderously. I telephoned him the day before, and because of his fear of my brother he agreed to open his own door before dawn, at four o'clock. It was not altogether through fear, for there was, too, a possibility of such an adventure as he always wanted, a girl coming to him alone and secretly in the night. He was one who would go down to the gate of hell to possess a woman, as I knew. And I sent him through the gate, and am glad. I have no remorse, no fear.

At the very last, I feared that the snow had ruined my plan, but then I saw how I might use it to make the plan more perfect. A man's footsteps, ceasing, and another track not going near Carter's house. Nothing to connect the two, but the killer vanishing at a certain point, not to be traced beyond it in spite of the snow. And the killing so bloodily, brutally done that it would be regarded as certainly the work of a man. Yet it was not one-hundredth part as brutal or cruel as the long, slow death my brother died, nor did Carter know one-hundredth part of the agony of mind my sister must have known before she went to her death. Because of those two, my only regret is that I could not make him suffer more.

Though I tell you this, I know you will not understand fully, and will not acquit me as I acquit myself. It is not in your blood, not in the race to which you belong, but to which I owe only half myself, to understand. And if I do not kill your love for me, some day I should bear you children, and perhaps, years hence, this truth I write now would come to your knowledge, and then life would no longer be worth living for you. So I know I must let you go, must go myself, and all the miracle of these days I have had with you must end.

It is nearly dawn again. How many more dawns must come and pass before I can bring myself to send you away from me, send you to keep the promise I made you give? Not at first, not for a long while perhaps, but in the end you will keep it, and I shall not be jealous or hurt. Living, I shall be glad that you have found a lesser, quieter, and perhaps surer happiness than I would have given you. Dead, I shall be as near you as God will let me be, loving you as I love you now.

Dear—still my dear, because you do not yet know that I shall find strength soon to make you go from me—I tell you again that I have no remorse and no fear. I have kept a promise, executed justice. If my act should become known, my escape from human reprisal is already planned, a certain, swift way, to the eternal justice of which I have no fear.

I write because of what you said to me this afternoon, that the "murderer" would be traced—write because, in spite of my belief, it may be true. And as I write, the sense of your presence in the room is very strong. I think, if I look up, I may see you standing with your arms held out to me, and I may come to you, feel you holding me—a very folly of longing, of hunger for the sight of you and the touch of you, and to give all you could ask of me—

Nearly dawn, and in a very few hours you will come to me again.

Good-bye, Hugh.

MARGUERITE.

He looked up, and became conscious that someone else was in the room, quite near him, moving about. It was Mrs. Pennefeather clearing away the tea-things. He heard the rattle of cups—was it cups rattling, though? Nothing appeared normal: neither sights nor sounds were real to him, then. He folded the sheets of the letter he had read, replaced them in the torn envelope, and put it in his pocket, not knowing what he did. The deaf old woman finished arranging the things on the tray and went out with it, closing the door behind her. He heard the click of the lock—but was it a lock's clicking? It was such a sound as might be caused by the mechanism of a pistol, if someone cocked it in readiness for use—in readiness to kill.

She had said—what was it she had said? Yes, that she had gone only for a little while. She would come back to him. . . .

After a long interval in which he could neither think clearly nor feel deeply, he rose to his feet and went to the window to look out. Movement restored some clarity to his mind, and he felt that he was beginning to understand. Not to understand fully all that she had written, but just beginning. Marguerite—not his Marguerite, now. . . .

Then again he saw the letter she had put down on the desk, and read the written words, not fully understanding them—

DEAR MISS WEST,

I regret that, for my own sake, I have been compelled to break the promise I made to you over two years ago, and to disclose the fact of your real identity. At an interview which Inspector Head had with me this morning, he made it quite clear that in some way he connected your brother with Edward Carter's death, and was trying to find Peter Vesci.

Do not for one moment think that I attach any suspicion to you, or that I have done this other than under what to me is compulsion. I know nothing and suspect nothing, but am compelled to safeguard myself, and in the letter which I have written to Inspector Head, I am requesting him to keep your secret as I have hitherto kept it.

I am sending the letter I have written to Inspector Head, together with this to you, by a messenger, who will call first at your home to deliver this, and then will go on with the letter for the inspector. I trust that this action on my part will cause you no inconvenience, and regret very much that I am compelled to make the revelation.

Sincerely yours,
FRANCIS MORTIMER.

She had gone, but only for a little while. She would come back to him, here in this room. . . .

He turned away from the window, went to the end of the settee, and stood looking down at it. It would not . . . would not hold them both again. She was not his Marguerite, now.

If he had—wait! He must get this clear. If he had told all the truth at the inquest, he would not be here now, stunned beyond feeling, incapable of reasoned action, and almost past the power of connected thought. If he had told all the truth. . . .

"I swear before Almighty God to tell the truth, the whole truth, and nothing but the truth—"

Damned in his own sight for evermore, a perjurer, uselessly—he had lied to no purpose after all! *He had lied on oath!* Sophistry regarding it was as useless, now, as his lying.

Somebody had rung the bell. Denham turned, and saw the top of a car—not Marguerite's car—over the top of the casement-cloth curtains drawn across the lower part of the window. By going nearer, he could see down into the car, see who had come to the house—but he did not want to go. He wanted to hide, to get to some place where he could not be seen—he who never in his life had feared to look another man in the eyes wanted to hide himself! Hugh Denham—was he Hugh Denham, straight-living little Adela's brother, and son of old Robert Denham, who had been respected for his uprightness by all who had known him? Hugh Denham, wanting to hide himself?

Again the bell rang, and this time Denham went to the door of the room and opened it. He heard no sound from the back of the house, and after a few moments he drew back, leaving the door half-opened, and stood with his back to the settee in helpless indecision. Then, for the third time, he heard the bell, and with it a thundering clatter that seemed violent enough to break in the panels of the door. As he started forward, he heard Mrs. Pennefeather come hurrying into the entrance-hall, and again he drew back. She would open the door.

He heard her sharp ejaculation, as of horror, and then Inspector Head's voice, rasping, incisive—

"Where is Miss West's room—her bedroom?"

Then more steps in the hall. Mrs. Pennefeather passed the door of the sitting-room, going toward the stairs. Head followed her, carrying something—somebody—almost wrapped from sight in a coat, and, where the coat failed to hide, there showed a charred, horrible semblance of a human form. Not Marguerite—that awful thing could not be Marguerite. Besides, Marguerite had said she would be gone only a little while. Yet Head had asked for Marguerite's room. . . .

Other men were out there, talking in lowered voices, so that what they said was no more than a murmur to Denham as he stood in the sitting-room. After another long interval—it seemed long to Denham, frozen here to incapability of action or of clear thought—Head's footsteps sounded coming down the stairs and along the hall. He paused outside the open door and looked into the sitting-room. Then he entered, and Denham stiffened to erectness to face him.

"Were you waiting for Miss West?" Head asked.

Denham cleared his throat. "Yes," he answered.

But was it he who answered, or had some other spoken the word? He did not recognise the syllable as spoken by his own voice.

"She is dead," Head said clearly, incisively.

Denham stared fixedly at the man before him.

"Dead?" he echoed.

But the news was hardly any shock to him. Beyond a certain point, the human mind is incapable of reaction to sudden shock, and Denham had been driven to that point. He was numbed, past feeling, for the time.

"Mr. Denham"—Head took a step toward him, and his voice was coldly sharp, like a bared blade—"how much did you know?"

Denham gathered his wits and shook his head. "Nothing," he answered, and the reply sounded as if he had expected such a question.

"Nothing." Head drew back again, and spoke after a long pause. "No. Then—I think—we shall not want you."

He meant that Denham would not be wanted at the inquest, but to the man he addressed it appeared that Head was telling him he would not be arrested. He felt behind him and laid his hand on the back of the settee—the settee that would not hold them both again!

"I—it is as you wish." He was finding speech increasingly difficult, but it was easier than he had anticipated to look Head straight in the face. And, he realised, he no longer wanted to hide himself.

"No," Head said, "I don't think we shall want you. The drive from the end of Treherne Road, and how it ended—I think that will be enough. Well, Mr. Denham, it's no use your waiting to see Miss West."

"No," Denham assented. "It is no use."

Abruptly he started forward from the settee, passed the inspector, and went toward the opened front door. Two men drew back from the doorstep to let him pass, and in one of them he recognised Sergeant Wells, who, like Head, was grimed of face and had ashes and stains on his clothes. Both he and the other man were bareheaded, a circumstance that impressed itself on Denham's mind as curious. Another man, also bareheaded, sat in the car by the gate.

"She is dead," Denham said to himself.

He, too, was bareheaded, he realised. He had left his coat and hat on the chest in the hall—the chest that contained a pistol, and a rope, and some clothes that Marguerite would have destroyed. But he would not go back. He would never enter that house again.

"She is dead!"

"Living, I shall be glad that you have found a lesser, quieter, and perhaps surer happiness than I would have given you. Dead, I shall be as near you as God will let me be, loving you as I love you now."

* * * * *

"You stay here for the present, Borrow. I'm going straight to the station to report. There is a telephone, I see—ring through to Doctor Bennett, and get him or his partner to come here at once. I'll communicate with you from the station, later. Come along, Wells."

They went out to the car, and Jeffries drove off. Head saw Denham opening the front door of his home, saw him enter the house and close the door as they turned the corner into Treherne Road.

"Did you see him come out of Miss West's house, Jeffries?" he asked of the man beside him.

"Yes, sir. No hat on, I noticed."

"He'd left it with his coat in the hall. What did you think of him? How did he strike you, as you saw him then?"

"Well, sir, since you ask me—I once saw a man taken down from the triangle after he'd been given ten lashes. Mr. Denham's face reminded me of that man's. The look in his eyes, I mean. No disrespect to the gentleman, but it did."

"It's not a bad description, Jeffries. In my opinion, he's getting far more than ten lashes. He looked to me like a man who had lost everything, and was just beginning to realise it."

* * * * *

Denham opened the door of his home silently, stole into the hall, and closed the door again with infinite care. But Adela, glancing up from her book as she sat in the drawing-room, had seen the top of his head when he approached the house.

"Hugh, Major Fenwick has sent me a brace of pheasants—we'll have them to-night. Does Marguerite like pheasant?"

(The little normal things of life—life that must go on!)

"She is dead." The words spoke themselves, using his voice, and it sounded as had Head's voice when he spoke the words.

"Hugh!" He heard the book thud to the floor, saw Adela appear in the doorway. "Oh, Hugh! My dear—"

She came toward him, but he gestured her away. After a pause in which she stared at him, he spoke again—

"My punishment is greater than I can bear."

Then he turned and went toward the staircase, walking as a man might walk in sleep, and groping before him with his hands.

THE END

RAMBLE HOUSE's

HARRY STEPHEN KEELER WEBWORK MYSTERIES
(RH) indicates the title is available ONLY in the RAMBLE HOUSE edition

The Ace of Spades Murder
The Affair of the Bottled Deuce (RH)
The Amazing Web
The Barking Clock
Behind That Mask
The Book with the Orange Leaves
The Bottle with the Green Wax Seal
The Box from Japan
The Case of the Canny Killer
The Case of the Crazy Corpse (RH)
The Case of the Flying Hands (RH)
The Case of the Ivory Arrow
The Case of the Jeweled Ragpicker
The Case of the Lavender Gripsack
The Case of the Mysterious Moll
The Case of the 16 Beans
The Case of the Transparent Nude (RH)
The Case of the Transposed Legs
The Case of the Two-Headed Idiot (RH)
The Case of the Two Strange Ladies
The Circus Stealers (RH)
Cleopatra's Tears
A Copy of Beowulf (RH)
The Crimson Cube (RH)
The Face of the Man From Saturn
Find the Clock
The Five Silver Buddhas
The 4th King
The Gallows Waits, My Lord! (RH)
The Green Jade Hand
Finger! Finger!
Hangman's Nights (RH)
I, Chameleon (RH)
I Killed Lincoln at 10:13! (RH)
The Iron Ring
The Man Who Changed His Skin (RH)
The Man with the Crimson Box
The Man with the Magic Eardrums
The Man with the Wooden Spectacles
The Marceau Case
The Matilda Hunter Murder
The Monocled Monster

The Murder of London Lew
The Murdered Mathematician
The Mysterious Card (RH)
The Mysterious Ivory Ball of Wong
    Shing Li (RH)
The Mystery of the Fiddling Cracks-
man
The Peacock Fan
The Photo of Lady X (RH)
The Portrait of Jirjohn Cobb
Report on Vanessa Hewstone (RH)
Riddle of the Travelling Skull
Riddle of the Wooden Parrakeet (RH)
The Scarlet Mummy (RH)
The Search for X-Y-Z
The Sharkskin Book
Sing Sing Nights
The Six From Nowhere (RH)
The Skull of the Waltzing Clown
The Spectacles of Mr. Cagliostro
Stand By—London Calling!
The Steeltown Strangler
The Stolen Gravestone (RH)
Strange Journey (RH)
The Strange Will
The Straw Hat Murders (RH)
The Street of 1000 Eyes (RH)
Thieves' Nights
Three Novellos (RH)
The Tiger Snake
The Trap (RH)
Vagabond Nights (Defrauded Yegg-
man)
Vagabond Nights 2 (10 Hours)
The Vanishing Gold Truck
The Voice of the Seven Sparrows
The Washington Square Enigma
When Thief Meets Thief
The White Circle (RH)
The Wonderful Scheme of Mr. Chris-
    topher Thorne
X. Jones—of Scotland Yard
Y. Cheung, Business Detective

Keeler Related Works

A To Izzard: A Harry Stephen Keeler Companion by Fender Tucker—Articles and stories about Harry, by Harry, and in his style. Included is a compleat bibliography.

Wild About Harry: Reviews of Keeler Novels—Edited by Richard Polt & Fender Tucker—22 reviews of works by Harry Stephen Keeler from *Keeler News*. A perfect introduction to the author.

The Keeler Keyhole Collection: Annotated newsletter rants from Harry Stephen Keeler, edited by Francis M. Nevins. Over 400 pages of incredibly personal Keeleriana.

Fakealoo—Pastiches of the style of Harry Stephen Keeler by selected demented members of the HSK Society. Updated every year with the new winner.

Strands of the Web: Short Stories of Harry Stephen Keeler—29 stories, just about all that Keeler wrote, are edited and introduced by Fred Cleaver.

RAMBLE HOUSE's LOON SANCTUARY

A Clear Path to Cross—Sharon Knowles short mystery stories by Ed Lynskey.

A Corpse Walks in Brooklyn and Other Stories—Volume 5 in the Day Keene in the Detective Pulps series.

A Fair Californian—Novel by Olive Harper about a young woman's quest for gold — a quest that turns into something completely unexpected.

A Jimmy Starr Omnibus—Three 40s novels by Jimmy Starr.

A Niche in Time and Other Stories—Classic SF by William F. Temple.

A Shot Rang Out—Three decades of reviews and articles by today's Anthony Boucher, Jon Breen. An essential book for any mystery lover's library.

A Snark Selection—Lewis Carroll's *The Hunting of the Snark* with two Snarkian chapters by Harry Stephen Keeler—Illustrated by Gavin L. O'Keefe.

A Young Man's Heart—A forgotten early classic by Cornell Woolrich.

Alexander Laing Novels—*The Motives of Nicholas Holtz* and *Dr. Scarlett*, stories of medical mayhem and intrigue from the 30s.

An Angel in the Street—Modern hardboiled noir by Peter Genovese.

Automaton—Brilliant treatise on robotics: 1928-style! By H. Stafford Hatfield.

Away From the Here and Now—Clare Winger Harris stories, collected by Richard A. Lupoff

Beast or Man?—A 1930 novel of racism and horror by Sean M'Guire. Introduced by John Pelan.

Black Beadle—A 1939 thriller by E.C.R. Lorac.

Black Hogan Strikes Again—Australia's Peter Renwick pens a tale of the 30s outback.

Black River Falls—Suspense from the master, Ed Gorman.

Blondy's Boy Friend—A snappy 1930 story by Philip Wylie, writing as Leatrice Homesley.

Blood in a Snap—The *Finnegan's Wake* of the 21st century, by Jim Weiler.

Blood Moon—The first of the Robert Payne series by Ed Gorman.

Bogart '48—Hollywood action with Bogie by John Stanley and Kenn Davis

Butterfly Man—1930s novel by Lew Levenson about a dancer who must come to terms with his homosexuality.

Calling Lou Largo!—Two Lou Largo novels by William Ard.

Cathedral of Horror—First volume of collected stories by weird fiction writer Arthur J. Burks.

Chalk Face—Curious supernatural murder thriller by Waldo Frank.

Cornucopia of Crime—Francis M. Nevins assembled this huge collection of his writings about crime literature and the people who write it. Essential for any serious mystery library.

Corpse Without Flesh—Strange novel of forensics by George Bruce

Crimson Clown Novels—By Johnston McCulley, author of the Zorro novels, *The Crimson Clown* and *The Crimson Clown Again*.

Dago Red—22 tales of dark suspense by Bill Pronzini.

Dark Sanctuary—Weird Menace story by H. B. Gregory.

David Hume Novels—*Corpses Never Argue, Cemetery First Stop, Make Way for the Mourners, Eternity Here I Come*. 1930s British hardboiled fiction with an attitude.

David&Son: Peregrine Parentus and other tales—Collection of tales and memoirs by Avram Davidson and Ethan Davidson, some published for the first time. Introduced by Grania Davidson Davis.

Dead Man Talks Too Much—Hollywood boozer by Weed Dickenson.

Death in a Bowl—1930's murder mystery by Raoul Whitfield.

Death March of the Dancing Dolls and Other Stories—Volume Three in the Day Keene in the Detective Pulps series. Introduced by Bill Crider.

Deep Space and other Stories—A collection of SF gems by Richard A. Lupoff.

Detective Duff Unravels It—Episodic mysteries by Harvey O'Higgins.

Devil's Planet—Locked room mystery set on the planet Mars, by Manly Wade Wellman.

Dime Novels: Ramble House's 10-Cent Books—*Knife in the Dark* by Robert Leslie Bellem, *Hot Lead* and *Song of Death* by Ed Earl Repp, *A Hashish House in New York* by H.H. Kane, and five more.

Doctor Arnoldi—Tiffany Thayer's story of the death of death.

Don Diablo: Book of a Lost Film—Two-volume treatment of a western by Paul Landres, with diagrams. Intro by Francis M. Nevins.

Dope and Swastikas—Two strange novels from 1922 by Edmund Snell

Dope Tales #1—Two dope-riddled classics; *Dope Runners* by Gerald Grantham and *Death Takes the Joystick* by Phillip Condé.

Dope Tales #2—Two more narco-classics; *The Invisible Hand* by Rex Dark and *The Smokers of Hashish* by Norman Berrow.

Dope Tales #3—Two enchanting novels of opium by the master, Sax Rohmer. *Dope* and *The Yellow Claw*.

Double Hot & Double Sex—Two combos of '60s softcore sex novels by Morris Hershman.

Dr. Odin—Douglas Newton's 1933 racial potboiler comes back to life.

E. R. Punshon novels—*Information Received, Crossword Mystery, Dictator's Way, Diabolic Candelabra, Music Tells All, Helen Passes By, The House of Godwinsson, The Golden Dagger, The Attending Truth, Strange Ending, Brought to Light, Dark is the Clue, Triple Quest*, and *Six Were Present*: featuring Bobby Owen.

Ed "Strangler" Lewis: Facts within a Myth—Authoritative illustrated biography of the famous American wrestler Ed Lewis, by noted historian Steve Yohe.

Evangelical Cockroach—Jack Woodford writes about writing.

Evidence in Blue—1938 mystery by E. Charles Vivian.

Fatal Accident—Murder by automobile, a 1936 mystery by Cecil M. Wills.

Fighting Mad—Todd Robbins' 1922 novel about boxing and life

Five Million in Cash—Gangster thriller by Tiffany Thayer writing as O. B. King.

Food for the Fungus Lady—Collection of weird stories by Ralston Shields, edited and introduced by John Pelan.

Francis M. Nevins—Two omnibus volumes of novels featuring his legal sleuth Loren Mensing: *Publish and Perish / Corrupt and Ensnare* and *Into the Same River Twice / Beneficiaries' Requiem*.

Joseph Shallit Novels—*The Case of the Billion Dollar Body, Lady Don't Die on My Doorstep, Kiss the Killer, Yell Bloody Murder, Take Your Last Look.* One of America's best 50's authors and a favorite of author Bill Pronzini.

Keller Memento—45 short stories of the amazing and weird by Dr. David Keller.

Killer's Caress—Cary Moran's 1936 hardboiled thriller.

Knowing the Unknowable: Putting Psi to Work—Damien Broderick, PhD puts forward the valid case for evidence of Psi.

Lady of the Yellow Death and Other Stories—More stories by Wyatt Blassingame.

Laughing Death—1932 Yellow Peril thriller by Walter C. Brown.

League of the Grateful Dead and Other Stories—Volume One in the Day Keene in the Detective Pulps series.

Library of Death—Ghastly tale by Ronald S. L. Harding, introduced by John Pelan

Lords of the Earth—A novel of meddling dabblers in the occult invoking the ancient powers of Atlantis. J.M.A. Mills' sequel to *The Tomb of the Dark Ones.*

Mad-Doctor Merciful—Collin Brooks' unsettling novel of medical experimentation with supernatural forces.

Malcolm Jameson Novels and Short Stories—*Astonishing! Astounding!, Tarnished Bomb, The Alien Envoy and Other Stories* and *The Chariots of San Fernando and Other Stories.* All introduced and edited by John Pelan or Richard A. Lupoff.

Man Out of Hell and Other Stories—Volume II of the John H. Knox weird pulps collection.

Marblehead: A Novel of H.P. Lovecraft—A long-lost masterpiece from Richard A. Lupoff. This is the "director's cut", the long version that has never been published before.

Mark of the Laughing Death and Other Stories—Shockers from the pulps by Francis James, introduced by John Pelan.

Mark Hansom Novels—*Master of Souls, The Ghost of Gaston Revere, The Madman, The Shadow on the House, Sorcerer's Chessmen & The Wizard of Berner's Abbey.*

Max Afford Novels—*Owl of Darkness, Death's Mannikins, Blood on His Hands, The Dead Are Blind, The Sheep and the Wolves, Sinners in Paradise* and *Two Locked Room Mysteries and a Ripping Yarn* by one of Australia's finest mystery novelists.

Miles Burton novels—*A Smell of Smoke, Death Leaves No Card* and *Death Paints a Picture.*

Mistress of Terror—Fourth volume of the collected weird tales of Wyatt Blassingame.

Mr. South Burned His Mouth—Gentry Nyland's only novel: a thriller.

Molly and her Man of War— Romantic novel with a difference, by Arabella Kenealy.

Money Brawl—Two books about the writing business by Jack Woodford and H. Bedford-Jones. Introduced by Richard A. Lupoff.

More Secret Adventures of Sherlock Holmes—Gary Lovisi's second collection of tales about the unknown sides of the great detective.

Muddled Mind: Complete Works of Ed Wood, Jr.—David Hayes and Hayden Davis deconstruct the life and works of the mad, but canny, genius.

Murder among the Nudists—1934 mystery by Peter Hunt, featuring a naked Detective-Inspector going undercover in a nudist colony.

Murder in Black and White—1931 classic tennis whodunit by Evelyn Elder.

Murder in Shawnee—Two novels of the Alleghenies by John Douglas: *Shawnee Alley Fire* and *Haunts*.

Murder in Suffolk—A 1938 murder mystery novel by the mysterious 'A. Fielding.'

My Deadly Angel—1955 Cold War drama by John Chelton.

My First Time: The One Experience You Never Forget—Michael Birchwood—64 true first-person narratives of how they lost it.

My Touch Brings Death—Second volume of collected stories by Russell Gray.

Mysterious Martin, the Master of Murder—Two versions of a strange 1912 novel by Tod Robbins about a man who writes books that can kill.

Norman Berrow Novels—*The Bishop's Sword, Ghost House, Don't Go Out After Dark, Claws of the Cougar, The Smokers of Hashish, The Secret Dancer, Don't Jump Mr. Boland!, The Footprints of Satan, Fingers for Ransom, The Three Tiers of Fantasy, The Spaniard's Thumb, The Eleventh Plague, Words Have Wings, One Thrilling Night, The Lady's in Danger, It Howls at Night, The Terror in the Fog, Oil Under the Window, Murder in the Melody, The Singing Room.* This is the complete Norman Berrow library of locked-room mysteries, several of which are masterpieces.

Old Faithful and Other Stories—SF classic tales by Raymond Z. Gallun

Old Times' Sake—Short stories by James Reasoner from Mike Shayne Magazine.

One Dreadful Night—A classic mystery by Ronald S. L. Harding

Pair O' Jacks—A mystery novel and a diatribe about publishing by Jack Woodford

Pawns of Destiny—Psychological drama by Kay Seaton.

Perfect .38—Two early Timothy Dane novels by William Ard. More to come.

Prince Pax—Devilish intrigue by George Sylvester Viereck and Philip Eldridge

Prose Bowl—Futuristic satire of a world where hack writing has replaced football as our national obsession, by Bill Pronzini and Barry N. Malzberg.

Ralph Trevor novels—*Murder in Silk, Front Page Murder, Easy for the Crook, The Deputy Avenger,* etc.

Red Light—The history of legal prostitution in Shreveport Louisiana by Eric Brock. Includes wonderful photos of the houses and the ladies.

Researching American-Made Toy Soldiers—A 276-page collection of a lifetime of articles by toy soldier expert Richard O'Brien.

Reunion in Hell—Volume One of the John H. Knox series of weird stories from the pulps. Introduced by horror expert John Pelan.

Ripped from the Headlines!—The Jack the Ripper story as told in the newspaper articles in the *New York* and *London Times*.

Rough Cut & New, Improved Murder—Ed Gorman's first two novels.

R. R. Ryan Novels — *Freak Museum, The Subjugated Beast, Death of a Sadist, Echo of a Curse, Devil's Shelter* and *No Escape*. Introduced by John Pelan.

Roland Daniel Novels — *Ruby of a Thousand Dreams, The Girl in the Dark,* and *A Roland Daniel Double: The Signal and The Return of Wu Fang*.

Ruled By Radio — 1925 futuristic novel by Robert L. Hadfield & Frank E. Farncombe.

Rupert Penny Novels — *Policeman's Holiday, Policeman's Evidence, Lucky Policeman, Policeman in Armour, Sealed Room Murder, Sweet Poison, The Talkative Policeman, She had to Have Gas* and *Cut and Run* (by Martin Tanner.) Rupert Penny is the pseudonym of Australian Charles Thornett, a master of the locked room, impossible crime plot.

Sacred Locomotive Flies — Richard A. Lupoff's psychedelic SF story.

Sam — Early gay novel by Lonnie Coleman.

Sand's Game — Spectacular hardboiled noir from Ennis Willie, edited by Lynn Myers and Stephen Mertz, with contributions from Max Allan Collins, Bill Crider, Wayne Dundee, Bill Pronzini, Gary Lovisi and James Reasoner.

Sand's War — More violent fiction from the typewriter of Ennis Willie

Satan's Den Exposed — True crime in Truth or Consequences New Mexico — Award-winning journalism by the *Desert Journal*.

Satan's Secret and Selected Stories — Barnard Stacey's only novel with a selection of his best short stories.

Satans of Saturn — Novellas from the pulps by Otis Adelbert Kline and E. H. Price

Satan's Sin House and Other Stories — Horrific gore by Wayne Rogers

Second Creation — The first volume of selected short stories by Gordon Eklund.

Secrets of a Teenage Superhero — Graphic lit by Jonathan Sweet

Sex Slave — Potboiler of lust in the days of Cleopatra by Dion Leclerq, 1966.

Sideslip — 1968 SF masterpiece by Ted White and Dave Van Arnam.

Slammer Days — Two full-length prison memoirs: *Men into Beasts* (1952) by George Sylvester Viereck and *Home Away From Home* (1962) by Jack Woodford.

Slippery Staircase — 1930s whodunit from E.C.R. Lorac

Star Griffin — Michael Kurland's 1987 masterpiece of SF drollery is back.

Stakeout on Millennium Drive — Award-winning Indianapolis Noir by Ian Woollen.

Strands of the Web: Short Stories of Harry Stephen Keeler — Edited and Introduced by Fred Cleaver.

Summer Camp for Corpses and Other Stories — Weird Menace tales from Arthur Leo Zagat; introduced by John Pelan.

Suzy — A collection of comic strips by Richard O'Brien and Bob Vojtko from 1970.

Tail of the Lizard King / Kaliwood — Two novellas by Adam Mudman Bezecny paying homage to the sleaze genre.

Tales of the Macabre and Ordinary — Modern twisted horror by Chris Mikul, author of the *Bizarrism* series.

Tales of Terror and Torment Vols. #1 & #2 — John Pelan selects and introduces these samplers of weird menace tales from the pulps.

Tenebrae — Ernest G. Henham's 1898 horror tale brought back.

The Alice Books — Lewis Carroll's classics *Alice's Adventures in Wonderland* and *Through the Looking-Glass* together in one volume, with new illustrations by O'Keefe.

The Amorous Intrigues & Adventures of Aaron Burr — by Anonymous. Hot historical action about the man who almost became Emperor of Mexico.

The Anthony Boucher Chronicles — edited by Francis M. Nevins. Book reviews by Anthony Boucher written for the *San Francisco Chronicle*, 1942 – 1947. Essential and fascinating reading by the best book reviewer there ever was.

The Barclay Catalogs — Two essential books about toy soldier collecting by Richard O'Brien

The Basil Wells Omnibus — A collection of Wells' stories by Richard A. Lupoff

The Beautiful Dead and Other Stories — Dreadful tales from Donald Dale

The Best of 10-Story Book — edited by Chris Mikul, over 35 stories from the literary magazine Harry Stephen Keeler edited.

The Bitch Wall — Novel about American soldiers in the Vietnam War, based on Dennis Lane's experiences.

The Black Dark Murders — Vintage 50s college murder yarn by Milt Ozaki, writing as Robert O. Saber.

The Book of Time — The classic novel by H.G. Wells is joined by sequels by Wells himself and three stories by Richard A. Lupoff. Illustrated by Gavin L. O'Keefe.

The Broken Fang and Other Experiences of a Specialist in Spooks — Eerie mystery tales by Uel Key.

The Case in the Clinic — One of E.C.R. Lorac's finest.

The Strange Case of the Antlered Man — A mystery of superstition by Edwy Searles Brooks.

The Case of the Bearded Bride — #4 in the Day Keene in the Detective Pulps series.

The Case of the Little Green Men — Mack Reynolds wrote this love song to sci-fi fans back in 1951 and it's now back in print.

The Charlie Chaplin Murder Mystery — A 2004 tribute by noted film scholar, Wes D. Gehring.

The Cloudbuilders and Other Stories — SF tales from Colin Kapp.

The Collected Writings — Collection of science fiction stories, memoirs and poetry by Carol Carr. Introduction by Karen Haber.

The Compleat Calhoon — All of Fender Tucker's works: Includes *Totah Six-Pack, Weed, Women and Song* and *Tales from the Tower,* plus a CD of all of his songs.

The Compleat Ova Hamlet — Parodies of SF authors by Richard A. Lupoff. This is a brand new edition with more stories and more illustrations by Trina Robbins.

The Contested Earth and Other SF Stories — A never-before published space opera and seven short stories by Jim Harmon.

The Corpse Factory — More horror stories by Arthur Leo Zagat.

The Crackpot and Other Twisted Tales of Greedy Fans and Collectors — The first retrospective collection of the whacky stories of John E. Stockman. Edited by Dwight R. Decker.

The Crimson Butterfly — Early novel by Edmund Snell involving superstition and aberrant Lepidoptera in Borneo.

The Crimson Query — A 1929 thriller from Arlton Eadie. A perfect way to get introduced.

The Daymakers, City of the Tiger & Perchance to Wake — Three volumes of stories taken from the influential British science fiction magazine *Science Fantasy*. Compiled by John Boston & Damien Broderick.

The Devil and the C.I.D. — Odd diabolic mystery by E.C.R. Lorac

The Devil Drives — An odd prison and lost treasure novel from 1932 by Virgil Markham.

The Devil of Pei-Ling — Herbert Asbury's 1929 tale of the occult.

The Devil's Mistress — A 1915 Scottish gothic tale by J. W. Brodie-Innes, a member of Aleister Crowley's Golden Dawn.

The Devil's Nightclub and Other Stories — John Pelan introduces some gruesome tales by Nat Schachner.

The Disentanglers — Episodic intrigue at the turn of last century by Andrew Lang

The Dog Poker Code — A spoof of *The Da Vinci Code* by D. B. Smithee.

The Dumpling — Political murder from 1907 by Coulson Kernahan.

The End of It All and Other Stories — Ed Gorman selected his favorite short stories for this huge collection.

The Evil of Li-Sin — A Gerald Verner double, combining *The Menace of Li-Sin* and *The Vengeance of Li-Sin*, together with an introduction by John Pelan and an afterword and bibliography by Chris Verner.

The Fangs of Suet Pudding — A 1944 novel of the German invasion by Adams Farr

The Finger of Destiny and Other Stories — Edmund Snell's superb collection of weird stories of Borneo.

The Gold Star Line — Seaboard adventure from L.T. Reade and Robert Eustace.

The Great Orme Terror — Horror stories by Garnett Radcliffe from the pulps

The Hairbreadth Escapes of Major Mendax — Francis Blake Crofton's 1889 boys' book.

The House That Time Forgot and Other Stories — Insane pulpitude by Robert F. Young

The House of the Vampire — 1907 poetic thriller by George S. Viereck.

The Illustrious Corpse — Murder hijinx from Tiffany Thayer

The Incredible Adventures of Rowland Hern — Intriguing 1928 impossible crimes by Nicholas Olde.

The John Dickson Carr Companion — Comprehensive reference work compiled by James E. Keirans. Indispensable resource for the Carr *aficionado*.

The Julius Caesar Murder Case — A 1935 retelling of the assassination by Wallace Irwin that's more fun than Shakespeare's version.

The Kid Was a Killer — Caryl Chessman's only novel, based on his own experiences.

The Koky Comics — A collection of all of the 1978-1981 Sunday and daily comic strips by Richard O'Brien and Mort Gerberg, in two volumes.

The Lady of the Terraces — 1925 missing race adventure by E. Charles Vivian.

The Lord of Terror — 1925 mystery with master-criminal, Fantômas.

The Man who was Murdered Twice — Intriguing murder mystery by Robert H. Leitfred.

The Melamare Mystery — A classic 1929 Arsene Lupin mystery by Maurice Leblanc

The Man Who Was Secrett — Epic SF stories from John Brunner

The Man Without a Planet — Science fiction tales by Richard Wilson

The N. R. De Mexico Novels — Robert Bragg, the real N.R. de Mexico, presents *Marijuana Girl, Madman on a Drum, Private Chauffeur* in one volume.

The Night Remembers — A 1991 Jack Walsh mystery from Ed Gorman.

The One After Snelling — Kickass modern noir from Richard O'Brien.

The Organ Reader — A huge compilation of just about everything published in the 1971-1972 radical bay-area newspaper, *THE ORGAN*. A coffee table book that points out the shallowness of the coffee table mindset.

The Place of Hairy Death — Collected weird horror tales by Anthony M. Rud.

The Poker Club — Three in one! Ed Gorman's ground-breaking novel, the short story it was based upon, and the screenplay of the film made from it.

The Private Journal & Diary of John H. Surratt — The memoirs of the man who conspired to assassinate President Lincoln.

The Ramble House Coloring Book — Twenty illustrations to color in, each adapted from one of Gavin L. O'Keefe's cover designs.

The Ramble House Mapbacks — Recently revised book by Gavin L. O'Keefe with color pictures of all the Ramble House books with mapbacks.

The Secret Adventures of Sherlock Holmes — Three Sherlockian pastiches by the Brooklyn author/publisher, Gary Lovisi.

The Secret of the Morgue — Frederick G. Eberhard's 1932 mystery involving murder and forensic science with an undercurrent of the malaise that's driven by Prohibition.

The Sign of the Scorpion — A 1935 Edmund Snell tale of oriental evil.

The Silent Terror of Chu-Sheng — Yellow Peril suspense novel by Eugene Thomas.

The Singular Problem of the Stygian House-Boat — Two classic tales by John Kendrick Bangs about the denizens of Hades.

The Smiling Corpse — Philip Wylie and Bernard Bergman's odd 1935 novel.

The Sorcery Club — Classic supernatural novel by Elliott O'Donnell.

The Spider: Satan's Murder Machines — A thesis about Iron Man.

The Stench of Death: An Odoriferous Omnibus by Jack Moskovitz — Two complete novels and two novellas from 60's sleaze author, Jack Moskovitz.

The Story Writer and Other Stories — Classic SF from Richard Wilson

The Strange Thirteen — Richard B. Gamon's odd stories about Raj India.

The Technique of the Mystery Story — Carolyn Wells' tips about writing.

The Tell-Tale Soul — Two novellas by Bram Stoker Award-winning author Christopher Conlon. Introduction by John Pelan.

The Threat of Nostalgia — A collection of his most obscure stories by Jon Breen

The Time Armada — Fox B. Holden's 1953 SF gem.

The Tomb of the Dark Ones — Adventure in Egypt where ancient forces are roused from æons of slumber. A J. M. A. Mills novel from 1937.

The Tongueless Horror and Other Stories — Volume One of the series of short stories from the weird pulps by Wyatt Blassingame.

The Town from Planet Five — From Richard Wilson, two SF classics, *And Then the Town Took Off* and *The Girls from Planet 5*

The Tracer of Lost Persons — From 1906, an episodic novel that became a hit radio series in the 30s. Introduced by Richard A. Lupoff.

The Trail of the Cloven Hoof — Diabolical horror from 1935 by Arlton Eadie. Introduced by John Pelan.

The Triune Man — Mindscrambling science fiction from Richard A. Lupoff.

The Unholy Goddess and Other Stories — Wyatt Blassingame's first DTP compilation

The Universal Holmes — Richard A. Lupoff's 2007 collection of five Holmesian pastiches and a recipe for giant rat stew.

The Werewolf vs the Vampire Woman — Hard to believe ultraviolence by either Arthur M. Scarm or Arthur M. Scram.

The Whistling Ancestors — A 1936 classic of weirdness by Richard E. Goddard and introduced by John Pelan.

The White Owl — A vintage thriller from Edmund Snell

The White Peril in the Far East — Sidney Lewis Gulick's 1905 indictment of the West and assurance that Japan would never attack the U.S.

The Wonderful Wizard of Oz — by L. Frank Baum and illustrated by Gavin L. O'Keefe.

The Worst Man in the World—Frank Richardson's comic novel about the woes of a Scottish baronet and his quirky extended family, as well as touching on whiskers and Jack the Ripper.

The Yu-Chi Stone — Novel of intrigue and superstition set in Borneo, by Edmund Snell.

They Called the Shots — Collection of authoritative articles by Francis M. Nevins exploring the action movie directors of the late silents through to the late 1960s.

Time Line — Ramble House artist Gavin O'Keefe selects his most evocative art inspired by the twisted literature he reads and designs.

Tiresias — Psychotic modern horror novel by Jonathan M. Sweet.

Tortures and Towers — Two novellas of terror by Dexter Dayle.

Totah Six-Pack — Fender Tucker's six tales about Farmington in one sleek volume.

Tree of Life, Book of Death — Grania Davis' book of her life.

Trail of the Spirit Warrior — Roger Haley's saga of life in the Indian Territories.

Twelve Who Were Damned — Collection of weird menace tales by Paul Ernst.

Two Kinds of Bad — Two 50s novels by William Ard about Danny Fontaine

Two Suns of Morcali and Other Stories — Evelyn E. Smith's SF tour-de-force

Two-Timers — Time travel double: *The Man Who Mastered Time* by Ray Cummings and *Time Column* and *Taa the Terrible* by Malcolm Jameson. Introduced by Richard A. Lupoff.

Ultra-Boiled — 23 gut-wrenching tales by our Man in Brooklyn, Gary Lovisi.

Up Front From Behind — A 2011 satire of Wall Street by James B. Kobak.

Victims & Villains — Intriguing Sherlockiana from Derham Groves.

Wade Wright Novels — *Echo of Fear, Death At Nostalgia Street, It Leads to Murder* and *Shadows' Edge*, a double book featuring *Shadows Don't Bleed* and *The Sharp Edge*.

Walter S. Masterman Novels — *The Green Toad, The Flying Beast, The Yellow Mistletoe, The Wrong Verdict, The Perjured Alibi, The Border Line, The Bloodhounds Bay, The Curse of Cantire, The Curse of the Reckaviles, Death Turns Traitor, The Wrong Letter* and *The Baddington Horror*.

We Are the Dead and Other Stories — Volume Two in the Day Keene in the Detective Pulps series, introduced by Ed Gorman. When done, there may be 11 in the series.

Welsh Rarebit Tales — Charming stories from 1902 by Harle Oren Cummins

West Texas War and Other Western Stories — Western hijinks by Gary Lovisi.

What Was That?—Ghostly murder mystery from 1920 by Katharine Haviland Taylor.

What If? Volume 1, 2 and 3 — Richard A. Lupoff introduces three decades worth of SF short stories that should have won a Hugo, but didn't.

When the Bat Man Thirsts and Other Stories — Weird tales from Frederick C. Davis.

When the Dead Walk — Gary Lovisi takes us into the zombie-infested South.

Whip Dodge: Man Hunter — Wesley Tallant's saga of a bounty hunter of the old West.

Win, Place and Die! — The first new mystery by Milt Ozaki in decades. The ultimate novel of 70s Reno.

Writer, Volumes 1, 2 & 3 — A *magnus opus* from Richard A. Lupoff summing up his life as writer.

You'll Die Laughing — Bruce Elliott's 1945 novel of murder at a practical joker's English countryside manor.

You're Not Alone: 30 Science Fiction Stories from *Cosmos Magazine*, edited by Damien Broderick.

RAMBLE HOUSE

www.ramblehouse.com fender@ramblehouse.com
10329 Sheephead Drive, Vancleave MS 39565

I *always look for the* 'RAMBLE HOUSE' *when I want a* PLEASANT BOOK*!*

Your troubles are at an end when you choose a Ramble House novel. No more doubts ! No more disappointments ! A Ramble House novel will give you hours of happy reading. Next time, just say to your librarian, "A Ramble House, please !"

www.ingramcontent.com/pod-product-compliance
Lightning Source LLC
Chambersburg PA
CBHW030319020726
47493CB00004B/1082